The Bookshop
on Autumn Lane

WITHDRAWN.

T0204353

JUL 1 4 2017
BO

Also by Cynthia Tennent

Skinny Dipping Season
A Wedding in Truhart

The Bookshop on Autumn Lane

Cynthia Tennent

LYRICAL SHINE
Kensington Publishing Corp.
www.kensingtonbooks.com

LYRICAL SHINE BOOKS are published by

Kensington Publishing Corp.
119 West 40th Street
New York, NY 10018

All Kensington titles, imprints, and distributed lines are available at special quantity discounts for bulk purchases for sales promotion, premiums, fund-raising, educational, or institutional use.

Special book excerpts or customized printings can also be created to fit specific needs. For details, write or phone the office of the Kensington Sales Manager: Kensington Publishing Corp., 119 West 40th Street, New York, NY 10018. Attn. Sales Department. Phone: 1-800-221-2647.

Lyrical Shine and Lyrical Shine logo Reg. U.S. Pat. & TM Off.

First Electronic Edition: October 2016
eISBN-13: 978-1-60183-645-8
eISBN-10: 1-60183-645-7

First Print Edition: October 2016
ISBN-13: 978-1-60183-647-2
ISBN-10: 1-60183-647-3

Printed in the United States of America

*This book is dedicated to the special children
who color our world with love.*

*Particular thanks to my fellow writers, Kelly and Sheila,
who keep me from panicking when faced with a blank
page.*

Chapter 1

I, Gertrude Louisa Brown, being of sound mind, and with no children or spouse to claim my inheritance, do hereby bequeath the bulk of my investments, bank accounts, and cash to the Harrison County Furry Friends Rescue Shelter in memory of my beloved cat, Piewacket. My remaining asset, Books from the Hart, located at 16 Main Street, Truhart, Michigan, and all its contents including my books, I bequeath to my niece and namesake, Gertrude C. Brown, in hopes that she will finally understand the difference between an ant and an Aunt, and being dammed and damned!

The lawyer said that her premature death, at the age of seventy-three, occurred in the lonely interior cabin of a cruise ship bound for Nassau. Aunt Gertrude's heart gave out in the middle of the night. The maid who found her the next morning reported that she clutched *Moby-Dick* to her chest, her place in the last chapter still saved between her thumb and forefinger.

If she hadn't died from a heart attack, I'm sure Aunt Gertrude would have died of boredom from reading the world's dullest bit of required high school reading ever.

The cruise had been the first and the last vacation she ever took.

The book, along with a lawyer's letter and Aunt Gertrude's last will and testament, sat in my P.O. box in Oakland for almost a year before I discovered them. I thought about throwing them both in the trash right there at the post office. But I was tired of sleeping on friends' couches and eating canned beans. And there was Angkor Wat to think about.

A *tap-tap* tapping woke me from the restless sleep that had plagued me since Bozeman. I pulled my dharma quilt up and rolled over in the limited space. Aunt Gertrude's copy of *Moby-Dick* fell from its perch on the emergency break. I had been using it to bridge the gap between the bucket seats. The break latch and the gearshift cut into my hip. It was the only thing I hated about manual transmissions.

Brightness seeped through my lacy pink sleep mask. I lifted the corner a fraction of an inch, then lowered it. Was it morning already? I usually didn't start my day until at least midmorning. Even then, I needed a major dose of caffeine to help clear the fog.

Tap-tap. A furry whip hit me square across the face. Its tempo increased and I felt like a car at a soft cloth auto wash. I pushed the fur away, but it came back with greater speed.

"Stop—oof." A hairy paw impaled my lap, taking the breath from me. It was followed by a high-pitched bark. Not the raspy, panicked bark issued the night before when a cat had jumped at us. This bark meant excitement.

I lifted my mask and shoved *Moby-Dick* under the seat. I stretched my long legs over the steering wheel. "How many times do I have to tell you? Your space is in the backseat, and mine is here. No crossing the line."

The old collie dog wasn't paying any attention to me. My eyes followed the source of his enthusiasm to the figures standing outside.

"Helloooo," a female voice called in a cheery, wake-up-it's-morning kind of way. I hated the way morning people sounded like a commercial for breakfast sausage.

The dog jumped back in my lap. He followed the fingers tapping on the windshield with his nose.

Something flashed in the sunlight beside me. "Are you okay in there?"

I rolled the old-fashioned manual window crank down. "Peachy."

"Maybe we should call J. D. or the sheriff. If he's a vagrant or homeless they would want to know." A man pressed his hands and face up against the window and peered inside my bedroom, the car.

I folded my legs beneath me and sat up.

"Oh look, he's awake."

And not a man. I readjusted my head scarf that kept my long red hair from tangling. Like I did every morning, I flipped down the visor, letting my fingers settle on the travel brochure with the pictures of temples rising out of the rain forest.

Someday soon, Mom.

Truhart was a blip on the radar. A stopover.

My traveling companion nudged me with his wet nose and let out a mild whine. "All right, buddy. Let's go."

I opened the door. Three figures stepped back while all five foot eight inches of my curveless body unfolded. Or attempted to. My legs were stiff. No matter how I lay across the front seats of the old '73 Beetle, there was never enough room to truly stretch out. After a bad night in Utah, I toyed with trading in Lulu for an SUV. A reclining front seat or cargo area would be the ultimate luxury. But I could never part with Lulu. In a world overtaken with indistinguishable sedans in silver and black, the bold yellow Beetle was one of a kind.

I scrunched my toes inside my wool socks and felt the rough surface of the concrete beneath me. Lifting my arms, I slowly stretched back and forth, feeling older than I should at twenty-eight.

"You're a girl." The man wore head-to-toe navy clothes and reminded me of the Maytag man.

"Some call me one." I leaned forward and blinked at the name tag embroidered on his left chest. "Jody."

"Joe," he corrected me.

The dog whined behind me and I turned back to help him out of the car.

"One of these days you're going to have to do this on your own, dog." I grabbed his middle, helping him navigate the distance between the seats and the ground. "What's going to happen when I'm not here anymore, huh? You need to discover your canine roots and get some balls, dude. Otherwise you're going to be at the bottom of the food chain."

A familiar chorus of *ooos* and *aws* erupted over the good-looking boy and I grabbed my boots from the backseat, glad to have a moment to collect myself before facing the small crowd that was gathered around me.

"Oh, it's Lassie."

"What a pretty dog."

Like he always did when someone gave him a little attention, the dog lifted his neck a little higher and raised and lowered his ears several times. He was such a poser!

I leaned against the car and stuffed my large feet into the army boots.

An oversized woman with pink-rimmed glasses ruffled her hand through the dog's fur. "What a good girl you are!"

We both had gender issues this morning, but he got all the glory for being beautiful. If they knew what a wimp he was they would have laughed. He could barely get in and out of the car without my help. Last night he had been afraid of his own tail.

A curvy middle-aged blond woman stood next to the voluminous woman. She was the only one who didn't coo over the dog. She put her hands on her hips and surveyed me from the messy red hair wrapped in a scarf to the long, flowing calico dress I had slept in. Ruffles stuck out of the hem at wrinkled angles and covered my shapeless legs. The boots I had just stepped into were unlaced.

"You took a wrong turn somewhere, honey. Woodstock is several states over," said the blonde.

"And several decades late," another man added. Look who's talking. He could have walked straight out of the fifties with his brown suit and pomade.

"Don't be mean, Regina. Let's find out where she came from first," said Joe.

A crowd grew around us. A man wearing a flannel shirt and shorts and a woman holding the hand of a young boy drew closer. Where had they all come from? I looked down the street. The door to the diner was propped open. Several people stood in the open doorway. I guess I was more popular than the morning news.

The dog broke loose from the hands that reached out for his silky coat. He wandered over to the curb and the fire hydrant I hadn't noticed last night. It was right next to my car. He squatted and eliminated like a girl. Poor guy. He didn't even know how to lift his leg like a real man-dog.

I read my Mickey Mouse watch. Fifteen minutes late. Not bad for me. I was tall enough to see over the crowd to the building down the street. A figure stood in the doorway. I should be relieved she was there. But I wasn't. The flutter in my stomach made me want to squat by the hydrant too.

I should have pulled into the alley and parked last night. But I had spent a lot of time in cities over the past few years. An alley, even in a small town like this, was no place for a girl who slept in her car. I purposely parked up Main Street so that the last thing I saw as I fell asleep wouldn't be the building where the woman stood waiting. As far as I was concerned the more distance I put between me and that place, the better. But that was irrational, considering it was my destination.

I pointed at the fire hydrant and then a no-parking sign. I could not afford a parking ticket. "Do they take that kind of thing seriously here?"

"We take fire safety seriously. No exceptions," said the man in the navy work uniform.

"I'll move it." The space behind me looked legal. I jumped into the passenger seat and, without turning the car on, shifted into neutral.

Hopping out, I made my way to the front bumper. "Excuse me." I nodded to the open space behind my car. The small crowd looked confused. I ignored them and put my hands on the hood and pushed Lulu backwards.

"What the—" The blond lady jumped out of the way.

"She has a problem with reversing," I explained.

Once she was in a legal space, I reapplied the emergency brake.

"Did you sleep in your car last night?" the little boy asked boldly. His face held a mixture of respect and awe.

"Andrew, shhh. That's not nice."

I placed my foot on the wheel so I could tie my boot laces and winked at him.

"There's a motor lodge at the corner of M-33 and Pine Road," the suited man said with a frown.

"And a charming inn on Winding Road," added the ample-sized lady. I envied her pink glasses. I had passed up a similar pair at a flea market last month.

"I'll remember that."

I could tell them that I never stayed in hotels. Ever. But most people didn't understand that. My car was fine. Couches weren't so bad. A bed: that was heaven. But the last time I had the chance to sleep in a bed, an ass had been in it. When I left him, I'd taken his dog and a bout of insomnia with me. Since then, the dog and the insomnia had become my constant companions.

Back from his adventures on the curb, the collie wagged his tail and licked my hand.

"Hungry, dude?" I reached into the backseat and grabbed a Chinese takeout box and an old plastic bowl from a small cooler I kept on the floor. Turning the box upside down, I dumped the block of rice in the bowl and set it down on the cement. "There you go."

My furry friend loved rice. If I was with someone who ate meat, I usually asked them for leftovers so he could have a little protein to go with his starch. But I hadn't been around any meat eaters in the past couple of days, so I was going to have to break down soon and buy him better fare.

When I looked up, I was assailed by various expressions of horror. "You're feeding him that?"

"He likes it."

The large lady with the glasses opened her purse and pulled out two small strips of paper. "Here, take these. A friend of mine sells homemade doggie treats. That first one will get you a twenty-percent discount. The other one you can use anywhere, but the Family Fare has double coupon days on Sundays, so if you're still in town then, come on by."

Coupons for dog food. Well, this was embarrassing, but I was never one to refuse charity. "Thanks."

While the dog gobbled up the last of the rice, I freed a jean jacket I'd used as a pillow from the car. The words *Hell's Kitchen* were inscribed on the back. I put it on and pulled out a toothbrush that I kept in a small baggie in the pocket. No one looked like they were interested in getting on with their own business and I was pressed for time. So I went about my morning routine with an audience. I reached into the cooler for my water bottle and a tube of toothpaste, which for some reason always ended up in my cooler instead of the bag. I squeezed a sliver of toothpaste on the toothbrush, closed the cap, and set the tube back in the cooler.

"Excuse me." I walked over to a grassy area on the side of the street and proceeded to brush my teeth, rinsing my mouth and spitting it out on the grass when I finished. I knew I was being stared at, but it wasn't new for me. Especially here. I was Aunt Gertrude's freaky fuzzy-haired redheaded great-niece. I had been in trouble from the moment I came to town fourteen years ago. I was going to have to get used to being gawked at all over again.

When I finished, I returned to the car and the dog and basically did everything in reverse. I closed the door to my bug. The crowd watched me avidly. I lifted my shoulders and ran my tongue across my minty-fresh teeth. "Recommended by nine out of ten dentists."

The curvy blond woman clutched her hand to her large chest as if she'd been shot. "Oh my gawd! I knew it was going to happen sooner or later. Truhart is becoming home to hippies and homeless people. What will our summer residents think when we have bag ladies lying around on the streets?"

"What will his lordship think?" the wide woman added. His lordship? How curious. Maybe there was some sort of strange cult thing happening in Truhart. I wasn't exactly opposed to cults. I had been on the fringe of several. More as a spectator than anything.

"We've got to get that community center going sooner rather than later, George," the blonde said.

George, the brown-suited man, cleared his throat, preparing to make a speech. "Young lady, as the mayor of this town, it is my duty to inform you that we don't take lightly to drifters. Now, while there isn't technically a vagrancy clause in our city bylaws, we do take drugs and other deviant behavior seriously. I could call the sheriff, but you might find it goes easier if you move along to the next town."

"Yeah. Try Harrisburg!" someone in the back said.

I held up my Pikachu key chain. "Oh, I'm not homeless. I just couldn't make it past the front door last night."

"What front door are you talking about?"

I pointed down the street where my appointment stood. "Books from He—I mean Books from the Hart."

A collective silence descended on the crowd. The large woman with the coupons stepped forward. "Wait a minute, I remember you. Are you Gertrude Brown's long-lost great-niece?"

"Long, yes." I stood tall. "But not lost." I had known where I was for the past several years. Most of the time, at least. There were a few times in Montana where I had taken a detour into parts unknown and ended up sleeping under the stars. Those had been some of the most beautiful wrong turns I had ever taken.

The busty woman cupped her hand over her mouth and whispered something to George. I heard the words *dim-witted* and *slow*.

I should have expected that reaction. But it had been years since I had heard those words. It made the tips of my fingers tingle when people used them in regards to me, or anyone else for that matter. I clutched Pikachu with both hands and told myself not to kick the woman. I grabbed my vintage military rucksack from the backseat. The shaggy collie leaned against my knee and I would have reassured him that he would be okay here, but he wasn't mine so it would be overstepping my role. I patted his back instead. "Come on, dog." Together we walked down the street toward Hell.

Even after all these years, it was amazing how little had changed. Truhart had never been crowded, but I didn't recall it being so vacant. The years since my mother died and my father dumped my brother, Leo, and me on my Aunt Gertrude didn't look like they had been good to the town.

We arrived late last night. Rush-hour traffic on I-75 in Detroit had been a mess, and by the time we got through it, Mickey was pointing both hands to the twelve. Almost exactly midnight. The night shadows had taken over the empty center of town and the streetlights weren't working—or maybe there were no streetlights. I had stared out Lulu's front windshield with the strange feeling that the dog and I weren't alone. Something unearthly floated in front of the windshield. The hair on my arm shot straight up. Perhaps Aunt Gertrude's ghost was coming to haunt me in new ways she hadn't thought up when she was alive. On closer inspection, I realized it was a torn plastic bag floating across the hood of the car.

It was ridiculous for a woman of my age and experience to sit in a parked car at midnight like a coward. I had climbed Pico de Orizaba, the tallest mountain in Mexico, at twenty-three, bungee-jumped from the bridge to nowhere in southern California at twenty, streaked naked through the streets of San Francisco at nineteen, and run away from my guardian at sixteen. This one little thing, I could do.

At the front door, Pikachu caught the light from the sliver of moon that rose above Main Street and winked back, doing his best to encourage me. I placed the key in the lock, but it wouldn't fit. I felt in my rucksack for my penlight and clicked it on. Rust and years of dust had worn away the hardware around the knob. But the cylinder where the key fit was new. Someone had replaced the lock.

Without warning, a black form jumped out from the top of the awning. A single raspy bark from the old dog was followed by a sharp feline screech. "Piewacket?" It couldn't be. There was no way the cat could still be alive. Unless it hadn't used up all its lives.

It jumped into the shadows and was gone.

A frosty ripple went up my spine, as if someone were trailing a block of ice along my vertebrae. A brisk breeze stirred the brittle leaves on the trees nearby. I refused to be scared of black cats and old curses.

I returned to Lulu and called Reeba Sweeney, the real-estate agent at Respect Realty. Her company had been given the job of maintaining the property by the administrator who handled Aunt Gertrude's estate. It was late, but her letter said to call anytime. So I did. She sounded angry at first. But when I gave her my name she changed her tone and promised to meet me at the store in the morning. I was secretly relieved. Another night of cramped sleep in the front seat was better than a sleepless night in Aunt Gertrude's upstairs apartment.

Now, squinting at the bright September sunshine, the morning didn't improve my spirits. I shook off my craving for a cup of coffee and walked past the vacant grocery store that abutted Aunt Gertrude's building. The bookstore was the last commercial structure in Truhart's business district. Echo Lake's public beach and dock rose up at the end of the street. Several acres of vacant land lay behind the store. I used to hide in those woods and smoke cigarettes when Aunt Gertrude went on what I called a "reading rampage."

A small figure stood on the curb, a smile plastered to her face.

The dog paused, as if he thought the black cat might jump out again. If I didn't have a small crowd of people following me, I would have told him to buck up and take it like a man. I kept my mouth shut. No need to embarrass him in front of his new admirers.

I hopped up the crumbling curb and marched toward the front door. When I was younger, two windows on the top floor and the larger storefront window on the first floor made me think the store was alive. The notion was stronger now. The paper on the large front window was ripped in a U, giving it a grotesque smile.

I looked up, expecting to see the blood-red shroud of the awning. Instead, I saw the sky through jagged holes. Years of rain and snow had taken their toll. I leaned to the side, wondering if I could still see the words scrawled across the front window of the two-story building. The ones that were supposed to make me proud because they were my own name. But all I could make out were *Books from . . . H . . . owner Gertrude . . .*

She had called this place Books from the Hart in a contrived reference to the town she had lived in her whole life.

I always called it Books from Hell.

The odd little dark-haired woman, wearing a coat that looked like a honeycomb, stepped forward and offered her hand. "You must be Gertrude Brown. I'm Reeba Sweeney."

I had to bend low to reach her and wondered if this was what it felt like to meet a hobbit. "Sorry I woke you up last night. And please, call me Trudy." Never, ever Gertrude.

She wrinkled her short nose with a loud laugh. "No problem. Sorry I couldn't get away to open up for you."

"I was surprised the lock had been changed."

"Uh . . . yes. Just recently. Someone broke in and got a little rowdy."

"Really? Was anything missing?" If I was lucky, everything would be missing.

"No, but—well, you'll see."

She handed me the key and it took several attempts to turn the knob. A few people behind me snickered.

"Maybe someone should help her," the larger woman whispered.

"Sshh!"

With a hearty jiggle of the wrist and a little muscle, I made the deadbolt give up its resistance. I turned the handle and pushed the door open. Stale air rushed out the building as if a tomb had been unsealed. A bell, strangely off tune, tinkled weakly on the door. Laughing at me . . . like always.

The dog stuck his nose in the air, alert to a scent that was new and foul. I took an uneven breath. The things here couldn't touch me anymore. I reached out to the wall beside me and flipped the light on. And just like that, the room came to life.

Books. From ceiling to floor. From the doorway to the back hall and beyond. Piles of books. Mountains of them. No room to walk. No room to breathe. Everything that had haunted my childhood stared straight back at me.

"Whoa . . ." someone said, breaking the silence.

A man bumped into me from behind. The earlier assemblage had followed me. I wasn't sorry they did. It helped to have company.

"Marva, stop pushing!" said navy-blue Joe to pink-glasses big lady.

I plastered myself against the wall, delaying my entrance into the store, as Marva shoved her large bulk to the forefront and halted on the threshold. "Lord almighty!"

"What is it?" someone said.

Marva turned around and faced the group on the sidewalk, stretching her hands across the doorway. "Don't anyone step past me. You're liable to get hurt."

"I don't know if it's that bad—" I started.

"Yes it is. Joe, you remember those books Gertrude stacked straight up to the ceiling?"

"You could barely squeeze from the As to the Ps." He stretched his neck, trying to see over her shoulder.

"I was fine with the Ps; it was you who had trouble, Joe," she said.

"For God's sake, would you stop talking about my prostate in front of the whole town," said Joe.

"Get on with what you were saying, Marva," said the mayor.

"Now George, I wasn't talking about Joe. I was talking about the Ps. Like James Patterson or Susan Elizabeth Phillips."

"Or Mario Puzo," someone added.

Ugh, people who read! I was surrounded by them wherever I went.

"And what, Marva? Come on. I got a breakfast I need to be at in ten minutes," said the mayor from the back of the mob. My stomach growled at the mere mention of breakfast.

This was ridiculous. I was boxed in between Marva and the doorway, and was feeling claustrophobic. Time to get over my fears. I ducked under her arm and took my chances on the mountain of books near the window. I sat on top and studied the room while the curiosity seekers kept talking in the doorway.

Marva waved her hand. "Do you all remember what this place used to be like? You remember, Regina? Little tiny aisles and towers of books that were several rows deep?"

"Yeah. Gertrude wouldn't let us pull anything ourselves. We had to call her if we needed help," Joe said behind her.

"That's right. If you needed a book, you had to tell her first. And then she'd give you all the reasons why you shouldn't read that book. She was always pushing the highbrow stuff on me. Said I read too much trash." I let my gaze pause on Marva and wondered where she bought her pants. They were cotton-candy pink and matched her glasses. I kind of liked them.

"Gertrude told me I was going to get nightmares from all the horror stories I read," Joe said.

My stomach growled. I remembered that I had a half-eaten piece of fruit leather in an inside pocket. I pulled it out, peeled back the wrapper, and gnawed on it. My collie friend pushed through the crowd when he heard the wrapper open. I held it away from him. "You ate already."

Someone in the back explained, "I started to go to the library. I mean, I hated to go to Harrisburg and all. And that one librarian was even meaner to me sometimes than Gertrude. The others are nice, mind you. But I couldn't handle her lectures."

"The librarian in Harrisburg?"

"No. Gertrude's."

"I can't say I blame you, June." Marva still held her hands across the doorjamb. "But now you have no choice. You will have to keep going to Harrisburg until this place gets cleaned up." She lowered her arms and stepped aside. I had taken a large bite of the fruit leather and my mouth was full. Everyone had a clear view of me sitting with my skirt spread out before me on a mound of mass-market paperbacks. I felt like Little Miss Muffet.

"This is worse than I could have ever imagined. It looks like she was a . . . a . . . ."

"Hoarder," someone finished.

I could have told them that years ago. My aunt loved her books as if they were her children. She adopted each one of them out to only worthy readers, and refused to let people take their chances on anything unless they had a serious interest in reading the books they bought. This meant that she scared most customers away.

She scared me too. But for different reasons.

"What are you going to do with all of this?" asked Marva.

I finished chewing, swallowed, and said, "I plan on selling it. You wouldn't happen to know any interested buyers, would you?"

"Yes. I can help you with that!" The real-estate lady worked her way toward the front of the crowd. She was almost as wide as she was tall, so several people had to plaster themselves against the doorway to make room.

I thought I heard someone mumble "sell-out Sweeney" as she passed.

Marva squinted at me over the top of Reeba Sweeney's head. "Don't be in too much of a rush, now. You never know what you might decide to do once you spend a little time here." She looked down her nose at Reeba Sweeney and then down at her watch. "Whoops, time for work. Well . . . Good luck."

"I've got to get to a meeting with the city council," said the mayor.

Reeba Sweeney grabbed his elbow. "I haven't received your donation to the Harrisburg Festival of the Arts, George."

He looked from her to me and then at the ground. "In the mail."

The crowd was gone so quickly, I wondered if it was something I said. But one look at the room around me made me understand why. Who wanted to suffer from accidental mummification under thousands of dusty books?

I was left sitting on my tuffet, curious to hear what Reeba Sweeney thought about selling the place. I pulled the wrapper over the remaining portion of my fruit leather and tucked it back in my pocket. My four-legged friend found the only bare spot on the floor and lay down with an *ooomph*.

Reeba Sweeney cleared her throat and stepped around me, careful not to trip on the magazines at her feet. "I hope you understand. Clients won't want to pay top dollar for this store. This place needs a lot of work."

"Mmm-hmmm." *A lot of work* was an understatement. I thought about the travel brochure tucked in my car's visor and prepared to bargain. I was forming a loose plan in my head. I needed to do some homework to figure out if it would work out. There were plenty of refuse-collection companies in business these days.

"You'll be happy to hear that I have a potential buyer who may be willing to give you cash."

I was taller sitting than she was standing, even in her heels. "Cash?"

"Cash. But first you'll need to clean the place out. He will want to know the floor and walls are structurally sound. The way it is now, no one would know if there were a hole straight through to the cellar. After that, you can be on your merry way to—wherever you came from?"

That wasn't going to happen. I rarely returned to the same place twice. Except Truhart, unfortunately.

"How much is this buyer willing to pay?"

She named a disappointing price. "I can barely get to Ohio with that amount. I was hoping to get more."

She blinked. "You're surprised?"

"I'm hoping for at least double."

"Maybe it's been too long since you were in this town, Trudy. This place isn't worth that kind of money. Look at the vacant grocery next door and all the buildings that are empty on Main Street. You can't be too picky about prices in this market. Even when it is cleaned up, no one will pay double. The paint is peeling, the shutters are hanging off. And you haven't even seen the upstairs apartment yet. You think this is bad, just wait!"

I thought about the plans I had made. Plans I had nurtured ever since Aunt Gertrude's lawyers had caught up to me. I needed that money. My dreams weren't going to change in a few short weeks. I had time to clean up and get a good price.

"I'll let you know when and if I decide to list the property with you. In the meantime, I appreciate your meeting me with the key."

"*If* you'll list with me?"

Before I left California, I had asked my friends how things were done. "Reeba, I hope you understand. I'm not going to make any decisions until I talk to a few other Realtors and get a feel for the market."

Reeba Sweeney's face no longer displayed a sales-pitch smile. In fact, her expression reminded me a lot of Aunt Gertrude's when she first found out I didn't like to read. She pulled a card out of her purse and handed it to me. "Office hours are from nine to five. Leave a message if you don't reach me," she said pointedly. I guess I was no longer a valued customer who could call her in the middle of the night.

"Where are you located?" I flipped the card over.

"Harrisburg!" she said. And she brushed a speck of dust off her coat and walked away.

Chapter 2

I sat on my nest of books. Echoes of Aunt Gertrude's voice drifted around me the same way tiny dust motes caught the light and floated around the room.

The last afternoon I had been here, Aunt Gertrude pointed her bony finger at me and called me lazy. If she'd stopped there, I would have made my usual escape to the woods or the shore of the lake. But she kept going. The words *stupid* and *lying* exploded from her lips. In a way, I don't blame her. All her frustration at being saddled with an ungrateful teenager broke to the surface. But she made me so angry that I marched upstairs and stuffed my things in my mother's old Samsonite suitcase.

I never thought I would be back.

Something dark moved in the doorway. Probably the cat I had seen last night. The old collie made a halfhearted attempt at a bark. Then he wagged his tail and looked at me, as if that counted as the kind of thing a fine watchdog would do.

"That was pathetic," I told him. I scanned the spot where the form disappeared.

That was when I noticed a tall form leaning against a tree on the other side of the street. His face was shadowed, but his arms were crossed in front of him in a pose that should have looked casual, but was more . . . intense. I was getting tired of being a spectacle. I rose from my literary chair, losing my balance and dislodging dozens of books. Once I was sure I wasn't going to do a nosedive into *The Great Gatsby* or— *Huck Sawyer* or whatever that book was. I looked up again. He was gone. Strange. But then again, this whole town was a bit strange.

On the bright side of things, we might be able to find the bed. Running water and a mattress would be heaven, even in this place.

I scaled the shifting paperbacks and hardcovers in an effort to get to the back room where the stairs to the apartment were. But it was almost impossible. No way could the old dog do it. "Come on, buddy, back to Lulu we go." The back door would be a straighter shot.

I pulled around to the alley that was nestled between a large field sprinkled with jack pines and the back of several empty buildings. Next to the field was a tennis court that was missing a net. Beyond it was an ice cream store and the faint blue streak of a lake through a stand of trees. I recalled that there was another lake nearby. The two had matching names. Echo and Reply. I don't know how they got those names. I used to scream from the shores of Echo all the time. No one ever replied.

I parked between a telephone pole and a pile of old wooden pallets, making sure that I could move forward if needed. Lulu wasn't at her best these days. She hiccupped every time I shifted gear. I grabbed my cooler and my old green Samsonite suitcase that contained my meager belongings. The collie perched on the seat and lowered his head. I sighed and reached down to help him.

"Aren't you guys supposed to leap tall fences and chase sheep across the glen?" He sent me a baleful look and I shook my head. I guess we were all typecast to some extent.

At the back door, the old aluminum storm door came loose in my hands. The dog skittered away as it clattered back against the door-jamb.

"This is just flippin' awesome."

I'd be lucky if anything worked properly. I removed the door and placed it against the aluminum siding. The key fit the new lock and the knob turned easily. Grateful for small favors, I pushed on the door. Nothing happened. I pushed with all my weight. It budged a few inches. I stuck my face through the opening.

It wasn't a pretty sight. Whoever had broken into the place had brought a tornado with them. Books were heaped everywhere. I had a fleeting moment of panic. Would anyone know or even care if I was lost forever? Other than Reeba Sweeney, not a soul in this town would miss me. No one would worry until Thanksgiving when I failed to make my biannual call to my father in New Jersey. Even then, he would probably make some comment about how unpredictable I was and assume I had decided to walk the Appalachian Trail.

I shoved with my shoulder and made enough room to slip through. Beside me, the dog whimpered. I crouched down. "We can either get started or spend another night in the car. What's it going to be?"

I was talking more to myself than to the old collie and I knew it. I had come to the proverbial fork in the road. And the truth was I had no real choice to make.

The bookstore was mine. It had been mine for the past year. In her infinitely warped sense of justice, Aunt Gertrude had left me with the one thing she knew I wouldn't want.

I could give up and walk away. Tell the lawyer I wanted no claim to the store, its contents, or its back taxes.

Or I could take a chance. Fix it up. Sell it. I could have the last laugh. After I paid the taxes and reimbursed my father for the money he leant me when I had my appendix out last spring, I would be clear and free. I could finance my trip to Asia. And then say good-bye to Truhart forever.

I had never been someone who had been averse to risks or taking chances. In fact, very little frightened me. But for some reason, this store scared the crap out of me.

I squeezed through the door. The front room had been bad enough. But it was almost tomblike in the back room. The sound of my own breathing and the panting of the dog at my knees filled the space. Outside, a car revved its engine at the only traffic light in town. The faint sounds of someone laughing down the street traveled on the wind. There was life out there.

My gaze wandered to the stairway that led to the apartment upstairs. I had no idea what to expect up there. More books? A dead body?

The dog moved past me. He sat down in front of a particularly hefty book and raised his ears. His dark eyes framed by the sable mask made him seem intelligent when he stared at me that way. He looked more ready to do this than I did. And if the wimpiest dog in the world was ready to take on the challenge, how could I walk away? We had come halfway across the country, after all.

"All right, buddy. But don't say I didn't warn you."

I reached down and grasped a book at my feet, clearing a path for both of us.

Chapter 3

There was nowhere to put the books that were piled everywhere. Never one to let tiny problems keep me from getting things done, I opened the door and threw them into the alley. It would do until I had a better option. I made a mental note to look into the cost of renting a dumpster, or even better, a junk-hauling service. If that didn't work, I could always start a bonfire.

I cleared enough space and eventually reached the bottom of the staircase. My hands were dust-covered, my back was sweaty, and my hair was coming loose.

I took a water break twice, sharing my bottle with the dog. I let him lap it up midair, caring little that I spilled on a dictionary at his feet. The tome was so old it probably still included the words *spiffy* and *golly*. By the time I reached the stairs I was out of patience. I brushed aside the books and let them tumble down the open rail to the floor below.

By then, the dog was asleep next to my suitcase in the middle of the path I had made. At least one of us seemed content. Too groggy to care about the falling books, he opened his eyes, made sure I was still nearby, and rolled on his side with a moan, dead to the world.

Finally I stood at the top of the stairs, in front of the door to the upstairs apartment.

"Oh, please, let there be a shower and clear path to it," I said to no one. I held a precautionary hand over my face, turned the tarnished brass handle, and pushed.

"Crap."

Since when had Aunt Gertrude become such a pack rat? Sure, I remembered the small apartment being cluttered with things she collected over the years. But never like this. Aunt Gertrude had either lost her marbles at the end, or the intruder Reeba Sweeney mentioned had been a very messy squatter.

Everywhere I looked there was junk.

Cereal boxes, baskets, cans of food, empty containers, dead plants, and grocery bags littered the ground. Pill bottles, tissue boxes, and pots and pans cluttered the counter of the small kitchenette. Piles of blankets, coats, magazines, and shoes were scattered across the couch and chair in the living area. And, of course, more books. Ironically, a broom stood near the door. The cleanest broom in the county, for sure.

I pulled my hand away from my nose, testing for biological hazards and dead animals. A stale, mildly sour smell permeated the air. I was grateful that there was no stench of rot. Spying the refrigerator, I decided to hold my gratitude. Unless Aunt Gertrude had an epiphany before she left on her cruise, chances were I'd be scrubbing that for the next month.

I pulled off the scarf that covered my hair and wiped my face. Suddenly, this was overwhelming. The prospect of walking away looked brighter and brighter. It was going to take a lot to get this place cleaned up and ready to sell. Maybe Reeba Sweeney could sell as is and I could take a loss.

And then what?

Hunger sent yearnings for rice noodles in Vietnam and curry in Thailand through me. Flashes of wise monks and hidden temples gave me courage.

I spotted a small path through the main room and stepped with one foot in front of the other, as if I were on a balance beam, toward a window above the couch. Climbing on the armrest, I steadied myself against the wall and reached for the window latch. Then I threw up the window sash and let a wave of fresh air spill into the room.

I made my way further down the path to the bedroom. Clothes and books and magazines again. Boxes in the corner. But there was a bed. A glorious, marvelous bed. Only a few clothes rested across its surface. I climbed over a pile by the window, slipping and sliding on things I could not name, and once again opened the window.

I hopped over a broken chair to see if the bathroom was still intact. I flipped on the light to reveal a dingy room with—what else? Books. But at least they weren't in the toilet. There was some access to the sink. And even though there were rust spots and corrosion all over the white porcelain fixtures, the water was working. Reddish-brown liquid burst from the pipes in gargling spurts that eventually cleared and became even.

Within minutes I had every window in the apartment open. Fresh air wandered to the furthest corners. Raising my arms above my head, I took a deep breath and did the mountain pose. Breathing in and out, I let that single yoga move wash over me.

Okay. This was doable. Armed with a breeze and an idea of what I needed to do, I tackled the one room I wanted most. The one I could finish by the end of the day. The bathroom.

I set down the sponge I had used to scrub the tub, grateful that Aunt Gertrude had hoarded cleaning supplies. There were five duplicates of every bathroom cleaner in existence under the sink.

I dried off with the towel I had retrieved from Lulu. I hadn't had a shower since that campground outside Joliet. It felt wonderful to be clean.

While I blotted my long hair, I studied the books that covered the floor. Aunt Gertrude apparently favored books that looked like short-story collections and old magazines for her bathroom reading. The thought of her sitting in here until she finished made me laugh. I attacked the stack between the toilet and sink, tossing the larger books out the window to the alley below.

A muffled grunt caught my attention.

A high-pitched bark erupted from the floor below me. My sleeping friend heard something too.

"Hello? Anyone out there?" I yelled. No reply. I must have imagined it. I picked up another handful of books and tossed them.

A shout erupted from the alley. Did I hear someone say "bloody"?

A man lay sprawled across the mound of books and magazines I had just thrown away. Wrapping the towel around me, I shoved my feet in my boots and tromped down the staircase and out the back door to investigate.

A tall, golden-haired man lay on his back, arms and legs flailing about. Black-rimmed glasses hung from one ear. He held a hand over his nose.

I skirted a pile of magazines to get to him. "Can I help you?"

He gawked at me and adjusted his glasses. With better vision he inspected me from my wet head to my boots. A silly grin split his face. I wasn't used to that kind of unveiled male appreciation. It made me wonder if he had sustained a concussion. Either way, I would take the compliment. I selfishly basked in the light of appreciation.

I shook my hips, half joking. "Like what you see?"

His face turned red and he whipped the glasses off again. "No. No!"

"You don't like what you see?"

"No. I mean, yes. I'm not really looking at anything at all. Not that you're nothing, that is. I . . ." His voice trailed off.

I extended my arm his way. "Let me help you up."

The knot of towel at my armpit slipped and he shook his head. "It's all good. Just go back to holding the tow—" He rolled over.

"I thought you weren't looking?"

"I'm not. Now." He came up on his hands and knees and tested the sturdiness of the ground before he unfolded his long body. When he finished, I had to tilt my head back. He stood on several layers of books, but I suspected that he was tall even without his pedestal. He was lean too. He held a book in his hand.

"Are you trash picking?"

"Of course not. I saw these books and I was—" He stopped himself and sighed. "I must seem like a blithering idiot. I sincerely apologize for interrupting your—uh—bathing."

I knew his type. Even though his clothes were out of alignment from his fall, his khaki pants, blue oxford shirt, and brown sweater vest made him look like he had just come from the library. His broad shoulders almost shattered the image. But his nervousness sealed it.

"No need to apologize or act all formal on this side of the pond," I said, referring to his British accent. "Especially when I'm the one who just threw a hardcover on your head."

He placed his glasses back on his face. "Well, it was my fault too. I forgot to check the weather report for falling books." Humor? Interesting. He was younger than I thought. Square jaw, long nose. Close-cropped amber hair with hints of sunshine. Early thirties, maybe.

"Hey, were you standing in the front of the bookstore earlier? I think I saw you across the street."

He stepped off the stack of books. He was still tall. "Could be. I was . . . walking by a while ago."

The dog whined loudly from the open back door. "That's the dog's way of protecting me," I explained. Just to prove his viciousness, the old collie wagged his tail and came to investigate.

"I'm shaking in my shoes." He put a hand on the dog's back.

Something caught his eye. He put his glasses on and reached for the magazine under my feet. A soggy Richard Nixon smiled at us from the front cover of the *Saturday Evening Post*. "This issue is fairly rare, I believe." He yanked on the pages. I stepped back and he shook the magazine. Water dripped off of Dick's five-o'clock shadow.

I hung my head upside down and shook my hair. "Didn't he have some kind of problem with water? Water . . . water . . ."

"Watergate?"

"That's it!" I said, flipping my head back. My hair caught the breeze.

A muscle in his jaw flickered. That same look of appreciation that had put me in a tizzy earlier passed over his face. His smile could have come with a martini—stirred, not shaken.

"Why don't you come inside and sit down for a moment? You could really be hurt."

He rubbed his forehead and gazed at the open door. "Well, if you insist. But how do you know I'm not using the weak excuse of a concussion as an opportunity to pinch all your worldly goods?"

"Because I'm never that lucky," I said, laughing. He could pinch me and my worldly goods any time.

"I think I'm too dizzy to get that."

"That's all right. Most people don't get me." I walked toward the door, but he paused.

"My name is Christopher Darlington, by the way. Just in case you feel the need to know my name before I commit a crime."

He was so darn proper that I felt like curtsying. For once I decided to use my full name. "I'm Gertrude Brown."

His eyebrow shot up and he leaned forward, as if he hadn't heard me. I suppose even to a Brit it was an unusual name.

"I'm named after my great-aunt Gertrude, who lived here. My friends call me Trudy."

Whatever I said seemed to please him. A full grin spread across his very appealing pale lips. "My friends call me Kit. Christopher was my uncle."

Something in common and we'd only known each other for two minutes. "Pleased to meet you, Kit." I held out my hand.

"Likewise, Trudy."

There must have been static from that pile of old books. A shock ran up my arm when our hands touched. We both jumped back, surprised.

And my towel dropped.

Nudity was an embarrassing predicament when I was young. I avoided it in the locker rooms during gym just like every other teenage girl. But when I was nineteen, I spent two years in California, working at various auto garages in the Castro and Haight-Ashbury districts of San Francisco. There, I learned that clothing was a socially constructed idea that I had been taught from an early age. I didn't walk the streets nude every day like some of the characters I befriended. But I enjoyed the freedom of participating in several events to celebrate the natural state of the human body.

At first it had been awkward. But by the time I participated in the "World Naked Bike Ride" and "Saint Stupid's Day Parade" I found nudity to be fun and enlightening. Among the sea of short, large, hairy, and sagging bodies, I learned that my own lanky, small breasted body was just as normal as everyone else's. It was liberating.

When my towel dropped, I picked it up and kept going. "Come on in. I can't offer you a seat. But I can offer you a book."

The dog ran ahead of me and barked at Kit to follow. He wiggled so much that I had to nudge him so we could pass through the door.

Kit seemed to be having trouble keeping up. He kept sucking in air and clearing his throat. I took pity and rewrapped the towel more firmly.

Making extra room for my guest, I kicked several books out of the way. When I turned around, it was to find that Kit had taken a great deal of interest in the back door and its hinges. His ears were red.

"The towel's back."

When he pivoted toward me the sun caught his glasses and I couldn't see his expression. Whatever embarrassment lingered disappeared the moment he noticed the books that filled every corner of the room.

"Good Lord."

"Simply shocking," I concurred in my best British accent.

He ignored my impersonation and scanned the room. "This is . . . impossible."

"Impossible? I'd call it many things. Ridiculous. Outrageous. But impossible? I'm not getting that same frequency, Kit."

He climbed over a pile of books near the door that separated the front and back room to get a better view of the store. "It could take years to go through all these books."

"I sure hope you're wrong. I'm giving it a few weeks."

"Your aunt lived here?"

"It wasn't quite so bad fourteen years ago. It was a bookstore. Used and new. She had a lot of books even then. But they were neatly piled up in the shelves and in stacks. Now it looks like there was a great big earthquake."

"What on earth happened?"

"Squatters, supposedly. Although I have a feeling the property management neglected it until I claimed the old place. The upstairs apartment is just as bad. I made it into the shower, however, as you can see."

The old collie had taken to Kit. He sniffed his private parts.

"Hi girl." Kit patted his head and tried to redirect his nose.

"Boy."

"Sorry."

"Everyone does that because he is so pretty."

"What's his name?" He stroked an apparent sensitive spot behind the dog's ear. I was almost jealous as I watched the dog melt in his large hands.

"He doesn't have a name."

"That's odd."

Kit returned his attention to the books. He reached down, stacking them into neat little piles. He seemed on edge as he straightened the books at an inhuman speed. Maybe he really was a librarian.

"Are you looking for something?" I moved closer and kicked a large book—with a picture of Martha Stewart on the cover—out of my way.

"No. No—yes, actually." He stopped and adjusted his collar. "Sorry. I should have explained earlier. When I saw the books littered in the alley, I couldn't help myself. Are they yours?"

"Not if I can help it." I tilted my head and read the spine of the book he held. It took me a moment to make out the words. *"Naked Birds and Antelopes?"*

"You mean *Native Birds of North America?"*

I felt heat creep to my face. "Hmm. You like that stuff?"

"Yes. Especially books on literature . . ." He blinked. "And uh . . .

things about the region. Logging. Local customs . . . famous authors."
He searched my face. "Even ornithology like this," he added weakly.

A long, tangled strand of hair was dripping down my neck. I
flipped my head back and forth to get rid of the excess moisture. "Or-
nith—what was that?"

"Ornithology. The study of birds." He said it as if I should know
the word.

"Oh." I couldn't hide the disappointment in my voice. Nothing
like a discussion on birds and books to cut off my estrogen.

He was handsome in a very Britishy sort of way. But a bit of a
weeny, after all. I wasn't one to judge, of course. But my personal
preference ran to cars and engines and anything that I could explore
without the need for a manual. Usually men who liked that stuff
came with tattoos and bulging muscles.

His eyelids lowered to where my towel had slipped. Was that fog
on his glasses? Or maybe he was trying to figure out if he would
make it out of this place alive. Since it was clear there was no danger
of him being a serial killer, I nodded my head toward the stairs.
"Come on upstairs. You can take anything you want. I'm guessing
Aunt Gertrude saved the best books for her own apartment."

He followed me up the wooden steps. My towel wasn't the fluffy
kind that reached the knees. It was the standard "one size fits all"
from the dollar store. I was well aware that I was somewhat exposed
to the man behind me. I didn't care about my nudity, but goose
bumps broke out on the backs of my arms anyway. I was probably
just cold. Still, was he peeking? I turned my head sharply. The top of
his head and the back of his neck were all that was visible as he con-
centrated on each step.

I waved my hand when we reached the top of the steps. "Here
we are."

He stepped in front of me and took in the view. He passed his
hand over his eyes. His cheeks were ruddy and red. I'd never seen
someone so excited about books. Yep. I was definitely safe with him.

"I'm pretty sure I saw several books with birds on the cover near
the window. Go ahead and look. Take anything you see. I'll finish
getting dressed," I said, unwrapping my towel and grabbing my suitcase. I was bothered by my virginal reaction on the stairs. Just to
prove I was still the same "Anything Goes Trudy" my San Francisco
friends called me, I left the door to the bathroom open as I changed. I

heard Kit Darlington clearing his throat and then the unmistakable sound of books and clutter being moved about.

"What brings you here?" I pulled on my dollar-store panties with pink pandas all over them. There was a pause and I wondered if he heard me. "What are you doing in Truhart?"

"Research."

"Really? On birds?"

Another silence. "Ahhh . . . that and more." He sneezed.

"Are you allergic to dogs?" I stepped into my leggings.

"Dust."

"Sorry. Everything in this place is dusty. It's been sitting for almost a year." I slipped my arms into an oversized olive-green tunic I bought at a secondhand shop in New York a few years ago. He sneezed again.

"If you want, I can see if Aunt Gertrude has some apple cider." I combed my fingers through my damp hair and moved into the main room.

He wasn't where I had left him. He was scrutinizing a pile of books under the table in the living area. He jumped and turned with a guilty look on his face.

"I thought I saw another bird book." He had nothing in his hands. "Apple cider, did you say?" His tone was so polite I wanted to offer him tea and crumpets. What was it with the English? They were so proper it made you lift your pinky finger and straighten your posture when you were around them.

I smoothed the front of my shirt. "Apple cider. You can mix it with water and drink it three times a day. It helps all the mucous and stuff that come with allergies."

"I have an antihistamine for allergies."

"Those aren't good for you, you know. All those chemicals are bad for your body. At the very least you should use a neti pot."

I moved close and turned my back to him. "Do you mind?"

"Mind what?"

"Can you button that top button in back? It's so much easier when I have someone to help me."

I lifted my wet hair and felt his warm hands at the base of my neck. That same rush I felt on the stairs traveled down my back. Only this time it didn't feel like goose bumps. It felt like velvet.

I stepped away and turned toward him. I could see a smattering of blond hair on his lower arms where he had rolled up his sleeves in perfect folds that must have taken many years of practice. I shouldn't be attracted to him at all. He was way too clean-cut. But he wasn't totally nerdy. The deep blue eyes behind the black-rimmed glasses and the square jaw that needed a shave proved that. I giggled. I was being ridiculous. I mean, he was into birds!

An old boyfriend of mine had been into birds too. Our last day together he told me he was going for a walk in the woods. He returned holding a gun and a half-dozen sparrows upside down as if they were weeds. He made fun of my horror and claimed they were the rats of the sky. It still made my blood run cold to think I had slept with the man.

I narrowed my eyes. "What exactly do you like about birds?"

"Birds? Ah . . . I am fascinated by birds. Specific ones that are . . . native to this area."

"Really? You mean like where they can be found so you can shoot them or like their mating rituals and stuff?"

"I don't own a gun or shoot anything. And I always find mating rituals fascinating." His eyes wandered to the front of my sweater. I hadn't bothered with a bra. There was nothing there. I was almost as flat as he was.

He coughed.

"You better be careful with those allergies, Kit." I pulled my hair into a loose knot.

He moved to the back window and cleared his throat. "Is that your car outside?"

"Yup. That's Lulu."

"Lulu?"

"She's a classic."

He put his hand over his mouth, but I could see a smile. "You named your car but not your dog?"

"Well, he's not really my dog. And Leo named the car. A long time ago."

"Boyfriend?"

"Brother." Leo had been gone for several years and thinking about my only sibling still made my chest hurt.

"What are you going to do with all of this?" He studied every piece of junk in the room. Even a basket with papers falling out. He lifted the stack and peeked between the sheets.

"When I first saw this mess, I briefly considered calling that TV show about hoarders to come over and check it out. But I'm pretty sure that will take more time than I actually have."

"Time?"

"Yup. It's all going in the trash as soon as I get a dumpster here."

His head jerked up. *"What?"* He backed up against a large pile of books, almost falling over. "Do you mean you are throwing all these books away?"

"That's the plan."

"You are going to take them by the handful and toss them?" He uttered each word separately. His tall frame blocked the sunlight from the window. With the light coming behind him, he reminded me of my father when I left vegetables on my dinner plate.

Out of habit I stood up straighter. "Yes." The word *sir* had been on the tip of my tongue.

But the mirage ended when Kit sank down until he was sitting on a book stack. "Let me understand this, Trudy. You want to throw all the books in this bookshop away?"

"Yes."

"Why?"

I had the urge to apologize for disappointing him. "I know it isn't PC. That's *politically correct*, in case you don't have that term in England. Everyone loves the idea of bookstores and the nostalgic memories of getting lost in the stacks and reading Nancy Hardy or the Drews or"—his face was blank—"or whatever kids liked in England when you grew up. And I know how romantic bookstores are in movies. But I can't afford the walk down memory road."

"Because?"

"Because I have a building to sell. And a trip to Asia to plan. Books don't sell anymore. Everyone knows that."

"That isn't technically true."

"I spent the summer here fourteen years ago. We had no more than ten people who regularly shopped in this place." I paused and thought about it. "I guess I should be fair. I never hung around long enough to take notice. And this town isn't exactly Boston. Have you seen the other buildings on Main Street? Nothing sells in this town unless it has an engine and runs on dirt, snow, or water."

"I hear they're trying to change things."

"Are they still talking about a community center? They were talking about that fourteen years ago."

Adjusting his position, he pulled a book from beneath him. He checked out the title and opened the first page, then set it aside. "Exactly what do you have against books?"

"Nothing. They make great seats."

He stood up and grabbed a book from an overflowing laundry basket. "Why the rush? I mean, there are probably some splendid books in this space."

"I thought about that. But most of these books are used. There isn't much value in this place except for the property it sits on." Even that was sketchy, judging by the empty buildings on Main Street.

His gaze floundered around the room, as if he were having a panic attack. Poor guy. A sensitive type. He ran a hand over his chin. "Wasn't there a—a famous author who used to live around here?"

"Who cares about that old dude?"

"A lot of—" He lowered his chin and stopped himself. "You should consider other options. Charities are always looking for books. And there are surely other uses for them."

"Finding a home for everything here would take months."

"Not really. It's all the things that aren't books that are causing the biggest eyesore." His voice was husky now. He had moved closer as we talked. A hint of cologne mixed with something else was making me want to lick him. If heat had an aroma, that was the other ingredient I smelled.

I shook my head and stepped away. "No. I want it cleared out quickly. Then I can sell it."

"What's the rush?"

"Travel. Life. It's all waiting for me."

He didn't respond. His glasses were in his hand and he was scanning the disintegrating volume that had broken apart in his hand. He rifled through several loose papers, the smile gone from his face.

"Everything all right?"

He mumbled something to himself.

"Earth to Kit?" I said again.

His blue eyes darted my way and I was struck by their intensity. A gust of wind sent the curtains billowing and knocked over the broom. As suddenly as the breeze came up, it disappeared.

Kit blinked, coming back from where he had been a moment ago. He walked over and righted the broom.

"Thank you. I'm going to get settled this afternoon and start cleaning out again tomorrow."

Kit gazed around with the same hungry expression the dog did when I unwrapped my fruit leather earlier. I took pity and offered him a crumb. "Feel free to stop by any time before I empty this place. You see a book you want? It's yours."

He put a finger to his lip. "I might do that."

He was almost at the bottom of the stairs when I called down to him. "Hey!"

He turned around.

"You forgot your bird books." I held out several that he had put aside earlier.

"Oh yes, of course." He ran up the steps and took them from me. "I almost forgot."

The sound of his footsteps going back down the back stairs were slow and deliberate. He took his time leaving. When I heard the back door close, I peeked out the window and caught him looking in the trash again.

Academics were such obsessive sorts. In love with the written word. Too bad. The dog leaned against my leg. His companionship was much more my style. Limited vocabulary. Simple needs.

Beyond the alley came a sweetly captivating melody. A tiny yellow-breasted bird flapped its wings from where it was perched on a low-lying jack-pine branch. It was beautiful with its bright-colored breast and a dark mask around its eyes. I checked to see if Kit had seen it. But he was looking down at the books at his feet.

Chapter 4

The old collie sat down, cocked his head, and whined. With those dark eyes rimmed by graying fur, he looked at me like I was supposed to know what he was thinking. I hated it when he did that. Human speak was tough enough. But dog speak did not come naturally to me. Since we'd been together, I worked hard to interpret his sounds and gestures. Usually I figured he was hungry. But a nagging sense that I wasn't understanding him kept bothering me.

I ruffled his ears. "Come on, carnivore dog. Let's find you some meat!" Poor thing. It would have gone easier on him if he had been thrust on a meat-loving person who lived on acres of green grass and had sheep to chase. But he was stuck with a homeless vegan like me.

I left the doors unlocked, hoping for a book thief, and headed toward the one restaurant in town that appeared to be open. Along the way, we passed the vacant grocery store that abutted the bookstore. The sign above the door was gone now. It had been called something like Kreap's Grocery Store when I lived here, but I always thought of it as Creepy's. Not because I couldn't read the name properly, but because it was dark and empty, even then. A Laundromat called the Sit and Spin stood on the corner. If Aunt Gertrude's washing machine in the cellar didn't work, that would be handy. On the opposite corner stood a small building with a sign that read *Colon Cleaners*. That stopped me in my tracks until I saw the faded outline of a Y at the end of *Colon*. At least someone in this town had a sense of humor.

The other stores on Main Street were few and far between. False clapboard fronts were the genius of some 1970s architect who should have been run out of town. It was supposed to evoke a lumber-town character, but instead it made Truhart feel like a Western ghost town.

The only thing missing was a tangled ball of tumbleweed rolling down the street.

The end of Main Street was the only place that showed signs of life. *Cookee's Diner*, the sign on the roof read. Several cars parked in angled spots in front guaranteed people, and the smell of something cooking on the griddle promised a tasty treat for my furry friend. I hoped they would have something for me. Even in a large city, it wasn't always easy to find food with no milk products, eggs, or honey. I couldn't imagine what it would be like in a small town like Truhart.

I knelt down in front of the dog. I didn't own a leash. And even if I did, I wouldn't have tied him to it. Not after the way I found him.

"Stay if you want to keep hanging with me, dude. Otherwise, good luck." He raised his ears and tilted his head. He had heard me say that before. Yet he always waited exactly where I left him when I returned. Old faithful. He might be old and wimpy, but he was going to make someone a great companion someday.

A bell above the door jingled. The soothing aroma of coffee and the haze of fried food filled the diner. Beside a front window were three large booths covered in faded blue vinyl. I glanced up at a sign above the counter: *Large Booths for 3 or More*, and felt a kinship with the two men sitting at the largest booth at the end of the counter. I loved people who ignored the rules.

A tall, balding man stood behind the counter. He was dressed in a white T-shirt, white pants, and a large apron that said *If you don't like my cooking lower your standards.* He greeted me. "Our waitress isn't back from picking up her granddaughter. But I can help you when you decide what you want. Whatever you want, we can fix it. But we try to impress our newer customers by giving them menus." He handed me a menu, then returned to the other end of the counter. The men in the booth were arguing. The cook got in on the debate.

While they talked, I pretended to read the menu.

"—I don't care if the county looks like a cesspool, I'm not paying more taxes to make the mayor's wife feel like she lives in Paris," argued a wiry, white-haired man wearing a faded plaid button-up under gray coveralls.

"I agree. But a community center and a better-looking downtown might attract more business and summer tourists," said the cook.

"We've got an ice cream stand and putt-putt golf. That's all they need, Mac," said a small, angular-faced man. He wore the same kind of gray overalls as the man across the booth from him.

"The lake is our big attraction. Not some sort of chic shopping district," said his buddy.

"Did you just use the word *chic*?" asked the cook.

The white-haired man looked over at me and winked. "I learned it from my wife. Every time she watches that HGTV channel, she moves furniture around and paints a room."

The cook pointed at me with a greasy spatula. "We need a woman's perspective. You're not going to defend that, are you? *Chic* is a stupid word."

I raised palms toward them to show I took no offense. "I don't own a couch to move or a TV to watch, so no defending here."

"A lady after my own heart," the cook said, lifting a spoon in the air. "Now food is different. Definitely worth spending time and money on. What can I get you, my dear?"

"How about oatmeal and coffee?"

His mouth turned down.

I looked outside and saw my friend, with those two furry ears and dark eyes of longing, looking through the door. "To go, if you don't mind. No butter, no cream or milk."

The cook reached for a pot from the rack and turned to the stove. "Breakfast so late? Are you sure? You're tall but you look like a good wind could blow you over. Can I fix you an omelet and hash browns on the side?"

"No thanks, I don't eat eggs."

"Allergies, huh?" he asked over his shoulder.

"No, vegan."

That made him stop with his spoon in the air. "Vegan?"

"Isn't that some sort of weird satanic ritual?" one of the men at the booth said. The other man chuckled.

The cook stepped in front of me and lowered his body until his elbows rested on the counter. "I have never met an actual vegan. I've certainly never cooked for one. What don't vegans eat again?"

"Meat, fish, poultry, or any other animal by-products."

"Eggs?"

"None." I shook my head. My no-egg policy had already been established, but I knew I'd have to say it again until it sank in.

"Is it because they are a rooster away from being baby chicks?

You do know that the eggs aren't fertilized, don't you, honey?" He said it as if I was ten years old and finding out the truth about Santa Claus.

"I know. It's because I like and I respect chickens."

"So do we. I respect a good chicken sandwich," said one of the men at the booth. They both laughed. I was used to it. I crossed my arms and sighed.

"No egg-eating at all, huh?"

"No eggs."

The cook's dark eyes, framed by thick eyebrows with wayward strands of hair, made him look kind. I didn't want to insult his own views on food and animals.

"It's my *thing*. I don't like to see animals harmed in any way. I have concerns about their treatment and living conditions. Oatmeal is filling, so I'm good."

The small man decided to keep up the comedy skit. "Those oats are rolled and tortured before they get in your bowl."

"Stuff it, Vance!"

"What? Oats are alive. Besides, who orders oatmeal at a diner?" he muttered.

"My customer comes first and I won't have you treating anybody with disrespect." The cook picked up a coffeepot and grabbed a Styrofoam cup.

"Jeez, Mac, ever since his lordship came to town, everyone's been all about manners and respect."

A woman with startlingly bleached short hair walked in from a back room with a young girl in hand. "Vance, Murdock. I didn't realize the garage was closed for the day?"

"Now Corinne, we're only having fun."

"Fun, my—" She looked down at the girl and bit the top of her lip.

"Hi, Uncle Murdock." The girl said it so sadly it made the men at the booth frown.

"Hi, peanut." He sent a questioning look at the older woman.

The girl had the beautiful wide-set brown eyes and perfectly shaped round face that accompanied Down syndrome. Wet tears rimmed her eyes and she was hiccupping as if she were still recovering from a long cry.

The man called Murdock cleared his throat. "No disrespect intended to the lady, Corinne. We're just funnin' with her."

"No problem, I'm used to it," I said.

The woman led the little girl to a booth. As they passed me I smiled. The girl stared at me and I caught the hint of interest on her face.

"Here's a crayon and some papers to draw with." She was briefly distracted as the woman helped her draw shapes.

"The school ended up sending her home again?" Mac asked as he placed the coffee in front of me.

"That P.E. teacher made her sit in the corner of the gym during relay races. She was still crying when I got there."

I sipped the coffee, remembering times when I had suffered a similar fate in school. It was horrible when you wanted nothing more than to be included. Classmates were very perceptive. They figured if an adult could exclude a kid from the class so easily, they could too. The teacher decided you didn't belong in gym, spelling, or social studies, and the kids made sure you didn't belong at their lunch table, recess, or anywhere else.

Mac placed a bowl and spoon in front of me. He nodded toward the sidewalk. "I assume your friend isn't vegan." Then he put a plastic bowl with several pieces of chicken in front of me. "Bring the dish back when you're finished."

"Thank you." How did he know? I looked down at the bowl and felt my mood lift like the girl's with her crayons and paper. Sometimes it was the little things that made life better. I wanted to say more, but he was already back at the stove.

When I exited the diner, the dog stood up and wagged his tail. He circled me as if I were a GI returning from an overseas post. "I've only been gone a few minutes, take it easy." He was a neurotic mutt. I never knew if it was his fear of hunger or of being alone that made him act that way.

I settled on the curb next to him and we ate in companionable silence. When he finished, in something like thirty seconds after he started, the dog burped and lay down next to me. "I don't know why I put up with a carnivore canine like you."

"What's his name?" I looked up. The little girl stood next to me.

She was one of the few people who had gotten his gender correct.

"I don't know." I looked back inside the diner to make sure someone knew she was with me. The older woman stood behind the glass door and watched us.

"You don't know his name?" A shy smile was washing away her tear-stained face.

"Unfortunately, no."

She shook her head. "Everyone has a name."

"What's yours?"

She looked back at the door, making sure it was okay to keep talking to me. The woman nodded at us. I was amazed by the trust the lady put in a virtual stranger like me. But then again, this town was so small, they probably didn't understand the stranger danger that city-wise folks worried about.

"My name is Jenny."

"I'm Trudy." I held out my hand and she shook it with a grin and giggled.

Then her attention was back on the old collie. She crouched down and smiled at him. He wagged his tail. He was a ham. He loved attention.

"He needs a name . . ."

"He isn't my dog. So it doesn't seem right for me to name him."

"Who's is he?"

"Nobody's. He's still trying to find a home."

"He doesn't have a family?" Her smile disappeared.

"He belonged to someone I knew, but that man didn't seem to want him." The backstory on that was not kid-friendly.

I had just returned to Oakland after working as a roadie with a post-psychedelic surf-rock band when the package from Aunt Gertrude's lawyer caught up with me. I decided to stay with an old friend until I could get Lulu out of storage and hit the road for Truhart. I had forgotten about my friend's ugly love affair with tequila. That night, I lay on his couch listening to the rain beating on the roof, and counting the minutes until morning. When I heard a series of whimpers from outside, I went to investigate. I discovered the old collie tied to a shed, his fur so wet and muddy that I couldn't tell for sure if he was even a dog. He wouldn't come near me, even when I enticed him with a soggy piece of bread. I kept trying different foods until he couldn't resist the bologna. I cut the rope and loaded him in Lulu.

It took me a week to untangle his matted fur and even longer to get a little meat on his bones. But only a day to win his trust and friendship.

"Do you want to pet him?"

Jenny nodded. I reached for her short fingers and held her hands until she relaxed. Then I placed her hand on the dog's back and let her bury her fingers in his fur. Her eyes widened and her mouth opened as she clenched and unclenched her fist. The dog turned his head and nudged her hand with his nose. She fluttered her lashes and stiffened.

"It's okay. He's a good boy. He won't hurt you."

Then he licked her wrist. She laughed and pulled her hand away. It took several more tries to reassure her that the dog wouldn't do anything more than lick her hand. Jenny reached out her hand. The dog extended his neck until his nose was in her palm. He licked her fingers.

She looked me squarely in the eye. "He needs a name."

Her simple words held such conviction that I felt like I was in the presence of a philosopher. There was no way I could let her down. "I guess we can give him a temporary name until his family decides."

Jenny clapped her hands together. "Yay!"

We stared at the old boy, trying to figure it out. He lifted his head and posed with his ears up. A natural-born charmer.

"He doesn't look like a 'Spot' or 'Rover' does he?"

She shook her head. "Where is he from?"

"He came from a place called Oakland. We could name him Oakey. But I don't think he wants to remember that place. Do you have any ideas?"

She ran her tongue around her lower lip as she tried to think of a name. "I don't know."

"Hmm. He came to live with me the same day I received a package in the mail. A letter and a book." I don't know why I still had that book. Something about it being the last thing Aunt Gertrude ever saw kept me from tossing it.

"What was the book called?"

She was on to something, this very special girl. "*Moby-Dick.* I never read it. But I know the story. It's about a whale and a ship. I don't like the men in the book much. But I like the whale."

"What was the whale called?"

"He had the same name as the book. Moby Dick."

She giggled at that.

"How about just Moby? That's not a bad name, is it?" I asked.

That seemed to please her. She put her hands above his back, not quite touching. "Moby."

And like that, he was christened. I went back to my breakfast and by the time I finished my oatmeal, Jenny was sitting on the curb next to me, her hands stroking the dog's back.

"You can pet Moby whenever you see us together. I'm going to be living over there for a while." I pointed down the street.

"Yay!" She wrapped her hands around the dog's neck. Not many dogs would put up with having their neck squeezed. But this guy didn't have a mean bone in his body.

"Careful, Jenny!" The waitress came up behind me.

At first the stark difference between the woman's bleached-out hair and her dark eyebrows struck me as odd. When she smiled a little line above her lip appeared and her eyes warmed up. "I'm Corinne Scott. And it looks like you met my granddaughter, Jenny."

"I'm Trudy Brown."

"Why does that name sound familiar?" she asked, taking the empty bowl from my hands.

"I was named after my dad's aunt, Gertrude Brown."

"You're the niece?" She looked me up and down. Her eyes darted to Jenny and she chewed her lip. Was she concerned about me being around her granddaughter? My reputation preceded me. The entire town probably knew about my crazy habits and inferior mind. Even from the grave, Aunt Gertrude had ways of making me miserable.

It was time I got back to clearing out the store. "It was a great breakfast."

But Corinne wasn't listening. A small crowd had formed across the street. A dozen ladies stood in a circle. There was no mistaking the feminine twitters that reached my ears. I had been around actors and bands long enough to recognize the sound. It could only be made by women under the command of a powerful master. The sunlight reflected off his gilded head in the center of the gaggle. When he was in the store going loony over books, I had never considered him a chick magnet. Evidently, there was more to Kit Darlington than I originally thought.

He said something and bursts of high-pitched laughter followed. In the military they called it *rapid dominance*. This was shock and awe of a different sort. Should the military ever need to take over a female nation, he would make a great general. He saw us standing across from him and waved. I saluted.

Corinne stared at the group with a faraway smile on her pencil-lined lips. The bowl tipped in her hands and I reached out to steady her grip. "Are you okay?"

She looked down at me for a split second and shoved the plates in my hand. "Jenny, go back to your crayons. And Trudy, thanks for taking the dishes in." Then she walked across the street to join the women.

I stood with my mouth open, trying to understand. The cook appeared at my side. He took the bowls from me and shrugged. "It happens all the time since he came to town."

"Really?"

He nodded. "I'm Mac, by the way."

"Mac?" I tried to hide my amusement.

"I know, go ahead and laugh. A bald guy named Mac who is the cook at the diner. It's a big cliché." He leaned down until he was closer to my ear. "Actually, my name is Ambrose. Ambrose McAllister. But everyone started calling me Mac when I moved here."

"I'm Trudy Brown, Ambrose."

"No. Call me Mac like everyone else. Otherwise, they might confuse me with a fancy pants like that guy."

"Okay, Mac." I clutched my army sack purse. "I still have to pay—"

He stepped back. "This one's on me. That smile on Jenny's face is worth a bowl of oatmeal."

"Thanks. That's not necessary, though. She brightened my own day."

"I'm also offering a shameful bribe, Trudy Brown. I would love to hear more about what it means to be vegan."

"Only if you can explain that phenomenon," I said, referring to Kit and the ladies.

"His lordship."

"What?"

Jenny raised her finger and pointed toward the throng. "His lordship."

I let the words sink in. Was Kit some kind of crazy English lord with the power to hypnotize anyone with a hint of estrogen? Jenny appeared unfazed. I'd like to say I was too. But my skin still tingled at the memory of his gaze on my towel-clad body.

I put a hand on Jenny's shoulder. "How about we get you back inside. I believe your crayons await, fair princess."

She seemed to consider that. Then she put her hand in my grip and let me see a gummy smile.

Something woke me. The nightmare again. The one where every day was the first day of school. Where every classroom was brimming with smart kids who never made mistakes. The one in which the teacher called on me to read aloud over and over and over.

A clattering noise sounded from outside. I tore off my night mask and sat up, drenched in sweat. A cold, wet nose found my hand and the dog, Moby, crawled toward me from the foot of the bed. Whether he was comforting me or I was comforting him wasn't clear.

The noise was probably a book falling from its perch. Or the loose shutter I noticed yesterday. I waited for the sound again, but there was nothing.

I left the bed and went to the window to see if anyone was outside. The street was dark and empty. Flipping the switch at the stairway, I called, "Hello?"

Only books.

When I returned to the bed I willed myself to banish the old dream back to my subconscious. The problem was, the old dream wasn't far from the reality that had been my school experience. My teachers never spent much time worrying about a girl with poor reading skills. It was easier for them to blame my problem on the revolving door of army-base schools I had attended rather than the expense of getting tested for a diagnosis of dyslexia.

If a class involved reading out loud, I would fake a sudden bout of nausea and head to the clinic. When I was older, I learned to skip the class. Getting detention for missing school didn't matter when I was already flunking out.

Meeting Jenny today must have stirred up those old memories.

If I lay very still and focused on my breathing I could relax. I felt Moby's chin on my leg. He seemed to be waiting for me to settle down. Even so, it took me a long time to get back to sleep.

Chapter 5

The next morning, I crouched by the front door and poured Coca-Cola over a rusted hinge. I found the can in the toilet tank, where I'd hidden it from Aunt Gertrude all those years ago. I couldn't stop smiling about it. Neither she nor any plumber had ever discovered it nestled between the float and the overflow tube, like a stowaway in the brig of an old ship.

The liquid coated the hardware, and I marveled at the power of cola to rid surfaces of rust. Satisfaction ran through me as I scrubbed the hinge with one of Aunt Gertrude's toothbrushes and watched it slowly eat away the corrosive buildup. With a little elbow grease, the gleam of metal appeared and years of grime and oxidation were washed away. My guess was the hardware on the door hadn't been seen to since before soldiers stormed the beach at Normandy. Raising myself to the tiptoes of my vintage army boots that could have been in the same battle, I drizzled more on the top hinge. The movement dislodged the old San Diego Padres cap that kept my hair in place. I ignored it and scrubbed. Several strands of red curls caught the breeze and whipped me in the face. I scrunched up my lips and tried to blow them away from the side of my mouth.

Leo used to call me *spaghetti-head* when we were little. It turned out to be one of the kinder nicknames for me. My classmates had other words. *Agent orange*, *blood-sucker-head*, and *red devil* were some of the worst. By the time I was twelve, the teasing bothered me so much that one morning before school, I cut off all my hair. When I stared at myself in the mirror, even *I* knew it looked horrible. When my mother saw me, she burst into tears. I ran to her and buried my face in her stomach, apologizing over and over. I don't know which one of us was more upset. Mom let me stay home from school that day. We visited the beauty shop and the poor beautician did what she could to clean up my hack job. Mom and I played dress-up the rest of the day. It was one of my last good memories of her. The following year, my brother and I were dumped on Aunt Gertrude. By then my hair had grown to my shoulders. Ever the diplomatic one, Aunt Gertrude had taken one look at me and declared that it reminded her of the copper pads people used to clean their pans. Being called names wasn't even a blip on my radar of worries by that time.

I finished scouring the hinge and reached down to retrieve the cap.

A pair of perfectly polished European leather shoes came into view.

"Does the door always like drinking Coca-Cola in the morning?" Kit Darlington leaned against the side of the building holding a Styrofoam cup and a bag.

I set the can on the ground. "It gets rid of rust and creaking. See." I pushed the door and it opened without a sound. I had rolled out of bed an hour earlier, still trying to adjust to waking up just short of noon. I wished I had pulled on something other than my worn Earth Day T-shirt and my hole-riddled jeans this morning. He looked like he had just stepped out of an Aston Martin.

"Interesting. Here's a better substitution for Coca-Cola in the morning." He handed me a cup of coffee.

"You're a lifesaver. I haven't had my morning fix yet. Thank you."

"Mac says hello." I nodded. I had popped in the diner after dinner last night and shared some of my vegan wisdom with him.

"Oh, this smells wonderful. Do you want to come inside, so I can sit on my tuffet to enjoy this?"

"Your what?"

"Books." I held up my hand. "After you."

Moby rose from where he'd been laying in a stripe of sunshine inside the door. Kit patted him on the head and fished out a couple of sausages from the bag. "Here you go, boy. This is for you from Mac."

"You've got a friend for life, now." There was no room to go deeper into the store, so we stood in the small space by the front windows.

Kit straightened a stack of books until they formed a chair and brushed off the top tome. "Here's your settee."

"Am I going to owe you a tip for bringing me coffee and finding me a seat?"

He scanned the room. "I kept thinking about you and this horrendous mess. I thought I would see if you needed a hand this morning."

"This place could use a dozen hands to get it cleaned up. But you don't have to help me, you know." I lowered myself and lifted the lid, inhaling the beautiful smell of java.

"It's no problem t'all. Just sit, relax, and tell me where to get started."

"This isn't normal for me."

"Drinking coffee?"

"No. I've never known a man who wanted me to sit while he cleaned."

"What kind of duffers have you been dealing with?"

I smiled into my coffee at the term. "Not too many of the good kind of duffers, I guess." For the past year, I had been reminding myself of all the reasons why I never wanted to hook up with a man again. Now they weren't just creeps, losers, assholes, and tools. They were duffers too. I would add that term to my vocabulary. I worked hard at using appropriate and interesting words. It helped to make up for all the times I mixed them up by accident.

I watched him from the corner of my eye as he stacked books against the wall. He tilted each spine sideways so he could see the cover. Then he placed them into piles.

I waved my cup at the floor in the middle of the room. "Just make an aisle in the center of the floor so I can move. Throw everything in a pile against the wall."

"You can't treat books that way!"

"Why not?"

He stopped. "You aren't getting a dumpster yet, are you?"

I took another sip. "No. Not yet. But I thought I would start throwing some of these books away now. This stuff is ancient. I'm pretty sure there are travel books from the 1950s in that pile. Can you imagine what would happen if someone tried to take one of those to New York or L.A.?"

"They'd be looking for streetcars and the Knickerbocker Building." He relaxed and went back to work.

"Ooh-la-la. History. I'm impressed."

He shrugged. "It's ingrained since birth. Everywhere you turn in England there's a history lesson waiting for you. It gets rather tiresome after a while."

"Is that why you studied birds?"

"I didn't—no."

"I was wondering: How does one make a living in or-tho-lo-g-y?"

His smile froze at the mention of his specialty. "Or-*nith*-ology."

"That's what I said. You didn't hear me correctly." I looked down at my coffee and swirled it violently. I hated the way I always mixed up words.

"I'm not a—well, I'm actually a professor. Of American . . . uh, studies. I'm on sabbatical until January. Maybe longer."

I scrunched up my face and shuddered. "A professor? I should have known."

He raised his head. "Are you making fun of me?"

I waved my cup and took a big sip. "No, of course not. So where do you teach?"

"Cambridge." He mumbled it so matter-of-factly that I almost choked.

"No shit," I sputtered. "Should I call you Professor or Doctor or something?"

"Please don't. Only my students call me *doctor*."

I imagined him in front of the chalkboard, with a classroom of female students sighing and writing *I Love You* in the margin of their notes. Even I would be tempted to go to school if he was the professor. "Dr. Darlington. Nice!"

The corner of his mouth twitched. "Makes me sound like a total prat, doesn't it?"

"Don't take it too badly. It's better than *your lordship*."

"Oh, so you've heard that one?"

"Hard to ignore it when everyone I meet in this town mentions you. What is that all about? I mean, I know you're British. But how did they make the leap to calling you *my lord*?"

He tilted his head, trying to read one of the titles, and mumbled. "I keep telling them to stop." He picked up another book. "Perhaps you should organize this. It might help if you decide to give books away. I'll stack fiction in the shelves against this wall, and we can put nonfiction on the other side. If we come across children and young adult, let's put it in the back shelves."

"Why not just throw it in the alley? Trash comes in a few days."

He steepled his fingers to his lips as if weighing his words carefully. "Trudy, may I respectfully suggest that you give it a little time?

Sell the books cheaply. Or give them away if you prefer. There are a number of charitable organizations that would love to receive books."

"I wasn't planning to—"

He narrowed his eyes and focused on my T-shirt. "It is the responsible thing to do for the environment."

Now he had me. I had been guilted. Since the moment I decided to throw the books in a dumpster, I had been faced with a nagging sense that I was doing something wrong. I was the queen of vintage shopping, garage sales, and thrifting. Growing up, we had moved so much that giving away our clothes, toys, and household items to other military families was a way of life. Everything was recycled.

He straightened and came toward me. "You will spend about five hundred dollars on a dumpster, right? At least cover the cost by trying to sell some of this. And think about it. You could help all those kids and their families who have no books to read."

I crossed my arms. "I don't have that much time."

He squatted in front of me until we were eye to eye. "Asia, is it?"

"Angkor Wat. I've wanted to go since I was thirteen." But with my mom.

"Isn't it still the rainy season in Southeast Asia?"

"It's almost over."

"Then you have time. It's only September. The next rainy season doesn't start again until late spring."

He was probably right. I wasn't crazy about the lowball offer from Reeba Sweeney's client. And no one else was banging down the door to see the place. But I wasn't ready to give in just yet. Unfortunately, the prospect of staying in Truhart any longer gave me the creeps.

"Why do you care so much?"

"It was just a suggestion." He stood up and bit his lip. The sunlight hit his glasses, obscuring his eyes. "Do you mind if I stop in sometimes and look around? Your aunt may have some—ah—interesting books that might help me in my research on the area."

"What are you researching? Midwestern ghost towns?"

"Old logging towns of the Midwest. Turn-of-the-century culture." He grabbed a pile of books and sorted them.

"And birds?"

"That too." He grabbed a stack of books at his feet.

"Hey, I didn't promise anything."

"Certainly." There was a new spring in his step as he moved around the room.

"You look happy."

"There's nothing better than spending the day among books—at least for me."

This was going to stink! The last thing I wanted to do was play librarian. But it made sense. If I got it organized, we could open up the doors and have one gigantic fire sale. I'd make enough pocket change to pay for a dumpster. Maybe even lure a tempted buyer in the process. Then it was off to Southeast Asia. The one place I could lose myself and find myself at the same time.

I set my coffee on the window ledge. "If I do decide to sell the books I would give it one week. No more."

"Mmm." He wasn't listening to me. I watched him leafing through a pile of papers and thought of a million excuses not to get near anything that resembled a book.

"Maybe I should get the broom and start sweeping."

"No sense in doing that until we have more floor space for you to actually sweep."

"Who knows what we'll find underneath this stuff." Maybe he was the squeamish sort. "Watch out for mice. We might have to remove some residents who weren't included in the will."

He glanced up. "I can get some mousetraps for you this afternoon."

I recoiled. "Traps? No way. That's cruel! I'm sure I can find a way to shoo them out the door without snapping their heads off."

He looked over at the dog, who was asleep near a stack of magazines. "Your nameless dog isn't doing his job if there are mice around."

"He's no longer nameless. A little girl fixed that yesterday. Meet Moby. And he wouldn't hurt a fly, poor old boy."

Kit reached over and rubbed his ears. Moby rolled over onto his side and lifted a paw, happy to be scratched. "He's a sweet chap. How did you two find each other?"

I didn't feel like going into the whole story. "We were both going in the same direction. Away."

"Moby. Hmm. Funny name. But it suits him, I think."

He turned back to work and I pretended to be busy cleaning off my pants. After several more minutes of stalling, he pointed to a heap nearby. "If you clear that area, you'll be able to get to the front door easier."

"You're really into this. It's so pointless," I moaned. I started the slow process of organizing books anyway.

Minutes felt like hours as I slowly sorted and stacked. The midday sun was high by the time I placed a book in the children's pile.

Kit reached out and stopped me. "That goes in the adult pile."

I pointed at the cartoon on the cover. "It's a kids' book. There's a cartoon on the cover."

"Nope. *Breakfast of Champions*. Kurt Vonnegut. You've heard of him, right?"

I scoffed, "Who hasn't?"

He sat back on his heels. "Sorry, I didn't mean to make you uncomfortable."

"Don't be silly. Every semiliterate person on this side of the pond knows him." I looked down at the sandy hair that covered his arm and swallowed. My head was pounding and I felt the sting of frustration behind my eyelids. "We've been at this for ages. Maybe I should get started upstairs. The apartment is what really needs cleaning first."

He studied my face. "That would be fine."

I stepped around him and almost tripped on the children's pile, as if the books were reaching out their manacled hands on purpose.

I heard Kit behind me. "Uh, are you all right?"

"I'm getting a headache."

"We could both use a break soon." He followed me.

"I'm only working a bit longer, then I have to grocery-shop."

"I'll help you get started in the living area," he said as we reached the top of the stairs.

"Suit yourself. Maybe you should have gone into the cleaning business instead of teaching." He ignored my grumpy comment.

Glad to have something besides words and titles to distract me, I moved aside a stack of paper grocery bags and opened a cabinet. Cleaning was not my favorite task. I was always grateful I didn't own a home to tidy. I would have to get used to the fact that I did now. At least temporarily.

Plastic cups, mugs, and glasses of all sizes lined the shelf. It was messy, but in the scheme of things it was the most normal-looking part of the apartment. Above the glasses a fine coat of dust covered the old Corelle dishes I remembered from years ago. I grabbed one of the five dish soaps under the sink and filled the basin with warm, soapy water. When I finished, I threw in the pots and pans and the utensils. Then I cleaned off the shelves. It was good to work with dishes. They had no pages or words.

Kit had cleared enough room on the couch to sit. I set the last dish in the wire rack and plopped down on the couch. "Let's take a break." Kit sank down next to me and I raised my eyebrow. "No sneezes this time?"

"I went to the chemist and bought antihistamines before coming this morning." Seeing the disapproval, he smiled and stretched out his long legs. "Don't get cheeky with me, now. I don't have time for homeopathic remedies. I happen to like instant relief like the rest of the world."

"Do you know how many chemicals you put into your body with that pill?"

"Almost as many as you put on the doorknob."

"Touché."

"Don't speak French. It gives me indigestion."

"Typical Brit." Was I flirting?

He gazed at me from lowered lashes. "No need to be sarcastic now. I get the impression that you are not enjoying this."

"Sorry, my aversion to cleaning is almost as strong as my aversion to this store."

"What did you do for a living before you came here?"

"I worked for several touring bands and theater companies."

"You're an actress?"

"Oh right." I let the sarcasm drip off my words. "Do I look like an actress?"

His eyes wandered from the top of my head to my boots and I felt as if a spotlight were raking me. "Well, with your titian hair and dark eyes you do remind me a bit of that actress who starred in that movie about the, ahh—lady of the night. The one who lived in the hotel with the man and then she turned classy."

I had no idea what he was talking about. But I loved the word *titian*.

"There was that scene with her in the tub and headphones on."

"You mean *Pretty Woman*?"

"That sounds like the one."

"Ha! An old boyfriend used to say the same thing. But my hair is much redder and, well—my boobs don't even have cleavage half the time."

"Yes they do. I mean, no!" He removed his glasses, trying not to look at my chest and I saw a hint of red creeping up his neck. "So . . . you aren't an actress. What exactly do you do in these theater companies?"

"I'm a techie. I run the light boards and help with the sound engineering. Sometimes I even help the carpenters with the set design."

Surprise split his face into a smile. "Really?"

"You sound like you don't believe me. Girls can be mechanics and engineers these days, Professor."

He dismissed my tone. "No. It's just that—pardon me if this sounds like I'm whinging, but aren't plays part of the arts, like books and literature? Your idea to toss these books in the trash is a bit like throwing your livelihood in the trash, isn't it?"

"I suppose you could think about it that way. But plays and movies are alive. At least to me. Books and I don't get along, though. My aunt always forced these super-boring books down my throat. I was here less than two years, but it was awful. She never owned a television or let me go to the movies in Gaylord. It was always 'sit and read.'" I did a fairly good imitation of my aunt. She had been a large-boned woman with buggy eyes and a shrill voice that still popped into my dreams, turning them into nightmares.

He was quiet for a moment. "Maybe she wanted you to learn to love books. Lots of people do. I do."

I slapped him on the knee. "I won't hold that against you." Beneath my fingers, I felt surprisingly well-defined quadriceps. I lifted my hand, trying not to let him see how his nearness affected me.

"So, tell me about this aunt of yours. If you disliked her so much, how is it you came to inherit the store?"

I put my head on the back of the couch and stared at the ceiling. "It was revenge."

"I don't quite follow."

"When my mom died, my emotionally challenged father dumped my brother and me on my great-aunt Gertrude. He had to return to duty overseas. Never having raised kids herself, she was at a loss with teenagers. My brother was seventeen by then. Able to fend for himself. But me, I was thirteen. Almost fourteen. Awkward. Used to being among other girls who understood the perils of being uprooted by the military every year." I was also disappointingly stupid. At least, that's what my aunt said. I now knew what my condition was called. But back then, I had never been in one school long enough for anyone to figure it out.

"Why didn't she give the store to someone else? Your brother or your dad?"

I didn't want to talk about Leo. "It would have made sense to give the store to my father. But Dad remarried and then retired back in the States. If there was one person Aunt Gertrude hated more than me, it was Dad's new wife."

"That bad?"

"No. She's a sweetheart. But she isn't American. Aunt Gertrude thought she married Dad for a visa."

"Blasted foreigners. So, I guess you were the only logical choice."

"If she were nicer, Aunt Gertrude would have given it to the town. But revenge was more her style. Even in death she wants me to read."

"So . . ." He frowned at the glasses in his hands. I probably sounded ungrateful. "Your aunt never married? I heard some rumor about a writer in town . . ."

"Oh, that. Yeah. It's crazy, but Aunt Gertrude had an affair with a famous writer when she was younger. Have you ever heard of Robin Hartchick?" It always freaked me out to imagine Aunt Gertrude having sex. To me, she was nothing but a prune with female parts. But she actually had a lover once. Good thing I had already finished my coffee, because picturing Aunt Gertrude in the same bed I slept in—doing stuff—well, it would have made me gag.

"What happened?"

I laughed. "She was dumped!"

"Really?"

"Yeah. I'm almost positive that he was the only lover she ever had."

"That's very sad."

"She was like twenty when the affair happened. I haven't thought about it for a long time. I guess she was younger than I am now."

"A young, impressionable small-town woman and a worldly author. One could almost feel sorry for her."

"If you knew Aunt Gertrude, you'd feel more sorry for *him*."

Kit gazed at me with a strange intensity. "You don't mean that."

I wanted to stick his glasses back on. Maybe it was easy to understand the power an attractive, worldly male could have on a young woman. The difference was that I was older and more experienced than Aunt Gertrude had been. If I wanted to—which I didn't—I could have a fling and move on without being wounded in the least. But I was in a long celibate phase of my life at the moment.

Kit studied his fingernails. "Robin Hartchick. Come to think of it, I did hear he spent his summers in Michigan. *Spring Solstice* is considered one of the greatest pieces of twentieth-century fiction. He wrote only one book . . . supposedly." He paused. "She never heard from him again?"

"Well, duh. It was Aunt Gertrude. Nobody with half a brain would stick around. He's dead, of course. A one-hit wonder. A boring writer."

He rubbed his chin. "His book was a rather important shift in American literature."

I narrowed my eyes. "Why do you know so much about it?"

"Everyone has read Robin Hartchick."

Except me. I stared at his profile. Without his glasses on, he was perfect. Aquiline nose, ridge at the forehead. Strong jaw. Kit bloody Bond!

If I was going to spend more time in Truhart, at least I had something better to look at than a bunch of books.

Chapter 6

Istood before a disappointing organic-produce section and tried to decide where to start. It had been a while since I had access to a full kitchen. In my cart were several cans of beans, whole-wheat tortillas, and a box of organic soy-grain bars. I threw a bag of carrots and celery in and wondered if the Family Fare had polenta or tofu.

"Do you think she needs help?" Two ladies huddled at the end of the aisle, heads together, trying to keep their voices low. I heard them anyway.

"Marva says Gertrude spent hours trying to teach her how to read. She didn't never get it right."

"Maybe we should ask if she needs help."

I gripped the handle of the grocery cart. Forget the tofu. Moby was waiting patiently in Lulu. I would grab whichever bag of dog food looked like it was healthy and get out of here.

"I heard she was sleeping in her car, of all places—"

I didn't stick around to hear the rest. My ears were ringing enough already. Fortunately, the dog food was on the opposite side of the store. I passed the dairy items, until I was at the pet aisle. Then I scanned the bags for the senior dog food. My budget was limited, but I couldn't bring myself to scrimp on Moby's food. He was somewhere around nine or ten years old. An octogenarian. I could eat cheaply and be fine. He needed better nutrition. Someday I would find him the perfect family. One with green fields and sheep and lots of money.

"Can I help you find anything?"

There she was again. Marva. The owner of the pink-rimmed glasses I had admired just yesterday, stood behind me. Had she been following me?

"Nope, I'm all set." I grabbed a bag of dog chow with the words *all natural* in large block letters and I brushed past her in search of the checkout.

I made a circle around several customers who were milling in front of a Halloween display and pulled my cart up to the cash register. I was almost finished unloading the items in my cart when the checkout lady asked, "Do you have a super-saver shopping card?"

I weighed the advantage of getting a saver card against the benefit of getting out of the store unscathed. "How do I get one?"

Marva appeared beside the cashier. My eyes wandered to the toucan pictures printed on her pants. She adjusted her glasses and took a form from behind the register. In a slow voice that was even louder than when she had been in the dog-food aisle, she explained the process. "I can fill this out for you, honey. Just give me your information. Or better yet, your license. That has all the information we need."

She was trying to be nice. But it felt condescending. An old breathless feeling rose in my chest. "It's all right. I can fill it out."

She held the form closer to her chest. "No problem at all," she said, nodding her head at two customers who appeared behind me. "You ladies don't mind if we take a little time here, do you?"

I turned to see two gray-haired sisters—they looked like twins—standing behind me. "Oh, we don't have anything going on today. Do we, Brenda?"

"Well, we are supposed to—"

"Like I said, nothing at all," said her sister.

"Thanks, Barbara." Marva nodded and straightened her purple smock.

"Yeah, thanks a lot, Barbara," I said. She smiled, failing to hear the irony in my tone.

Marva pushed her glasses up on top of her head and leaned down, resting her elbows on the conveyor belt.

"Name. I got this part. Gertrude Brown, right?"

"How *did* you remember me?"

"Address? The bookstore, right?" Her glasses slipped off her head to her nose. She pushed them back to the top of the head. "You wouldn't happen to remember the address—no, never mind. I can look it up. I'll just leave this blank—."

"Sixteen Main Street."

She seemed to doubt my memory. "We'll see. And not to confuse you, but we're changing the name to Autumn Lane. Just for October. I wanted it to be called Haunted Avenue. But Annie Adler and Flo Jarvis thought the youngsters might be scared and well..." She caught my blank stare and cleared her throat. "And your e-mail address?"

"I don't have one."

Her eyes popped. "*What?*"

"I don't have one." What was the point in telling her I thought that the internet and e-mailing were a waste of time?

"Do you have a phone number?"

"Yes." I gave her my non–smart cell phone number and declined to tell her it was a pay-as-you-go model. I always forgot to charge it.

"Birth date."

"Look, how many questions are on that form?" If it weren't for the dog food I would have torn it in two and left.

"This is the last one, honey. Don't worry." She tilted her head and sent an 'I told you so' look to the women in back of me.

I gave her my birth date.

"A Halloween baby. How interesting!"

"And I'm twenty-seven years old!" I added. She nodded her head, glad that I could add.

She stepped away and I sighed, relieved to have that little pity party over with. "Here you go, Ginger." She let the checkout lady scan the zebra code. "And there are coupons for that dog food too. So you will save seven dollars and thirty cents."

"That was forty-five dollars and twenty cents. Now it's less seven dollars and thirty cents." She could have hosted a children's TV show with that slow and deliberate voice she was using on me. She pointed at the final price on the screen in front of me. Numbers were sometimes as bad as letters. If she had just told me the final amount, I would have been fine.

I felt cold sweat at the back of my neck. It joined the invisible belt that was cinching my chest, making me breathless. I longed for my car and Moby and a long stretch of road.

I pulled out a flowered change purse. It had been my mother's. My hand shook. I lifted out several twenties and placed them on the belt. "I don't have any change," I said at the same time that all my change decided to drop out of the purse, bounce onto the counter, and fall to the floor.

"Of course, that happened," I said, reaching down to pick up the coins at my feet.

The lady behind me said, "Count it out for her, Ginger. Poor thing—"

When I straightened up, Ginger was holding up a few bills in her hand. "Don't worry, I'll make change for the twenties."

"I can do it—" I started to say. But she was already handing me my two singles and a dime. "That is two dollars and ten cents change." She smiled brightly and sent the ladies a dazzling grin, as if she had just managed to save an entire third-world country.

"Thanks," I responded flatly. One of the twins behind me clucked at my rude tone.

Wheeling the cart and the dog food out the door, I hit a sharp downward slope by the curb. Rather than let the cart get away from me, I stepped on the back and took a joyride before it came to a stop near the handicapped spaces. The ladies watched me from the automatic double doors. I had just reinforced their views on my mental state.

When I was little, I combated those kind of looks by sticking out my tongue. I was tempted to do it now. But Moby whined from Lulu's open window and stuck his own tongue out for me.

I loaded my groceries onto the floor of the backseat. Moby sniffed the air above them and put his nose inside a bag.

"Don't get any ideas."

His tongue orbited the outside of his mouth and he made no attempt to cover his thoughts. Thinking better of my grocery placement, I pulled a bag off the floor and put it in the front seat where I could keep an eye on it. It was then that I noticed the truck that sat in the parking-lot lane in front of me.

At first I couldn't believe what I was looking at: A garbage truck with what appeared to be teddy bears, plastered all over it. And they thought *I* was crazy? I stomped my foot at the ridiculous way the driver had parked. I had been so careful to position Lulu facing out, like I always did. But whoever owned this absurd-looking truck had parked right across Lulu's front bumper. Like everything else in my day, things were not going as planned.

There was no one in the driver's seat of the truck. I gazed back at the front of the Family Fare. No garbage men with stuffed animal fetishes were anywhere in sight. The spectators were still standing by the doors. They had no idea how much better this show was about to get.

I clutched Pikachu, wishing there was some way to make this look normal.

I shifted Lulu in neutral and unlocked the emergency break to release it. Then I jumped out of the car and began the sadly familiar routine of manually reversing my car. I moved to the front bumper, grimacing at the fact that it was dust-covered and bug-splattered. Lulu needed a bath.

The proximity of the cars parked behind me meant that there wasn't enough room to do it with one try. Once the front bumper was clear of the car next to me, I walked back and turned the steering wheel. "I don't suppose you could be useful and learn how to do this," I said to the dog, who waited patiently for me to complete my reverse. Then I returned to hugging the front bumper and pushed the car again. Lulu moved into the aisle of the parking lot just as a sheriff's SUV pulled up behind me. Pretending it was perfectly normal to push a car out of a parking spot, I kept my head down and completed the job.

As I moved back to the driver's door, expecting to get arrested any second now, I heard a deep voice ask, "Everything okay, ma'am?"

I was surprised by the sympathetic eyes of the young officer leaning out the window of his SUV. Next to him sat a curly-headed blonde. She said something to the officer and he exited the SUV.

"Can I help?" he asked. "I can call for a tow."

"No. I'm fine now."

"Did you stall? Need a jump?" His eyes traveled from the front bumper to the back and the lopsided grin on his face showed an appreciation for my vintage yellow Beetle.

"No. She's just a little quirky, that's all."

His eyes strayed to the blonde in the passenger's seat. "Quirky, huh? I know how that goes."

The blonde waved. She was about my age. The officer could barely take his eyes off her. I patted Lulu. "Worth the inconvenience, though."

He started to say something, then he caught himself and was back to business. "I'm Deputy Sheriff Hardy. You must be Trudy Brown."

Instead of letting his assumption offend me, I smiled. "I guess word of my unconventional arrival has already spread through town."

"Some of our most highly respected residents have made unconventional arrivals." Judging by the glint in his eyes, I wondered if he was referring to someone close to him.

"J. D. . . ." the blonde warned from the SUV.

He put his hands in his pockets and pretended he didn't hear her. "If you ever need to get her checked out, you'll find the doc on M-33, a quarter-mile down from Main Street."

"The doc?"

"The name on the front window is Auto Doctor. But we just call it Doc's. His garage doesn't look like much, but he can work wonders."

"I'll make sure to remember that. Thanks."

A single high-pitched bark came from the car.

"Nice dog." He moved back to his SUV.

"You want him? He's looking for a home," I offered.

"I've got my hands full already." The blonde said something and he laughed.

As I left the parking lot, I glanced at the front door of the Family Fare. Several faces still watched me. I stuck out my tongue after all.

I drove away, triumphant. Ten minutes later, Lulu hit a rut and began to putter out.

"Aww, I hate to see a dead bug." A familiar-looking white-haired man said, coming out of the garage holding a bag of candy corn.

"What are you talking about? You make a game out of killing flies with the Shop-Vac," said a stocky young man who followed him.

"Jesus, Richard, what year were you born again?"

"That's a little detail I thought you would remember, Dad," the young man bit back.

While the two argued, I put Lulu in neutral and grasped the emergency brake. My brave car had struggled in gasping fits on the two-lane state highway until we finally made it to the Auto Doctor. She still had life in her, but she was like an old lady. The miles she had traveled since California had forced her into the slow lane.

Moby jumped to the front seat and wagged his tail at the sight of two new friends. I stuck my head out the open window. "Remember me?"

"Hey, it's the vegan."

"Murdock, right?"

"Actually, that's just what my big sister, Corinne, calls me. Most people call me Doc."

With his receding white hair, height, and large nose that might have been broken a time or three, the name fit him better. "Doc it is. I'll steer if you don't mind pushing her."

He helped me move Lulu into the empty bay in the garage. I secured the brake. When I stepped out of the car, the young man gawked at my boots and vintage jacket. But Doc never took his eyes off Lulu.

"Is that a super-Beetle?"

"What?" A third mechanic rolled out from underneath a Chevy. I remembered him too. The man who wore the matching gray coveralls at the diner. Vance. At the sight of Lulu, Vance's eyes lit up and he dropped his tools. "Joe O'Shea told me he saw one in town yesterday. Seventy-four?"

"Seventy-three," I said.

Still on his back, he rolled the creeper toward the bug and looked under the chassis. "Original floor pan and suspension?"

"Yes." I couldn't keep the pride out of my voice. Lulu was very special.

"How did you keep it from rusting out?"

"She's a California girl. My brother also kept her in the garage most of the time he owned her."

Doc walked around Lulu in a full circle. "You drove her from Cali?"

"Yes. But she's feeling the stress. Besides the wear and tear of the trip, California potholes are nothing to the craters around here."

Moby barked from the backseat. Doc stopped to pet him through the open window. "No need to get snippety. We'll give you some attention too, girl."

"Boy," I corrected.

The man on the ground rolled over and stood up. The top of his head barely reached my shoulder. "And the car is a girl, I'm guessing?"

I waved my hand across the hood and grinned. "Meet Lulu."

"You and your family have come to the right place."

Family? I kind of liked the thought. A foster dog and a car. Nice. "She's been losing power for the past few miles. I'm pretty sure I left a trail of smoke on M-33."

The younger man, Richard, wiped his hands on a towel attached to his belt and I wondered why. They were clean from his palms to beneath his fingernails. He swaggered over to the front of the bug and sent the other men a smug look. "Why don't you just get yourself some coffee and watch *Ellen*? We'll let you know what's wrong with it."

"I don't think—"

"That smoke was probably engine coolant. Your head gasket is most likely blown," he said, searching for the lid handle. "But we'll take a look for you, right, Dad?"

Doc rubbed the dog behind his ears. He winked at me and curled his lip. "Sure, son."

The young man lifted the hood of the Beetle and jumped back. "What the—"

The two older mechanics doubled over, laughing.

I had to admit, it was pretty funny. The way his mouth dropped open, you would have thought he'd discovered a dead body under the hood.

I walked around the car and opened the trunk. I tapped the engine. "Are you looking for this?"

He peered around Lulu and turned a distinct shade of pink.

"And just for the record, this is an air-cooled car. There is no coolant in the engine." I turned to the older men. "Everything looked fine to me the last time I had the engine out. But my guess is I may have burned a valve. Also, I have not been able to put her transmission in reverse since Montana. But I don't think that is a related problem."

Doc held a hand out to me. "I love a woman who knows her way around an engine. You've already met Vance." He nodded at the tiny man who continued his high-pitched giggle. Doc slapped the boy on the back. "And this boy here is my son, Richie. He's either seventeen or eighteen. His mom knows. Go easy on him, honey. He's a Beetle virgin!"

He leaned down to Vance and said under his breath, "He thinks with his brain in his pants the same way a Beetle does."

Vance laughed even harder. Doc continued: "When he's not working here, he's working on his punts. He's a better football player than a mechanic. So we'll have to give him credit for something."

I shook his hand. "I'm Trudy and my friend here is Moby."

Vance was trying to look in the car, but Moby kept licking his face. "There's a cat in the office, but he's pretty good with dogs. Can we let him out?"

Once Moby was sniffing around the garage in search of the cat, we turned our attention back to business. I took off my colorful coat and rolled up my sleeves. Doc and Vance took turns sitting in Lulu. Vance acted like a boy with a crush. He sat in the driver's seat flipping switches, engrossed by every detail.

At one point he flipped down the visor, pausing to study the picture of Angkor Wat on the brochure. "You goin' somewhere?"

"That's the plan."

"I don't know my geography much, but this doesn't look like a place you can get to in a bug."

"No. That trip will take a little coordination and lots of money." Which reminded me. "She's still got life in her. But maybe we could work out a little bargain, Doc."

"Bargain?" He pulled on his chin and I decided to wait to discuss it further.

I explained to the men how Lulu stopped reversing in Montana. And then how the power started to drop off in Iowa. "I was hoping it was just an adjustment. Then she started running rough today. The smoke off the back end makes me pretty sure she has burned out a valve."

Doc whistled and Vance scratched his head. "That's probably the cause. We can check the cylinder pressures and take a look."

"I don't have access to the internet. Can you help me order parts when we're done?"

Vance pointed to the computer on a stand against the wall. "That is one thing Richie does well. The internet."

Richie had been distracted by his smartphone while the men were exploring Lulu. He held it up and gave me a crooked smile.

I rubbed a bug, a real one, off the hood with my sleeve and thought of a way to minimize my repair costs. "Here's the other problem. I'm limited on cash for now. I could try to fix it myself, working on the heads with the engine still in the car. But it would be much easier to access the transmission with the engine out. I can't drop the engine by myself and if a replacement cylinder head is required, that's going to be a good chunk of change—never mind the cost to fix the transmission. Can I do some of the labor and knock off some of the cost?"

Doc shook his head. "You sound like you know your way around a car, but there's liability and expensive tools at stake."

I sighed. "I understand. But will you at least think about it?"

He looked at Lulu and back at me. "Let's take a look first. We'll see what we can do."

For the next hour, with the help of Doc and Vance, I performed the delicate operation of showing them around Lulu's engine. I explained to them how I had already rebuilt parts of the old engine when I first acquired the car.

By the time we had fully discussed VW Beetles and the elegant simplicity of air-cooled engines and manual transmissions, the guys and I were old friends. We moved to the chairs in the waiting room and drank coffee, comparing notes on the classic cars we had known over the years. Who needed the ladies at the Family Fare when I could have company like this?

Richie left for football practice. Doc offered me candy corn and asked, "So I don't get it. You inherited that bookstore from your aunt?"

Only one subject could dampen my mood and he had just doused me. "Unfortunately."

"What are you going to do with it?" asked Vance.

"I'm cleaning it out and then I'm selling it."

"Rumor is Reeba Sweeney has an interested buyer. Is that true?"

"It was a lowball offer. I'm not sure it's going to work out."

"That will make a few people happy."

Doc nodded. "My wife, for one."

"My mother too," added Vance.

"Because?" I really didn't want to know what the women thought. But I couldn't help being curious.

"Supposedly, the interested party is Logan Fribley."

"Who's he?"

"He runs a pawnshop in Victor. Bought one building ten years ago, and now it takes up half the town."

"Along with an adult bookstore and a casino," added Vance.

The men were watching me carefully for a reaction. It wasn't my business to care what happened to Truhart. I just needed to sell. I sipped my coffee.

They had already seen my travel brochure. "I want to travel. I need a good offer."

"What about Lulu and Moby?" asked Vance.

"Lulu can live in my dad's garage in New Jersey, and Moby . . . Well, I don't suppose you know anyone who has a little land and a few sheep?"

Moby was asleep with his head on my boot. He looked up. He already seemed to know his name.

"Moby doesn't look like he wants to be separated from you anytime soon," said Doc.

Moby liked everyone. But Lulu was my worry at the moment. "Can I keep Lulu here until the parts come in?"

"I have room on the side of the garage."

The sun was low in the sky and it was time to go home. I still had groceries in the trunk and a gross refrigerator to clean. Home ownership came with a lot of work and I was already dreading tomorrow and the prospect of more books. Hopefully, I could slap a *For Sale* sign on the front window soon. Every hour in Truhart brought a new snag in my plans that was making Angkor Wat seem further and further away.

I dreamed I was flying over an endless ocean. At first I was happy to drift with the wind and soar through the clouds. But my wings grew heavy and stiff. They weighed me down. I couldn't find a place to land and flew lower and lower until I thought I was about to drown in the dark sea.

I awoke to a muffled sound from the room below. "Moby?"

I reached for my face and pulled my sleep mask to the top of my head. "Moby!"

The dog appeared at the open door of the bedroom. His ears were up and he was panting.

"Where were you, boy?" In the dim light that came from the doorway, I saw him standing by the bed. Then he licked my hand.

"Chasing mice? I hope you got 'em."

He put his head on the mattress and I helped him onto the bed. Once he was settled against me, I lay awake, unable to get back to sleep. I passed the early hours of the morning staring at the ceiling, planning my trip to Southeast Asia, and remembering a day in second grade when I came home from school in tears.

I stormed through the front door and lamented to my mother that we were supposed to give a report about someplace in the world that we found fascinating. At first I wanted London. But Bobby Griggs, the boy who called me fire-head, got it. Then I wanted Paris. And Susan Schenkie, the teacher's pet, beat me to it. One by one, all the places I knew about were taken. My arch-enemy, Juliette Strayer, told me I shouldn't even bother doing the report since my projects always stunk anyway.

My mother soothed my face with a cool washcloth and held me close. "You know, Trudy, those are fine cities that those kids picked. But they don't hold a stick to the City of Temples."

My ears perked up. "The what?"

"Angkor Wat. The City of Temples. Some people believed it was the largest city in the world at one time. Far larger than any old Paris or London." Mom described the moats and the towers and the hidden art inside. She told me how the other temples in the region had been swallowed by a rain forest for centuries. By the time she explained the elephant gates and the way the structure aligned with the stars and moon, I had forgotten all about Paris and London. Together we created a report that blew the rest of the class away.

Not only was that report the highlight of my school career, but Angkor Wat became a symbol of all the good things that lay ahead. Mom and I decided we were going to visit Angkor Wat when I graduated from high school. We collected pennies in an old pickle jar and planned our route. Every house we lived in, the first thing we taped to my bedroom wall was the travel brochure of Angkor Wat. On bad school days when life got the worst of me, Mom would kiss me good night and put her hand on the picture next to my bed. "Just remember, we're going to Angkor Wat, Trudy."

Even when Mom's hair was gone and she was suffering from

the ravages of chemotherapy, there was still Angkor Wat. I taped the brochure to her hospital wall and told her we would be there soon.

Closing my eyes, I pictured the old brochure clipped to the back of Lulu's visor now.

Soon, Mom.

Chapter 7

From my vantage point, straddling the second-story windowsill, I could see the empty county road and Echo Lake peeking through the bare branches of a dead elm tree. An American flag waved listlessly in the mid-day wind in front of the ice cream store on a street beyond. The town belonged in a Stephen King novel. The only thing missing was a low-lying fog.

The little bird I had seen the other day appeared on the eave above me. "Hello, little fellow."

He looked down at me and angled his head back and forth. A shadow scurried below us. "Be careful, there's a cat somewhere around here," I whispered.

He flapped his wings and flew away. Funny guy. I shook my head and returned to the shutter. It hung by a single screw from the second story. If it was the source of the noise that had been waking me up in the middle of the night, I was determined to take care of it. Sleep was too precious these days.

I shifted the dangling shutter until it was positioned properly and fished in my tool belt for a screw that was the right size. Then I placed it against the frame, using the back of my wrist and forearm to hold the shutter in place. With my free hand I pulled out the screwdriver from my belt loop and placed the blade in the head of the screw and twisted with all my energy.

"Are you trying to kill yourself?" Kit Darlington stood in the alley below me, looking like he had stepped out of a British roadster commercial.

"Just fixing a loose shutter and getting a bird's-eye view while I'm at it."

"Get off the windowsill before you fall, you crazy, wingless creature."

I swung my feet around until they hung all the way out the window. "I'm fine."

"Very funny. But really. You're going to hurt yourself."

"Don't worry, I know what I'm doing. I used to sit here all the time when I wanted to escape Aunt Gertrude." At night I would crawl onto this overhang at the front of the bookstore and sit for hours, thinking of all the ways I was going to fly free.

"Shouldn't you be out studying important American things like people who wear shorts in winter and other oddities of the Midwest?"

"I'm at a lull in my work and thought I would stop by."

I was pleased he had returned today. Not just for the help. But for the company. For some reason I felt like we were a team. Two strangers in town. And even though he was adored and I was, well . . . scorned, we were outsiders. We belonged to a more rational world beyond this two-bit town. We needed to stick together.

"Feel like lunch? I'll buy? Then I can help you the rest of the afternoon."

That did the trick. Free meals were perfect for my budget these days.

I quickly washed my hands and smoothed my ponytail in the bathroom mirror. Then I looped my tool belt around the banister and greeted him at the back door, trying not to feel self-conscious in my work clothes. We left Moby to nap away the afternoon, and walked down the street.

I matched my stride to Kit's and watched our shortened shadows move beside us. "For how long did you say you were here again?"

"Just a month or two . . . while I do some research in the region. I'm waiting to be accepted as a visiting fellow at the university in Ann Arbor."

"Visiting fellow? Sounds impressive." I slowed down. "Research, huh? I can't imagine what would be so interesting about this place."

He kept walking. When he didn't stop, I ran to catch up.

Either his research wasn't going according to plan or there was something bothering him. He didn't seem to want to talk about it any further. "Sensitive, huh?"

We reached the diner and he held open the door for me. "What was that, Trudy?"

I stepped inside and halted, my question forgotten. Every available booth in Cookee's was occupied. By women. The crowd ranged in age from ten to ancient.

"Wow, we must have hit happy hour."

Kit stiffened. "I forgot. It's Wednesday, isn't it?"

And then it happened. When we first entered, the sound of women trying to talk over each other had been so loud it drowned out the jingle of the bells above the door. As soon as Kit was spotted, everything shifted. Muffled whispers and heavy sighs spread from the door to the back of the room. The Kit Darlington phenomenon.

Mac saw us. He shook his head and pressed a spatula down on a piece of meat with a powerful *hiss* that was the loudest sound in the hushed diner.

"Your weekly fan club meeting has just convened," I said.

Kit ignored my sarcasm and said under his breath, "Maybe we should go somewhere else."

Marva, of the pink glasses, flapped her hands at a large booth. "Bridget! Move over and let his lordship have a booth." Ladies grabbed their dishes and scattered out of a cubicle like a flock of birds being shooed away by a tomcat.

"Yoo-hoo. There's an empty seat over here." Marva grabbed a napkin and tried to clean off the table.

Kit smiled at the disenfranchised ladies who were trying to squeeze into a booth for four that was already occupied by three. "There are only two of us. We don't want to take up one of the large booths. We can wait until a table clears."

"Oh, no one pays attention to the signs. Right, ladies?" Corinne Scott smoothed her apron and grabbed a couple of menus. She shouldered Marva out of the way and waited for us or, I should say, *him* at the newly vacated booth.

Kit started to object. But I was hungry. I nudged him with my elbow. "A free booth. How convenient."

I slid into the seat and took the menus from Corinne. Other than coffee, organic bars, and home-cooked veggie tortillas, I had eaten very little since yesterday. Kit sat across from me and looked like he wanted to do me bodily harm.

Corinne waved her hand across the room. "Wednesdays are ladies' days. They've all had their usual coffee and doughnuts. So you two just go about your meal and ignore us, my lord."

Kit wiggled his index finger in the air and tried to be nice. "Now, remember. No more calling me that. Just Kit."

She put a hand to her chest and giggled. An attractive waitress with too much eye makeup stepped in front of Corinne. She set a cup and saucer in front of Kit. "I'll bet you would like some tea."

"Thanks, Tiffany," he said in a weak voice.

"I would love a glass of water," I added. She didn't even glance my way.

"I can bring you something to go with your tea if you want. Lemon? Sugar?" She leaned closer, giving Kit a nice view of her ampleness. Her eyelashes actually fluttered.

"Sugar. Not lemon." Kit's blue eyes matched the sky in the window behind him. The British accent alone was a chick magnet. But his eyes were his secret weapon.

I plopped my rucksack down on the table between them, almost spilling the tea.

"Who is that with his lordship?" someone whispered behind us.

"Gertrude's niece."

"The nutty homeless one who was sleeping in her car—"

"Shhh."

I brushed my cheek to swat the fire that had ignited on my face. Kit didn't seem to have heard the conversation. Thank goodness.

Corinne returned and practically pushed Tiffany out of the way. "Do you need a minute?"

Kit flashed her a charmer. "No. We'll order now. Trudy, here, appears to be withering away from hunger."

A familiar prickle of unease traveled up my spine. "That's all right. We can take a moment if you want."

Kit picked up the menu. "I'll go first if you need a moment. The sooner we order, the sooner you will get your food and we can get back to work." His meaning was clear. He wanted to get out of the diner and the swarm of admirers as quickly as possible.

I cursed myself for coming here in the first place and stared at the menu. The words blurred in front of me. I sat on my free hand, trying to keep myself from reading with my forefinger and felt sweat building at the back of my neck.

Kit took only a brief moment to scan the menu. "I'll have the Dinty Moore with corned beef."

"I'll have the same," said a frail old lady in the overcrowded booth behind Kit. It was hard to ignore her amazing hat. There were lures stuck all over the brim.

Corinne grabbed Kit's menu and turned to the fly-lady. "Flo. I just placed your order. You said you wanted a BLT."

"I changed my mind." She put her chin in her hand and smiled at Kit. That hat was so realistic I felt like picking the bug lures out of her fishing hat and sticking them in a tree for the birds.

Someone behind me spoke up, "I'll have one too."

"Why not order a round for everyone?"

"What was that, Trudy?" I was growing irritated. Didn't these women have places to go?

"Nothing." I grumbled and studied the menu again. Kit and Corinne waited for me to make up my mind. I hated it when people watched me read. It made things worse. I resorted to my fallback choice. "You know—I'll just have fries, thanks."

"Which ones?" Corinne nodded toward the menu. But I kept my focus on her.

"The regular, plain fries."

She pointed to the menu. "Which ones?"

"Small?" It was a shot in the dark. But I must have hit it, because she wrote something down on her notepad.

"Is that all? I thought you said you were starving?" Kit teased.

I was just about to lie and tell him I had lost my appetite when Mac called out, "Make sure they know the soup of the day, Corinne."

Corinne poked her short, bleached hair with her pencil and looked up at the ceiling as if to apologize. "Mac's been on some sort of organic-food kick today. I can't imagine what he was thinking. He made black-eyed peas and collard green soup, if you can believe it."

"With vegetable stock," Mac said, nodding my way.

I beamed at Mac. "I'll take a bowl of soup as well as the fries."

Kit scratched his head and looked back and forth between Mac and me. "Vegetarian?"

"Vegan. It means—"

He held up his hand. "I know all about it. My sister is vegan."

That was a relief. I hated having to explain vegan-ness all the time. I reached out and shook his hand. "The brother of a fellow vegan is no enemy of mine."

That made him laugh. "You remind me of her. Cheeky."

I thought we were done with the Kit worship. But buxom Tiffany interrupted my moment. "Here is the sugar and some milk."

She was practically in his lap. Tiffany walked away and her hips moved in a universal invitation.

Kit's eyes followed her and I cupped my hand over my mouth, calling out, "And water, please."

Marva approached and slapped a newspaper down on the faux-wood veneer of the table. "I thought you might like to see the local paper. It only comes out once a week, but there are all sorts of events and human-interest stories listed."

"How thoughtful of you," Kit said.

"My nephew, Calvin, is on the front page of the sports section. He's the quarterback on the high school football team."

"The football team, huh?" I could see him trying to hold back his amusement over the soccer vs. football thing.

Marva made tiny bounces on her heels. "Football is just about as American as you can get, my lord. Why don't you come to a game? I would love for you to be my guest Friday night. It's under the lights in Harrisburg."

"Under the lights?"

"There's a band and cheerleaders and you would love it. We even have a bonfire afterwards on the public beach."

"I'll make sure to bring some hot tea in a thermos just for you, your lordship," said the older woman behind him.

I added my two shillings. "And don't forget a brolly. If it rains he'll need to cover up."

Mac snorted from behind the counter. He flipped me a thumbs-up.

Kit tapped my foot under the table.

"Dr. Darling—ah, I mean Kit—is always prepared for the weather. Tut-tut, it looks like rain and all that British stuff, you know?"

Good thing I had on boots. His foot grew heavier. "I have never been to a high school football game. Have you, Trudy?"

"Never." It was true. My brother was a tight end for one season on the Harrison County high school team. But my aunt wouldn't let me go anywhere on a Friday night until I brought my grades up.

Marva cocked her head sideways and added an afterthought. "You could come too."

"Peachy."

Kit handed me part of the paper. "Here. Do you want to read the outdoor section?"

I glanced down at an article on hunting and let the paper fall on the table in front of me. I wondered why he would want to include me in the invitation for the football game. Maybe he needed me as a buffer for the paparazzi.

Marva suddenly focused on me. "Gertrude, I've been meaning to stop by the store."

"Trudy," I corrected her.

"Trudy. Cute. Do you remember me from yesterday? My name is Marva O'Shea." She spoke very slowly and loudly as if I was deaf and old.

I imitated her. "Oh. Yes. Hello. Marva."

I kept my face straight. She didn't know whether I was making fun of her or not.

"Trudy. I wanted to tell you that we, the community center committee—the Triple C's, we call ourselves now, thanks to Elizabeth over there"—she nodded to the curly-headed blonde from the sheriff's SUV yesterday—"we are going to host a Halloween house."

Well, that sounded like fun. I had helped out on the set of a few horror movies when I lived in L.A.

"You should know about it, since it might affect you," said Marva.

"Oh, I'm not afraid of ghosts," I joked.

She put a hand on my arm with the tenderness of a grandmother. "No, my dear. They aren't real. It's all fake."

Deciding to play along, I let disappointment play across my slumped shoulders. "It is?"

"You see, we are all going to decorate and pretend that the house is haunted and then we are going to charge money for people to come through the house before Halloween. We're decorating Main Street too. We're renaming the street Autumn Lane. We are trying to bring in people from all over this side of the state."

"Get on with it, Marva! The reason we want you to know is that we are using the empty grocery store next door to the bookstore as the haunted house," interrupted Flo, the owner of the bug hat.

Marva explained to a confused Kit, "The Furry Friends Rescue Shelter used to host a haunted house. But they received a big donation this year and said we could host it instead. We just hosted the Timberfest last summer so we are feeling pretty good about our ability to organize things. The old grocery store has been vacant since the Family Fare was built. That's where I work. Not the old store, of course. The Family Fare—oh, you know that. Anyway, it's bank-owned now. The old grocery store is. But we get permission from the bank to hold the Halloween house there as long as we pay for the extra insurance and all the cleanup afterwards. If all goes well we are going to make it a Santa's workshop at Christmas."

I was starting to feel bewildered now. But I kept my smile plastered to my face. "So I'm going to be living next door to a haunted house?"

"Exactly. But remember, my dear. It isn't real. And we are going to call it the house of horrors." I envied the Triple C's and their project. Ghosts were a lot more interesting than books.

When Marva left, Kit picked up a spoon and began to doctor his tea. I played "spin the salt shaker" while he added heaping spoons of sugar. After several moments, I felt the strange sensation of being under glass. I looked up. Every woman leaned toward us as if the room was tilted in our direction.

I slumped in my seat and stared at them. But they ignored me. Their focus was entirely on Kit.

"Seriously?" I asked under my breath.

He lifted his head. "Something wrong?"

"Nope." I sent him a squinty smile and leaned forward, propping my elbows on the table in front of me. It would have been bad for his ego to point out the obvious.

Someone in the booth behind us said, "His smile is so dreamy."

I tapped the table with my fingertip. My mouth was beginning to go dry from lack of water. I eyed the water pitcher at the end of the counter and thought about getting it myself.

I rested my chin in my hand and tapped my fingers to my cheek.

Kit had finally finished doctoring the tea. He took a sip of the tea and pushed it away.

"Aren't you going to drink that?"

"Hmm?" Kit lifted the paper, as if high school football was the most fascinating thing in the world. He eyed the tea sideways without moving his head, but said nothing.

"Your tea is going to get cold," I said loudly. "You'd better drink it, Dr. Darling-ton."

He picked up the cup and lifted it to his lips again. But I wasn't fooled. His action was just like the sip that actors pretended to take on stage. His Adam's apple didn't even move.

I leaned forward and whispered, "You don't like tea, do you—"

"Shhh. You don't have to be so loud."

It was wonderful to discover something that wasn't so perfect about him. "Admit it. You wanted coffee! You don't like tea."

He scanned the room. Fortunately, somewhere between my stare-down and his first sip of tea, most of the ladies had lost their fixation with our booth. "It's not my favorite."

"Not your favorite? You look like you hate it."

"I don't hate anything. I just don't care for it. I grew up with the bloody stuff jammed down my throat at every meal."

"Tell them you hate the stuff."

"It's not my favorite, but I can drink it—"

I moved the paper away from his face and dislodged the teacup by accident. The tea sloshed across the table and into Kit's lap.

He raised himself out of his seat and looked down at his pants.

I put a hand over my mouth. "Oh, no. Right on your crotch."

Several of the women around us cried out as if I had shot Kit. Three women grabbed their napkins and ran over to help. Kit stood up.

I tried not to laugh. "Want me to blot it for you?"

"Trudy—" he warned me. He tried to keep the ladies' hands away from the stain that had developed around his fly and I let a giggle loose, which earned me angry stares.

"I'll just go to the restroom," he said as if nothing out of the ordinary had happened.

I sent him a charming smile. "Stupendous, old chap. I'll hold down the fort."

Kit sent me a wary glance and slipped out of the booth. I must admit that I appreciated the stiff upper lip. He put on his glasses and strolled to the men's room as if he had all the time in the world. His path was tracked by his adoring followers.

Corinne arrived with a towel to clean the mess. I pushed the soggy napkins to the edge of the table. While she wiped up the spill, I heard two ladies talking at the counter. "She's just like she used to be. Remember how difficult she made Gertrude's life?"

"I don't know what his lordship is doing with her. Maybe he feels sorry for her."

The whispered comments brought back emotions I hadn't felt in a long time.

Corinne finished cleaning up the spilled tea and left before I could ask for water. A moment later she placed Kit's Dinty Moore on the table with a fresh napkin. "Does he need anything else?"

"Oh, I think *he* should be all set." I looked at my steaming plate of soup and fries growing cold on the counter behind her and wondered if she would bring it to me any time this century.

Tiffany moved around Corinne and placed another cup of tea on the table next to the sandwich. I smiled brightly. "Just keep the tea coming, he loves it."

The ladies waited breathlessly for the men's bathroom door to open. I hoped he came out dragging toilet paper on his shoe while zipping his fly.

I picked up the Tabasco sauce from the basket on the table. I knew it was wrong, but the angry teenage version of myself was rearing her ugly head. I was tired from being surrounded by words. I was irritated with the way the women fawned over Dr. Darling and pitied me. And I was hungry. Even Mac seemed to have forgotten about me. Before I could stop myself, I unscrewed the cap on the hot sauce and lifted the top of Kit's Dinty Moore.

I stood with Kit behind the diner, patting his back and trying to keep from laughing as he gasped and wheezed. Handing him the water I had procured in a to-go cup, I waited while he downed half of its contents.

"Did you do that?"

"It must have been the Dinty Moore." I patted my full stomach. "My soup wasn't spicy at all."

"I've only known you forty-eight hours and already you're playing practical jokes?"

"It was just a drop or four of hot sauce. You didn't have to eat it."

"I didn't want to hurt Corinne's feelings."

"That's stupid."

"No. That's called being polite."

"Why didn't you just tell everyone the truth? You could have said you don't like tea and you could have complained about the hot sauce."

"I didn't want to cause a stir."

"Pardon me for telling you this, but you have a little problem with honesty."

That seemed to bother him. He squinted at the ground and took a raging sip of water. It sloshed out of his mouth and over his chin. He wiped his chin with his sleeve. His lordship didn't look so fancy now.

When he finally calmed the heat on his tongue, he grabbed me by the hand and marched me down the street.

I let him lead me without complaint, secretly relishing it. When was the last time someone held my hand?

At the back door of Books from Hell, I leaned against the wall. He stepped in front of me and I could swear the hot sauce was steaming between us. He put his hand against the doorframe beside my head and I felt trapped. In a good way.

"Trudy, there is something . . ." His voice trailed off.

My nose barely reached his chin and I tilted my head up. "What are you going to do to me?" My voice was husky and the invitation was there. His nostrils flared and he tilted his head until our lips almost met. I waited.

A high-pitched bark interrupted us. Kit stepped back. He ran his hand through his hair and shook his head as if he were trying to clear his thoughts.

I slumped sideways and swallowed my sexual angst. "Don't look like that," I said. "You can always blame your faltering judgment on the Tabasco sauce."

Then I opened the back door. Moby bounded out and greeted us. "Great job, boy. You saved me from a drooling lunatic."

Kit didn't say anything. It was obvious he regretted what almost happened. I would too if I were smart. But smart was one thing I had never been considered. And as much as I wanted to abide by my new rule of no men in my life, I was willing to make an exception. Because it felt really good to stand so close to him. I loved the distraction of him. And I wanted more. I wanted to run my hands through his hair and see if it was as silky as it looked. I wanted to know the power of the muscles I felt beneath his clean-cut clothes.

I wanted to know if the feel of his mouth was as beautiful as the words that came out of it.

A wet tongue licked the Dinty Moore juice on my fingers and I returned from the cloud layer. Maybe I should clear my head.

I turned toward the lake. "He wants a walk."

A few moments later Kit fell into step beside me. We passed a large field of maple and popple trees that were starting to lose their leaves. Bright red, orange and yellow mixed with dark pine needles in a quilt of vibrant hues. Autumn in the northeastern quadrant of the United States was a singular experience. I had forgotten about it while living in California. I breathed in through my nose, loving the smells of the nearby forest in the cool breeze.

Moby ran up ahead. "So, I still don't understand why the ladies call you *his lordship*. I mean, I know you're British and there's the whole obsession American women have with British men and the royal family. But it seems like a bit of a leap to call you *his lordship*."

My question made him groan and touch his lip as if he were still in pain from the hot sauce.

"I didn't put that much on it. Try honey or baking soda."

"Another home remedy?"

"Don't change the subject. What kind of misunderstanding took place for you to become *my lord*? Did you and the priest mix up the sermons? Did you black out and turn into that famous young pop singer?"

"Who?" He was confused.

"Never mind. Just explain. I'm curious."

He put his hands in his pockets. "It's just a bit of rubbish, actually. When the lease for the house I'm renting was made up, it was accidentally placed in the wrong name with the wrong title."

"That's weird."

"It was a bit of a pain. But by the time I made the corrections and told the agent that I wasn't a viscount, the papers had already been drawn up with the titles."

"A what-count?"

"A viscount. It's spelled V-I-S-C-O-U-N-T. But it's pronounced *vie-count*. It is actually a courtesy title nowadays."

We were almost at the public beach. It was empty. He picked up a stick and threw it for Moby. "So, do you still want to get some work done in the bookshop today?"

I moved around him until we were toe to toe. "Wait a minute. It can't be that easy to get fancy titles mixed up. Who was the real viss- viecount you were mistaken for?"

He paused, opening and closing his mouth. "The viscount of Knightsbridge."

"Wow. That sounds like something that would be hard to mix up."

"That's what I thought." Moby returned with a stick in his mouth and Kit wrestled it from him and threw it again. "We need to clear an area so you can get from front to back of the store without tripping."

"What we need to clear up is this idea that you're royalty."

I moved toward a bench on the beach and sat down. I had so many questions and so far none of his answers fit. He came all the way from England to bird-watch and study the lumberjacks, but he barely talked about birds and logging. He seemed far more interested in helping clear the books in the store. The women in town loved him and he was embarrassed by it. Or maybe he was so used to being adored that he didn't care. Or was it something else? And now this strange situation with his title. I wasn't normally a suspicious person, but I was very confused by this man.

"Which cottage are you renting that caused a mix-up?"

"It's over there." He pointed across a cove to a large cedar house with two-story windows and a deck on two levels.

My mouth fell open. "That's not a cottage. That's a mansion."

"It's not as big as it looks. And it's the off season. It was cheap to rent."

I glanced at his expensive shoes. "Right. When are you going to invite me for cocktails?"

Kit ignored the question and sat down beside me. We watched Moby run back and forth along the beach.

"So, since we're asking questions, why do you hate it here?" he asked.

"I don't hate it here."

"Yes, you do. If I didn't already know how much you want to sell the bookstore, I would have known by the way you acted at the diner. You don't like this town, do you?"

"If *you* lived and traveled all over the world and *you* were dumped here when you were fourteen, you'd feel the same way."

"That bad?"

"Just for me. I'm used to everybody being new. I'm an army brat. But here, everyone knew each other. Did you notice how everyone seems related? Just wait until the football game. You'll see."

"Some people find that comforting."

"My dad was stationed in Texas . . . Oklahoma, Italy, Germany, England, and South Korea. My brother and I were so used to moving that we never even unpacked when we were posted. We slipped in and out of friendships almost as quickly as we grew out of our shoes. Permanence was being allowed to put nails in our walls."

"I can see how Truhart would be different for you."

"*Different* is an understatement."

"Difficult, then. And you'd just lost your mum. Right?"

I stared out at the water, watching as the autumn wind sent white-capped ripples across the lake. Moby eventually grew tired of sniffing in the reeds near the dock. After my mom died and Dad sent us here, at least my brother and I had each other. For a while. But he had been seventeen. He could drive. He had friends and ambitions. Little sisters weren't high on his list of priorities. And that was perhaps the main reason why the year and a half I spent in Truhart felt so strange and off-kilter.

I picked up a stick and absently tapped it on my knee. "At first I thought *you* stuck out like the queen at Walmart, my lord. But now I am rethinking things. Is it possible you feel right at home here?"

He laughed at my comparison. "Actually, the queen wouldn't look so out of place at Walmart. But, yes. I do feel at ease. Things here are a bit newer, though. I like that. Big cars and lots of high school sports. We don't have as much of that. In both places, though, there's a strong sense of community."

"Really? You feel at home here?"

"Actually, yes. I lived in the same village until I went away to school."

I waited for him to say more. He didn't, so I nudged him like an old pal might have. "In a castle?"

He elbowed me back. I guess neither one of us was ready for true confessions.

I threw up a truce flag. "Apologies, my lord. No more teasing . . . Today."

"Thank you."

"Shall we walk back before he lies down in the sand?" I asked, nodding at Moby.

"I imagine sand on a collie would be quite difficult to extract."

"Yeah. I'd have to rinse him several times to get it all out."

"Kind of like hot sauce in the mouth, don't you think?"

"Smart-ass."

Chapter 8

On Friday night, Kit picked me up in a Ford F150 pickup truck. He had stopped by Books from Hell twice since our lunch at the diner. I told him I could handle Aunt Gertrude's wreckage myself. He should be off studying horticulture and such. Only I screwed up the word and called it "horrorculture." Which somehow fit, considering the upcoming haunted house. When he did nothing more than grin at my gaffe, I forgot everything. His expression was so sweet and understanding it made me feel warm inside. I was developing a major crush on him. Despite his little white-lie politeness problem, the man was flawless. It bothered me that my infatuation put me in the same category as Marva O'Shea. Perfect wasn't usually my thing. I liked shabby fixer-uppers.

"Thanks for the ride. Hopefully Lulu will be her old self soon." I played with the controls on the dashboard, "I thought you'd be driving something small and sleek."

He revved the engine. "Are you kidding? I love American four-wheel drives. When I saw this in the rental-agency lot, I paid extra just to get it."

I winced at the way he handled the truck as we drove to the stadium. "Don't forget to drive on the right side of the road."

"You mean the wrong side of the road," he complained.

I ignored his comment and flipped on several switches, playing with the interior lighting. "You may want to take your turns a little slower. Truck driving is a lot different than driving your Mini Cooper."

He seemed affronted by my comments. But he slowed down at the next curve. When we pulled into the stadium parking lot, we were hit by the unmistakable odor of barbecued meat and popcorn.

At the ticket booth Kit insisted on buying both our tickets. He smiled at the woman in the booth and made some inane comment about the weather.

She perked up. "I love your accent. Where are you from?"

"Ohio," I said, before he could respond. This earned me a frown from both of them.

As we searched for a seat, we were hailed by the crowd of women standing in the bleachers. They flapped their hands madly and shouted, "Over here! We saved you a seat." Sitting in the football stands with Kit was going to be another repeat of the Kit fan club.

The pecking order was immediately obvious. Kit was flanked by Marva O'Shea on one side and the mayor's wife, Regina Blood- worth, on the other. Behind Kit, Corinne sat with Jenny and a group I recognized from the diner on Wednesday, including Flo, her fishing hat replaced by a foam "number one" hat. They sat on a blanket spread across the seats and handed a thermos back and forth.

Kit gestured for me to squeeze in next to him. "Budge up, every- one," he said, laying the accent on thick. "Let Trudy in."

"Sure." Marva smiled. "There's plenty of space, Trudy."

I shook my head and sat at the end of the row. "I'm fine. This seat has a better view." I indicated the empty row in front of me. Kit drew his brows together, but he was swallowed up by the women around him who talked over each other trying to explain American football traditions. They introduced him to dozens of people in the stands and politely included me each time. Despite that, I felt invisible in the crowd.

I knew the gist of the sport, that the football needed to make it to the other end. I watched the game with detached interest. But I couldn't help but wonder at the flock of ladies around me. It was strange how lit- tle attention they paid to the game. They plied Kit with tea and called out to friends. I wondered if any of them even knew the score. Sev- eral times Regina Bloodworth bragged that her husband, in the press box behind us, was presenting an honorary award to an alumnus of the class of 1948's state semifinalist team at halftime. Hopefully, the man would make it until then. He sat in a wheelchair on the sideline, looking as bored as I felt.

Before the end of the second quarter, Marva took orders for re- freshments. "The line really picks up at halftime. But Joe is flipping burgers. He'll make sure to get to us before the rush. Excuse me, Trudy."

I was forced to stand out in the aisle as she and her considerable girth moved past me. After several ladies went to the restroom, Kit slid across the empty void.

I held out my hand.

At first he was confused. Then his eyes lit up. "Brilliant, love."

He passed me his Styrofoam cup and I dumped his tea over the side of the bleachers when no one was looking.

When I returned he put an arm around my shoulders. "This is rather fun, isn't it, Trudy?"

"There are no words," I said, nodding my head and enjoying his touch.

"You went to high school here?"

"Unfortunately." He removed his arm as someone entered our row.

Halftime started. The frail former football player shook hands with the mayors of both Truhart and Harrisburg. The older man kept trying to pull his hands away, but the mayors clung to him as they smiled for the cameras.

"Poor bloke," Kit said.

I knocked his elbow with my own. "What about you? I'm guessing you were too busy studying to play many sports in school."

"Me? I dabbled in sports, actually."

"I wasn't talking about ping-pong."

His mouth twitched. "I enjoyed a little football of my own. And rugby. Even though I wasn't really good at it. And cricket. I loved cricket."

Cricket? It figured. "Did you dress like you were going to the Ascot races when you played that as well?"

"What's wrong with this?" He looked down at himself. "Are you criticizing my clothes?"

"No. It fits your personality perfectly." He wore a button-up blue shirt with a maroon wool pullover sweater. A gray scarf was tied around his neck. It was a chilly evening and it made sense to bundle up. But still . . . "You look like a professor."

"I have on a jumper. And I *am* a professor."

"Jumper. You kill me. Look around, dude."

He scanned the crowd. It was a chilly night. Baseball hats, fleeces, sweatshirts, windbreakers, and Harrison County High School letter jackets seemed to be the dress code of the evening. "I'm not that out of place."

"I feel like I should give you a pipe and a Sherlock Holmes hat." Not really. He looked hot. But I liked teasing him.

His eyes traveled over me in turn. I wore my army boots, tights, argyle socks, a long peasant skirt, and a flannel shirt with my favorite tapestry coat.

"I suppose I should have worn my Boy George coat." Was that a sense of humor again? At least he was comfortable enough to quit the polite stuff around me.

The energetic beat of the drum line during the halftime show made it impossible to carry on the conversation any further. We watched and cheered the band, the best part of the game so far, in my opinion.

As halftime came to a conclusion, Marva returned, followed by a small pack of teenage boys carrying cardboard trays filled with burgers, soda, and nachos slathered in orange cheese. "Thanks, boys," she said when they passed the food to the ladies who had returned to their seats. She gave each of them a quarter and they looked amused as they pocketed the coins.

"Thanks, Mrs. O'Shea."

"Now, you pay close attention to Ms. Scott's nephew, boys. Richard Scott. He may be skinny, but he has a lot of power in that kick. You remember that when you're on the varsity team. It's not the size that counts. It's the skill."

"We'll remember that." One of the boys said something to the others as he turned away. She didn't have a clue how amused they were by that comment. I guess I wasn't the only person people made fun of in this town.

Kit returned to his place when Marva waved him over. She passed him a burger.

I called over to Corinne. "Where's Jenny?"

"I told her to sit with her friends. She's over there with a few of them from school." Corinne nodded below us to the end of the stands. Jenny sat in a row of bleachers that was almost empty. But she didn't seem to care. She watched the game starting up again and clapped along with the cheerleaders. Scattered around her were several other girls who could have been anywhere from ten to eighteen. A bright-haired girl clapped from a wheelchair that was placed at the top of the ramp. A tall girl next to her held the handle and sipped soda. A curvy girl with a shaved head and a nose ring leaned back against Jenny's knees and let Jenny pat her head to the beat of the cheers.

I rose from my seat and walked through the bleachers, dodging up and down the rows in-between spectators. When I finally plopped down next to Jenny, she smiled and said, "Hi Trudy. Did they make you sit here too?"

I looked over her at the girl with the shaved head and our eyes met.

"I wanted to sit with the cool people."

That made her laugh. "I wish you could have brought Moby."

"Dogs hate football."

"Cause they can't fit it in their mouths, right?" Good point.

Jenny introduced me to her friends. Gina, who held Stacy's wheelchair, and Bibi, the fierce one with the nose ring. While I watched the game and tried to understand the play, the girls around me were focused on something else: The cheerleaders. Even Bibi, who slouched against Jenny with her hands in her pockets, watched the cheerleaders with a long face.

Jenny held out her popcorn. "Want some?"

I took a handful and one of the boys, who had carried trays for Marva, passed into the row near us. "Hey, look at the sped row."

Jenny's face fell and she stared at the ground. Sped? Then I remembered what it stood for: special education.

"Get lost, loser!" Bibi flipped up her middle finger.

Jenny giggled and said, "Good job, Bibi. My cousin does that."

One of the boys crossed his eyes and made a face at us.

"Down in front, lard face. You're blocking my view. I can't see the game!" I grabbed a handful of popcorn and threw it at the boys. The girls thought that was hilarious coming from a grown-up. They joined me in throwing popcorn.

A lady behind me huffed. "That's so rude—"

"Who is that?" another woman asked.

"Gertrude Brown's niece. She's loonier than Michigan's lakes."

I stuffed popcorn into my mouth and chewed furiously.

A particularly popular cheer began and the crowd joined in. "Oh, I know that cheer." Jenny started chanting along. So did the other girls.

Except Bibi. She made fun of the team mascots and changed the words to the cheer. "Go Huskies, it's okay, we'll use our Trojans another day!"

Stacy and Gina laughed. Jenny said, "That's not the right words, Bibi. It doesn't make sense that way."

Bibi leaned against Jenny and said. "Sorry, girlfriend."

Jenny put her hands on Bibi's shoulders and turned to me. "I wish, I wish, I wish I was a cheerleader."

Bibi kept her eyes on the field. "You'd be better than they are, Jenny. Look, they don't even look at the crowd. They just watch each other."

Jenny pointed at one. "And the football players. Look, that one keeps looking at my cousin Richie."

"Well, he's pretty cute," Gina said.

Jenny put a hand to her nose. "Gross." They all giggled.

Bibi stared at my feet. She had been covertly checking out my wardrobe since I first sat down. "I like your boots. Where'd you get them?"

"An old army surplus store. I got them years ago, before they were even cool to wear."

I found myself enjoying the rest of the game. The girls were funny and sometimes gross. And I felt right at home. The game ended in a field goal for the Harrison County Huskies that left them two points up over the Alpena Trojans.

In the stands above us, no one cheered louder than Jenny. "That's my cousin! Woo-hoo! That's my cousin Richie! He won the game!"

Her enthusiasm made even the snarky woman behind us laugh.

We filed out of our seats and I felt Kit's hand on my elbow. "Did you have fun?"

"I did." I actually meant it. "You?"

"It was interesting. A little slower paced than our own football. But it had an excitement that was really quite invigorating. And much more social, I must say." He tilted his head toward the ladies ahead of us.

We filed out of the stadium and moved toward the parking lot. Reeba Sweeney and two other women were gathered around a large SUV that had its back gate up. They waved to us as we passed. The night was growing cold and I paused to reach inside my rucksack for my old mittens. Then I dropped one and crouched down to pick it up.

"Did you see her?" The nasally voice behind me made my ears hurt.

"How could I miss her?" Reeba's familiar voice answered. "I may not be the right one to judge, of course, but that bright red hair and those awful clothes don't exactly make her look normal. She belonged right in that row with those kids."

"That coat looks like my grandma's carpet. Her hair makes her look like a clown."

I stood, smoothing the coat that reached my knees, and shrugged. I happened to love this overcoat. It was Mom's. The owner of a store in Greenwich Village had tried to buy it from me once. He claimed he had a celebrity client who would pay big bucks.

"What does he see in her? Is it just pity?" asked the third woman with a booming voice. She wore a full-length mink coat and ran her hands up and down her collar.

"It's not like he's attracted to her. I told him she might be odd when he asked about the bookstore," said Reeba. The three women continued to talk over each other loudly, as if they were still in the bleachers.

My back burned with a mixture of anger and embarrassment. Thinking of Reeba talking to Kit about me made me feel suckerpunched. I paused in the shadow of a large van and tried to catch my breath as people moved past me.

Suddenly Kit was beside me. His voice carried over the cool evening breeze. "I didn't get a chance to say hello, Ms. Sweeney."

Reeba and her friends froze. "Oh—I didn't see you there, Dr. Darlington."

"I figured as much," said Kit. His voice held a different tone. Gone was the flirty British lilt. In its place was something stern, almost austere.

"You met my friend, Trudy Brown?"

"Yes. Of course. I let her into the store the first day she arrived." Reeba sent me a brittle smile.

"We know all about her," the fur coat said under her breath. She still sounded like she had a megaphone.

"Good. Then you'll know how wonderful she is. One of the kindest people I've met in the county."

I felt a roaring in my ears and tried to shake off the feeling that I was fourteen years old again. Sitting in the school social worker's office while he made platitudes and clichés out of how my mother's death must have affected me.

Reeba nodded her head like a puppet. "Of course, we'll remember that."

He put his arm around my shoulder and sent them a killer smile. "Good. Don't forget it."

We pulled into the alley behind Books from Hell and I jumped out of the truck. Even though he didn't deserve it, I almost slammed the back door in Kit's face.

"You wouldn't talk the whole way home and now you try to smash my head. Are you mad about those inane women in the parking lot?"

Moby watched our argument from the stairs. Confused by Kit's loud voice, he barked and I walked over to the step and buried my face in his neck.

I wished I had beaten Kit to the back door. If only I could have put a barrier between us, I could make Dr. Darling go away. "I'm just tired."

Kit reached out and patted Moby on the back. Moby licked Kit's hand. I turned and started up the stairs. "Good night."

The sound of Kit's shoes brought me to a halt. "Would you stop following me?"

"I want to make sure you're all right."

"Why? Because you're afraid someone like me will do something crazy?"

"What are you talking about?"

"You know exactly what I'm talking about. You don't have to pretend now. You heard what those gossips in the parking lot said about me."

"You shouldn't care what they say. It doesn't matter."

How could he act like he had no idea? "What? Not care that they called me dumb? Stupid. The fact that I belong in a row with—" I stopped myself. God forgive me, I was doing exactly what I had accused everyone of doing to me. Categorizing people in easy-to-define ways that had nothing to do with who they really were.

"Is that what this is about?"

At the top of the stairs, I gave up hope that he would leave anytime soon. I opened the door to the apartment and stomped inside.

"I know your aunt didn't exactly help you with her attitude about reading, but just because you don't like books doesn't mean you are stupid. Don't be so hard on—"

"Is that what you think my problem is?"

"You told me already. You didn't do very well in school. But it's obvious that you aren't stupid."

I laughed and realized how close I was to losing it. I sounded like an inmate in an insane asylum. If they heard, the ladies would be falling all over themselves to hire me for their house of horrors.

"It was more than that." I struggled to find the words and gave up.

Kit turned on a nearby lamp. I wished he had left me in the dark.

He waited for me to explain. The only sound in the room was Moby's heavy panting.

"I haven't known you that long, Trudy. But what I see is an intelligent woman standing in front of me."

"Stop pat—patronizing me. I hate it when people do that. You sound like one of the psychologists my father's new wife made me see, trying to assure me that it wasn't my fault I was so illiterate." I threw my sack on the couch and ran my hands through my long hair, yanking out the scarf and throwing it on the floor.

"I don't understand." Kit stood with his palms up, gaping at me as if he thought I was a wild animal who might bolt.

"I can't read. Did you figure that out yet, Professor?"

"That is ridiculous. You were categorizing the books with me."

"Sure I was. It was easy if it had a book cover. Anyone can tell a children's book from an adult book if you look at the cover and the size of the thing and the pictures. Unless the adult-book cover is in a cartoonlike print. Did you notice the trouble I had with Kurt V— whatever his name was?"

He pulled his glasses off and moved closer. "Why didn't you say anything?"

"Because I didn't want you to know. But it didn't matter. Reeba Sweeney made sure you knew all about me."

"She said you had trouble learning and hated school. That your aunt was always complaining about you. That's it."

"Well, now you can all have a good laugh. I can't read and I inherited a flippin' bookstore. Ha. Ha. Ha!"

I had used up the last of my energy. I sank onto the couch on the last "ha". I suppose I should look at the bright side. If I scared

Kit away with my craziness, he would leave and I could go back to throwing books away and selling this place.

Kit continued looking at me with an intensity that made me uneasy. He sat on the arm of the couch. Facing me.

"You have dyslexia?"

I let his question hang, surprised that he had figured it out so quickly and, at the same time, surprised that it took him so long.

"Yes. Thank you for the tip."

"You realize that isn't your fault."

"No. It isn't. Would you be a dear and explain that to Aunt Gertrude?"

"My God, you were never diagnosed, were you?"

"When I was twenty—a mere fifteen years too late."

He paused. "Well, there are ways to overcome it now. Technology has done a lot for people who have trouble reading."

I felt a familiar anger bubbling up inside me. Here it was again. If people rationalized it they could dismiss it. They could dismiss the pain I felt. And then I would be invisible again. I had a label stuck to me as permanently as a tattoo. No, it was more than that. It was embedded beneath the skin. Inside, where no matter how much I told myself it wasn't my fault, I knew I could never be like everyone else. Have a conversation with friends about my favorite book. Order from a menu without studying it for ten minutes. Even look up the players on a high school football program someone handed me.

"There are wonderful things like audiobooks and dictation applications. And I even heard there is a new font to help dyslexic people read." Kit was trying to make me feel better and I was getting madder by the second.

"A new font! Wow, I'm cured."

"People don't necessarily have to read to get good jobs," he said.

"Oh, yeah. I always put dyslexia at the top of my résumé."

"And lots of successful people have dyslexia."

"Give me a break."

He was on a roll. "Books are overrated anyway, Trudy. Just like you were explaining to me. Plays and television and other forms of entertainment are—"

I was off the couch. "Don't try to make me feel better, you ass! Do you have any idea how it feels to love stories but not be able to read them? I know the words are there and it kills me."

"What about letting people help. I'll be happy to—"

I launched myself at Kit's chest. "It's not the same!"

"Trudy." He opened his arms and met my attack.

"I can hear them if I'm lucky. If someone reads them or I see Shakespeare or any other version of the story that some hack hasn't screwed with."

He rubbed his hands along my back. "There are good recordings."

"But a new book can take years for the words to be recorded. And even then, it's someone else reading them. A voice that isn't mine. A shitty substitute!"

"I'm sorry—"

"When I was younger I wanted to read *Harry Potter* in the worst way! I watched my friends laugh and read and joke and I even once waited until midnight just to hold the next book. A book I couldn't read."

I just wanted to be like everyone else. I buried my hands in his sweater. "It doesn't help when people tell me how I can overcome it!"

"Then, I won't," Kit said softly in my hair.

His sweater smelled like a football game and the cool September air. It reminded me of growing up, for some reason. Not just the painful times inside these walls. But other times when there was someone to lean on.

There were so many classrooms where I learned to cover up for the fact that I couldn't read. Usually the teachers dismissed me as being behind after moving. I used to work hard to remember other people's book reports so I could recite those same book reports the following year on another army base. My mother would help me type my homework sometimes. If she knew I couldn't write she never said a word. She told me I was smart and helped me get through each grade level. But when she was gone there was no more covering up. Aunt Gertrude made it crystal clear that I was illiterate.

"I don't know why I'm telling you all this now. Lots of people have problems that are much worse. It's just this place. This town and all the memories brings out the worst in me."

"Your aunt doesn't sound like the most patient of women."

"She wasn't."

"Were you close to your dad at all?"

I rested my head on his shoulder. "My dad didn't know what to do after my mom died. He was still deployed overseas, and there was no one to be with us. So he dumped my brother and me on her doorstep. In some ways, it wasn't her fault. What did she know about raising teenagers?"

"I'd like to think she might have figured out that there was a reason you couldn't read."

"I kind of made her life difficult."

"You? I can't imagine." The sarcasm in his voice made me laugh. And I swiped away a tear that rolled down my face and pushed out of Kit's arms.

"Your brother? Was he at all helpful?"

"He was a wonderful big brother. Really, he was. But he was hardly ever around." And then he enlisted.

"When did you realize it wasn't your fault?"

I wanted to say "never," but there was a moment when I discovered that there was a reason behind my failure. One of my teachers at Harrison County High School had recommended a tutor who had been successful in helping people overcome their reading problems. At first Mrs. Blodget had scared me to death with her polished black hair and her gravelly cigarette voice. But she turned out to be kindhearted and perceptive. It didn't take her long to realize that I had a reading disability.

I moved to the window and put my hand on the cool glass. "I was in tenth grade, but reading at a second-grade level. A tutor tried to explain her suspicions to Aunt Gertrude. Aunt Gertrude thought if I worked harder I could overcome it. She nixed any future tutoring. She made me sit and read aloud each night. Do you have any idea how painful that is to a fifteen-year-old?"

"It must have been mortifying."

"She just didn't understand it. I know that now." Our relationship might have been different if I had been formally diagnosed when I was younger.

Kit came over and leaned against the wall beside me. "What happened to you? You left here, right?"

I nodded. "Technically, I couldn't leave until I was sixteen. But I packed up and went to live with a friend in Texas months before my birthday. Her parents were always good to me and my dad didn't contest it." Aunt Gertrude had been hurt by that. Looking back, I think she thought she could somehow pull me out of the abyss of ignorance and fix me.

"Did you get the help you needed?"

"In California. When I was twenty. That's when a reading specialist worked with me. But that was expensive."

"Did it help?"

"I still have some of the tools she used. I take them out every once in a while and practice reading. But it's slow. And it's embarrassing to do when people watch me. I get uptight when I feel rushed. I still stumble over my words too. Have you noticed how I mix up my syllables and sounds?"

"Maybe if you explain—"

I halted him with my hand. "I know. Yes. That is the easy way to handle it. And sometimes I can. And sometimes it's just too complicated. Dyslexia is kind of a spectrum thing. Not everyone who suffers from it is the same. Mine seems worse than most." People had a way of asking all sorts of questions about my problem. They had this mistaken perception that I saw words backwards. But it was more like someone had tossed a deck of cards in the air and told me to read them before they dropped.

Moby gave a muffled bark from downstairs. "He needs to go out," I said.

"I'll come with you."

We followed Moby into the brisk night. Kit was quiet. He seemed to be thinking about something important. My anger was spent. The cool air felt good on my skin now. Like my mother's washcloth on my face after I cried.

Music and laughter came from a bonfire at the public beach. We veered away from it and stopped on an empty spit of land that bordered the lake. A mist hung over the water. The sound of crickets mixed with cicadas interrupted the sound of the post-football revelers.

"I'm sorry I exploded."

"Don't be sorry."

"I'll be better as soon as I get out of this town."

As we watched Moby search through the underbrush near the shore, Kit took my hand. "So Trudy. Tell me more about your plans after you sell the store?"

"Travel."

"Don't military children usually want the opposite?"

"Oh, you mean like a home they'll never leave?"

"Hmm."

"What is a home? Just a piece of land with a house."

"I think of it as a place you belong."

"I've felt more at home traveling in a car than I ever have under a roof."

"Lulu? Isn't she the same thing as a home, then? A place you belong."

"It's not the same. She has wheels and no mortgage."

He reached out and grabbed my hand. "Sure it is."

The breeze whipped my hair in front of my face. I couldn't bring myself to disturb the moment. I kept my hand in his and let my hair fly. "So, what about the little village you mentioned. The place where the Darlingtons are from? If it's so great to be home, why are you here?"

He let go of my hand and reached down and picked up a stick. He pulled back his arm and threw it. "I'm often gone for long periods of time. Even so, I love to know there is a home that still exists for me when I am ready to return."

"I wouldn't have a clue what that feels like." I shrugged and picked up a rock. I threw it as hard as I could. It didn't travel as far as Kit's stick and landed just a few yards past the shore.

"Having a home is kind of like this beach," Kit said.

"How's that?"

"You can throw yourself as far as you want, like the rock and the stick. But you'll catch the wind and the current and find your way back to land."

"Very deep, Professor." As if on cue, Moby pulled a stick out of the water and brought it back to our feet.

Kit chuckled and put his arm around me. "You know, Trudy, I think you are a bit afraid."

"What?" I pushed away from him.

"You heard me." He turned me around until our faces were inches apart. I could feel the heat of his breath and my heart sped up. I didn't know if this new intimacy was a good thing or a bad thing. And it was so unlike me to even think about my actions. I was definitely off my game. Before I could figure out why I was hesitating, he lowered his head to mine.

* * *

Our lips met with an explosion that chased away the lingering coolness in the air, making it feel like a scorching night in July. He tasted salty and sweet, and I felt like I had been starving until now. I buried my fingers in his hair. His hands wandered underneath my shirt, making paths across my back that left a trail of fire. His hair was thicker than I thought. Like corn silk crossed with cashmere. I ran my thumb across the nape of his neck and tried to follow with my tongue. He was just tall enough that I could reach the side of his neck while his own lips moved lower.

In the distance, Moby barked.

Kit kissed the area right beneath my ear. Heat and uber-sensitivity rippled across my breasts and below. I was ready to jump his bones right there and then. And based on the way he felt against me, he would have no objections. I reached down to his belt and he stopped.

"This is . . ." His hands had stalled on my back and he pulled away from me with a shudder.

Moby barked again.

"What's wrong?"

"I can't do this."

I tried to kiss him again. "I'm not like most girls. I don't need cotton sheets and a roaring fire."

He turned away. "We aren't a couple of teenagers."

Why did I have to fall for a proper Englishman?

Moby barked louder now. An angrier bark. I looked past Kit to see Moby running through the darker scrub nearby.

"Moby!"

But he ignored me and the white fur on his tail disappeared in the brush. A darker shadow nearby sent a shiver up my spine. "There's something there."

"Where?" Kit's hands dropped to his sides. He walked toward the area Moby had disappeared.

"Do you think he's all right?"

"Hopefully. The last thing you want is him discovering a skunk."

A shaggy collie and a skunk were not something I wanted to even consider. "Moby. Get back here!"

Before we reached him, something separated itself from a larger shadow and leaped out into the moonlight. For a moment I thought it was a skunk. But the white stripe was missing. The black cat.

Moby wasn't far behind it. He stopped a few feet from the cat, who faced him with an arched back and a straight tail. The cat erupted in a hiss. Moby didn't stick around long enough to find out what the cat planned to do with him. He ran straight for us.

"Scared of a little cat, boy?" He wove himself between my legs and back to Kit, seeking reassurance that we were there for him.

"Your dog is a bit timid."

"I told you. He's not *my* dog. But he's not the only one acting scared."

Kit stopped petting Moby and stood up straight. "Are you referring to me?"

"I don't see anyone else around here." I turned and started walking toward Main Street.

"Excuse me. But in what manner is what we were just doing timid?"

It was so unfair. I picked up my pace and Moby stuck to my side. I was doomed to be surrounded by men who slipped away from me like waves on a beach. Which was why I should have remembered that I was in my self-induced dry phase.

"Hello? Are you listening?" Kit was in front of me now, walking backwards while he waited for me to respond.

"It's not what you were doing. It's the fact that you stopped."

He slowed and I passed him. I heard him sputtering behind me. "You—well . . . Wait a minute, there, Trudy."

"It's all right, Kit. I get it. I was having a good time. You, on the other hand, must have felt differently."

"You don't understand." He caught up to me and reached for my hand.

"Our incredibly romantic discussion about owning a home and dyslexia dampened the mood, anyway."

"Hey. Just stop and let me explain."

We were almost at the store. I turned and faced him.

He adjusted his glasses. "It's just that I'm here for only a short time."

"So am I."

"You don't really know me. And I don't think it would be in our best interests to have any complications that would make me—"

He paused. What was he going to say? I stomped my foot. "Our best interests? Complications? What kind of complications?"

"It's just, you know, we just met and you're trying to clean up the store."

"I get it. You're a professor. You live for schedules and houses and order. I live in a broken-down bug."

"That isn't what I was thinking at all."

"Oh really?"

"Really." He reached out with both hands and cupped my chin. "I respect you. That's why I stopped."

I stood speechless, trying to figure out what he meant. No one ever used the word *respect* around me. Then he kissed me soundly. Not a breathless, drawn-out kiss like we had shared on the beach. But a firm, single kiss that held a promise. I felt it long after his lips left mine. He reached into his pocket and pulled out his car key. "I will see you tomorrow."

I watched him climb into the truck and pull away and tried to shake off a nagging suspicion. And an overwhelming sense of longing.

I touched the tip of my tongue to my upper lip. Something unique and pleasing tingled in my mouth. A new sensation awakened my body and rocked my insides.

Kit Darlington tasted like I imagined a home would taste.

Chapter 9

The next morning someone knocked at the back door. I looked down at Mickey. He pointed to the nine with his short arm. "Let me in. I come bearing gifts."

I met Kit at the back door and Moby practically tackled him in his excitement. So did I.

"I missed you too, boy," said Kit. He handed me a takeout bag. "How did you sleep?"

"Fine . . ." I grabbed the bag and sat on the stairs, watching Kit take a sip from what I assumed was coffee, not tea. "Except for being horny half the night."

He sputtered and almost sprayed a cookbook.

Last night I had dreamed of playing naked tug-of-war with Kit along the shores of Echo Lake, only to wake up at dawn, tangled in the sheets and kissing the pillow. I lay on my side and stared at the shadows of tree branches gyrating up and down like lovers.

"Hey, look." I pulled out a bowl and a covered cup with handwritten labels. "Muesli and almond milk."

"Mac seems to—ah, like you," Kit said, wiping his mouth. "He prepared it just for you."

"And a banana," I said, pulling it out of the bag and putting it up to my mouth, licking my lip in a not-so subtle way.

Kit pulled off his glasses and pretended to wipe them on his shirttail. I gave him a break and set the banana aside. "Having breakfast with you could become a lovely habit, Professor."

I savored the nutty texture of the cereal. And Kit. He looked good enough to eat in his faded jeans and navy crew-neck sweater. His face had the shadow of a beard that gave him a rather un-professorly look this morning. "Has anyone ever told you that when you don't shave you look like David Beckham?"

He raised an eyebrow. "Your imagination is amazing." It made him look even more like Beckham, but I knew he was tired of the admiring masses.

I poured more almond milk into my bowl. "Okay. Okay. I'll stop drooling over your macho looks and your cute little accent."

"Who says it isn't you who has an accent?" He made himself comfortable on a stack of old coffee-table books.

I raised the spoon to my mouth and considered Kit's effect on women. At first I had been disgusted by the way the women followed him around town. But I was well aware of his charm up close. He was sweet and smart—and tolerant of everyone. I thought about the way he sat in the football stands last night, nodding as Marva asked him if he knew the queen. He shook hands and acknowledged every person that was introduced to him. I had watched closely, hoping to find some crack in the niceness facade he wore like a second skin. But I realized that Kit was the real deal. A nice man. A gentleman.

"Respect," he had said last night. I wasn't used to men like that.

Forget respect. I wanted to ride him like a rodeo cowgirl.

"So where do we start this morning?" he asked.

"How about where we left off last night?"

Kit waved a finger at me. "Your humor takes some getting used to."

"Who said I was joking?"

His eyes widened. But his eyes lowered to my lips. "Take pity on me. I haven't even finished my coffee."

"All right. You want to know where we should start? How about we order a dumpster."

"Be patient, old girl. Remember, if you get this place in order, you can hold your sale and toddle off to wherever you want to go."

"Toddle?" I laughed. "That word just burst my David Beckham fantasy." Not really, but I didn't want him getting full of himself. I couldn't figure out why he was so interested in helping me, but I was tired of trying to understand him. And it was nice to have company.

I looked around the back room. Things were looking better, I had to admit. After the past few days of working, I could see all the way into the front of the store. It reminded me of the way it used to look. There were still piles on the floor, but it was an organized chaos.

"The main floor is looking better."

Kit rifled through a pile of papers and mumbled something to himself.

"What?"

He placed his glasses on top of his head to see the words in front of him. "Nothing. There is quite a bit of organizing that still needs doing."

Although the shelves against the wall were full, books were still scattered in piles around the wood floors. We—or rather, Kit—had organized the corners of the main room by fiction and nonfiction and adult and child. That was as far as we had gotten. But there were aisles to walk down and it was enormously better than it had been. At least the store was no longer a firetrap.

"It looks fine to me."

"Hmm. If you open for a large sale and really want your customers to find what they're looking for quickly, you should categorize some of the books."

"You mean like romance and erotica?"

That got his attention. He readjusted his position on the books. "Amusing, love. However, something tells me your aunt didn't have much erotica."

"Probably not. Hey, let's categorize in an unconventional way. Something fun."

He gave up what he was reading and scrutinized me patiently. "What would you suggest, Trudy?"

"By emotion. We can have the happy section, the funny section, the hungry section, and the sexy section."

He pursed his lips. "Where would Shakespeare fit? He is a little bit of everything."

"I don't know. Maybe the section for people who like guys in tights."

Kit tilted his head backward against the wall. "How about this? You eat. I'll tackle the pile of papers in the corner."

I leaned back on the step above me and watched Kit go through the papers. He sat on his pile of books and sorted the stack around him. I enjoyed the way his broad shoulders stretched the thin material of the sweater. For a tall, lean man, he was fairly muscular. I could see the outline of his biceps as he reached across the pile. His shoulders too. I wondered what he would look like with his shirt off. I knew a little about how his muscles would feel under my fingertips, but not enough. Putting the empty spoon in my mouth, I imagined the heat of his skin sliding across my tongue. Oh God. I fanned myself with my hand.

"Something wrong?" Kit turned to me.

"Nope. It's just hot in here."

"I'm cool. Are the windows open?"

"Hmm." I bit the spoon and willed myself not to sweat.

"There's a lot of random papers in this pile. Your aunt seems to have kept every bill she ever received. Book orders; a set of bookshelves she bought ten years ago. Even bills from bookbinders. Did she have a safe or anywhere else she might keep important documents?" he asked in a casual tone.

"Not that I can remember. Why?"

He kept his head down. "Just wondering. Some people have secret stashes of money or jewelry that they hide from everyone else. It would be very convenient for you if you suddenly discovered a hidden bank account."

"Believe me, all her money was already given to the Furry Friends Rescue Shelter. If Aunt Gertrude was hiding something under all this junk, she most certainly forgot about it."

"Like what? What might she hide? And what kind of things were already given away?" He stared at me. This serious line of questioning made me feel uncomfortable, for some reason.

"Why is this so important to you?"

He shrugged and went back to the papers. "Just wanted to help. Besides, I like books. Sometimes bookstores own first editions or other important documents. Could help my research."

"That sounds like something from a *Masterpiece Theatre* plot. Maybe we'll discover an original lumberjack diary from Paul Bunyan."

I heard the sound of voices from outside. I leaned forward to see out the front window. The figures of three women were outlined in the glass, peering through with their hands around their eyes, blocking out the sun.

I pointed at Kit with my spoon. "Your coven is outside."

Kit leaned out of view. "Don't tell them I'm here."

"Oh, come on. You love being the center of attention."

"It's embarrassing. Marva keeps asking if I am interested in selling a men's line of beauty products."

"With your looks and all that charm, you could." He could make a mint.

He hit his palm on his head and rolled his eyes upwards. "Women!"

Three hours later, we sat on the floor at the rear of the main room. My head was pounding again and all thoughts of Kit and sex had disappeared.

I put my head in my hands. "I've had it with books. Most of this stuff is junk and you know it." I was whining. But the thought of doing this much longer was making me feel sick.

"Think of them as more than just paper and binding."

"What are they? Sugar and gold? You're being ridiculous."

Kit dropped a book in my lap. "Look, here is a book that you would appreciate."

"Just tell me the title. My head hurts."

"Practical Jokes and Other Nonsense."

I picked it up and hurled it at him. "If someone has to actually read a book about jokes, they've already failed at comedy."

"How do you know? You haven't read it. Everything you want to throw out was crafted by someone. Each book is ideas and philosophy and imagination and . . . well, art!"

"You really think *Practical Jokes and Other Nonsense* is art?"

"To a comedian, yes." He looked around for the book in question. Locating it in the pile at his feet he picked it up, opened it and started reading. *"The aim of a joke is not to degrade the human being, but to remind him that he is already degraded."*

"That isn't a joke."

"Yes, it is. It's on us."

"It didn't make me laugh. It made me feel sad."

"Well, George Orwell said it," he said, flipping the pages. "So he was thinking about all the dystopian philosophy."

"Oh, great. dysto-thing. That's really funny stuff."

I moved to stand in front of Kit. "About all the things last night . . . I was angry and I said some things about books and reading. You can say what you want about my warped views, but you have to admit, some of the books that critics love the most are super-boring."

"I don't agree. Every book has some merit."

I picked up a random book at my feet. I handed it to him. "Find something worthwhile somewhere in this."

He turned it on its side to read the title: "*Gather around Me* by Gerry Stuckey. All right." He flipped the pages of a book that looked like no one had cracked it open since it was first in print a century ago. He found something and smiled. "Here. *'I lifted the hair from her neck and unbuttoned the pearl buttons one by one until I could see the base of her spine. Then—'*"

"You're making that up!"

"No, I'm not." He held it out and continued reading. *" 'Her land-scape unfolded in curving folds of rapture. I was lost before the journey even began.' "*

I was about to ask him to read more. Then I caught myself and sat back. "I'd rather watch the movie."

"I got your attention, though. Didn't I? You, of all people, should be the last person who wants to throw out old books."

"I don't know what you're talking about."

"You don't? You love old things. You're sentimental. Where did you get those boots? And that old coat hanging on the back of the door?"

"That's different. These clothes are still useful. Those books aren't."

"That is ridiculous."

"Oh yeah? Do you see anyone else in this town banging down the door, trying to get to these books?"

"I guarantee you that once we tidy up and get this place in order, this store will be full of people."

"You overestimate your powers. The only people I want banging down doors are the Realtors. Reeba Sweeney is coming back with another offer as soon as I clean up."

He ran his fingers through his hair. "Just give me . . . give it time."

"Time? Angkor Wat is waiting. I cleaned the magazines out of the tub and the cookbooks out of the oven. Upstairs things are starting to look normal."

"There's still a lot that needs doing."

"Not really. I've fixed the door, taken down the old awning. I'm going to give the front window a fresh coat of paint. As soon as I make my way to the basement I'll even be able to do my first load of real laundry. The store is almost ready to sell."

Kit froze and his mouth dropped open. "Basement?"

"Don't look so upset. I know it's going to be an awful job. We can ignore whatever mess is down there and make a walkway to the washing machine . . . if it still works. I haven't been down there at all."

He bit his lip and stood up, gazing around the store. "I didn't even see a set of stairs."

"You can't see the cellar entrance unless you go around the outside of the building. It's hidden by brush and weeds. Reeba Sweeney's agency was hired by the administrator of Aunt Gertrude's trust to handle basic maintenance until they found me. They had the water and heater turned on for me. But that's it. I'm pretty sure they let squatters live here. I've been avoiding the basement since I arrived."

Kit looked down at the floor, as if he were imagining what could be down below us. "Well, there's no time like the present."

"I'm not finished here."

He had the back door open and was out the door before I could say anymore.

I tossed the rest of the magazines in a plastic bag. Why was he so interested? That strange feeling of uneasiness returned. Moby and I followed him.

"Just because you offered to help the first day doesn't mean you have to continue helping me clean Books from Hell. It's a beautiful fall day. Perfect for bird-watching and other research."

"What?" He stood outside and shifted his glasses to his nose absentmindedly. They caught the glare of the sun behind him and for a moment I couldn't see his eyes. "—birds?"

"Yes."

"They're doing great." He rubbed his hands together. "Let's tackle the basement."

"We really don't have to do this."

He walked around the corner. Leaves crunched under our feet and he found the area where weeds and bushes had grown over a set of faded blue cellar doors. I had forgotten to put my hair up today and the wind blew it around my face. I tried to control it while Kit reached into the bush and forced one side of the cellar door open. Moby jumped back and then moved forward, sniffing the opening.

"This isn't locked?"

I shrugged. "I guess not."

That seemed to bother him. "Why wouldn't it be locked? Anyone could get in and steal from you."

"How sad. They might take books." I said it in a deadpan voice that caused him to look at me sharply.

"You are a smart aleck sometimes, Trudy, you know that?" he said with a frown before turning back to his task.

I grinned and watched his backside as he struggled with the cellar door. I could see the muscles outlined in his broad shoulders and looking lower I was gifted with even more of an eye treat.

I sighed. Here was that feverish feeling again. Maybe he would change his mind about "respect". I had visions of the two of us wrapped around each other.

"Trudy?" Only the top half of Kit was visible now as he stared at me from several steps down the cellar. "You all right?"

I swallowed. "Fine." Then I followed him into the recesses of hell.

"It's a huge mess, isn't it?" I asked descending the wooden stairs.

"Well, I guess we should have counted our blessings when we were working upstairs." He pulled on a string that hung from a light-bulb. I gasped: There was junk everywhere. Old clothes racks, boxes, chairs, tables, and Christmas decorations made with dried pasta.

"It didn't used to look this way." I don't know how Aunt Gertrude could let things get so bad down here. The washing machine and dryer in the corner looked like they were built when Nixon was still president. All the room needed was a wringer and a crank.

"I guess I'll just keep hand-washing or use the Sit and Spin," I said. Bummer.

"You're so handy. You could try to fix it."

"I don't have much experience with washing machines," I explained.

"Is anybody down there?" I jumped at the sound of Marva's voice.

"Of course there is, Marva, why else would it be open?" another familiar voice said.

Kit ran a hand over his face.

"You never know. The young people around here are always up to no good."

I made a face at the women who couldn't see us and called, "It's just Trudy, hoping to be up to no good with Kit . . ."

"Up to what?" A thick ankle followed by a thicker set of thighs descended the ladder.

"I don't know if I've ever been down here." Marva O'Shea reached the bottom of the wooden stairs.

"Sure you have." Flo's head appeared, outlined by the morning sky at the opening of the cellar. "Remember the year Gertrude was in charge of storing the pop for fish fries at the Elks, Marva?"

Kit was looking at them like they had started speaking in a foreign language.

"Oh, now I remember," Marva said. "Cripes almighty, but we had to let it de-thaw for hours in the winter. That was the last time we gave her that job. The only people who liked frozen pop in the middle of the winter were the Yoopers."

"Aren't you a Yooper?" Flo asked Marva.

"No, I'm from Cheboygan." She held up her hand and pointed to the tip of her index finger.

Kit buried his chin in his neck and peered at me sideways, beseeching me to translate as if the women were speaking in tongues. I grinned. I remembered the Michigan lingo very well and explained it. "*Pop* is soda. The Elks is an organization that has fish fries on Fridays. *De-thaw* is de-ice. And Yoopers are the residents of the Upper Peninsula."

"And this is Michigan," said Flo proudly, holding her hand through the doorway. "A mitten."

Marva ignored us. "I remember being down here. But it didn't look like this at all. I don't understand it. Gertrude was never as messy as all this. Between the bookstore and the cellar, it's like she lost her marbles in the last few years of her life."

"She never had any mar—"

Kit clapped his hands together and bumped me out of the way. "So, ladies, what can we help you with?"

"We just started working on the house of horrors next door and saw the cellar door open." Marva lifted several sheets that were covering the clutter. "Oh, this would be perfect for the haunted house. Trudy, could we borrow this?"

"Only if you keep it."

"And those jars too," said Flo. "We can try to make something scary look like it's living in them."

"Maybe there already is something living in them," I commented.

Marva pulled out an old picture of some long-lost ancestor from the early twentieth century. "Oh, look! This would be perfect over the mantel."

"We don't have a mantel," Flo said.

"We can make one." Marva handed her the picture and the sheets.

"I keep hearing you say we're gonna make stuff, but you have no idea what you're doing and none of the men have time to help," Flo explained. "Hunting season is right around the corner. Everyone's getting their hunting blinds ready and scouting their trails for bucks."

Just thinking about it sent a shiver down my spine. Another reason to get out of town before the season ramped up. I remembered very clearly how the center of town looked in hunting season. Deer hung from truck roofs and poles placed in the center of town. From my bedroom window above the store, I could see the bodies swinging in the breeze at night. I had nightmares the entire month of November when I lived in Truhart. And I wasn't even a vegan then. I used to wake up crying, dreaming that it was my mother swinging from the pole. Aunt Gertrude would hush my whimpers from the next room and tell me to go back to sleep. Leo, my big brother, sometimes came in and slept at the foot of my bed when it was bad. He tried to explain that the deer population was out of control and hunting was a form of conservation. But I never understood what he meant.

"Are you all right, Trudy? You look sick." Kit touched my hand.

I took a deep breath, blocking out the images of Bambi swinging from trees. "I'm sorry, you were talking about a mantel?"

"If we ever get around to it, yes. We have pieces of old mantels, but we need to put them together," said Marva.

"One of dozens of things we still have to do in the next week," said Flo.

Kit looked at me with a calculating gleam in his eye while the women named all the projects they still had to tackle before the haunted house opened. "Trudy is excellent with tools and building things, you know."

A silence descended on the cellar. Marva pushed her glasses higher up on her nose. "Well, this is rather complicated, my lord. It takes more than just someone who likes crafting—"

He interrupted: "She works with stage crews that design sets and engineer lighting."

Two heads pivoted toward me. Flo and Marva stared at me as if they were reassessing my worth in the world. I climbed over an old chair and made my way to the ladder. Time to escape.

"Trudy?" The question hung in the air. I turned. Marva stood behind me with a half-smile. "Would you be able to help us?"

"Sorry. I have work to do in the bookstore."

I was met on the top step by Flo. She extended her hand to help me on the last step. "We would be so grateful if you could help us." A wrinkle at the corner of her mouth deepened as she smiled. "Just a few days? And then we could come over and help you organize the rest of the store. We can help each other."

"It's almost organized, thanks to Kit." Why should I feel obligated to help? Most of the women in town didn't even like me. They thought I was stupid.

Kit helped Marva up the stairs with her load. She was amazingly nimble for such a large woman, but she took advantage of his gallantry and held his hand as if he were a flipping duke. Surprisingly, it didn't irritate me as much as it had a few days ago. It was rather endearing to see her giggle at his touch.

"Maybe you need a break from working in the store," Kit said to me. The meaning behind his words was obvious. He was right. I needed to get away from all the books and do something I enjoyed.

"It's for a good cause. All the proceeds go to our community-center fund. We want to build a place with activities for children and adults alike. There will be a gym and a craft center and a therapy room for some of our special-needs kids. We want to set up educational classes for our four-legged friends, like Moby. We'll have puppy-training classes once we get going."

"A place for the community to come together," added Marva.

I brushed imaginary dust off my overalls. "That's a great thing. But I have other problems to deal with."

Marva turned to me. "Don't be in such a rush to sell to Reeba. Be careful, Trudy. She wants to lowball you and make a hefty profit selling the whole building to that Fribley guy."

Flo put a hand on Marva's arm and shook her head. "That's not Trudy's problem."

Her words made me pause. "Is anyone else interested in the building?"

Marva pulled her arm away from Flo. "That's what we're trying to tell you. We are trying to raise enough money to make this a community center."

"This building?"

"Yes," both women said at the same time.

"To be honest, we have to start small. Just the grocery store for now. We are renting it for the month. And then we want to set up the Santa's workshop in December. We think we can buy the grocery store by spring. The long-term plan is for us to purchase both stores. If we can keep Fribley from getting his hands on your store we might have a chance. He wants both properties together. That's like selling out half of Main Street. We already have some donations. If we can raise just a little more we can start with the grocery store and *then* the bookshop. Turn this whole block into the kind of place Truhart needs. Don't you see?" Marva pushed her glasses up her nose with a fierce jerk.

Flo sighed. "If this place ends up like Reeba wants, all we will get is a bunch of pawnshops and adult stores and God knows what else. It would be another nail on the coffin of our town."

"And that's scarier than a house of horrors!" Marva said.

I did not care. I did not care. If I said it to myself it would be true. But still . . . "Just how much money have you raised?" I asked.

Marva mumbled something.

"What?" I couldn't hear what she said.

Flo started to speak and then shut her mouth. I looked at both of them. "That bad?"

"We have almost twenty-five-hundred dollars! I know it isn't much. But we'll have so much more if we can get this haunted house going."

Kit put his hands in his pockets and shook his head. "It really would be a great project. I wish I could help you. But I have two left thumbs."

Moby tipped the scales. He had been lying down at the entrance to the cellar, lazily enjoying the cool morning air. But on cue, he nudged my hand and wagged his tail. I had been thinking about the fact that I didn't have a home for him. I should put a flyer up at the Family Fare.

A community with dog classes would be a good thing. Maybe they could hold classes in animal cruelty during hunting season too. And host an animal-adoption event.

"I'll tell you what," I said. "I'm not going to budge on my selling price for the store. If someone is willing to pay it, then I sell. But I can help you with this haunted house."

Kit grinned. I could see the little gears moving in his academic mind. He was pleased.

"Deal," said Flo. She held out her hand again. I took it and realized that, for the first time, this crappy little town and I were going to be on the same side.

Marva and Flo followed me into the bookstore, telling me all about their plans for the haunted house. When we entered the back of the store we skirted the piles Kit and I had categorized.

I joked about the mess. "Maybe the ghosts want a few books."

Florence pulled something out of a book mountain. "Oh, it's Ray Bradbury! I loved *Something Wicked This Way Comes*."

"I did too. Have you read *The Martian Chronicles*?" asked Kit.

Flo's eyes lit up. "Of course! But I thought you would be more into someone like Thomas Hardy or E. M. Forster."

"Way too stodgy." He shook his head and bent down to explain. "Trudy here says no one will care about these books."

She clutched one to her chest. "Really?"

I did not like his argument "Take what you want now. It will make for fewer books to throw in the trash."

"No. Don't throw them away." Flo's eyes were wide in panic.

Marva dug into a pile and pulled out her own favorites. They included several cookbooks from at least fifty years ago. Kit gave me an I-told-you-so look.

A half hour later, with more women wandering in from next door, I knew I had lost my argument for trashing everything.

In the center of it all was Kit. Smiling and making small talk about interesting books and magazines. It dawned on me again: He was just too damn nice. I was burning to know what a man like him was like when his barriers were down. I pictured him in bed . . . with me.

I fanned my face.

I knew he was tired of their silly questions. In fact, if I didn't see the way a muscle in his jaw tightened whenever Marva asked him about the royal family, I would have thought he was having the time of his life. He let her talk on and on about absolutely nothing. I studied Kit. He wanted to avoid the ladies earlier and now he was sweetening them up. He was acting like a phony.

I should be flattered. At least he wasn't that way with me, I thought as the day clouded over.

Chapter 10

"You're not killing her good enough."

"What?" It was Mary Conrad's third attempted murder and she still couldn't get it right.

"Like this." Flo took the knife, smeared more ketchup on it, and raised it over her head. "Get mad and let her have it." She slashed the knife through the air and slammed it into the gut. Intestines spurted out of an open wound. "There!"

The corpse screamed and sat up. "Hey!"

"Sorry, Bridgette." She had five inches of padding and another two of her own personal padding to cushion the blow. But Bridgette was not happy with the messy innards made of spaghetti.

"Did that hurt?" Flo asked.

"No, but it scared the bejesus out of me!"

Flo shook her head. "You have to stop screaming, Bridgette. This haunted house is for the kids, not you! Every time we add another prop you run around screaming like you've never seen a haunted house before."

"I haven't!"

"Then what the blazes are you doing working this one?"

"I want to help. And Marva promised I could be dead so I wouldn't have to see anything. But being stabbed is scary."

Flo jammed the knife into her palm. "This is made of rubber. I can barely feel it."

June Krueger popped her head up over the partition. "Trudy! We need you over in the insane asylum."

I resisted the urge to point out that I was already in the insane asylum. Besides the zombie zone, where Flo, at the ripe age of eighty-three, led the undead, there was the bloodsucker's bedroom, headed appropriately by Regina Bloodworth, who kept trying to change the theme to "sexy vampires" so she could wear her favorite costume. An eccentric older woman named Addie Adler created the terrifying clown corner. She kept missing the point of making the clowns scary. She refused to add sharp teeth and red eyes to the clown corp. Instead, she wanted the clowns to learn how to juggle. I had yet to meet the woman in charge of the witch's wing, but everyone said she was the nicest woman in Truhart. She owned the Amble Inn.

The insane asylum was run by who else? Marva O'Shea.

I drew back the curtain and entered the land of the crazies.

Marva pointed at a small armchair made of two-by-fours. "Joe hasn't made this electric chair right."

Joe stood at the table saw, frowning at his wife. "I cut it exactly like you told me. So if you don't like it, blame yourself. I followed your measurements."

"There's no way you followed them. That chair looks like it was made for a pygmy."

Joe dropped a two-by-four on the floor. "I've had it. You wanted me to help and I helped. But all you've done is criticize me. I've got three dishwashers and an oven to look at this afternoon and I'm late already."

Marva waved him away. "Then go."

Joe looked at me and said, "Feel free to shove her behind in the chair if she keeps acting this way, Trudy. I'll be happy to flip the lever!" He stomped away and ignored Marva's angry huff.

"He's such a baby."

I picked the two-by-four off the ground and took my measuring tape out of my tool belt. "Do you want it the size of a regular chair?"

"Bigger. Like a throne."

I pulled a pencil out of my pocket and pictured a chair the perfect size for our local royalty, Kit. While I measured and marked the wood, I imagined him sitting on the electric chair at my mercy. My imagination took a turn and once again I was overheating.

Kit deserved punishment for getting me involved in this project. Everywhere I turned, flustered women told each other what to do. A few people left in tears. More than a dozen had done nothing more than stand in the corner and gossip.

But truthfully, I was having fun.

Besides creating weird props and working with my hands, something I absolutely loved, the ladies were treating me differently. When they saw how easy it was for me to construct scary scenery and heard my ideas for enhancing the haunted house, they began to treat me with respect. I didn't let it go to my head, of course. I was still an oddity they hadn't figured out. But I was useful now. Every now and then I caught Marva and Flo looking at me as if I had grown a new head. They were curious. They had me pegged when I was on my side of the wall. But here I was, in the loony bin right with them.

"And don't forget to add straps and ties at the hands and feet." Marva was still talking. "We want this to be the scariest feature in the whole haunted house."

"This is for people over sixteen, right?" I asked.

"Mature viewers only!" Marva said. "We're going to have a tent outside for the little tykes."

"Good idea!" Everyone was getting into the theme so much that I was beginning to understand how serial killers got started.

I pulled out a scrap of paper and began to trace a chair.

I drew Marva a rough sketch. I had worked on almost every haunted room in the store, but something about the asylum fascinated me.

Marva looked over my shoulder. "Is his lordship coming by today?" Kit's request to lose the title had caught on with everybody except Marva.

"He says he's busy in the bookshop."

"Why doesn't he ever come and see our masterpiece?"

"I don't know. Don't ask me . . ." My voice trailed off.

The ladies asked him over each day but, for the past week, he kept making excuses. It suddenly occurred to me that I may not be the only haunted soul in Truhart.

I popped my head in the bookshop. "Time to eat, Professor." His head was buried in one of the boxes of papers he had pulled down from the attic yesterday.

He started to say something and I put my hand up. "You owe me lunch after getting me involved in the nuthouse next door."

"In a little—"

"Even Shakespeare ate!"

It was a nice day and I made Kit take the long way to Cookee's. We passed by Doc's and I shooed a black cat off Lulu's hood. "Must be Doc's cat."

Kit patiently listened to me explain all the ways I had nurtured her over the past few years. I left her with a fond caress and a silent promise to return soon.

When we finally sat down in a booth, Mac announced he had a surprise for me. "Wait till you see what I found on the internet."

Twenty minutes later he placed a mushroom risotto with squash in front of me. "Locally harvested," he said proudly.

I was majorly impressed with his expertise. It was delicious. I tackled the dish with gusto. Meanwhile, Kit picked at his fries and stared across the street at the bakery.

"Something bothering you?" I angled around to see what he was looking at. Hay barrels. A few skeletons swinging from a post. A stuffed dummy wearing a monster mask.

"Does that bother you?" He was confirming my suspicions.

"Huh, what?" he said, bringing his eyes back to me.

"The Halloween decorations. Do they creep you out?"

"Yes . . . I mean, no!" A guilty expression passed over his face and he put the bun back on his burger. "It's a bit odd to me how people get into this gruesome holiday."

"Uh, if I remember correctly, the tradition started in England. So don't blame us."

"Scotland and Ireland, to be exact. We had almost obliterated the holiday with Guy Fawkes Night, but thanks to the Scots and Irish, it's back in vogue now."

"I don't know about the history behind it, but it's fun to be scared, don't you think?"

"No."

I remembered Marva's complaint that Kit wouldn't visit and thought about his reaction to the decorations. I should have realized it sooner.

Kit was afraid.

He watched Truhart transform from sleepy-town to haunted-town with an obvious lack of appreciation. Well, well. He gave me a hard time about my aversion to books. Hypocrite. He had his own issue.

If he expected me to accept the idea of selling books, he was going to have to accept Halloween. Come to think of it, Kit was as nervous around Halloween as he was around me. Every time I teased him about kissing me he adjusted his glasses and changed the subject. I knew he wasn't immune to me. He watched me when he thought I wasn't looking. He had responded to me by the lake. There was no way it was my imagination. But there was one way to prove it.

An idea formed as I ate and I couldn't get it out of my mind.

It involved me and Kit and an electric chair.

"Relax. It's all fake, nothing is going to hurt you." I held his hand as we walked through the carnage of fake corpses and creepy things.

"I am relaxed," Kit said.

"Then why is sweat rolling down your neck? It's sixty degrees in here."

"I've been moving books all day. That's hard work."

"You haven't moved a single book in the last half hour."

"Hmmph." He almost tripped on a skull. "Why am I here again?"

"I'm giving you a private tour so you can conquer your fears. Most of this is just papier-mâché and flour."

The majority of Truhart was at the football game. But we had both declined to go. It was a windy night and light rain mixed with snow didn't make the prospect appealing.

Kit surveyed the room. "You've done a great job. If I were watching *Macbeth* I'd give you a standing ovation."

"Thanks. But that's not the only reason I dragged you here. I need a little help with something." I bit my lip. Ever since I had started cutting and hammering the electric chair, I had been obsessed with one thing: Getting Kit in it.

"Don't tell me. You're finally going to bury me for suggesting you help the Triple C's out with the house of horror."

"Close." We were in the corner of the room. I pulled back a curtain. Kit expelled a deep breath. I don't know what he expected, but it was just a wooden chair and a white sheet. We hadn't added the scary asylum people or the blood yet. Even then the effect wasn't complete without the flashing lights and the scary soundtrack I was helping Flo create.

"So, this is just a chair?"

"It is," I said. "But it's going to be an electric chair."

"What do you need me to do?"

"I need you to sit in it."

Kit arched an eyebrow. "That's all? You've been begging me to come here all evening and you just need me to sit down?"

"Yes." I smiled. "I need to make sure I have the right measurements. And you can relax and forget your fears at the same time." Only the fears I was thinking of included the fear of me.

He stood over the chair and put his hand on the backing, testing it for sturdiness. "Looks fine to me. Let's go."

"Not so fast, Professor. I need to know it's the right size."

"Then can we go?" He turned around and slowly lowered himself into the chair. "All good?"

I walked around him in a circle, picking up some of the materials I had procured earlier today. "It seems like it's the right size. How does it feel?"

"Shockingly comfortable." He clasped the end of the armrest with his hands.

"Humor. That's the way, Professor. Now you're relaxing." I took a piece of thick cloth and tied it around his wrist. "See. This isn't so bad, is it?"

"All I need is a good book and a hot toddy." If he only knew.

Pulling out a pencil, I marked the correct spot on the wooden frame and knotted the material. When I finished I stepped back. His chest rose and fell and his breathing was erratic.

"Now the other side." I took another long scrap of cloth and did the same with Kit's other hand. "And the feet."

I could feel Kit's eyes on the back of my neck as I knelt down and tied his ankles to the frame at the bottom of the chair. "No, that's too low. Hold still. Let me readjust this one." I tied the length a little closer to his calf than his ankle.

Sitting back on my heels, I tilted my head and studied the electric chair with Kit sitting in it. His mouth was open and his cheeks were flushed.

He wiggled in the chair. "Trudy . . ."

"How do you feel?"

"Shocked."

"Do you like it?" I ran my tongue across my lower lip.

"I'm warming up to Halloween. But—"

I put my finger in the air. "For once, don't think, Kit. We both need to tackle our fears." I pulled my hair out of its bun and shook it out. "It's getting hot. Hmm. I should probably place something across you to make sure you can't get away."

I ran my hands across his chest. "I'm tired of you getting away from me." He watched my hands and his nostrils flared.

"What can I use to keep you right here in this chair, Kit?"

"You." His eyes were glazed. My seduction plan was working.

I straddled his lap and let my lip run across his collarbone. "Are you going to be good? Or am I gonna have to make you beg?"

"Beg?" His voice was hoarse. I ran my hands in his hair and kissed him. He tasted like toasted grain and delicious man. He strained against the bonds and arched his back trying to get loose.

"Ah, this is what I need." I unbuckled his belt and slid it off him. Then I backed away and wrapped it around his middle and secured him to the thin post at his back.

I stepped between his legs. "What are you going to do now, Dr. Darling? Respect me?"

"Maybe we should forget about respect," he croaked.

I leaned forward until my lips were almost touching his. His eyes widened. I raised my hand and traced a light line from his jaw to his collarbone. Slowly, I unbuttoned the first few buttons on his shirt.

"Just a suggestion. You could do the same," he whispered. He was looking at me with uncontrolled lust. His smooth skin felt like fire on the back of my knuckles. His uneven, husky breathing and half-lidded eyes told me all I needed to know. This was no polite act from Kit. There was no mistaking his body's reaction. I liked the honesty. And now I knew his desire was as strong as my own.

I lowered my head and pressed my lips to the point at the bottom of his neck where the pulse was visibly throbbing. Then I kept going, punctuating each button with a kiss. Until there was no more shirt left.

I put my hands on his shoulders and climbed into his lap again. "Poor prisoner. Maybe you need a little lap dance before I get started."

I nipped him behind the ear and he growled, "I'm a fabulous tipper."

He buried his head in my neck and ran his tongue along my collarbone. I arched my back and rubbed myself against him. My advantage was unfair, straddling him like this. I slid down until I was on my knees.

Unbuttoning the front of his pants. I asked, "Is it time to flip the switch?"

His smoldering eyes were the only answer I needed.

* * *

Someone caressed my face. It tickled. In a good way. I smiled, thinking about the way Kit and I tripped over each other on the way to the upstairs apartment last night. The electric chair may have shocked Kit, but his performance afterward had stunned me as well. When I untied Kit . . . finally, it was to discover a whole new side of him. He was insatiable. Wild. Starving but never sated. I wasn't as experienced as Kit thought. But something about his reaction to my seductive play was different than anything I had known. The intensity was surprising. And wonderful.

Fingers brushed aside a strand of hair that had fallen over my eye and a cool breeze grazed my cheek. Not fingers. I opened my eyes to see something white billowing over me. The curtain.

Strange, I hadn't left the window open.

I rolled onto my side and reached for Kit. It was still dark. But there was nothing beside me but a crumpled sheet and a lopsided pillow.

"Kit?" Suddenly the bed felt too big and very empty. But it wasn't just Kit's absence that made a void. Moby was gone too. I had become used to him taking up half the bed.

I rolled off and nearly knocked over my old box of condoms we'd almost used up. I padded barefoot and bare naked into the living room. "Hey, guys?" My toe bumped into a stack of books I'd forgotten about. Damn things.

I turned on a lamp. "Where are you?"

Well, nothing like being loved and left. And he'd taken my temporary dog companion too. They couldn't be far. Downstairs I flipped the light switch and gazed around the store. But no one was there. Not even my friendly ghost. The back door was partially open. I pulled on my tapestry coat and slipped my feet in the boots I had kicked off last night in my frenzy to undress.

Outside, a cold wind tangled my hair. I clutched the front of the coat. The moon was low on the western horizon and a faint glow had started in the east. Mickey was somewhere in my pile of clothes. It must have been close to sunrise.

Several early birds were beginning the day. They called back and forth in light, lilting songs. I wasn't much for the wee hours, but this morning made me appreciate the beauty of the predawn light.

I scanned the fields behind the store, but all I saw was the faint shadow of the tall grasses blowing in the wind. Main Street was quiet.

Too early for anyone else to be awake yet. Even the traffic from M-33 was silent.

As I walked down the middle of Main Street toward them, naked but for the coat and boots, I thought of all the things I was going to tease Kit about. I looked toward Echo Lake. I could make out movement and a faint outline at the spit of land by the shore.

He stood on the sandy beach, his hands in the pockets of the very same pants I had removed in less than two seconds last night. His shirt hung loose and flapped in the breeze. With the dim glow of the lake behind him, he looked like an apparition.

Moby saw me first. He jumped over a pile of driftwood someone had used for an old bonfire. Wagging his tail and his body with it, he nuzzled my hand, seeking forgiveness for leaving me in the middle of the night. Kit watched us approach with a brooding expression that reminded me of a gothic hero in a BBC film. I wrapped my arms around him. His shoulders were stiff. I took the hint and stepped back.

He nodded toward Moby. "He needed to go out."

"Really. He usually has a bladder the size of a horse."

The wind kept playing games with my hair so I turned and faced it, freeing my hands enough to clutch my coat more tightly.

From my vantage point I could see Kit's profile as he stared out at the lake. He stepped back until we were yards apart.

The silence settled over us and felt stifling.

"So Kit—"

"Trudy, I—"

We spoke at the same time.

"Sorry?" he asked.

"Nothing. What was it you were going to say?" A heaviness settled on my chest. It was ridiculous. I didn't care about this morning-after stuff. I was fine enjoying sex and moving on.

I stumbled over my words. "If you don't want to do anything else together—fine. I mean, lots of people have sex once—I mean one night." We actually did it more than once. "Feel free to move on to someone else, one of your loyal followers—it's all fine. It was just mutual pleasure. I don't believe in relationships and bonds that made people speak and do things they don't mean. I'm not like that—"

He cleared his throat. "I was just going to say that I didn't mean to be so—so ardent last night."

"Ardent?" What kind of word was that to use?

"You know what I mean. I was just a little avid. I didn't mean to be so . . . it wasn't like me to be that way. I didn't mean it to happen."

And there it was. Dropped like a bomb between us.

"You regret it?"

"*Regret* is a word that expresses sorrow that something happened. I don't feel that. But I do feel that it can't happen again. You. Me. We are here for just a short time. And we have responsibilities that don't necessarily . . ."

"Don't necessarily what?"

"They don't fit together."

I tossed my head and turned toward the lake. The wind whipped my hair into tangles that would take time to comb out. I didn't feel like looking at him. All sad and full of whatever the word was that wasn't exactly regret.

"Whatever. It was good. No worries." And I thought we fit together pretty good.

"Trudy, don't take it the wrong way. Maybe you'll understand in time—"

"Time?" I laughed. "Hey, Kit. Don't make this into a big deal. I'm no shy virgin and I was the one who attacked you in the chair. I'm here for a short time and you are too. You wanna have some fun while we're here, I'm up for it. You want to part ways and just put books on shelves and drink tea, that's fine too."

He put a hand on my bare neck. "I don't mean to sound so cold—"

"Don't be silly." I shrugged off his hand and reached down and picked up a stick at my feet. "Hey boy, go get it," I said. I threw the stick as far on the grass behind us as I could.

Moby ran after it and sniffed. Instead of bringing it back, he sat down and began to chew. Even the dog didn't want to play with me. "So it's like four in the morning or something. I'm going to try to go back to bed," I said.

My throat felt funny. I couldn't say anything else. I must be losing my ability to have a proper one-night stand. I turned to go.

"Come on, dog." I suppose I should be grateful that the dog would come to my bed. He didn't have to. He was as free to leave me as Kit.

"Wait a minute, Trudy." Kit grabbed my hand. "I don't want you to go back alone."

I dug my nails into the fabric of my coat. "Don't be polite, god-damn it!"

"What?"

"Stop thinking about how I feel. What do *you* want?" Despite my intentions, my anger was rising to the surface.

"I don't want to leave you alone like this."

"I've been alone for the past fifteen years. I can take that. What I can't take is your polite pity. I am not one of the ladies of this town. Don't treat me that way!"

"I don't treat you like them." His glasses caught a faint glimmer of light from the horizon.

"Yes you do. When you act the way you think you should, instead of the way you want to—you treat me like them. You act like a fake!"

"That is ridiculous. Did it look like I was faking it last night?"

I poked him in the chest. "No. That felt real. Then this morning you turned back into a fraud."

"Being cautious and thinking something through does not make me a fraud. I'm not prevaricating."

"Pre—? Whatever! I just want you to be honest."

The wind blew his hair up. I resisted the urge to smooth it down. His shoulders slumped. "Honesty can be very complicated."

"I find it very simple. You start by doing and saying what you want."

"What *I* want? Ha! If you only knew. You wouldn't be happy with me . . ." His voice trailed off in the breeze.

I turned back to Main Street. "I should have known. You aren't capable of being honest with your feelings."

"You have no idea what I am capable of." He moved around to block my path.

"You're right. Because you never let anyone know."

"Wait. I don't want you to go."

"You don't? Why? Because you don't want me to be alone and feel bad, my lord?"

"No!" In the pre-glow of dawn his eyes looked black and fierce.

"Then why, for God's sake!"

"Because right now I want to make love to you again. That's what I want. I want you!"

"You do?" I put my hands on my hips and my coat fell open.

"I do!"

"Then come over here and prove it."

He closed the distance between us in two steps, wrapping his hand around my bare hip and pulling me close with one rough movement. We collided in an exquisite crash that made my senses explode. Before I could tease him his lips were on mine in a kiss that was hard and urgent.

If he thought he was ardent before this, he was single-minded and bold now.

He reached down and lifted me, grinding his hips against me and forcing me to wrap my legs around him. I clung to him and arched my back, crying out when his lips travelled down my neck.

Everything spun away from me; time, place, sounds. My world was Kit. In my eagerness to get his clothes off I unbalanced us. We fell backward and I braced for the impact. But Kit had me. He cushioned my fall, making the sandy beach as soft as a down pillow.

Kit looked down at me with a satisfied smile and slowed his pace. His kisses grew softer as he peppered me with his tongue and his touch until I cried out. He took his time. He savored my body with a focus that made me feel amazing. As if I were special.

When we came together part of me cracked open. Like a new fissure at the bottom of the ocean, Kit exposed something inside me that was ablaze like hot lava.

With my coat spread beneath us, and the first blush of morning behind his head, I felt like the luckiest woman in the world.

Chapter 11

I woke up to the warmth of sunshine and Kit's smile. "How long have you been staring at me?"

"Since the first morning I saw you in that towel." He kissed me on the nose and then moved to my lips. They weren't the only part of my body that was pleasantly raw. I could feel the delightfully chaffed skin and whisker rash all over.

When the kiss ended, Kit looked down his adorable aquiline nose with hooded morning eyes. The heat in the apartment hadn't kicked in yet. The air was crisp and I burrowed under the blankets and snuggled, savoring the warmth and the smooth, hard places of his body. As if on cue, the grind of a garbage truck and the pounding of someone hammering next door reminded us that the morning was almost halfway gone.

"Let's stay in bed and forget the world outside."

Kit smoothed his fingertip along my brow. "I have a better idea. You finish that chair and I'll organize the west side of the store. Then you can come to my place tonight. We'll open a bottle of wine and relax by the fireplace."

"It turns me on when you get bossy like that!" I ruffled his hair.

"We have some things to talk about—"

"Forget the blimey talk, you silly Brit. Tea and crumpets are for talk. But wine and a roaring fire are for sex!" Then I rolled off the bed and fumbled in the closet for my clothes. For once my words had made an impact. Kit sat on the edge of the bed watching me quietly. He grabbed his pants from the floor and almost fell over as it took him several tries to get his feet in the right holes. I laughed and pulled on an old sweater and jeans.

"I love the way you wear clothes," he eventually said after he fastened his pants. He sat down and ran his hand along a silk scarf with butterflies I had left on the bedpost.

"The credit goes to my mother."

"Really?" He seemed fascinated. I pulled out a Japanese silk *yukata* robe from the closet. "A lot of this is hers."

"Even the boots you always wear?"

"God no. Just the good stuff. I like to shop at vintage stores and supplement her pieces, of course. All the boots and shoes are mine. My feet are bigger than hers were . . . and I lost her shoes when she—" I paused and shook my head.

The morning sun played on the back of Kit's hair, making me blink. "She what?" he asked.

"She loved shoes."

"Tell me about her."

I don't know why I felt compelled to open up. But last night had changed things between us. I snapped the button on my old jeans and grabbed the butterfly scarf.

I brought it to my face. "Sometimes I imagine it still smells like Mom." I folded it reverently and placed it on a box. "When I was young, she let me play dress-up in her closet . . ."

"Women and their clothes . . ." Kit drawled.

"Says the man who could be a J. Crew model."

"Tell me more."

I sat down next to him and hugged my knees to my chest. "Mom was warm and funny and thrifty. But her guilty pleasure was clothes. The one advantage to living overseas is that, whether we were in Europe or Asia, there were always great places to shop. Korea had amazing markets for finding off-label clothes. Germany was great for handmade clothing. Shoes were best in Italy. Mom spent her free time hunting for great bargains and vintage clothing. I got to go along whenever I wasn't in school. My favorite moments were at home, playing dress-up in the mirror.

"But her shoes were the best. I begged and begged her to let me wear them to school. But she always said 'no'."

Kit pulled my toes into his lap and rubbed. "I can't imagine you would have looked normal wearing grown-up shoes to school at that age."

I closed my eyes, enjoying the foot massage. "I tried once. I left the house one morning when she wasn't looking. We were the same size then. I wobbled all the way to school." It seemed so long ago.

"What happened?"

"My teacher looked at me strangely. The kids in my class laughed at me. But I didn't care. I was wearing the beautiful black four-inch pumps that I loved. I fell twice. By noon my feet were throbbing. By the end of school I had started forming blisters. I took them off on the way home, regardless of the fact that it was cold enough to snow in Itaewon."

Kit dropped my feet and pulled me close. "Did she find out?"

"Don't all mothers have that sixth sense? When I got home, she was waiting. She looked down at my blistered, red feet and took the shoes from me." I could still picture how she let them dangle off her index finger.

"Was she mad?"

"Not really. She helped me spread lotion on the blisters. I remember she said, 'Shoes are the one thing you can't really borrow, Trudy. It's not just the fit. People's feet have different places to go. You have to wear your own shoes in life.' "

Kit pulled me onto his lap. "Your mother was a wise woman."

"You would have liked her." I put my head on Kit's shoulder and felt a peace I hadn't felt in years. It was good to talk about her. "My father gave all her beautiful shoes away after she died. I was so mad. I stuffed as many of her clothes as I could into that old Samsonite suitcase and covered them up with my own clothes so he wouldn't see them. I was lucky to have something left of her to save."

"Good for you. I suspect you carry more of your mother with you than her clothes, though."

That was a beautiful thought. I wrapped myself in it and stayed in the circle of his arms, letting the warmth envelope me.

After a few minutes, I said, "You'll appreciate the fact that her favorite reminder after that came from a book. Something about never knowing a person until you wore their shoes or walked around in their skin or something like that."

He put his arms around me. *To Kill a Mockingbird.*

"I should have known. A bird story."

He kissed my nose and held me close, sensing my need to pause and catch my breath. Talking about my mother was like unraveling another layer of myself. For someone comfortable with nudity, it was a strange feeling to be exposed this way. I felt raw and naked.

"I think you need another pair of shoes. The ones you had on yesterday were—" Kit looked down at my feet and his eyes went wide. "You did pick up all your clothes you dropped by those two coffins, didn't you?"

I froze. "I didn't even think about it." We tumbled out of bed and dressed like silly children, giggling the whole time.

Before he left, he cupped my chin in his hands. "See you later."

I liked the way he said it. It sounded like it came with a guarantee. I trailed my finger along the tip of his perfectly formed ear. Nothing on his body that wasn't perfect. Even his toes were shaped like Adonis's.

When he was gone I stood and stretched. It was a beautiful morning and I was ready to return to the Nightmare on Main Street next door. While Moby ate breakfast, I crept into the store from the back door and grabbed my clothes. The lone person in the insane asylum was the lady who had been with the deputy sheriff the other day. The only clue she might have seen me was a crooked grin that she covered with her hand.

I dumped my clothes in the apartment and held the back door open for Moby. We both needed a long walk.

Years ago, before I first came, there had been a fire at an old barn a mile away. It had swept across the field, almost reaching town. By the time I arrived in Truhart, nothing remained of the field but a charred and barren stretch that matched my mood during that fourteenth year of my life. Now nature had returned to the land. The autumn grass was golden and brittle and the sun flickered off the jack pines that had grown tall among the brush.

Moby ambled from tree to tree, sniffing and marking his territory. I walked with my hands in the pockets of my coat, trying to stop smiling like a silly teenager. The shy little bird who was becoming my friend flitted above us, singing a sweet repetitive song over and over. Like a gentle reminder no one understood.

This . . . "thing" with Kit was not normal for me. Despite the impression I gave off, I hadn't slept with scores of men. The ones I had been with had been convenient. Like friends with benefits. I was with those men because we shared things. A love for vinyl records, a summer of working in a theater company, or a trip along the trailhead to Sentinel Dome in Yosemite. Ironically, Kit and I had absolutely nothing in common. We were as different as Lulu and the sleek black Ford truck he drove. Despite that, I felt something that I never felt with the other lovers in my life. He was so—nice. And smart. And decent. And sexy. I wanted to know him, read his moods. Understand him. His obsession with books, his affection for all things American, the fact that he hated tea and loved football. I wanted to find everything that made him happy and feed it to him on a platter, just because. And even though I felt no affection for those things and probably never would, I wanted to watch joy play across his face and know I had helped put it there.

Maybe I would look back some day and say, *Oh that was my Truhart phase—the time I cleaned out a bookstore with the British guy and we slept together.* But, I doubted it. This didn't feel like anything I had experienced. This time with Kit felt like I imagined Angkor Wat would feel. Like a temple in the jungle where I could discover something wonderful.

He challenged me to think about so many things. To accept what I had been avoiding. Not just about Aunt Gertrude and the store and the town. Being with Kit was like having a mirror around. I didn't need to look at myself to get through the day, but having the option of looking at my reflection made me more sure of who I was. I felt better because of him.

I giggled and raised my face to the sun. "What the hell am I doing?" It was more of a hope than a complaint. I looked down to see Moby staring at me with raised ears, as if he wanted to answer me. Instead he wagged his tail and put his nose back down to the ground.

I kicked a pinecone and shook my head. I was overthinking this. "Come on, boy. I'm hungry. Let's get some grub."

We rerouted and had almost reached the back of Cookee's when I heard the little bird again. I had an old packet of oyster crackers in the pocket of my coat I had been saving for Moby. I smashed the packet with my fist, making the pieces more manageable for the little guy, and spread the crumbs on the ground.

"I'm going to have to remind Kit to tell me all about chickadees in the Midwest," I whispered, trying not to scare him. I held Moby and watched the little guy eating just four yards away. When I turned to go I almost ran headfirst into the lens of a camera.

"Oh!" I reached out and steadied the frail man with the hooked nose, whose camera I'd almost run into.

"Shh . . ." he said with a finger over his mouth. He pointed behind me and I looked back at the little chickadee.

"Isn't he cute?" I whispered.

"Do you know what that is?" he asked.

I shook my head.

"That's a Kirtland's warbler," he said with wide eyes.

"A what?"

"A Kirtland's warbler." He said it again, with reverence. "Very rare."

The tiny bird must have sensed our attention. He grabbed a crumb and flew away.

I turned to the man. "Rare, you said?"

"Kirtland's warblers have been on the list of endangered species for years. They can only be found in the spring and summer in this region of the state. That little guy is very late flying south. Just like me."

"Really?" A buzzing started in my ears.

"Whole ecotours are scheduled around those little guys. I've been looking for them all summer. I can't believe I was lucky enough to get close and snap a good picture of him." He held out his digital camera for me to view.

I nodded absently. "Are you absolutely sure that was a Kirt—Kir—"

"Kirtland's warbler?" He pulled a field guide out of his pocket. "Absolutely. See? The yellow breast, the blue-black wings, little broken outline of yellow around the eyes."

I studied the field guide. The picture fit. He was right.

"And then there's that lilting sound with that little upturn at the end as if he's asking a question."

"I heard the song just now." I heard it several times, in fact. I had pointed it out to Kit.

"They love to make their home in a jack-pine forest. People thought they were extinct for a while. But they are making a grand comeback. I can't wait to show my friends in the Keys when I head out next week."

I thought about the first day I'd met Kit. It was the first time I'd seen the warbler. And Kit hadn't even noticed. He was too busy looking at books.

"Do many people outside the area know about them?"

"Birders and nature lovers do. Here." He handed me the binoculars. "Can you see him at the edge of the clearing?"

I put the binoculars to my eyes. But I wasn't really looking. My mind was thinking about Kit. Something had been bothering me since I first caught him in the back alley. His fascination with the store and the books. And his strange disregard for the little bird.

I handed the binoculars back to the older man. "You seem to know a lot about birds."

"Oh, I know a lot about this area. I get so excited about these things that everyone teases me that I'm the local expert on the flora and fauna of the county. Name's Nestor Nagel." We shook hands. "It's hard not to love the area. Truhart has some of the best morel-mushroom picking in the state. Our rare plants like trillium and lady's slipper are the pride of the county. And then there's that little guy." He pointed to the bird, who was back again.

I didn't want to ask. But I had to. "Have you by any chance spoken with the professor from England about all this?"

"His lordship? Oh, I've heard all about him from Marva O'Shea. But I can't say as I've had the pleasure. I head down to the Keys tomorrow. So I guess it will have to wait until next spring."

I walked him back toward Main Street and wished him luck.

Then I returned to Books from Hell.

The appetite I had earlier was gone. I let Moby inside the bookstore, my attention caught by the stacks against the wall. Kit had been very thorough in his organizing. He had taken each book one by one, opened up the first few pages, and then stacked them in the correct pile. I had teased him once that he was going to get a crick in his neck from looking down so much.

I didn't know much about people who studied birds. But it seemed to me that most whatever-ologists spent more time looking up. Not down.

I burst through the side door of the garage. "Where is Richie?"

Doc greeted me. "Trudy! I was going to stop by the haunted house and talk to you about Lulu."

I wasn't concerned about Lulu right now. I had passed her parked in the side lot. "Is Richie working today?"

Doc nodded toward the office. "Until noon. Then he's got practice. The team lost big last night. So they have extra workouts today."

I was already at the office door. "Richie."

Richie looked up from his phone with a guilty expression on his face.

Behind me, Doc bellowed, "Richie, what the hell am I paying you for? Get off your phone and get back to cleaning out the back room."

Richie set down his phone. "I was just checking something."

"Check on your own time." His father walked away and I caught the way Richie's gaze followed his dad. I probably used that same expression dozens of times when my aunt was alive.

I pulled up the chair next to Richie and lowered my voice. "Can you just do one thing for me before you start the back room?"

He looked doubtful. "I don't know anything about cars, Ms. Brown. You must have figured that out already."

"Yeah, but you know other things. You know how to look something up for me, right?"

He twisted his lips and lowered his brows. "Uh, yeah."

"I don't have a smartphone. Can you look up someone?"

He pushed his phone toward me. "Feel free to do it yourself. I've gotta start on the back room before my dad fires me."

"No. No. That will take too long for me. I have dyslexia."

His mouth dropped open. "Really? Isn't that where you read backwards?"

"Not exactly. But it makes reading difficult."

"Man! That sucks! And you own a bookstore."

"Tell me about it!"

Richie was looking at me with a whole new fascination that owning Lulu had never done for me. "Hey, that's why people think you . . . um . . . have problems."

"Exactly. That's why they think I'm dumb." I pushed the phone back toward him. "Can you look someone up or not?"

He picked up the phone and lifted his thumbs over the screen. "Who?"

"Christopher Darlington."

"The weeny English-lord guy? Sure." He thumbed the name and watched as the screen popped up with information. "There are a few Christopher Darlingtons. This one was born, like, almost a hundred years ago. Can you narrow the search?"

"Try birds."

He shook his head. "Nope."

"Wait. That's wrong. He's a professor. Try Cambridge."

His eyes lit up. "Hey, here's his lordship." He turned the screen toward me so I could see the picture of Kit. It was a studio photo, the kind they use in yearbooks. He looked serious. And very professional.

"What does it say?"

"Let's see . . . Christopher Darlington. Cambridge University. Professor of North American Studies."

I knew that part. "What else?"

"Here's an article in the *Cambridge News*. It's titled *Professor of American Studies Steps in Muck over American Author*." He turned the screen toward me. I shook my head. Something burned in the pit of my stomach. "What does it say?"

He clicked on it so it appeared larger. "Let's see . . . *Christopher Darlington, professor in the Faculty of English, has made a bold statement that may land him in a quagmire in the literary community. His postulation that renowned American author Robin Hartchick wrote a second novel was enough to raise eyebrows on both sides of the pond. But his declaration that he will find the elusive treasure brought about scorn in the literary community—much of which came from his own father, Sir Charles Darlington, professor emeritus of British literature, Britain's own national treasure.*"

Kit wasn't here to research local culture, or birds, or anything about the region. He was in Truhart for one very specific purpose. And like a fool, I had invited him into the store and played right into his scheme.

I had become accustomed to people who made me feel inferior. I thought Kit was different. The sting of his deception was almost unbearable.

I stood inside the front door, watching Kit rifle through the pages of a book. His brows were furrowed and he was talking to himself. He shook his head and moved it to a pile beside him.

"Did you find it yet, Professor?"

"Find what?"

"Kirtland's warbler. Ring a bell at all?"

"Is that a children's book?" he said absently, moving a stack of books against the wall.

"It wasn't written by Robin Hartchick. I know that. But maybe another lost book of his showed up since yesterday?" Kit's hands froze on a stack of loose papers.

The stillness in the room was broken only by the sound of someone practicing a scream in the haunted house next door.

"Trudy—I wanted to tell you that first day."

"Then why didn't you?"

"I was going to."

"When? After we had sex again, or after you sold this nonexistent manuscript at Sotheby's?"

He carefully took his glasses from the top of a nearby stack. "I don't care about the money."

"Or me?"

He stood up, setting down the books that he had been holding. "I didn't want that to happen. I felt terrible knowing that we had—had been together and you didn't know the truth. I was actually going to tell you tonight."

"Bull!" I marched over to him.

"I completely understand how mad you feel right now. I would be too. I tried to explain, but so many things got in the way and you—"

He stopped mid-sentence, for a very good reason. I slapped him. A red mark bloomed on his cheek. "I threw myself at you? Is that what you were going to say? You must have had a great laugh, Dr. Darlington, American literature professor at Cambridge. Not only were you secretly searching for the elud—I mean eluser—" What the hell was that word in the article Richie read to me? I substituted, "*lost* manuscript, but you were screwing *a* Gertrude Brown under the same roof that Robin Hartchick did."

"Trudy! It wasn't like that. I *wanted* to be with you."

"Because I was the dumb-ass who couldn't figure out what was going on. Right? Were you laughing about it when you left this morning?"

"No!" He reached a hand toward my shoulder, but I twisted away.

"Don't touch me ever again!" I kicked a pile of books that he had just so carefully stacked. "You know what I'm going to do with all these books? I'm going to throw them in the garbage! I hate them! I hate this store! I hate you!"

Moby whined and curled up near the stairs.

"Get out," I said in a low voice.

"Listen to me. I came here looking for the book. Yes. But I met you and everything was different. I wanted to help and I didn't want to fool you. If I found that lost manuscript, I planned on giving you the money anyway and nothing would be harmed. I would be proven correct to my skeptical colleagues and you would have enough money to travel for the rest of your life."

"Everyone thinks you are a fool for believing it exists and stating it publicly. You're desperate because your career and reputation are on the line."

"Yes, that's true."

"Admit it."

"I admit it freely."

"This has nothing to do with anyone but you."

"Well, at first it didn't. Then I met you."

"I should have followed my instincts when I first saw you. You're a pompous ass, my lord. Now get out."

"No. I can't leave you like this. I need to make you understand." He straightened his glasses on his face. They stayed crooked and there was a sheen of perspiration on his forehead despite the cool room around us. He didn't look handsome right now. He looked like a man who'd gambled everything and lost.

"Why weren't you honest from the start? Why didn't you just tell me you were looking for a lost book?"

"When I got here, you made it very clear you hated books and wanted to get rid of the store. You acted like you didn't care whether there was an important book here or not."

"I would have let you search."

"For two days maybe. Then you would throw everything in the trash."

"That's right. I'd be gone by now if you hadn't talked me into cleaning out the store. You made me think it was for my benefit. You acted like you were helping me. I can't believe how I fell for it!"

"You have to under—"

"Leave," I repeated. Just so he knew I was serious, I reached down and grabbed a large leather-bound book. He put his hands up to shield himself. My aim was off. The book hit the wall and landed at his feet.

He stepped toward the front door. "I know you're upset, but when you calm down, we're going to talk. Not now, but tomorrow. In a fortnight we'll be laughing about this. It's not what it seems."

"Do you have any idea how you sound? You and your British words make me sick."

He stepped over a pile of books. "I can't help that."

"Yes you can. Just stop talking!"

He put a hand up to appease me. I lifted another book, winding up to throw it. "Okay, Trudy. I'll stop. But give me time. It's going to be all right."

His outline blurred in front of me. I swallowed past the gunk that clogged my throat.

"Just give me a chance to prove the manuscript is here."

I threw the book; it landed short. "Get out!"

He was at the door now. Just to make sure he kept going I picked up a larger hardcover book and lunged his way. Moby barked a warning—the traitor. Kit ducked out of the way, giving me a perfect view of a small group of females gathered on the sidewalk outside the store. My screaming must have even scared the loonies in the house of horrors.

"Do you know what you are, Dr. Darlington?" I yelled to his retreating back. I figured I might as well give them a show. "You are nothing but a lousy professor with a corny accent!"

He dodged my next missile and hurried down the street, leaving a sea of curious faces in his wake.

Chapter 12

The setting sun tinted the end of a bad day to puce. I sat on the roof outside the second-story window and let the mist dampen my old jeans. The cold, hard aluminum siding cut into my back. The discomfort was nothing compared to my shame.

How could I have missed all the signs?

I played the clues like a rerun, over and over in my mind.

The first day Kit had visited, he seemed nervous. I thought it was because I was wrapped in a towel. But there was more. He said he was looking for books on the region for his research. He lied for weeks. The humiliation made me burn inside.

But I felt more than shame. I was mad. Really, really mad. Madder than any word in Kit's huge vocabulary.

The last time I felt even close to this kind of anger was when I saw Moby chained to a stake just a few months ago. But that was because I loved animals. I believed they were all sacred creatures on our earth.

But now, I was furious for my own sake. I hadn't sat on this roof shaking with anger since I had lived with Aunt Gertrude. In those days, I would seethe with fury for hours.

And here I was again. Looking out over Truhart and feeling like the dumbest person on earth. I guess my life had come full circle.

I hoped Kit had bruises from my book missiles. I hoped he realized he had lost all possibility of ever finding that damn manuscript.

Thank God for Kirtland's warbler. If that little bird hadn't popped up, I never would have figured out the scam. No professor with an interest in whatever-ology would have visited Truhart without caring about a rare native species that was found nowhere else in the world.

Richie had uncovered several articles about Kit's theory. Kit believed that Robin Hartchick had written a novel before his famous literary masterpiece, *Spring Solstice*. While he originally thought that the manuscript might be somewhere in Paris, where Hartchick drank his life away, he hit a dead end in France. Did Kit sleep with some dim-witted Parisian girl before coming to that conclusion? Was that what led him to Hartchick's earlier haunts? The town where one of Hartchick's earlier ex-lovers lived? To Aunt Gertrude's store?

Other professors had called his theory bunk. Even Robin Hartchick's aging friends denied that the manuscript existed. Evidently, Kit had even defended his views in a BBC documentary. The kicker was when the Lord of Knightsbridge, Kit's own father, a renowned British literary historian, was interviewed. *Deluded* and *imaginary* were two words Kit's father used to describe his own son's theory. Nice guy. Evidently, Kit took after his father in the sensitivity department.

It was ridiculous, of course. If Aunt Gertrude knew anything about the existence of a Hartchick manuscript, my inheritance might have included a mansion and a large trust. Kit's opinion was pure rubbish.

From the roof I could see the bench across the street. Kit had been watching me from there that first day. Calculating. The professor wanted to prove himself to the world of literary heavyweights. I let that sink in. I might have felt sorry for him. In his mind, I was the only thing that stood between success and failure. An illiterate woman who was easier to seduce than to reason with.

I thought about the way he had looked at me the first time we made love. The intensity had been mind-blowing. Now I realized he had just been concentrating hard on the task at hand.

The darkness had settled in. The smell of smoldering peat from someone burning damp leaves reached my nose and made my eyes water. Long after dark, I crawled back inside, closed the window, and collapsed into bed.

Later, a series of cars revved their engines as they passed. Someone was having a party at a house on Echo Lake. The occasional loud beat of a pop radio station and laughter floated my way. It was irritating to listen to people having a good time. I stared at the headlights on the ceiling and tried not to think about Kit and the fact that it was just twenty-four hours ago when he had made love to me in this very bed. I woke in the middle of the night with my nose buried in the pillow that still smelled of Kit's faint musk.

Native Americans used sage to wipe out the smell of dead people.

I could at least use laundry soap tomorrow to wipe out a living person. I tore the sheets off the bed and tossed them out the back door.

I ended up in a huddled heap of blankets in the middle of the bare bed. Despite erasing Kit Darlington from my bed, I still had trouble sleeping. I smelled burning leaves, now. I reached up to wipe my eyes. I could fool myself into thinking I was over him. But deep down I knew it wasn't smoke that made my eyes water.

I placed a sign announcing a sale in the front door and propped it open with a dictionary. Then I waited for customers.

The house of horrors was quiet. It was a Sunday. The usual churchgoers were probably piling in their cars in their Sunday best instead of thinking up ways to terrify the town. The faint ringing of a bell erupted not far from Main Street. Moby had eaten his boring dog food, which made him amazingly happy anyway. He slept in the corner of the store on an old blanket. His old bones needed a cushion. He cracked his eyes open as I walked around the shelves. Then he shut them again, tired of watching me fidget.

There were still piles of papers, old magazines, and books in the front room. But they were stacked neatly along the floor against the walls. The shelves were full and organized by category. I had Kit to thank for that, of course. If I were someone who loved books and loved retail, I'd consider giving the whole place a go. See if I could make something of it. But I wasn't.

I could have been on a boat to Thailand by now. And it was Kit's fault I wasn't.

An hour later, I still waited for my first customer. Feeling restless, I grabbed my tool bag and took my bedsheets to the basement, leaving the front door unlocked. Who cared if someone stole a few books? That was the point, after all. For the next few hours I played with the old washing machine, taking it apart and repairing a damaged lid. Now the washing machine ran like a dream. I ran the test cycle, then stuffed the sheets inside and added extra laundry detergent for good measure.

On the way up the ladder, the stairway rail came off in my hand. I guess I needed to add one more item to my to-do list before I put the store on the market. Backing out of the cellar with the rail in my hand, I froze. A familiar pair of Ferragamo loafers appeared under my nose. I clutched the rail with both hands and remembered the way

I ran my hands up those legs when he was in the electric chair. I slammed his toes with one end of the wooden railing.

"Ouch!"

"Get off my property."

He hopped up and down and grabbed his foot. "You could have broken my toes."

"I could have. But I didn't hit you that hard. Lucky you. Now go."

He placed his foot back down on the ground and tested it. Then he leaned forward and peered down the ladder. "You got the washing machine to work?"

"Just in time. Now I can wash you out of my bed."

"What?"

"Never mind."

"Trudy, we need to talk." He extended a hand to help me with the long rail. I ignored his help and brandished it like a lance. He dodged out of my way.

I dropped the wood against the side of the building. Even that made Kit jump again. It gave me bitter delight.

With the addition of a very appealing shadow of stubble on his chin, Kit looked like he had stepped out of another menswear catalog. I, on the other hand, wore blue jeans and my brother Leo's XL gray wool sweater. I felt at a disadvantage. My disloyal senses were still going haywire from Kit's sex appeal and he was probably wondering how he had sunk so low with me.

I marched through the front door. "We never need to talk again. Get off my property or I'll call the sheriff."

"It's open to the public." Kit was right behind me, halting in front of the sign on the front door. He looked at it, and back at me.

"Why are you staring? Can't you read?" I walked over to the sign and pointed. It read, *Books for Sale. Cheep! Cheep! Cheep!* "I'm not picky about the price."

He shook his head. "Nothing. It's just—"

"Hey, you got birds? The sign says *cheep cheep*." The first customer walked through the door. I looked back at the sign and felt heat on my cheeks.

Kit pulled a pen out of his pocket and inked in three *A*s in place of the *E*s. When he finished, he raised the pen.

"Sorry. I spelled it wrong," he explained. Saving me from embarrassment was not going to earn him brownie points with me. "Everything's cheap now."

Several other customers wandered in. "Is there a limit?" someone asked.

I grabbed a grocery bag I'd saved from the Family Fare. "Feel free to fill this up."

Kit lowered his voice and followed me through the store. "Don't you think you should at least hear my side of things?"

"Why should I care about someone who makes a habit of lying?"

"Because we shared something and you mean a lot to m—"

"Cut the crap! You just wanted to look for a book."

"At first. Yes. I did. I put my reputation on the line for that book. My colleagues, my friends, my own father . . . Especially my father—they all think I'm insane."

"Aww, poor little Lord Christopher. Not everyone thought you were special and smart? I can't begin to imagine the pain."

"I know this sounds ridiculous, especially to you. But I made a public statement and I can't back down."

"You have such *big* problems."

"It would be a major find of historical significance."

"Who cares about world hunger and the environment when there is a book to find, right?"

He stopped and put his shoulders back. His brows drew together and his eyes narrowed. Was that anger? "I would never compare my problems to those kind of issues."

"Could have fooled me. Oh wait—you *did* fool me."

I stood behind a shelf at the back of the store. Kit followed and placed a hand on the shelf near my head. "There are many horrible things in the world. I haven't lost my perspective so much that I would ever forget that. But even in the midst of horrible things, people need humanity. They need beauty."

"I'm sure designer shoes and fancy novels make a big difference in a famine."

"Don't underestimate the power of the written word to lift people up for even a short time, Trudy. Don't underestimate the power of something made from passion and love, or from the connection to it, whether it comes from words or from a touch." His eyes burned into my own.

A book on a shelf was on its side. I spent longer than necessary straightening it so I didn't have to respond. I understood beauty. It overwhelmed me.

"Do you have any children's books? I'm always looking for reading material for my third-graders," asked a balding man at the end of the aisle.

"The children's books are over here." Kit led him to the section he had organized for young people. He even dug up several bags and boxes and helped him haul everything to his car. When he returned I was helping Joe O'Shea fill a bag for the local veterans organization.

"You aren't redeeming yourself by sticking around here. I want you to leave," I hissed when Joe moved away.

Kit touched my hand. "I was getting ready to tell you everything. Believe me. But I had to earn your trust and friendship first. I thought that was the only way you were going to care about that book. And then—well, then . . ."

"You realized it was easier to lie? Just like the tea and the hot sauce on your Dinty Moore? You seem to have a problem with a little thing called the truth."

A pretty dark-haired woman pulled out a piece of paper and interrupted us. "I was wondering. Do you have any books by Fern Michaels, Stephen King, Ken Follett, Kent Haruf?"

"Do I look like a crusty old librarian?" I knew I shouldn't be annoyed. But she was doing exactly what I feared people would do. Ask about books.

She put her hands on her hips and replied, "Crusty old librarian? What is that supposed to mean?" Then she stomped off. Joe, still filling a box with books in the corner, leaned in. "Uh, Trudy. Just so you know, she's a librarian in Gaylord."

So much for my amazing customer skills. Kit raised his eyebrow. "Why don't I stay and help?"

"Or not."

He ignored me and approached an older couple.

"Find any good books?" He used a chipper British accent that was becoming as irritating to me as sandpaper on a chalkboard. Even more grating was the way the man and woman smiled when they heard his accent and actually let him examine their books.

I raised my voice. "Glad to see you out after that bad bout of norovirus, Kit. I see the doctor cleared you from using a surgical mask."

He shook his head and laughed, winking at the older man. "Isn't she a hoot? You keep those jokes coming, my lovebird."

I stormed off to search for more bags. Ten minutes later I was pocketing several dollars from a customer, when I saw Kit leaning over the shoulder of a gray-haired woman. I called across the store, "You look much better in person than you do on the sex-offenders web site, Professor." The lady clutched her purse to her chest and ran out.

Within a half hour a small crowd had gathered in the store. Mac and Joe were highly entertained by our banter. The usual Kit Darlington fan club thought it was some sort of game. Armed with the attention of the crowd, Kit had started his own counteroffensive. As people walked in, he asked them if they wouldn't mind signing a disclaimer on behalf of the public-safety department before entering. The county wasn't responsible for damages should the crazy lady inside insult anyone.

He lifted his chin to one old man and showed him a bruise that I completely denied causing the day before.

A familiar curly-headed blond held a book on gnomes to her chest and kneeled down on the ground, scratching a very happy Moby behind his ears.

Kit joined her as if he owned the place. "Are you still interested in starting a book club, Elizabeth?"

I stepped in front of Kit. "I'm calling the sheriff if you aren't gone in ten minutes."

Elizabeth enthusiastically pulled her phone out of her purse. "I'll do it for you. What do you want to say?"

Corinne and Marva popped up from a nearby aisle. In fact, the whole store seemed to be waiting on the reason for our strange behavior. It was time to burst the illusion of Dr. Darlington.

"Tell the sheriff that the imposter from Cambridge has been scoping out the bookshop looking for a lost manuscript by Robin Hartchick. I don't want him on my property any longer."

Several women gasped. Mac snickered. "I thought something was odd with him."

Marva put her hand on her chest. "You aren't a lord from England who is here to study the old logging culture?"

Kit pressed his lips together. Fun and games were over. It was time that the rest of the people in town understood the deception.

He turned in a circle and addressed the room. "I'm a professor from Cambridge. That's not a lie."

I raised my chin. "But he's not studying local culture. He's looking for an imaginary book by Robin Hartchick."

Corinne spoke under her breath. "My nephew Richie told me all about it this morning. But I didn't believe him."

While she filled everyone in on the situation, I stood with my arms crossed in front of me, staring at Kit. "I did warn you to leave."

"This isn't finished, Trudy. *We* aren't finished."

I walked over to the front door and held it open for him.

He put his hands up and stepped backwards, all the way to the back door. He called from the back alley. "There. I'm off your property."

I walked through the store to the back door and slammed it in his face. Alone in the storage room, I leaned against the wall and let out a long breath. *The power of connection.* Kit had described beauty that way. I thought what we had was beautiful.

What he forgot to mention is that with all that power also comes pain.

At the end of the day, only a few customers remained. Richie knelt in the corner scrounging for old Cliff's Notes of *Great Expectations* that might help him in an English-lit class.

"Richie, can you look something up on your phone for me?" I asked.

He glanced over and bit his lip. "I don't know, Ms. Brown. I feel kind of sorry for Dr. Darlington. Are you going to 'out' anyone else in town?"

"No. Of course not. I need to make a phone call." The shelves were slowly emptying. "All right. What do I look up?" Richie held his thumbs above the screen.

"Dumpsters!"

He dialed the number of a waste-removal company in Gaylord and handed his phone to me. The owner offered to stop by and give me an estimate of what size dumpster I would need to use. When I told him where I was, he said never mind. He knew all about the store. His wife was in earlier. She told him I needed a medium-sized dumpster for the store and a trash compactor for my smart mouth. I asked him to apologize to his wife, the woman I thought was too pretty to be the Gaylord librarian.

The dumpster would arrive in a week.

By late afternoon, the crowd outside was gone. I filled a box with children's books to donate to the hospital in Gaylord when I heard the clicking of heels on the wooden floor behind me.

"Hello?" Reeba Sweeney stood inside the door. She wore a dark red dress with a green overcoat that made her look like a Christmas tree.

I straightened. "Good afternoon, Reeba."

"I just drove by on my way to an open house and saw the sign. Cheap books?"

"Yes. I am clearing out this week. Whatever doesn't go is going in the trash." I expected it by Wednesday.

Reeba leaned down and picked up a book with a picture of a businessman turned politician on the cover. "Can my interested buyer and I stop by when you are finished?"

"That would be great. You can already see the floors and walls now. And the upstairs is much better. Once I paint, I might get a decent offer. Especially if they see how much space there is inside."

She took a deep breath and looked around. Then she paused, as if the prospect of explaining the situation to me had already exhausted her. "I understand your enthusiasm. You've done a lot of work. But you have to be realistic here. I want to help you. I really, really do. But this is a business deal. I can't afford to negotiate an unrealistic sale just because I like you."

What a fake. "I'm hoping, after I clean it up, your client will offer what the property is worth."

She pointed at the wall. "There is an empty business next door. In fact, there are three other vacated buildings on this street. Truhart is not exactly Harrisburg. It's been hurting for years."

"Some of the ladies at the house of horrors think Truhart is ready for a big comeback. They mentioned a community center. There could even be a bidding war," I lied.

"Trudy, Trudy. A bidding war. That's adorable." Reeba shook her head. "I'm not going to say anything about that pipe dream. The community center committee, the Triple C's, are a nice group. But the unfortunate name sounds like their bra sizes. Everyone makes fun of them and their eternal optimism. I heard they even want to open a

Santa's workshop. Ha! Marva is so heavy she could be Santa." Reeba's loose neck skin jiggled when she laughed.

"They're worried that your client wants to open a pawnshop." I don't know what made me say that.

Reeba put a hand on her throat and giggled. At least, I think it was a giggle. It might have been a snarl. "That's precious. They hold garage sales every weekend, and they're complaining about a thrift shop."

"Pawnshop. There's a difference."

"Selling guns and knives is no different than selling old teacups and lamps."

"It is a little different, actually. And they aren't opposed to all those—"

"People in Truhart are so idealistic. It breaks my heart. They think that a ghost town like this will draw the attention of some wealthy developer who wants to build gyms and condos and golf courses, not to mention libraries and swimming pools for their kids."

"They just hope for something more family friendly and—" I bit my tongue and stopped myself. I needed her on my side. I needed to sell the store.

"Money is family friendly, Trudy. Putting food on the table is family friendly. You know that place next door? It used to be owned by a family. The Kreaps. They were salt-of-the-earth people. But they had a fatal flaw: Inflexible principles. They believed in quality. For everything. They wouldn't jack up the prices. Barely sold with a margin of profit. And look how that ended."

"A lot of family-run stores went out of business in the past twenty years."

"They could have sold to a big discount store at one point in time. But they refused. Now that family sells jams and pickles off the M-33 for pennies."

My jaw hurt from clenching it. I walked her to the door and held on to it, issuing an obvious invitation for her to leave. But I couldn't help asking one last question. "I wonder why Aunt Gertrude didn't sell to you years ago?"

"Your aunt was the most unrealistic one in the lot. She held onto this store and all the books inside as if it was the last defense against Armageddon. That cruise ship was the only vacation she ever took."

"Maybe doing what she loved was all the vacation she needed." Why did I suddenly feel the need to defend Aunt Gertrude?

Reeba almost tripped on Moby, who came between us. He let out a rumble that I had never heard from him before. His ears lay back and his tail stood straight out.

Reeba raised the book she held and Moby barked loudly. "Be sure to lock him up when I bring people to look at the store."

She marched out the store and I realized, too late, she never paid for the book she held. I knelt down and put my arms around Moby. "It's all right," I repeated over and over. But it wasn't for his benefit, it was for my own.

I could care less who bought the store. All I wanted to do was sell, pay off my debt to my father, and then take myself off to Southeast Asia, where I could pray to the gods of a deserted temple in the middle of the jungle.

I let Moby lick my face. I would be happy when I had no one and nothing in the world to care about but myself. Moby squirmed in my arms because I was holding him so hard. I let him go. He curled his tail and darted across the street. "Moby!"

I hadn't noticed him earlier, when Reeba Sweeney and I were talking. But Moby wiggled and swept his tail in excited circles as he greeted his buddy. Kit Darlington sat on the bench across the street.

He smiled and slanted his head my way. "Bad meeting, huh?"

I pulled a multigrain soy bar out of my pocket. "Come on, boy!"

After much coaxing and much grinning from Kit, Moby finally came back.

Then I shut the front door in Kit's face.

Chapter 13

Three days later, business was as dead as the fake corpses next door. I squatted by Moby's blanket. "Let's go into more debt and treat ourselves to a late lunch at Cookee's."

Moby raised his head and then went back to sleep. He had been out of sorts since I made him leave Kit's side on Sunday. I kept telling him he had bad taste in friends, and he responded by staring at me as if to say, *What does that make you?*

For the past few days a slow stream of customers had dropped by the store. I had been able to get rid of enough books that I could place all the books on the shelves now. Lowering the price to five dollars a bag helped. But business was slowing down. I waited impatiently for the dumpster and tried to ignore the fact that there might be a priceless manuscript somewhere in the store. It was ridiculous. Ever since Kit mentioned that the manuscript could be hidden anywhere, I found myself searching corners for some sign of a hidden manuscript.

October had settled in, sending waves of leaves down the street and bringing a chill in the air. The trees around Echo Lake were shedding amber and gold almost as quickly as a snowfall. The Halloween house next door was just about finished. I stopped in yesterday, when most of the ladies were gone, and helped place cobwebs around the exhibits. Main Street was looking more like a nightmare than a ghost town. Which was the point of everything. The haunted house was going to open in a few days.

After washing up and changing into a pair of tight-fitting plaid pants from a vintage store in Queens and an oversized green sweater, I left Moby still sleeping. I would bring a few tidbits back from the diner. Maybe then I'd be back in his good graces.

I did my usual detour and visited Lulu. Doc had said the parts were due any day. I couldn't wait to drop the engine and get her fixed. I ran my sleeve across her hood and wiped away the grime and buildup that came with sitting out in the open. I would have to search the cellar for a tarp.

Except for the whirling of the old Hamilton Beach blender, the diner was quiet for a Tuesday. Mac greeted me and Corinne waved from the mixer.

Mac grabbed a sausage and some rice from a pot further down and added both to a to-go carton. "You can give that to Lassie later. I'll keep it here."

A familiar curly-headed blonde sat at the end of the counter. She looked over at me and waved. "Come sit with me."

I moved down the counter and dropped down next to her. "I'm Trudy."

She held out her hand and smiled. "I know. I'm Elizabeth Lively." I waited for her to comment on the circus at Books from Hell the other day. Instead, she spun back and forth and grinned at me. "Don't you love these old swivel stools? My grandmother used to threaten me with washing all the dishes if I didn't stop spinning."

"You grew up here?" For some reason, she struck me as a city girl.

"I spent my summers in Truhart. Loved it so much I came back."

"Really?"

She raised an eyebrow at my sarcastic tone of voice. "It grows on you. Believe me. You lived here for a while, right?"

"Fourteen years ago. I hated it."

She tucked a strand of hair behind her ear. "I don't remember you. But I remember hearing about your aunt. Quite a character, people say."

Corinne placed a chocolate milkshake in front of Elizabeth. "Here you go. Your Froot Loops are coming up in a moment."

When she caught me staring, Elizabeth turned pink and shrugged. "Therapy."

Corinne filled a glass of water and brought it over to me, saying, "It's a long story, Trudy. She's a little OCD about some things like food and neatness. So she does the opposite as some wacko form of therapy."

Elizabeth took a long sip. "J. D. doesn't like junk food. So I come here to get my fix."

Mac was cleaning the griddle and called out, "She's a little crazy, but we all love her. Especially Officer Hardy." I remembered J. D. Hardy. He was the hunky deputy sheriff I met in the Family Fare parking lot.

Elizabeth twirled the milkshake with her straw. "Just ignore them. They love to talk about my little idiosyncrasies. It makes them forget their own."

"I have none," announced Corinne.

Elizabeth looked up from her straw. "Until you get near Marva. Then you two can't stop fighting."

Corinne curled her lip. "That's what best friends are for."

Mac wiped his hands and joined us. "Trudy, I bought an acorn squash that would be great with a garlic and tomato sauce over it. It's vegan. I saw it on the *Morning Show* last week. It looked great."

My mouth watered. "Mac, you could go head-to-head with any chef in California. And I'm not just saying that. Unfortunately, my budget is limited."

"No worries. You are my guinea pig. My buddy who works at the Grande Lucerne sent several customers our way last week. They were vegetarians who were looking for something off the beaten track. He says the foodies from downstate will love this place. It has everything. Quaint atmosphere. Interesting locals."

I glanced around the room with a whole new appreciation.

Mac smoothed his apron and grinned. "I've always dreamed of having a chance to do more than flip burgers on a grill and mix shakes in the old mixer."

Corinne groaned. "Just don't forget our regular clients, Mac. If you go all healthy on us, Elizabeth will have nowhere to eat."

When they left, Elizabeth turned to me. "I have a lot of friends who are vegetarians, but I don't know much about vegans. Have you always been vegan?"

I watched her sipping her milkshake and remembered how much I loved ice cream when I was younger. "You probably won't believe this. But I hated vegetables when I was little. Especially the green ones. If it was yellow like corn, or red like tomatoes, it could be covered up in a sauce. But no food coloring in the world would hide green vegetables."

Elizabeth grinned. "Every parent's nightmare."

"It drove my mother crazy. She would try to bribe me with all sorts of incentives if I would just please, please eat three bites of peas. But I would have nothing to do with them."

Elizabeth shook her head. "My little brother is still a picky eater."

"Hopefully he's not as stubborn as I was."

"So what did your parents do?"

I didn't like to remember those times, but for some reason I felt comfortable talking to Elizabeth. "If my dad was around, dinnertime turned into guerrilla warfare. He would point his finger at me and demand that I finish my vegetables. I would stare right back at him and shake my head. He was in the military, so you can imagine how angry he was that I didn't salute and follow orders. It was quite a standoff."

I took a sip of my water and remembered. My father used to turn his frustration on my mother. "What the hell kind of daughter defies her father like this?" he would ask her. "There are soldiers in the desert who haven't had fresh broccoli in months and she thinks she can waste it like trash?" Then he would place both hands on the table and lean forward until I could see the pores in his nose. "I'll tell you what will make you eat those damn vegetables. Sitting here. All night if you have to. Do you hear me?"

I hated vegetables almost as much as I hated him. I refused to eat them, even when the clock over the stove said 10:30 p.m. and I had school the next day.

Once, he got so mad that he pulled my hair until I screamed and then he shoved a piece of cold, soggy broccoli in my mouth. With a hand under my chin and another on the top of my head, he kept me from spitting it back out. I realized it was worse to keep it in my mouth where the taste made me want to puke. I had no option but to chew and swallow. I got my revenge. When my father stepped back with a smug look of triumph across his face, I gave in to the gag reflex and threw up all over the table.

I put my shaking hand in my lap. No need to tell that part of the story to Elizabeth. She was going to town on that milkshake.

"How did your aunt deal with your eating habits?"

"Aunt Gertrude wasn't much of a cook. My brother was the lucky one who got to eat at his friends' houses. Aunt Gertrude and I usually ate frozen dinners at the kitchen table."

"Poor kid. You must have hated that."

"Imagine complete silence. Her with a book under her nose, and me pretending to read."

"What changed?" Elizabeth asked.

"I ran away."

Her eyes grew wide. "Running away made you turn vegan? My brother ran away last summer and he still eats like a four-year-old."

Corinne brought Elizabeth a bowl, a cup of milk, and a small box of Froot Loops. I couldn't help looking at her stomach to see where she packed away all that food. She poured the cereal in the bowl and without looking at me she said, "I know. Don't say it. When I'm forty, this 'therapy' is going to make me fat."

"It certainly hasn't happened yet."

She patted her stomach. "Lots of swimming." She turned pink for some reason. Then added, "I'm thinking of starting a yoga group soon."

I would have loved that. But I wasn't going to stick around that long.

"Tell me, how did you end up quitting meat and dairy?" asked Elizabeth.

I lifted my shoulders. "It's no secret, I guess. I ran away from Aunt Gertrude when I was almost sixteen. I stayed with a family I knew when we were stationed overseas. They had moved back to a large farm in Texas."

The bell above the door rang. Corinne grabbed menus and water glasses and Mac started up the grill. But they kept one ear close.

"How was life on the farm?" Elizabeth asked as she tackled the Froot Loops.

"I would have been fine except for one thing."

"What was that?" Elizabeth asked with her mouth full.

"The pigs, the cows, the chickens. It was a large livestock farm. Not the kind of farm where I got to know Homer the cow and Wilbur the pig."

"Oh, no." Elizabeth looked at the hamburger patties Mac had just put on the griddle and swallowed.

Mac waved the spatula in the air. "No details, Trudy. This is still a meat-loving town."

I raised my hands. "The last thing I would do is preach to others."

"Good," he said. "I still have customers who like a rare cowboy steak."

I turned back to Elizabeth. "Anyway, you get the picture. The same stubbornness I felt about eating vegetables set in. I stopped eating meat within three weeks after my arrival. Unfortunately, my body wasn't very good at handling my new diet. I was eating no protein *and* no vegetables. My friend's family joked that *'woman could not live on potatoes alone.'* But it was no joking matter. My hair fell out. I grew weak. I was tired all the time."

Elizabeth's eyes were wide. "You poor thing."

"A cousin from California came for a visit and things changed. I had been hosing sewage and blood down the drain—" Mac slapped the spatula down and glared at me. "Oops, sorry. Let's just say I was working when I fainted in the slaughterhouse. Everyone made a fuss. The cousin made me his personal project. For the next week, all I heard, between mucking out stalls and washing sewage down the drain, was vegetable talk. Beans, legumes, and the best sources of nutrition.

"Finally, I swallowed my pride. I learned to like vegetables, with lots of spices added."

A familiar voice asked, "You never ate eggs or meat again?"

I looked behind me. Marva and Flo were seated at the booth. Doc and Vance from the garage were in the booth next to them. I had been so busy telling my story that I hadn't seen them come in.

I felt heat rising up to my cheeks. But Elizabeth put a hand on my elbow and squeezed. "Your story is fascinating. And it's good for even us meat eaters to hear."

"It's not gonna change my mind. I just ordered a hamburger," said Vance.

Elizabeth swiveled in her chair and stared at him. "But you have to admit, Trudy didn't tell us what she really saw on that farm. Don't you ever think about it?"

Doc leaned back and spread his arms across the booth. "I'm a hunter. We don't waste any part of the animal. And the deer population would get out of control if we didn't hunt each year."

"You guys are all full of macho. I run a bait-and-tackle store. We have all sorts of hunting things. But even I want to eat animals who had space to move and healthy food to eat," said Flo.

I interrupted before tempers flared. "I have nothing at all against meat eaters. Some of my favorite people are meat eaters. It's a personal choice. Like the way I dress or the car I drive."

A silence descended. Corinne came around the counter and sat on the seat next to me and swiveled until she faced me. "We don't get strangers very often, Trudy. And we forget how set in our ways we can be."

Marva spoke up. "Speak for yourself, Corinne. I see new people at the Family Fare all the time."

"Stuff it, Marva. I'm trying to apologize to Trudy here, and you're picking a fight?"

"I'm not picking a fight!"

While the two ladies argued, Elizabeth touched my knee. "What Corinne was trying to tell you is that we're sorry if the town was less than welcoming when you first came here."

Flo raised her voice over the argument. "With your odd clothes and the way you were sleeping in your car, we jumped to conclusions."

Doc shook his head. "I didn't think she was odd. Her car is amazing."

"But we never met a vegan," said Vance.

Marva leaned back and said, "And we didn't know about your dyslexia."

Flo put a finger to her lips and glared at Marva. "Shhh!"

"But Richie told us that Trudy told him. It's not a secret."

Corinne stood up with her hands on her hips. "That does it! Marva, you have the biggest mouth in—"

I started giggling. Elizabeth joined me. Mac arrived with my meal. "Don't laugh so hard. You might choke on your Froot Loops, Elizabeth."

I enjoyed Mac's latest creation and the discussion turned to whether anyone had ever tried kale and if it was true that McDonald's added kale to their milkshakes. Since I had banished Kit from the store and my life, my mood had been in the dumps. But now, I felt a new lightness.

The bell above the door rang and Jenny and her mother walked in. Jenny ran to me and gave me an unabashed hug. Her mother, Debbie, waved and ushered her and two young girls to a booth. The tiny brown-haired woman worked hard at two shifts at a hospital in Gaylord, while her husband, Corinne's son, worked for the county road commission.

"Day off school?" Mac asked.

Debbie nodded. "Teacher-planning day. I just took them to a movie in Gaylord and I promised the girls they could have dessert."

"Dessert and a movie, what a treat. What was the movie?" asked Corinne.

The girls clapped their hands. "*Pom-Pom Princess*," they said in unison.

"They just love cheerleaders. They know the high school cheers by heart and now I'll be hearing about the movie for weeks," Debbie said.

Corinne mumbled, "Too bad that Coach won't let them do just a few cheers with the team."

Elizabeth slapped down a tip. "That coach is very competitive. I know several other girls who got cut. Cherry Miller refused to try out."

Marva agreed. "Even Regina Bloodworth isn't happy with the coach. Her daughter was cut from the team when she gained too much weight to be the top of the pyramid."

I finished my meal and listened to the girls behind me talk about the movie and how much they wished they could be cheerleaders. High school was difficult enough. But not being included in any activities made it almost unbearable.

I pulled out my phone. I rarely used it and the battery was almost drained. But I had one friend who owed me a big favor for filling in for her on the lighting crew of a theater in Santa Barbara two summers ago. Sometime little girls needed fairy godmothers to come to their rescue. Or at least red-haired vegans.

Tiffany arrived, tying her apron. "I've got you covered for the rest of the night, Corinne."

I pulled out my rucksack to pay Corinne just as Tiffany reached for a teacup and a pot of hot water.

She skirted around me and greeted Kit, who leaned against the back of a booth by the doorway. "Come have a seat, my lord. Tea?"

I tensed. How the hell long had he been here?

He looked down the moment our eyes locked. "No thank you, Tiffany."

"No tea?"

Kit put his hands in his pockets as I brushed past him on my way out the door. "I should have told you the truth a while ago. I don't actually like tea," he said.

The Friday-night lights lit up the football field in Harrisburg. Everyone showed up to cheer for their team to make a play-off spot.

The second half of the game was getting ready to start and Harrison County High School was down by six points against the team from Boyne City. The smell of barbecue was strong in the cool night air.

And I was under the bleachers with a team of outcast cheerleaders.

I hadn't hidden under the bleachers since my freshman year in high school when I skipped out on my remedial English class. But this time things were different.

I couldn't wipe the grin off my face.

"These uniforms fit perfect, Miss Trudy."

"I thought they would." My girlfriend worked in the costume department of a theater in Chicago. It only took a couple of days for them to arrive in the mail. She said we had the use of the costumes until November.

The girls jumped up and down and squealed. "This is going to be so much fun!"

"*Ssshhh.* Don't let anybody hear you."

They hushed each other and giggled, making more noise than ever.

When I first told the girls about the costumes, I thought they would want to use them for Halloween. But they insisted that they wanted to be real cheerleaders and wear them at a game.

I mumbled to Corinne, who was beside me, "Are you sure we won't get in trouble?"

"The principal said as long as we stay on the fan side of the fence it's fine. I think he was thrilled that the girls were going to add a few cheers to the game. He can't stand the cheerleading coach."

"Anyway, who cares if anyone gets mad?" said Debbie, Jenny's mother. With excitement on her face she looked younger than she had when I first met her.

Actually, getting in trouble wasn't my biggest fear for them.

Jenny overheard us. "Will we get arrested?"

I put my hand on her shoulder. "Absolutely not."

"Bummer," her friend Madeline said.

"What, you *want* to get arrested?" I asked her.

"Yeah! It would be cool."

"Well, maybe the sheriff will let you go visit the jail cell sometime. But we aren't going to do that tonight."

My little squad was made up of hopefuls who failed to make the cuts during cheerleading tryouts. The girls ranged in age from thirteen to eighteen. Jenny and Madeline and Theresa were from the contained special-education classroom. Emily Bloodworth and friend Leah were told they were too heavy for the pyramids and jumps. Bibi, with her shaved head and her nose piercing, swore when she missed a jump in tryouts, ending her hopes of making the team. Stacy was in a wheelchair. And Gina simply didn't like the rest of the girls on the team, so she quit after a week. She was in charge of helping Stacy.

"*Psst*, Corinne," I said through my hand. "Are you sure their parents know about this?"

"They were so excited they offered to help. I told them to get their video cameras ready and enjoy the game."

After ponytails were readjusted and shoelaces were tied, I gathered my team together. "Are you sure you want to do this?"

"Yeah!" they yelled. And then they shushed each other.

"Umm . . ." I tried to figure out how to say what I was really afraid of. "You know, some people in the crowd might not cheer."

"We know," said Stacy.

"They might . . . even laugh."

"We know," said Madeline.

"What else is new?" said Emily.

Bibi raised her knee in a kung-fu move. "I'll kick them in the balls if they do."

"Well, you can't do that, you know." I bit my lip. In making this dream come true, I was putting the girls at risk. They could easily get mocked and belittled—or worse, incite the rage of some of these fans. Some kids, like the boys at the football game a few weeks ago, might even imitate them. Jenny, with her big eyes and sweet face, was vulnerable to all sorts of ridicule. And I wasn't sure how the crowd would react to Stacy in the wheelchair. People could be so mean.

Jenny put her arms around me and rested her head right above my heart. "Don't worry, Trudy. We're used to it."

A sharp pain stabbed my chest. I swallowed and hugged her, stealing a kiss on top of her head.

"Let's go kick some ass," said Bibi. She guided them to the path behind us that led to the front of the bleachers.

I stood in the shadows by the fence and watched the girls calmly line up in front of the infield fence by the home crowd. Their wavy outlines blurred in and out. I wiped the reflection from the bright lights out of my eyes. Those girls were braver than I had ever been.

At first no one noticed them as they stood with their hands on their hips, waiting for Stacy to give the signal. The official cheerleaders were finishing a cheer further down on the infield.

Stacy started the first line of the chant. "Hey team!"

"Hey team!"

"What's the score?"

"What's the score?"

"We don't care!"

"We don't care!"

"Let's play some more!"

They waved their arms up and down, without skill and out of sync. I stepped to the side of the bleachers where I could see the crowd's reaction. Further down, the real cheerleaders stopped and looked toward the home bleachers in confusion.

Some of the fans in the stands near me took notice. "Hey, look! There's another set of cheerleaders."

"Isn't that Jenny Scott?" someone nearby asked.

The girls repeated the same cheer. The coach shook her head and yelled at the ragtag team. But the crowd was warming up. I stepped toward the fence so I could better see the reaction of the spectators. People in the stands waved and shouted their support.

"Oh, look how cute they are!"

"You tell 'em, girls!"

One set of eyes was not on the girls, however. I felt the blue heat of Kit Darlington's eyes. I hadn't expected him to be at the game. An unreadable expression crossed over his face. Was he annoyed to see me? He was surrounded by the familiar faces I had gotten to know in the past few weeks: June, Marva, Flo. They could have each other, for all I cared.

"What should we do next, Miss Trudy?" Jenny ducked around the side of the bleachers.

I cupped my hands over my mouth and shouted the words. Jenny nodded and started the girls on the cheer. I was so proud of her confidence.

"Defense, defense, push them back. Defense, defense, sack the quarterback!"

Gina grabbed Stacy's wheelchair and spun her in a circle. Stacy waved and laughed and the crowd went wild.

The players on the field were noticing too. A few of the boys on the bench turned around, watching my squad, forgetting the game. One player stood up and raised his helmet in the air and shouted, "Go, Stacy!"

Bibi, looking very uncheerleader-like with her shaved head and nose ring, did an impromptu cartwheel. It wasn't great, but it made the crowd cheer harder at her effort.

"Show them the tinkerbell jump," I called out.

Meanwhile, the other cheerleading coach walked over to the side of the fence and scanned the area for someone who might be in charge. I backed into the shadow. She moved to the football bench and tried to pull over one of the coaches. The Boyne City team failed to make their first down and now Harrisburg had the ball. The coach put on his headset. He wasn't interested in the little problem with the cheerleaders. The real cheerleaders tried to crowd out my squad. But the girls held their ground with the help of the wheelchair.

The ragtag team waved their hands, loving the response of the fans. Now the girls were performing my favorite cheer. I had made it up.

"You! Bit off more than you could chew! Because your eyes were too big for your tummy too! But we're the Huskies and we're the best. Well, heck yes!"

They repeated it until the crowd caught on and repeated the last three words. I was so excited for them that I found myself cheering right along with the girls. I stood under the bleachers, peeking through the feet of the crowd and raised my arms up, doing all the moves.

The football went back and forth for most of the half. No one scored. With only a minute left, Harrison County High had the ball with a long way to go to the end zone. And then miraculously, the quarterback threw a long pass and it was caught. Touchdown.

The girls went nuts. They jumped up and down. Gina used Stacy's handles as a prop and jumped higher than everyone. My cheerleaders had electrified not only the crowd, but the players as well.

"Harrison County twenty-seven; Boyne City twenty-seven," said the announcer over the PA system. "The Huskies get ready to kick with thirty seconds left in the game."

I was vaguely aware of the team lining up for the kick.

Bibi led the girls in a new cheer. "Someone's gotta lose and you are it, the kick's gonna make it, so eat my sh—"

"No!" I said, running for the girls. But I was too late. Jenny yelled it the loudest.

I leaned against a tree in the public park at the end of Main Street. A large bonfire glowed from the beach. Music blasted from someone's pickup-truck speakers and the red cups and marshmallows were in abundance. Everyone celebrated the win. Including my errant group of cheerleaders. They danced together, chanting cheers that had no rhyme or reason, and having nothing to do with football but everything to do with victory.

After the field goal and the accompanying revelry, the principal had called both cheerleading teams together. I stood by their side as he and the cheer coach discussed the alternate team.

I recognized the young principal. He had been one of the loudest in the crowd cheering my rogue team on earlier. He seemed quite sympathetic to Jenny and her friends. He suggested that they hold off cheering during the first three quarters, and join the real cheerleaders on the other side of the fence for the final quarter of every game.

This did not make the coach happy. Fortunately, the girls had a very strong group of parents nearby. Corinne told the coach that if he did not allow her granddaughter to cheer, she was going to sue. It worked. The girls were even going to be given an older set of uniforms to wear.

The only caveat was that because of the last cheer, I was barred from helping the girls. It was a small price to pay.

The bonfire was more than a celebration of the football win. It was a victory for the girls. I should be celebrating with them. I wanted to dance too. But I tapped my foot against the tree root instead.

"Why aren't you out there with them?"

I didn't have to turn around to know the owner of the voice.

"They don't need me, Professor."

I kept my eyes on the girls who were chanting. "Go! Win! Fight!"

"How did you do it?"

"I didn't do anything. They wanted to cheer. They made it happen."

"With a little help," he said, moving closer until he stood next to me. I peeked at him out of the corner of my eye. In the glow of the fire I could see his suede jacket, russet sweater, and dark jeans that were cut perfectly in a European fit. On his feet were sleek boots that reflected the sparks from the bonfire.

I, on the other hand, wore a loose-fitting long skirt, a flowered blouse, and a baggy sweater that I had bought at a Salvation Army store. My hair was coming out of the loose ponytail I had tied it in before leaving the house. Together we could have been a cartoon for sleek and slouchy.

"And how did they get the uniforms?"

"Grease."

"Excuse me?"

"The play. *Grease.* A friend owed me a favor. They come from a theater she worked in."

"First the haunted house and now this. For someone who doesn't like to stay in one place, you certainly make an impression on the places you visit."

"You do too."

He chuckled.

"If you are looking for your lost book, I burned it." I pointed to the fire.

"I know you don't like me right now. But I think you are great, Trudy Brown." I ignored the way the warmth of his words spread through me.

"Not great enough to tell the truth to, though."

He glanced down at his feet. "I was wrong. I wasn't as brave as you."

"You were brave when you let me seduce you."

"No. I wasn't thinking about anything but myself then. Now I wish I had. I would never want to hurt you."

"You could have shown it in a better way than turning my dog against me."

"Your dog? Are you going to claim him now?"

"My temporary dog, I mean."

"Look. I didn't mean it to happen."

I held up my hand and stared at the fire. "It's all right, I'm over it."

"You are?" He sounded wary now. Typical man. Afraid he was off my radar.

"I've moved on."

"Really."

"Yes. See that guy over there by the pickup truck?"

"The one with his mouth open under the keg?"

"Not him. His friend. The cute one with the beard."

Kit grunted. "What about him?"

"He's my latest and greatest."

"No, he's not."

"Of course he is."

"That's Edge."

"Yeah." I had no idea who Edge was. But he was handsome and very nice whenever I saw him at the diner.

"You're not going out with Edge."

"How do you know?"

"Because he's dating a skier who just made the Olympic team. It's all his aunt talks about."

"Blah, blah, blah." He was such a know-it-all.

"So, what happened after that saucy cheer at the end of the game?"

I smiled at the memory. "I'm barred from all practices in the future."

"You? What did you do?"

"I had them do the last cheer."

"No, you didn't."

I put my hand on my hip. "What makes you say that?"

"The way you ran out to stop them."

I watched a spark fly into the sky, following it until it faded. "Whatever. I could care less about football."

The music was louder now. Several people danced in the open sandy area. I swayed to the music, wishing I could join them. Kit put his hands in his pockets and watched me. But I refused to meet his gaze. I watched the dancers instead.

"Ah, the pagan American ritual of celebrating a football victory. Kegs, bonfires, and music," he said after a while.

"They do the same thing in England. You are deliberately trying to make it look like only Americans celebrate like asses."

One of my favorite songs from the Cure came on the radio. It always made me happy!

Kit held his hands out. "Come on. I know you want to dance."

"What? Are you going to deign to join an American ritual?"

He took a deep breath and started to move awkwardly. "It seems that this large island is starting to influence me."

I laughed at the way his body jerked around. "You stink. If I'd known you danced so badly I never would have had sex with you."

"What does my dancing have to do with my performance in bed?"

"It's my little theory. Good dancers are good in bed. Bad dancers are not."

"Codswallop."

"Whatever. And now that I think of it, you *were* awful in bed."

"How was I *out* of bed? We made love off the bed several times." His voice was low. It made my neck tingle.

He was moving around me now. The music was loud and I tried to tell myself the beat was making me swing my hips; not Kit, not my own legs. We were still in the shadows, under the trees, where no one else could see us. I watched his spastic movement and could no longer stand still. I twirled and waved my arms, letting the rhythm inhabit me. I could feel the heat of the fire and another kind of fire where Kit moved beside me.

We were in sync. Back and forth in the same beat.

I couldn't see his face, and maybe he was staring at me as if I had come from crazyville. But I didn't care. I had been standing against the damn tree for way too long wanting to do exactly this. I moved my arms in circles like a pinwheel and turned until I was dizzy and laughing. Kit caught me before I fell. I clutched his shoulders and lifted my head. Before we knew it, we were back where we left off. He pulled me deeper into the shadows and captured my mouth, his hands on either side of my head, drifting lower to pull me against him.

We were part of the music and the beat and I couldn't think anymore. It didn't matter if I was letting myself be vulnerable or losing any sense of self-respect that I never had anyway. I surrendered to the feeling that was part of the moment—part of the now, which made me happy. My own pagan ritual.

Faint laughter came from the beach. Another song started. I couldn't find the beat this time. I stepped away, faking the ability to control the shots. "You knew how to dance after all."

My voice was calm, but I was mad at myself. Mad at the way I let him pull me into his arms.

"No, I didn't. I was just better when I danced with you, Trudy Brown." He gasped as if he was winded, his breath coming out in clouds.

"Too late. I dance better by myself."

Kit opened his mouth to say something. He looked at me like a dragon getting ready to shoot flames. Then he clamped his lips shut. He stepped away and moved toward the fire, leaving me in the cool shadows.

Chapter 14

The dumpster arrived Monday morning. The unfriendly man who delivered it hauled the container to the back alley without a word. When I signed the paperwork, he looked around the store and said, "You doing this yourself?"

The place was tidy. But there was just so much. Hundreds and hundreds of books lining aisles of shelves. I tried not to sound over-whelmed. "Yes."

"Good luck, lady! You need a forklift."

I figured out what he meant in less than three hours.

Magazines by the front door went in the trash first. I made so many trips back and forth that my boots left a dirty path. Even after a good cleaning the treads underneath the dust would probably show permanent wear by the end of the week.

My height should have been an advantage as I lifted and dumped everything over the seven-foot wall of the dumpster. But in no time, my shoulders ached from the exertion of an unused set of muscles. Still, I was making some progress.

By mid-afternoon, I no longer heard the metal clanging of the books hitting the bottom of the dumpster. They landed with a dull *thud*, on top of other pages. I peeked over the side, thinking I would see the refuse rising to the top, but was discouraged by the sight of just a shallow layer of paperbacks, coffee-table books, and boxes.

Arguing came from the open back door of the house of horrors. Curious, I poked my head inside. At least a dozen people were putting the last-minute touches on the haunted house. Marva and Flo, together in the corner, adjusted a corpse that was sitting up in a coffin. The arm fell out at an odd angle and Marva attempted to stuff it back in.

Flo stepped back. "That doesn't look natural."

"It looks just fine. How would you know what a corpse looks like when it sits up anyway?" Marva asked.

"My husband was ninety-five when he died. Believe me, all he did was sit up for the last five years of his life."

Marva looked over Flo's shoulder. She nodded my way and Flo turned. She lost her smile and clamped her lips together. Marva joined her in a frown and crossed her arms in front of her wide girth, making her breasts bunch up in strange clumps.

"What did I do now?" I asked.

Flo maintained her icy stare, but Marva had no trouble telling me. "We saw the dumpster. You're selling out."

"I told you I was going to sell right from the very first day I came to town. That's not a surprise."

Several other women dropped what they were doing and came to stand with Marva and Flo. Marva took that as a sign that she was in charge and widened her stance. "We thought you were going to take more time. Sell more books. That sort of thing. But you are caving in to that Reeba Sweeney faster than we can raise money. This town is going to be ruined if that pawnshop guy buys the store."

"And the next thing you know we'll have tattoo parlors and all the undesirables who sell witchcraft and drugs and violence that corrupt our kids."

"Who do I look like, George Bailey? The town problems are not my fault." I didn't want to point out that an attraction filled with dead bodies, serial killers, and monsters might also corrupt a few young people.

"And the books, Trudy. What about the books?" Flo added. Her eyes were filled with tears.

Flo's words surprised me. "You took boxes of books already, Flo. And I donated quite a few to the church and the hospital. There are barely any kids' books left. You all had a chance to take your share. Why are you angry about a bunch of books no one wants?"

June stepped forward. "What about the environment? I thought you were all about being green and helping save animals."

"Animals, yes. Books, no." I ran a hand up the back of my neck. They were being unfair. "Being vegan doesn't make me responsible for saving the world. Besides, Flo has a bait shop that sells hunting equipment."

Flo leaned against the corpse. "That's a non sequitur. Fishing and hunting is a controlled industry. We don't do anything that would hurt our land."

"Non-seq—? Whatever! I'm not hurting the land. The guy I ordered the dumpster from promised to send this straight to the paper recycling."

"He's probably going to dump it in the nearest landfill."

After meeting the driver, I wouldn't be surprised.

I didn't want to think about landfills and pawnshops and casinos. I didn't want to feel guilty. For the first time since I had arrived in Truhart, I was finally taking action. I had been wasting time. Thanks to Dr. Darlington and his secret agenda, I had moved and sorted books for weeks. And for what? Time was my price. The rainy season was almost over in Angkor Wat. I needed to get my plane tickets. Put Lulu in storage. And find a home for Moby. Then I could . . . could be happy. Right? I moved to the corpse and adjusted his arms.

Thinking about Moby made me feel like I had been punched in the gut.

I had asked several families who came into the store if they were interested in a free dog. But one look at his graying face and his slow walk and they said *no, thank you*. Nobody wanted an old dog. A cute puppy, maybe. But an old dog was too much work.

I changed the subject. "The house of horrors looks awesome. Are you ready for the opening Saturday?"

"The ghost June made fell apart and the cobwebs are drooping. Everyone is panicking." Marva adjusted her pink glasses. "Care to help us? Or are you too busy turning over the store to a slumlord?"

I bit my tongue and joined the final preparations, thinking about the trash pile with a halfhearted longing. I could be throwing books out. But after being targeted as a wrecking ball for the town, it seemed more important to help with the final pieces of Truhart's house of horrors.

I showed June how to make a cheesecloth ghost and pumpkins out of glue and flour. The whole process was rather messy, but oddly therapeutic. The most enthusiastic participant came by to help. Elizabeth Lively rolled up her sleeves, enjoying the process way more than the average person. She wanted to make a large ghost for the center of the room. Her attempts to lay the cheesecloth on the ghost arms without letting it stick to her skin made everyone giggle. There was more glue and glop on her than on the ghost. That seemed to make her particularly happy. When J. D. Hardy stopped by and laughed at her, she smeared glue all over his cheek.

His eyes swept the room in amazement. "This is incredible. I didn't know you all had such talent."

"Well, we had help." Several of the women, who had looked at me so accusingly earlier, pointed my way. Marva nodded and Flo actually smiled.

I turned my focus to pulling glue out from in between my fingers. And I wondered why I cared what they thought of me.

If I hadn't been worried about cleaning out Books from Hell, boosting my bank account, or getting Kit Darlington out of my mind, I might have had a good night's sleep. The last straw was Moby's barking. He woke me up in the wee hours of the morning.

I turned over and looked at the clock. 6:30. It was still dark outside. Where had the late nights and even later mornings from my previous life gone?

I rolled out of bed and pulled on an old pair of sweatpants and my tapestry coat and made my way downstairs. Moby sat at the back door whining and scratching to be let out. I opened the door and he let out a deep woof and ran into the alley.

"Oomph!" A muffled grunt came from outside.

The horizon was beginning to glow in a deep red color that probably meant something, if I understood the weather. Outlined in the glow was the ridiculous-looking form of a man trying to scale the dumpster like Spiderman.

"What are you doing here?" I asked.

Kit looked over his shoulder and swung a leg up and over the top of the ledge. "What does it look like I'm doing?"

"Dumpster diving."

"Is that what you Americans call it?"

"Yes. And whether it is in British or American, it's illegal when you are on my property."

"Well, here's the thing: I double-checked and the fact is, this is public property."

"No it's not. You're bluffing." I moved to stand at his feet. "I'm calling the mayor to find out."

"I hope he doesn't mind your bothering him this early in the morning after the football game on the telly last night."

"Football's on television on Monday nights."

"It's America. Football's bloody on every night this time of year."

"Fine, I'll call the sheriff's department. Someone is likely to be working."

Kit turned on his flashlight and illuminated a wide smile across his face. "Suit yourself. But chances are some deputy is asleep in his car and won't appreciate the early-morning call. Or worse, it could be J. D. Hardy. Rumor is he sent a man down a counter like a bowling ball just for bothering him a few months ago."

"That's not the real story, and you know it."

He clicked his tongue. "Feel free to test his temper. Call."

I hugged my arms across myself. The wind was calm, but a bitter chill was in the air. Sunrise would likely show frost on the field behind Kit.

He threw each leg over the edge of the dumpster, sitting on the top and assessing the next step. Then he jumped. I heard a loud bump and another curse under his breath.

"Sorry about the dog poop," I yelled. "It really is the most convenient place to put it."

"Trudy! You aren't serious, are you?"

I wasn't. But I wasn't about to tell him that. "Guess you'll find out."

I looked at the horizon. The last thing I wanted to do was to call George Bloodworth or anyone else right now. If Kit wanted to sit out here sorting through dusty old books in the freezing cold, he could be my guest.

Moby whined at my feet, portraying a Lassie-like loyalty to Kit. That dog acted as if the professor was in the same predicament as Timmy down the well.

There was always one way to get Moby's attention. I returned to the back door and grabbed a fruit leather. "Come on, boy. Let's leave the professor drowning in doggy doo-doo and take ourselves off for a *walk*."

That usually pepped Moby up. But I was ten yards down the alley before I realized I heard no familiar panting and scurry of the old collie. I looked back. Moby stood where I left him. I waited. Then I retraced my steps.

Moby wagged his tail and I narrowed my eyes at him. "See how you feel when I don't share my quinoa with you this afternoon."

"Quinoa, huh?" Kit said from inside the dumpster. He popped his head up over the top. "What kind of kibble is that for a dog like you? I'll get you a big, fat steak, boy. With lots of red meat and *blood* oozing out of it."

He said the last few words loudly on purpose. He knew that would bother me this early in the morning. I was just about to say something when he disappeared and I heard a loud bang. "Bloody hell."

"What happened? Are you all right?"

"Bugger. I lost my footing."

"Be careful in there, Professor. You don't strike me as someone who is particularly fr—frugal. I don't think the city has insurance for dumpster diving."

He popped his head up over the top of the dumpster again. "Frugal?"

"Fragile—I mean . . . You know what I mean."

He played with the words. "Fragile-fragile . . . agile?"

"*Agile.* That's what I said."

"I thought that's what you said, love." He grinned down at me and with his hair in disarray he looked surprisingly young. The light was getting stronger and I could see his breath vaporizing like smoke.

"I know that may come as a bit of a surprise to you, Trudy. But I am quite agile. I grew up in a very old building and I would climb all sorts of walls and turrets."

I blocked out all the reasons why I shouldn't be standing outside in the dawn of day. He didn't talk much about himself much. I was interested. "A castle?"

"I wouldn't call it that, exactly."

"How old was it?"

"Sixteenth century." He disappeared and I saw a faint glow that must be his flashlight. Then I heard the dull *thunk* of books being tossed about. The dumpster served as a kind of amplifier. Kit didn't have to shout at all. I heard everything inside as if it were a soundstage.

"Was there a moat?"

"It dried up over the years."

I sat on a small well tucked into the molding of the dumpster and crossed my legs. "So, how is it that a young man who grew up in a castle could be so interested in things in the colonies?"

"You already know that story from your research." I heard rustling as he dug deeper into the container.

"I know some of it from a teenager's smartphone. And some from you. You were sick of all the old stuff. The scary ghosts. *Macbeth*. Things like that. You love baseball. And football. You love four-wheel drives. And a good cup of coffee."

"What else do you need to know about me? That pretty well sums it up."

"I know you're obsessed with Robin Hartchick. But tell me the rest. Tell me your real story."

"What on earth do you mean?"

"*Why* are you so into Robin Hartchick and finding that manuscript?"

Silence fell, and I waited.

"Did you ever have that moment when you discovered something you loved so much you knew it was your destiny?"

I thought about the travel brochure on Lulu's visor. "Yes."

"That was me the first time I read *Spring Solstice*." Kit was close. I pictured him leaning against the Dumpster wall behind me. "By the time I turned the last page, I felt like Robin Hartchick was speaking directly to me. He wrote about the young man who didn't belong. How he journeyed across the Upper Peninsula of Michigan to find his way in a barren forest near a rocky shore. He wrote in a voice that felt like mine."

"But it wasn't enough to read the story and put it back on your shelf?"

"No. I wanted to understand the character. I wanted to live the *movement* Hartchick created in literature. I wanted to . . . I almost wanted to be . . ."

"American?" I offered.

"Yes, I suppose so. But it was more like I wanted to be Robin Hartchick. And by association, I didn't want to be . . ."

"You didn't want to be Christopher Darlington."

"It wasn't a conscious thought."

"It's a very sad way to feel." I knew that feeling very well, in fact.

"I still cherish my own heritage."

"I'm thinking that didn't go over well in the castle."

He chuckled. "My father. A most esteemed and knighted scholar. Did your research reveal that he had been knighted?"

"Yes. So, you *did* meet the queen."

"She's lovely, really. I liked her hat that day. Anyway, like I was saying, good old Dad was a famous scholar of English literature. He was horrified by my taste. American literature was a shallow imitation of what he believed in. He was good at covering that up with his colleagues, mind you. But he wanted me to appreciate his world. Sometimes I didn't think he could accept anything that wasn't four-hundred years old. But everything changed."

"How so?"

"The family home has always been impossible to keep up. It costs a fortune to maintain. My mother grew increasingly panicked over our funds. Last year, for a new source of income, she insisted we open for tours. It just about killed my dad. Imagine a bunch of tourists wandering around his beloved home in Bermuda shorts and sneakers. He projected all his anger on me. When I publicly stated I believed there was a lost manuscript, he stood up in front of the Association of Comparative Literature and called me delusional."

I had learned about that when Richie read the article to me at the garage. "That must have been awful."

"It wasn't my best moment. We were sitting in our formal wear, drinking champagne at the same table."

I closed my eyes and pictured Kit. Perpetually upbeat. Stiff upper lip. Always wearing a charming smile. I imagined him trying not to show how upset he was in front of a crowd of his peers.

Strange. Right now, with a metal wall between us, I felt closer to him than I ever had.

"What happens if you don't find the manuscript?"

"I keep looking."

"Aren't you afraid it doesn't exist?"

I heard him sigh from the other side of the cold metal. "At least I'm going after something I want."

"Even if it's all an illusion?"

"Many dreams are illusory, don't you think?"

"I don't know. I'm not the one standing in the trash looking for a Robin Hartchick manuscript."

"No, you're the one trading it all away for a trip."

We were back to the real problem now. "All you really cared about this whole time you were with me was the manuscript. Isn't that right?"

"I could ask a similar question. All you cared about was selling the store to get to Angkor Wat, right?"

"I didn't lie, though."

Kit started moving behind me. I heard a clanking and a rattling above me. I looked up to see his head popping back up. "For the record, Trudy, I tried at least a half-dozen times to tell you why I was really here. But you were too busy with your practical jokes and your free-spirited fun to hear it."

I jumped off my cold perch. "You know what? Be my guest. You can sit there with your old books and search for the dead guy's manuscript. Just watch out for the ghosts that are going to haunt you for all your lies."

"The only one haunting me is you. And do you want to know the answer to your question?"

I moved to the back door. "No."

He called after me. "The answer is *no*. The manuscript wasn't the only thing I cared about. I wasn't thinking about the manuscript at all when we were together. I happen to like being with you, Trudy Brown. I like the way you smell, the way your hair looks when you don't brush it. I like the sleepy way you look at me in the morning." He fell off a book and a clattering sound erupted along with a string of foul words.

I returned to bed, but not to sleep. I wanted to blame my insomnia on the clamor coming from the dumpster. But I knew that wasn't the problem.

It was getting harder to be mad at Kit. And very easy to let the lovely words he spoke from inside a trash container warm my heart.

Chapter 15

By noon the next day, the front half of the store was actually beginning to look like something other than a book-hoarder's lair. I took a break and sat on a pile of old magazines, eating a stale protein bar, and measured my progress. I could hold out my arms and twirl in a full circle without tripping or falling over books and boxes. I could see the gray walls and the dusty pine floorboards. With new paint, window cleaning, and TLC, the store might be quite appealing to an interested entrepreneur.

Kit was nowhere to be seen. With no one to make fun of, things were way too quiet. Moby sat by the back door, exhausted from our work this morning. He had followed me out the door each time I schlepped my crumpled box of books to the garbage. Several times he raised his head and pricked his ears, thinking he heard something. I knew he was listening for a familiar voice. But the alley was quiet. We were both a little disappointed.

My measly lunch was hardly satisfying. Whatever Mac served was probably amazing compared to old fruit leather and rice crackers. The sound of a car door slamming and then the *blip* of the door being locked made me look up. I felt an unsettling gnawing in my stomach that had nothing to do with my hunger when I saw the gold Lexus parked in front.

A sharp knock rattled the front door. I pictured Reeba Sweeney on the other side and weighed the merits of ignoring her. But Moby was already barking and I saw her peering through the front window at me.

I opened the door and pasted a smile on my face. "Hello, Reeba."

She stood on Christian Louboutin heels that barely brought her up to five feet, clutching her large Tory Burch purse, and trying to see over my shoulder into the store.

"I was driving by and thought I would check on you."

I stepped back. "As you can see, I'm making progress. I've got a dumpster out back now. This place is going to look great."

"Hmm." Reeba clicked past me and walked around the clear space I had created.

I followed her. "It cleans up really nice, doesn't it?"

"I don't see any cracks in the walls or major damage to the floor. But it's going to need work once you get it cleared. At the very least, you might need to re-sand the floors and paint the walls."

I couldn't imagine how much it would cost me to rent a sander. I brushed the tip of my boot across the wood. "I don't know. People pay top dollar for this worn, lived-in look these days. Some people even purposely buy salvaged wood to make floors look old."

She sent me a pitying half smile. "This isn't a decorator house, Trudy. Businesses want to know their investment is sound. They want quality. Not old and used."

I bit my lip. "I'll see what I need when I get to that point."

Reeba fished into her large purse and took out a folded piece of paper. "I have an alternative way to handle your sale. This is a solid offer from Logan Fribley. It's cash. As is. It's exactly what you need. You can accept it and be on your way with minimal fuss."

My mouth turned dry as I stared at the paper clutched in her fat fingers.

She waved it up and down. "It won't hurt to at least look at his offer."

I took it from her and unfolded it. As I stared at the number on the page, she explained, "Logan doesn't want a negotiating war. He is offering a flat price on the bookstore. I have to say, it is quite generous. It's actually much more than he is offering for the old grocery next door."

My head shot up. "He's buying next door too?"

She laughed and adjusted her frizzy halo of dark hair. "Honey, he's buying the whole block."

"But what about the community center? And the Santa's workshop?"

"What about it? I told you last time I was here. That committee's been talking about that for as long as I can remember. They don't have two pennies to rub together."

She must have read the doubt on my face. She stopped herself and changed tactics. "You are new here, Trudy. You don't have a history with the people of this town like I do."

Actually, I did. I should be grabbing the offer and running with it, based on my experience fourteen years ago. But I had a new bond with Truhart now. I didn't want them to lose their hopes for a community center. It was a good cause.

Reeba put a hand on my arm. Seeing her jangly bracelet and chunky rings sent an unexpected shot of ice up my shoulder. "I shouldn't be telling you this. It's not something that people like to talk about. And everyone knows I'm not a gossip. But some of the people next door . . . well, I don't think I can mention their names. Let's just say you may have been sitting with them at the football game a few weeks ago? They *may* not be the upstanding people you think they are." She raised her hands in quotation marks when she said the word *upstanding*.

I stepped back so she wouldn't touch me again. "That's not something I need to know."

"Maybe it is. Flo Jarvis's husband was one of the richest men in the county. But he *might* have cheated on his taxes. I'm not saying anything one way or the other, of course. But Flo *might* have inherited more than a bait shop if she hadn't been forced to pay all the back taxes he owed when he died. Some people might think she knew all about the tax scam when it was happening."

Reeba came closer. I took another step backward. Moby appeared at my side, leaning against my knee. Reeba checked herself when she saw the big dog. "Now, I'm not saying, but June Krueger and her husband *might* have lost their house last year." Her voice was high and lilting, as if she were telling a sick fairy tale. "They *might* have defaulted on their mortgage. All I can say is that they rent a house I own now. And I can't tell you, but they *might* have been late on the r—"

I put my hand up. "I don't need to know that kind of thing, Reeba."

"I'm not saying anything, just so you understand. People in this town *might* not be in a position to raise money for a ridiculous community center when they might not be able to pay the mortgage on their own houses. Maybe you should think twice before relying on them for help in selling this store."

Before I knew what I was doing, I raised the paper with the offer from Logan Fribley in front of her face. I tore it straight down the middle.

"I've decided to list with a different Realtor, Reeba. Tell Logan Fribley that he can send his next offer to me directly if he decides to increase his price."

"What?"

"Anyone who would talk about someone's personal finances with a stranger is not the kind of person I want to deal with." I realized I was shaking.

Reeba glared at me. "I am shocked and saddened by your disrespect. After all I have done for you, Trudy Brown."

"Done for me?"

"I went out of my way to get the keys to you that first morning you arrived." Reeba stamped her foot and raised her voice to a shriek that would have been perfect in the house next door. "I've been working hard trying to find buyers for this wrecked-out building. You wanted to sell as quickly as possible and I even convinced Logan to offer cash."

I took a step toward her. "Is it possible the lawyers who administered Aunt Gertrude's estate *might* have paid you for keeping this place up? Which you *might* not have done so well? *Might* you have realized that at the last minute and changed the locks before I got here to make it look like you did something?" I threw her passive-aggressive language back in her face. "How much money *might* you be making on an easy sale? Is it possible this building *might* not even officially be listed yet? If not, why are you trying to get me to accept a lowball offer? I'm not saying anything, mind you, but I can't help but feel that you *might* not be representing my best interests."

She curled her lip and raised her voice. "I have never been so disrespected."

"You said that already."

"You're making a big mistake to think you can talk to me that way." Her face was red and her jowls jiggled as she spoke.

I moved to the door and held it open for her. "Probably. I *might* have a conscience that lets me sleep better at night than yours. Now, go on. Moby *might* bite you."

She swept out the door and ran into one of the fake spiderwebs I'd woven in the doorway. It tangled up in her hair and she waved her arms around herself, frantic to get rid of the fake spiders. The words *crazy* and *stupid* were just a few words that came from her mouth.

She drove off in her Lexus, trailing a mass of webbing and spiders in her wake. The only thing missing was a broomstick out the tailpipe.

I should have guessed that my temper would come back and bite me in the butt. It wasn't more than an hour or two later that I received another important visitor.

"Trudy," Mayor Bloodworth said before I even opened the door. I had barely seen him and his brown suit since that first morning I arrived in town.

"Mayor, what an honor," I said. "Please come in."

He stepped inside and surveyed the store. Moby rose from his new favorite spot, where the last of the *National Geographic*s waited for me to sort. I was taking my time in hopes that I might find pictures of Angkor Wat.

Sheriff Howe followed the mayor, looking for all the world like he would rather be issuing a traffic ticket than standing with the town leader.

The mayor put his hands behind his back, rocking back and forth. He opened and closed his mouth several times. Then he turned his back to the front window and said, "It has just come to our attention that the dumpster you are using is parked illegally on public property."

I peeked over the mayor's shoulder and noticed the shrewd little woman sitting in the front seat of the Lexus parked on the curb. She stared straight back at me with a triumphant expression on her face, her vengeance cold in her beady eyes.

"I didn't realize there was anything illegal about parking it behind my store."

"The thing is," said the sheriff miserably, "you need a permit for a dumpster."

"I had no idea. The rental agency never said a word to me about it."

"We have to issue a ticket to you for every day you keep it on public property."

"What part of this block isn't public property? Can I use that?"

"Where we're standing. Sorry, there just isn't any piece of property that you own that would be big enough for a container of that size."

"I'll get rid of it soon. By the end of the week?"

The sheriff tweaked his mustache and looked grim. "I'm sorry. It's still something you need a permit for."

"How much will a ticket cost versus a permit?"

He named a figure. The permit was cheaper, but still not something I had much room for in my bank account. I had wiped almost all of my cash out with the rental.

"How much time do I have to pay the ticket?"

The mayor sighed and looked behind him. I didn't like him that morning I first met him. But now I wasn't so sure he was all bad. He looked as unhappy as the sheriff. As if he was stuck between a boulder and a place harder than that. Or in this case, between the bookshop and the lady in the car behind him.

He leaned forward and spoke in a low tone. "I know you want to sell for as much as you can get. And I'm not telling you what to do, mind you." He cast a sideways look toward the sheriff who took his cue and suddenly found himself interested in the women's-romance section of the bookstore.

"I know Reeba Sweeney wants you to sell to Logan Fribley," the mayor said.

"Then you know the price he offered wouldn't buy a shack in most towns."

"I know that too." He pressed his lips together as if he were afraid to say more.

"So, do you think I should sell?"

He looked over my shoulder at the car behind me. "I don't want a pawnshop. It's not good for the town. But I don't want another vacant building either."

I held my palms up. "I don't know what to do. I need the money. But not the way Reeba was pushing me."

"I admire you for holding out. I really do. But let me make one thing clear: Reeba Sweeney is going to make your life worse if you don't give in. She owns half the county. Most of Truhart is indebted to her for one reason or another."

"Including you?"

He looked down at his feet. "I'm not in debt in the traditional sense. But she helped me in my last campaign. If I alienate her she'll find someone to run against me in the next election. That's how she got rid of the last mayor."

I raised my finger toward his chest. He nodded. "Yep. She asked me to run against him."

I couldn't believe he had just admitted that.

Sheriff Howe cleared his throat. "You have a lot more support now than you think, George."

"Spoken like a man who is getting ready to retire to Arizona, Liam," said Mayor Bloodworth.

The two men stared at each other and the sound of someone pounding on the wall next door broke the exchange.

"Sorry, Trudy. My hands are tied."

Sheriff Howe stood up straighter, as if he'd made up his mind about something. "Last I heard, I was still the sheriff in this town. I am in the habit of giving warnings to people before issuing tickets. That isn't going to change today."

Thank God there was one person with a backbone in town.

Sheriff Howe scribbled an official warning and handed it to me. He put a finger to his hat. With a small salute, he said, "You have until tomorrow afternoon to get a permit, Miss Brown. The county offices are open from nine o'clock to four-thirty. Have a good day."

He walked out of the store and passed Reeba Sweeney's car without giving her a second glance. He slammed his car door, revved the engine, and put some weight on the accelerator. His driving said everything about his state of mind.

George Bloodworth adjusted his tie until it squeezed his neck. "Some people can afford to take the high road. I can't."

"Hey," I said. "At least you admitted the truth. Thank you for that."

When he left, I closed my eyes and wished myself thousands of miles away. More than anything I wanted to be on my way to Southeast Asia. Alone. Far from this nutty town and the people who made everything I ever wanted seem so complicated.

When the mayor left, I tried to figure out how much money I had in my checking account. The numbers swam in front of me, making my eyes water and my head throb. Maybe Doc would give me a deal on labor for Lulu's engine. I patted the checkbook in my pocket and walked toward Doc's.

In the garage's parking lot, I stopped by Lulu and ran my hand along her cold steel. Doc opened a side door and waved me inside. His brows drew together as he spoke. "Your new cylinder and valve came in, Trudy."

"Perfect timing, Doc. That's what I wanted to talk to you about."

Doc put his hands in his pockets and rocked. "It arrived this morning with a COD receipt."

"COD?"

"Your check bounced."

I lowered my chin and let it sink in. I knew my bank account was low. But I hadn't realized it was this bad. "Look, Doc, I'm really sorry. I'll get another check to you as soon as possible."

"Now is a good time."

"I can't do that."

He looked away from me. "Trudy, I want to let you do your own labor—but it goes against my policy. I can't break the rules. Even for Lulu."

"I'm a little short right now. I rented a dumpster and now I need to buy a permit and—I know you don't need to hear all this. But just understand, as soon as I sell the store, I'll have enough to repay you."

He rubbed the back of his neck. "In the meantime, I'm sitting here a few hundred dollars in the hole with a cylinder and valve I don't need."

"Give me time. Please."

"What am I going to do if I don't get the money, Trudy? I've got bills to pay just like everyone else."

I thought about what Reeba Sweeney said earlier. Was Doc one of the people who was in debt to her? It made me sad to think he could be behind on his bills and struggling to keep the viper away. And here I was, making things worse.

Vance slid from underneath a nearby Malibu. His smudged face didn't hide his feelings. "We don't do no free work, even for you. Maybe you could get a job cooking a vegan meal at the diner."

"Now Vance, don't go into that stuff about the diner again." Doc held up his hand.

Vance stood up, ignoring Doc. "I tried to order my Wednesday-night meat loaf and Mac told me he had replaced it on the menu. Something with eggplant and olives." He made a face. "And two couples wearing loafers with no socks and skinny jeans was sitting in my booth."

Doc threw him a towel to rub his hands. "You were alone, Vance. You know Corinne has a rule about that booth and more than two people."

"Since when did anyone pay attention to that?" Vance wiped his hands and glared at me.

"He's in a bad mood. Ignore him." Doc walked to the side door.

"Wait." The desperation in my voice was pitiful. "Can I at least still leave Lulu here?"

"She can stay where she is. But the snow and ice start soon. The Michigan weather is going to make her rust."

"I'll put a tarp over her. I'll find the money and then we can make a deal. Maybe you need some help around the garage? I've got a lot of experience."

His long face told me the answer before he opened his mouth. "I have no doubt that you could do the work, Trudy. You seem to know almost as much about fixing cars as Vance or me, here. But I don't have enough business to hire another grease monkey."

"What about light work? If Richie is busy with football, I could sweep the back room. Do any type of extra work you need."

Doc scratched his head. "I can't give you a job, Trudy. But if worse comes to worse, I might be able to help you sell Lulu."

Sell? Lulu had been Leo's. He named her. He planned on fixing her up when he returned from Afghanistan. She was all I had left of my brother.

"I can't sell Lulu."

Vance slid back under the Malibu and I heard him muttering, "—sacrifice her to rust."

Doc put a hand on my shoulder. "I know things aren't easy with the mess your aunt left, and the pressure you're getting to sell to Fribley. You have a lot on your plate right now, Trudy. But we like you. You've been a big help to the Triple C's and then Jenny and the cheerleaders. I hope you know, we're all rooting for you."

"Thank you." My voice cracked. When I left the garage I felt Doc's sympathetic eyes following me. He could have refused delivery for Lulu's parts. I knew that very well. But he hadn't. It had put him in a bad position. And it wasn't fair to lay my sob story at his feet.

I walked back to Books from Hell and I did a double take when I passed a Jaguar F-Type parked in front of Cookee's. It would have stuck out like an Armani suit at a thrift store. But a BMW 4 Series and a Cadillac CTS were parked nearby too. I was surprised to see so many people I didn't recognize sitting in the booths by the windows. I knew without asking that they weren't from Truhart. Vance's complaints came to mind. But maybe big tippers would be good for Cookee's. At least that's what I told myself.

Back at the bookshop I found an old blue tarp in the cellar. I carried it back to Doc's and covered Lulu with it. Just to show there were no hard feelings, Vance came out and quietly helped me secure it tightly. When I left Lulu, I silently promised her that I would be back to fix her. Even so, I felt like I'd just buried an old friend.

Shoving my hands in my pockets, I walked down to Echo Lake. I stood on the shore and wanted to scream across the gray waves. But my throat was too tight. And I wasn't fourteen anymore. A spring inside me felt like it was coming undone. All the mechanics that had made me tick for so long were snapping piece by piece. The old anger was replaced with something much more difficult to grasp.

Chapter 16

Bump. The noise came from outside. *Thud.* Another party down on the beach?

Rolling over, I reached for my sleep mask. But I had forgotten to put it on. The sound seemed distant. As if it came from the back of the store.

A wet nose nudged my hand and moved to my face. Moby. I looked around the shadowy bedroom trying to remember where I was. Who I was. I had been dreaming. But it escaped me now.

I wrapped my dharma quilt around me and went downstairs to investigate.

A faint glow flashed through the back window. A light radiated from the top of the dumpster. *Plunk.*

I opened the door and stepped outside. "Seriously? You couldn't wait until daylight to start your trash-picking?"

The outline of a bright head I knew way too well appeared over the top. "Unfortunately, I'm dealing with a limited schedule. And you have not been playing fair."

Moby tried to get past me, but I pushed him back inside. He was an uncertain ally and I didn't want him sucking up to Kit for more attention.

I leaped across the cold cement to the dumpster. "What are you talking about?"

"These books and papers are multiplying like rabbits. There's a book festival in Traverse City I have to attend for a couple of days. With my duties there, I'm never going to be able to keep on top of this."

I clutched the blanket closer. It was a mild night for October. But it was unusually windy. "I didn't know you actually had duties."

"I am still a professor. It's a famous book fair and I feel obligated to catch up on the newer authors in the American market. Plus, it's a place to network."

"Network? That sounds boring."

Kit held up a carry-out bag I had tossed inside the day before. "Terribly unfair, Trudy."

"Unfair? I didn't know there were rules here."

"You know what you did. Really, Trudy. Squash and rice?"

"That's eggplant and orzo, you fool." Moby hadn't been very interested in Mac's vegan meal.

"Well, it's slimy and disgusting either way. It almost ruined the papers in the box you tossed." His tone reminded me of the moaning sound I used to make when there were vegetables on my plate.

"What have you got in there, a lamp or something?"

"Actually, yes. I borrowed a camp lantern from Flo. At least I have one friend in this endeavor."

I put a foot on the bottom support of the dumpster and pulled myself upward so that I could see over the top. Inside, the lantern cast a dim, warm glow. Kit had strung it up across two ropes fastened on either side of the frame. An umbrella chair rested at an odd angle and was covered with a thick plaid blanket. It looked quite cozy.

"This is really pathetic. Are you camping out now?"

"I'm getting comfortable."

I nodded at the blanket. "It looks like you're taking up residency."

"If you are going to stand here and criticize me, then do it. But don't expect me to entertain you. I have work to do." His face was in the shadow, but his voice was laced with bitterness. Well, I was bitter too. Between Reeba's visit, the ticket, Lulu, and another nightmare, it had been a very bad day.

"Excuse me if my real-life problems interfere with your search for the lost ark."

He moved out of the shadow and examined my face. He seemed taken aback by my angry tone. Good. I was tired of the flirty sparring we had been doing up until now. Even in the glow of the lantern—with the stubble on his chin and the coat that could have come from an Orvis catalogue—he looked like a commercial for fine cognac. I wished I had more eggplant and orzo to dump on his head. Mickey was on the dresser and I had no idea what time it was. I suspected I wouldn't be able to sleep the rest of the night knowing that Kit was out here.

I started to climb down when he held something up. "By the way, is this your scarf?"

I shifted back. My silk scarf with butterflies was clutched in his hand. "That's mine—where did you find it?"

"Underneath a large tome on decorating the loo, to be exact."

"I must have dropped it in a box by accident." I held out my hand.

"Come inside and get it. I'm tired of talking to you through a metal wall."

"That scarf is worth something." And it was Mom's.

"So are these books." He tucked it in the pocket of his jacket and held up his hand. "Are you scared of being in here, or is it me? The dumpster is cleaner than you might think. And I don't bite . . . unless you want me to."

I stood on the side, trying to figure out if I was going to fight him for my scarf. I wanted to climb back into bed and pull the covers over my head in a dreamless sleep. But he was making me crazy. And in the end, the scarf was more valuable than my pride. I climbed until I was perched on top, facing Kit. He stood in front of me and put his hands on my hips to steady me.

"If it hadn't been for you I would have been putting a final coat of paint on the walls and polishing the floor by now. I'd be one step closer to Angkor Wat." I pulled in my lower lip, but he had already seen the pout.

"Poor baby. What happened?"

I took a deep breath and put my hands on his shoulders. "I have one day to fill this container and send it on its way. After that I get charged for a ticket if I don't have a permit."

"A ticket?"

"According to the mayor, this dumpster is illegal without a permit."

"You need money?"

I sighed. "In the worst way. Lulu's cylinder and valve are expensive. The check I wrote to Doc bounced. My bottom account has banked out."

"Your bottom—?" He touched my cheek and smiled. "Ah, my love, I can loan you money."

"Oh yeah, I forgot about your castle and your title."

He narrowed his eyes. "Is it just the money that is bothering you?"

"I'll make you a deal. For the cost of an airline ticket and six months of travel in Southeast Asia, I'll sell you the store and all the books in it right now."

"Sorry, love, I have enough to get you your permit," he said calmly. "But I told you already. My pockets are empty. I'm on a professor's salary. The bulk of my family's money is tied up in land and a house that belongs to the Royal Trust."

"You certainly dress well. And that house you're renting, that's not exactly cheap."

"That's what I can do on a professor's salary. Housing is paid for me. I'm given a stipend. But I don't have thousands of dollars sitting in an account somewhere to buy your store. Buying property means a loan and a mortgage."

I smiled sweetly and pushed him away. "Then I have no use for you."

I lost my balance and Kit grabbed me and steadied me. His hands were warm and firm. I wanted to trust they would keep me from falling. "Trudy, listen to me. Let me pay for this trash bin or whatever else you need for the moment. I can do that."

"And you get to continue your search for the lost book?"

He lost his smile. "I don't work that way."

He surprised me. "Really?"

"No strings."

I stared down at him. I wanted to believe him. It would be so easy. Without thinking, I jumped into his arms and made a dive for the scarf that hung out of his back pocket. But he was quick. He caught my hands before I could get to it.

"Mine," he said in a haggard voice. But he wasn't looking at the scarf: He was looking directly down at me.

"Not yours," I said, lifting my chin.

He hauled me against him. I put my hands on his chest. "Dr. Darlington, that is very macho. Not at all like a professor of literature."

"Even Shakespeare knew when words weren't enough." He put his hands on the back of my head and ground his body against mine. "Still want your scarf?"

"What scarf?"

Our lips connected in a crushing claim that was reckless and angry. The kind of angry that wasn't directed at each other. It was the kind of angry that came from inside. Angry that I wanted him so much I was willing to let my self-control go. Angry that I wanted him more than I didn't want him.

And what the lips started the body took over.

My hands ran up and down his back and under his jacket and shirt to the hard body that I already knew so well. One of his hands was buried in my hair and the other traveled over my back. He was like steel with a velvet veneer. And he was on fire.

I heard someone making little mewling sounds and realized it was me. I laughed at myself and Kit captured my mouth again. The world spun away in a dizziness and frenzy that reminded me of dancing and spinning in joy.

Cool air hit my stomach as he lifted my T-shirt, sliding his hands along my bare skin underneath. He pulled his mouth away from mine to let it trail down. Kneeling on some godforsaken uncomfortable mound of books, he found my breasts.

The camp lantern gleamed off the top of his head and I ran my fingers through his hair. I closed my eyes as his tongue fluttered back and forth across my nipples. They puckered in the cool air. I messed up his hair with my death grip on his head. He pulled away and slowly lifted my shirt further.

"Who is this very familiar-looking cartoon character on your T-shirt?" he mumbled as he held the fabric out of the way.

I looked down, trying to figure out what he was talking about. "Oh, that's just Bart. Bart Simpson."

"Boyfriend?" he asked with a saucy grin.

"Hero," I replied.

"But way too young to watch this." He tossed my shirt over a self-help book.

In only my pink-panda underpants, I watched Kit's eyes travel to my face. His eyes were feverish and I shivered at the thought of what was coming next. I reached for his shirt, but he put a hand on my wrist and stopped me. "This is my den. I don't have an electric chair. But I get to call the shots tonight."

"Be my guest," I said as I lowered my arms. Heat shot straight to my core.

Kit ran his hands up my arms and traced my collarbone. He leaned in and followed the path with his tongue. His fingers drifted lower and he took a deep breath and raised his smoky eyes. "May I?"

My mouth went dry. I swallowed and nodded. Or at least I think I did. Whatever it was, he took it as *yes*. I watched his hands run down my hips and inside the waistband of my silly panties. He lowered them and I stepped out, enjoying the return of his hands when they were off.

What his hands touched, his lips and eyes followed. I felt extraordinary. Cherished. I understood how a woman could feel worshipped. When he touched me in the most sensitive area, I shuddered. Kit's nostrils flared and he lifted his fingers to my lips. And what I did for Kit in the electric chair, he did for me . . . Only better.

The evening took an intriguing turn, like a porn movie set in a library. We made love among the paperbacks and hardcovers—some very hard covers. When it wasn't comfortable, we tried new positions, rearranging the books and the blanket to suit ourselves. It was an entirely different way to use books and I welcomed the way the rough pages bunched and shifted in front of my face when Kit kneeled on the blanket and pressed himself against me. He came into me from behind and I was so sensitive I almost lost control right there. He reached around and touched me with his fingers, bringing me to a climax that went on and on. I grasped the pages of an open book in front of me and wrinkled the corners of the pages with my fists. I held on to them for dear life as I cried out. Kit joined me moments later.

Afterward, when we were exhausted, we pulled my dharma quilt over ourselves and snuggled in our cave. The lantern waved in the wind and I wondered if anyone in the world had ever made love in a dumpster. And if so, had it been as magical as it had been for me?

Kit lifted his head and grinned at something above my head. He reached for a small book and checked the title on the spine.

"What is that?" I asked in a sleepy voice that made him kiss my earlobe.

"Some light reading." He flipped through the pages, trying to catch the light. "Want to read it with me?"

I shook my head. He adjusted his arm underneath me and began.

"She is a mortal danger to all men. She is beautiful without knowing it, and possesses charms that she's not even aware of. She is like a trap set by nature—a sweet perfumed rose in whose petals Cupid lurks in ambush! Anyone who has seen her smile has known perfection. She instills grace in every common thing and divinity in every careless gesture."

I closed my eyes and imagined that woman as he spoke. "Who is she?"

"You."

"No, it's not. I know that. It's a play, right?"

"Cyrano de Bergerac."

"I thought I recognized it. I made a balcony for it once in a summer-stock theater in Canada. She's Roxane."

"You have a good memory."

"Me? I can't remember words. But for some reason that part stuck with me."

He braced himself over me and the light shone from behind him like a halo. "Words are just the vehicle for the story. You get where you need to go in other ways, Trudy. That is what makes you so magnificent."

I didn't deserve that kind of pretty language. Most of the time we teased more than we were serious. I closed my eyes, afraid to see him mocking me. I didn't want to ruin the pretense that I was his Roxane.

The night was quiet. A breeze started and finished from different ends of the night sky. When I couldn't stand it any longer, I opened my eyes to see if he was smiling with that teasing look he often used.

But he was staring at me from unwavering eyes; a solemn, almost sad expression on his face. "I wish it had been different, Trudy."

He moved a piece of hair that the wind had flicked over my eye. "I wish we had met under the glitter of the streetlights by the Seine. On a warm night in Paris with the sound of music in the air.

"I would have seen you standing at the gilded railing. Your hair glowing in the lights. Your smile and the way you hold yourself when no one is watching would remind me of an enchantress, looking for all the world like you had a secret that no one else could share."

I touched his cheek and blinked back heat that made my eyes feel heavy. No one had ever described me that way. "I would have shared my secret with you, Kit . . . If I had met you on a Paris night."

I slept a dreamless sleep that was surprisingly refreshing. When I woke, my head rested against the soft pillow of Kit's shoulder and my hip was nuzzled between two hardcover copies of the encyclopedia. My guess was they were volumes 1 and 2, because volume 3 was under his head. The early-morning sky was tinted deep fuchsia and orange. I didn't want to move, not just because of the cool air outside the blanket, or because I was so comfortable in his arms. I was afraid if I left, reality would hit and I would never feel this way again.

"Good morning, Trudy." Kit's half-lidded eyes and lazy smile made him look adorably sexy.

"Good morning, Christopher." I liked the sound of his full name.

He pulled me to him, planting a soft but firm morning kiss on my lips. "I adore waking up with you."

I sent a rueful gaze to the encyclopedias. "Yes, but I am afraid my behind will be permanently marked with the history of—what's this?"

"Spanish sailing ships. But I fear, fair damsel, that your bum will be permanently marked with more than just the history of Spanish sailing ships," he said, touching a spot on my hip that looked a bit like a hickey.

"Peachy," I said, curling my lip.

Kit must have read my mind. He propped himself up on his elbow and said, "Maybe we should just stay here and ignore the rest of the world."

If only we could. I thought about the things that I had to do today. "Your books and festival are waiting for you, Professor."

A gust ruffled his hair. The wind was stronger this morning. Several leaves had blown into the container and skimmed across the top layer of books. We rose stiffly and wobbled on the unstable carpet of books beneath us. Scrambling over the mounds of paper and cardboard looking for our clothes, we stopped every few moments to touch each other.

When we were semi-dressed, Kit helped me over the ledge before tossing the chair and blanket out. He grabbed the lantern and hopped out in one leap. So agile. British secret agent Double-O Darlington.

Moby was awake. He whined from inside the store.

"He's been a good boy. Both of you come by the house when you are dressed and I'll give you extra cash so you can buy him a proper bone," Kit said.

The sun's colors were shifting. It drifted above the horizon now and the sky turned pink. I held my blanket to my chest. I didn't want to leave Kit yet.

He stepped close and cradled my face in his hands. "Now a soft kiss—Aye, by that kiss, I vow an endless bliss." Then he touched his lips to mine.

When he finished, I sighed. "What was that from?"

"Keats. I love American literature. But I am British after all." He winked at me and walked away.

I watched him disappear across the field toward the lake beyond and felt something inside me loosen. An overpowering feeling of freedom raced through my veins. I leaned back against the Dumpster and lifted my face to the morning sun.

When Kit read to me last night, an old rage that had weighed me down for years came unhinged. Now I felt a delirious lightness that reminded me of the way I felt a day not so long ago when I first started to forgive my father.

Dad had softened in his old age. Or maybe it was the new wife and children. There were two of them. One to replace the boy who had been blown up in the convoy ambushed in the desert. And another to replace me. The girl who refused to follow orders.

Maybe someday soon I would call Dad and tell him I ate vegetables now. I don't think he knew. I would promise again to repay him for the loan, even though he didn't want me to. And I would tell him I didn't hate him anymore for leaving me with an emotionally disconnected woman who knew nothing about raising children.

After Kit left me, branded by his kiss in the morning sun, I scaled the Dumpster and climbed back inside. I hunted around until I found what I was looking for: *Cyrano de Bergerac*. I clutched it to my chest and I clambered back over the edge before returning to Books from the Hart.

Chapter 17

"This feels weird." My hand tingled where Kit placed the hundred-dollar bills as casually as if they were pieces of gum. He must have kept large denominations around the way some people kept pennies in a jar.

We stood inside the lake house he was renting. He lifted my chin with his index finger and angled my face up. "Don't think twice about it. You need the loan and I'm not putting any conditions on it."

"Maybe I should find some other way—"

"When you sell the place you can pay me back, all right?" He lowered his head and kissed me. I was too busy worrying to enjoy it. "Are you sure I can't give you more for Lulu?"

"Yes." On that part I was definite. If the store didn't sell, I was going nowhere, so it didn't matter. I had all the time in the world to find work and pay for Lulu at that point.

"You are a stubborn wench!" Kit said with a grin, pulling me close. "Do you have time for a quick breakfast? I don't have to meet my colleague until later in the morning. Even better, I could forget the conference and stay." His hands strayed down my back.

"I have plenty to keep me busy. And the house of horrors opens tomorrow. I'll be making things bloody and gross for the rest of the day."

"Brilliant. Do you at least want me to drive you to the county offices?" Moby leaned against our knees and wagged his tail.

"I'm going to ask Elizabeth Lively for a ride."

"Come back later, then. I haven't had the opportunity to host you in a king-sized bed. Imagine the possibilities." My heart did a cartwheel.

When he kissed me again, I dropped the cash and almost told him to cancel. We could spend the day discovering new ways to use books. But he picked up the bills and stuffed them in my pocket.

"Come. At least have coffee."

While he prepared the coffee in the kitchen, I played snoop. The living-room fireplace was huge. The view out the floor-to-ceiling windows was incredible. When I wandered into the large dining room that overlooked Echo Lake, my attention was caught by all the books strewn across the table and the papers pinned to several project boards against the wall. Among them was a picture of Robin Hartchick as a young man. A newspaper article with a picture of a burned building. A magazine interview with a portrait of an elderly Robin Hartchick.

Kit stood with two mugs in his hands, watching me. "I'm getting ready to throw all that out."

"I see that." A trash can stuffed with dozens of handwritten sheets of paper sat by a chair. "So this is why you never invited me over. You didn't want me to see your paper trail."

"That was before you found out. Then . . . I didn't think you wanted to get within a mile of me. It's done, now."

"Can you at least explain more of what you were looking for?" I reached out and touched the magazine and papers that described Robin Hartchick's life, and tried to grasp Kit's fascination.

He made it easy for me. Putting down the mugs, he reached out and plucked the article from the bulletin board. "This is an interview conducted with Robin Hartchick right before he died."

"He looks awful, like he could have been in the house of horrors," I said.

"Yes, that's one of the reasons no one took him seriously. He mentions in that interview that his very best work, in his humble opinion—which was never humble at all—was a novel he wrote prior to *Spring Solstice*. But look at him. He could barely talk or walk."

"People thought he made it up?"

"Yes. He claims the manuscript was lost in a fire. They thought he was delusional."

I looked at the newspaper article that showed a picture of a burned-down building. "Is that the fire?"

"Yes. I dug up some information. There was a hotel on the west coast of Michigan that burned down. Your aunt was supposed to meet him there." He set the bowls on the table.

I got goose bumps looking at the charred, blackened building. It was a connection to a young Aunt Gertrude that I knew nothing about.

"Sip and I'll tell you." Kit sat down. He handed me the mug. Checking my face to make sure I was still interested, he continued: "Let me back up first. What do you know about your aunt and Robin Hartchick?"

"Some of it. Aunt Gertrude was swept off her feet by Robin Hartchick."

"She was young. He was ten years older."

"Hard to picture anyone falling for Aunt Gertrude, much less sweeping a lady as imposing as she was off her feet."

Kit didn't laugh at my comment. "Here she is." He pointed to a picture of her young face. She looked innocent and sweet. And almost beautiful. "That's the woman Hartchick fell in love with."

I stared at the portrait for a long time. I didn't know she had red hair. "Can I keep this?"

He reached out and tenderly wiped the corner of my mouth. "Of course. Did you know they met when he was on a hunting excursion in Michigan? He was from Chicago and she lived in Traverse City with her parents and her little brother, your father's dad."

"How did they meet?"

"No one I spoke with remembers. But they all say it was love at first sight." The color on his cheeks heightened as he spoke. "When she ran off with him, Gertrude's father basically disowned her. Did you know that?"

"My grandfather was quite overbearing, according to my dad." I didn't comment on the similarity in his son.

"For the next year they lived in the happy haze of 1960. Life was still good then. According to his autobiography, they lived over a store on Echo Lake. He wrote a novel and she worked as a waitress and supported them both. Then things went downhill."

"What happened?"

"He traveled to New York several times that year. He stayed for weeks at a time. According to people who knew your aunt, she waited patiently, believing that he was busy submitting his short stories to agents and publishers."

"And?"

"He was playing around on her. Robin Hartchick was famous for his womanizing later in his life. His five marriages illustrate that. He was a major-league philanderer, even back then."

"How did she find out?" I almost felt sorry for Aunt Gertrude. She was estranged from her family and living on her own in a town where she knew no one. And Robin Hartchick was two-timing her.

"You didn't know any of this?"

I shook my head. I wish I had. I'd like to think even a fifteen-year-old me would have been a little nicer to a heartbroken old woman. "In August of 1960, he called her and told her to bring the manuscript and meet him at a hotel in Charlevoix. The wealthy members of Chicago society summered there. Hartchick had an agent who was coming up from Chicago and was interested in reading a novel he had written. His first."

Kit leaned forward. "My sources say that when your aunt tried to check into the hotel, the clerk confused her with another woman. A woman who called herself Mrs. Robin Hartchick and routinely met Hartchick at the same hotel in Charlevoix."

I sat back and pictured Aunt Gertrude. Young. Innocent. And betrayed.

"The hotel burned down the night before he arrived."

"My aunt was in the fire?" I gasped. I curled my knee under me. This was horrible.

"She got out, but most of her things were burned. According to reports, the fire started in a fireplace in the lobby that wasn't properly cleaned. Your aunt met Robin at the train station in tears. She claimed the manuscript was lost in the fire."

I sat back in my chair. I thought the last twenty-four hours had been bad for me. What did I know? I was mad at Kit for his white lies. But Aunt Gertrude had found out the man she loved was cheating on her. Been in a hotel fire. And then had to explain why she lost the great American novel.

"There were no copies of this manuscript?"

"She brought the carbons with her. He couldn't believe she did that. She was very upset, evidently. Partly because he cared more about the manuscript than her. He packed up and left her shortly after that."

Kit was watching me closely. I kept staring from him to Aunt Gertrude's picture. What a sad and lonely life she had.

Kit put his hand on top of my own. "It was a long time ago."

I squeezed his hand. "So why do you believe the novel exists?"

"I believe that the fire was a convenient excuse. I think she saved the carbons but deliberately kept them from Robin Hartchick. It's very possible, when she returned to Echo Lake, she hid the copies, waiting for Hartchick to admit his cheating and give up his ways. I don't think she planned on keeping them from him or the world forever. But as the months went by and the news of his partying in New York reached her, maybe she just decided to keep them to herself."

My coffee was growing cold. I sipped it quickly as I thought about Aunt Gertrude.

The year I'd lived with her, I was so lost in my own grief over my mother's death that I didn't think much about Aunt Gertrude's life. From what I could remember, her only real companions were books. She surrounded herself with books and papers as if they were her friends. Her parents—my great-grandparents—died in the early 1970s. My father's dad, her brother, had kept in touch with her. But he died too. The only person left in her life was my own father . . . and my brother and me.

Dad warned us to be nice to Aunt Gertrude when he dropped us off in Truhart. But I hated her. And I hated her store. And I hated the town she lived in.

I scanned all the documents on the table and felt a little less angry with the poor old bird. Her wings had been clipped pretty badly.

After I left Kit's place, I returned to the bookshop. I walked around the store and ran my fingers over a pile of papers that were stacked against the wall.

Maybe throwing everything out could wait until I figured out what to do about my new feelings for Kit. And my new knowledge of Aunt Gertrude.

I didn't know how I could help in the quest for the lost manuscript. But I had forgiven Kit for deceiving me. I knew what it was like to want something that badly. He had dreams like I did. They just happened to be at cross-purposes. Maybe we could work something out that would satisfy both of us. If all went well we could both find a way to achieve our goals.

A few months from now, I could be in the jungles of Cambodia and he could be presenting his discovery to the literary world.

The thought left me oddly flat.

* * *

By late afternoon, I was too busy to think about lost manuscripts and Kit. When Elizabeth and I returned from the county offices, the house of horrors was in chaos. Just as Elizabeth parked her Honda in front of the old grocery store, we were accosted by ladies in panic. The bats were falling from the ceiling. The black lights were aimed at the wrong display and the coffin collapsed with Bridgette in it. Other than being mad at Marva for getting her involved in the house of horrors, she was fine.

The day became a frenzy of finishing details and calming the rabid panic that hovered in the air. At one point, Elizabeth and I made a run to the superstore in Gaylord to purchase more white makeup for the zombies. It turned out to be a nice break from the pandemonium. We played the radio loudly and she joked about the unpredictable mess her life had become.

By the time the sun was ready to set all the volunteers, including me, were exhausted. But there were still priorities. Harrison High School was playing a team from Grayling in a game that would decide who made it to the regional championship. I was too tired to go and looking forward to seeing Kit later. But no one else had any intention of missing it.

"We are as ready as we will ever be," announced Marva in a booming voice.

She was right. The old grocery store had been transformed to a respectably terrifying house of horrors.

"Everyone gather round!" Marva shouted.

She stood at the front of the store and waited for a circle to form around her. "The house opens at ten a.m. on the dot. Lori's Restaurant is providing a free lunch for volunteers. Zombies, witches, clowns, vampires and—oh, yeah—crazies."

"That's you, Marva," interrupted Joe. The men in the room joined him and a few even added their wives' names.

Marva put her hands on her hips. "You married me. So that makes you just as insane." It earned her a big kiss from Joe and whistles from the rest of us.

"So, as I was saying, we are ready to go. Don't be late. And don't forget to remind all your friends and their kids to come! I have flyers from here to Lake Huron, so hopefully we'll have a line of customers all the way to the county road."

As people shuffled out the door, Corinne pulled me aside. "Trudy, we never could have done all this without you. You've been working hard and we know it has taken quite a bit of time away from your own affairs."

"That's okay."

"No. We feel bad."

Marva came up behind Corinne. "We heard about your little . . . er . . . *problem* with Reeba Sweeney. We haven't exactly been understanding about your feelings and what you need. Just because we don't want the store to go to Logan Fribley doesn't mean you don't have the right to sell. We'd love to use it for the community center, but maybe another nice business will want it."

Corinne laid a hand on my shoulder. "And you did so much for Jenny and the girls and their cheerleading. So, they got together and decided to surprise you."

"Surprise me?"

Marva pushed her glasses up her nose. "Well, they had help from us. You didn't exactly need to get the makeup in Gaylord."

They took my elbow and led me out the front door. The dimming light of the late afternoon cast shadows on a small crowd that stood in front of Books from the Hart. Jenny, Bibi, Madeline, and all the girls who had cheered at the football game so passionately just a few weeks ago jumped up and down when they saw me. Moby was with them. He ran toward me, tail wagging. I crouched down and gave him a big kiss on the snout. "Sorry I was gone so long, boy. I hope you had a good nap."

Jenny wore a big grin on her face and grabbed my hands in hers, pulling me up toward the front door. "Miss Trudy! Come see!"

I smiled and let her lead me. Her excitement was contagious and I had no idea what she was up to.

Jenny giggled when we reached the door. She opened it wide and Bibi flipped on the light. "Ta-da!"

I froze.

The room was almost completely clear.

"We put books in the trash while you were helping out at the haunted house," said Jenny with huge pride in her voice.

"They're gone." I stood still, blinking rapidly and wondering if I was seeing clearly.

"We wanted to do something for you for a change," said Corinne.

"And it was a shitload of work. Even with some help from our parents. My shoulders are going to be sore for a week after this," Bibi said, rubbing her upper arm.

All these weeks, I wanted nothing more than to see books gone and the room bare. Empty. And now all I could think about was Kit. It would take weeks for him to sort through the garbage.

"Miss Trudy . . . Are you okay?"

No. "Yes, it's just such a surprise." I don't know where I found my smile, but I dug it up from somewhere. With my lips feeling as stiff as the mummy next door, I squeezed her hand and said, "You girls are wonderful. I just can't—can't thank you all enough."

Jenny leaped into my arms and hugged me.

"Awww . . . look, Jenny. You girls made her so happy she's speechless," said Marva. "We really surprised you, didn't we? Flo was the only one who wouldn't have anything to do with this. She loves books, you know. You'll probably hear all about it from her next time you see her."

"Now you girls, we have to dress and be in Grayling by seven o'clock. Leave Miss Trudy to enjoy her nice, clean store," said Corinne with a wave my way.

The girls took turns hugging me, with the exception of Bibi, who gave me a fist bump. When they left, I collapsed on the cold, hard bare floor. My numbness turned to hysterical laughs. Just a month ago, I would have given anything to be this close to purging Books from Hell. Now I found myself wondering how long it would take to carry everything back out of the trash.

The words from Aunt Gertrude's will came back to me. She must be laughing her ass off. I finally understood what Aunt Gertrude meant in her will. I was damned!

For what seemed like hours, I lay in an exhausted heap on the floor of the store, staring at the bare bulb in the ceiling.

"Aunt Gertrude, why are you still haunting me?" Moby appeared, blocking out the light with his furry head, and he licked my face. I pulled him close, happy to have a friend who understood conflicting loyalty. Especially as it related to a certain British man. With a grunt, he laid down and put his head on my thigh.

When I was younger I had always felt an uncomfortable sense of claustrophobia when I was alone in the store. Like being in a car that had been packed so tightly with luggage that you had to curl your knees to your chest just to fit. Now, with the pressure gone, I understood that some things here were worth caring about after all. Stories that made loneliness meaningful. Characters that filled the void. And beautiful words that lovers held close to their hearts.

I called out to the ghost of Aunt Gertrude. "If it's here, send me a sign!"

The wind rattled the front window and Moby whined. I finally roused myself from my stupor and poured dog food in Moby's plastic bowl. He sniffed it and walked away. "Not hungry, boy?" He sent me a baleful look and dropped his head.

I couldn't look at bare shelves and a clean floor another minute. Maybe I would be able to think better with something in my stomach and a little company.

Moby curled up by the back door. His ears were back, as if he was nervous about something. Other than a gusty breeze that was cooling off the evening, I couldn't hear anything that would upset him. I grabbed my old jean jacket and crouched down in front of him. "I'll be back soon, boy. Maybe I'll bring you a little ground beef to perk you up." He whined and watched me leave. I nearly changed my mind and turned around, but the stark room was too depressing.

Outside, the wind had picked up. I almost tripped over Doc's black cat that waited in the night shadows across the street. It screeched and took off in the direction of Doc's garage. The no-parking sign rattled in the breeze. A scarecrow swayed on the post outside the house of horrors. I headed toward the glow at the end of the street, careful not to trip in the darkness. It was the time of year that made it hard to tell late afternoon from early evening. It was probably bright and sunny in Angkor Wat. Warm too. I wish I had taken the picture off Lulu's visor. I needed a reminder of where I was going. Something to focus on.

A strong breeze tore through my hair and whipped my coat away from me. A cornstalk came loose from the light post at the end of the street. It flew past me on a burst of wind. Above me, a tree limb creaked. I held my coat closer to me and made my way down the road.

When I pushed open the door of the diner, the chime above my

200 • Cynthia Tennent

head was lost on a draft that tore the door from my hands, banging it against the frame. I fought to pull it shut. "Whew! That's a strong—" I stopped.

Cookee's was empty except for a family in the corner. A waitress I didn't recognize stood in front of the television, watching the weatherman give his nightly report. And a short, scrawny stranger stood at the stove flattening a meat patty. They were the only people in the diner. No Corinne. No Mac. Not even a trendy tourist.

"Where is everybody?"

"Who?" asked the waitress, her eyes still fixed on the TV.

"Mac?"

She glanced my way and dismissed me. I guess I didn't seem like a big tipper. "Everyone has the night off for the football game and Mac just got hired at the Grande Lucerne."

"What?"

She pushed away from the counter as a commercial came on. "Yeah. I guess they liked his food. I didn't. Neither did Bert, here. But who can guess at the taste of people with money?"

"So that's it? No more Mac?"

"Unless you want to pay forty bucks an entree on the other side of I-75. Yeah. No Mac. But Bert makes a mean slider."

I looked over at Bert at the grill. He was picking his nose. "No thank you. I'll just have a bowl of oatmeal."

"Oatmeal? We only serve that at breakfast," she said, staring at my coat.

"Okay. How about a bowl of rice or brussels sprouts?"

She put a hand on her hip. "Neither one of those are on the menu. That's gonna be extra if we have to make it special."

I stepped forward. "Mac never charged me extra to make something off the menu."

"I've heard that before. Haven't you, Bert?" She laughed and he joined in. Then he grabbed a bun from the top shelf with the hand he had just used on his nostril. Bert was going to make boogers, not burgers. I don't know why I thought that was so funny. I put a hand over my mouth. I think I was getting light-headed.

"Something amusing you?" The waitress scowled at me.

"Never mind." I probably had a can of beans somewhere under

the shelf in Aunt Gertrude's kitchen. A strong gust blew the door open and shut.

I walked out the door, leaving it flying in the wind as the waitress screamed from behind me. All the humor inside me quickly drained away. Nothing was funny now.

I made my way down the sidewalk, letting my hair fly every which way across my face. I didn't bother buttoning my coat and the bitter cold cut through my thigh-length rayon sweater. The first drops of rain hit my cheeks like pelting ice. I picked up my pace. No cars were parked on Main Street tonight. The Laundromat had closed and another letter on the dry-cleaning sign was hanging in the wind. With the exception of a surly waitress and a crude cook, it felt like I was the only person left in Truhart.

I was going to be gone soon too. The last glimpse I would have of Truhart would be out Lulu's rearview mirror. The diner would go on with Bert behind the counter now, cooking his disgusting fare. The garage would continue to service boring cars. The ladies would be doing whatever came next in their quest to raise money for a community center. And after the football season, girls like Jenny were still going to be sent home from school for crying when they were left out of gym class.

I walked past one empty building after another. The pizza place that had been for sale for over a year. The bakery that had been empty even when I lived here. The Chamber of Commerce defying the notion that there wasn't any commerce in Truhart.

I could have changed that, according to Reeba Sweeney. There could be a pawnshop. And if they were lucky, a cheap casino. Maybe an adult bookstore.

I never liked Truhart when I was fourteen. But it wasn't because of the town. It wasn't Truhart's fault that my mother died and my father didn't want us. It wasn't anyone's fault I couldn't read. Most people here were as down on their luck now as I had been back then.

The picture on the other side of Lulu's visor came to mind. Angkor Wat was an abandoned temple. It had once sat rotting slowly in the jungle with no one inhabiting it other than a bunch of wild monkeys. Absurdly, I was leaving one decaying town for another.

I cut between buildings and turned down the back alley toward the store. There was no glow coming from a camp light now. Kit would have been challenged by tonight's weather. Our bed of books would have been cold and blustery. The beautiful words he read me from *Cyrano de Bergerac* would have been lost on the wind.

I stopped in my tracks. I had placed *Cyrano de Bergerac* on the table in the back room. I let myself in the back door, leaving it open to bang against the side of the building. Moby barked and hovered at my knees.

"It's just me." He whined louder. But I wasn't paying attention. With a sense of foreboding, I stared at the table. The girls had been thorough. *Cyrano de Bergerac* was gone.

And along with all the other books, it was going to be drenched when the rain came.

A giant crack of thunder erupted at the same time several flashes of light illuminated the back alley.

Suddenly, I knew what to do.

I grabbed the flashlight from the desk by the back wall and headed out into the wind. The screen door crashed facedown and I left it. I headed toward Doc's. Lulu waited for me. The tarp I had secured days ago flapped in the wind.

"Just for one night," I said out loud, apologizing as I removed it. "Sorry, Lulu." I quickly untied the rope, ignoring the way my hands turned numb in the cold wind. When I was finished, I started back to the store.

The tarp flew apart and billowed in the wind as I walked down Main Street. I was forced to grasp it with both hands to keep from losing it. The first drops of rain were falling faster by the time I was back at the Dumpster. With the flashlight tucked inside my coat pocket, I went to work, managing to drape one corner of the container at a time. I felt for the grommets at each end of the tarp and threaded the rope through. The cleats on each corner of the container made it easier. I managed to secure the tarp and tie it off. When I finished, I stepped back and held up the flashlight. Another clap of thunder made me jump. Lightning followed in a surge of bursts that made the night seem like day. The tarp rose up in the wind like a parachute, but it stayed in place, protecting the contents of the Dumpster from the rain that fell harder now.

Satisfied that the covering was going to stay, I made my way to the back door. It slapped against the doorframe, rattled by the wind. I fought the wind until the door clicked shut. While the rain fell in sheets outside, I stood in the middle of the bookstore and caught my breath.

A strange feeling came over me as if something wasn't right. Even empty of books, the store felt too vacant. My eyes traveled around the room. It was dry. All the crazy weather was outside.

And Moby was gone.

Chapter 18

I stumbled along Main Street, searching for anything that might resemble a soggy collie. The rain pelted my face, making it painful to keep my eyes open. My clothes stuck to me like papier-mâché ice. My hair hung in clumps. The cuff of my pants dragged on the ground. And water cascaded down the inside of my collar, making a path down to my waterlogged boots.

I was plagued by the extra weight of the soaking rain. Every step I took was slower and slower. Like in a nightmare, I tried to run but I had trouble getting the right hop and make my legs move in unison. I couldn't imagine how Moby was managing. A full coat of cold, wet fur must feel like lead on a dog with old arthritic bones.

"Moby!" I called over and over. I barely heard the sound of my own voice, but dogs' ears were better, right? If Moby were anywhere nearby he should hear me.

Where would a scared dog hide? I checked in the bushes, under the bench across the street, anywhere that might offer shelter.

Sheets of rain intensified, blanketing the end of the street where the road dipped to the lake. The reflection off the black asphalt was deceiving. I landed ankle-deep in a puddle and almost lost my footing.

The lights from my flashlight shifted in the wind, making false shadows. A figure of a man stood by the door of the empty bakery. Struggling in the downpour, he flapped his arms back and forth. Relieved that someone else was out on this godawful night, I ran toward him. Maybe he had seen an old, frightened collie.

"Have you seen a dog?" I shouted into the gust as I approached him.

He didn't hear me. I placed my hand on his shoulder to get his attention. But his arm disintegrated from my touch and he came apart in my fingers. He careened sideways and a grotesque face spun and crashed into me. I screamed and arched backwards, circling my arms for balance, and slipped off the curb. I landed with a jarring *thud* on my backside. The flashlight flew out of my hands and went dim. With a racing heart, I felt for the ground and struggled to stand. Something with flowing strands of light hair bobbed facedown in the stream of rainwater that was turning into a river.

Dread formed in my throat. I blinked past the liquid bullets that sprayed my face.

I leaned forward with an unsteady hand. "Please, please . . . not Moby."

Lightning flashed just as I grasped the object. It turned over and the hollow eyes and sickly smiling teeth of a monster mask writhed in the water. I screamed and drew back, letting the deluge take the scarecrow away.

I swallowed icy rain and pulled myself together. If I was scared on a night like tonight, what was a poor, wimpy dog feeling? He didn't like being wet. Hell, he didn't like a rain shower, much less a thunderstorm.

I wiped my eyes and returned to my search, running up and down Main Street, from one end to the other, peering in every doorway, under each bench, and below any possible overhang that might give an animal shelter. I yelled his name until my voice grew hoarse. The street was deserted.

Almost.

Every cheesecloth ghost, every undead pumpkin, black bat, and perching spider came alive. I was caught in dozens of spiderwebs and tripped over cornstalks that were wilting in the rain. Halloween decorations that had been so funny in the clear light of day had transformed into a macabre specter in the storm.

I pressed on. I would gladly suffer through a million nightmares like this, if I could find Moby.

I raced back to the store, hoping against hope that Moby might have come home. But no soggy, tail-wagging old dog was there. Just a tarp on a Dumpster billowing in the wind. I considered my options and came up with nothing. No one was around. I didn't have anyone's number on my cell phone anyway.

Back on Main Street, I turned in the other direction. Water rushed around my ankles like a flood in a monsoon. Instead of turning night to day, the lightning only made Echo Lake at the end of the street blacker. Like a hole that swallowed everything up.

Moby was a horrible swimmer. When I teasingly lured him into the lake one afternoon, his heavy coat pulled him down, like a rock around the neck. If he had lost his footing or wandered to the shore, he could be in the lake right now.

I stumbled toward the beach and scanned the water. But it was impossible to tell if anything was lost on the waves. I struggled for breath. The wind buried the sound of my sobs.

"Moby! Moby!" Nothing came back to me. Not a bark or a whimper or a whine. I made my way down the lake road, searching for the one person who might be able to help me.

I pounded on the door, hoping I got the right house. Everything looked different in the dark. My hands were so cold that I couldn't even feel them against the wood.

The door swung open. My brain registered Kit's startled face before I blurted out, "Kit, I lost Moby."

"You *what*?"

He pulled me inside. I was shivering so hard I could barely make my lips move. "Have you seen Moby? He loves you so much. I thought he might come here."

Kit grabbed a blanket from the couch. "I just returned from the festival. For God's sake, Trudy. You look frozen."

"Is he here?" I asked as he wrapped the plush blanket around me. "Here?"

"He's—he's out there. And he's s—scared." My voice broke in a shudder.

I wrenched the blanket off. Kit put it back, wrapping his arm around my shoulders. "What happened?" He rubbed the soft flannel up and down and my skin prickled as it came back to life.

"The girls put all the books in the Dumpster. I'm so sorry. And then it was starting to rain, and I went to the diner—" Why was I telling him all this? It wasn't important. "Moby kept whining as the wind and thunder started. He hates storms! And I—I ignored his fear. I feel so badly, Kit."

He rubbed the blanket over my soggy head and pulled me closer. "Shhh, it's all right."

"No, it's not. He's out in the storm." A stream followed me as Kit guided me to the nearby couch. "Don't you get it?"

"Let me make a call to J. D. or Sheriff Howe. Just stay here."

He left me to retrieve his phone. His voice was low as he spoke, but I heard him describe Moby and where he had been seen last. When he returned, he said, "You stay here and get warm. I'll take my truck and try to see if I can find him."

"No. I'm going with you."

"You're half frozen. The weather is supposed to get colder and you—"

I was already at the door. "Let's drive to Doc's or the Family Fare. Maybe he went there."

He stomped after me. "You're shivering like a *Titanic* victim."

"Come on. Let's go."

"You stubborn girl. At least put on another coat." He grabbed his barn jacket from the peg by the door and helped me change into it before putting on a windbreaker.

We ran to the truck, splashing through the puddles that formed on the gravel driveway, and jumped in. The rain on the roof made me feel like I was inside a drum barrel. Even with the windshield wipers oscillating back and forth at full speed, it was still hard to see past the cascading rain on the glass. The headlights cut through the downpour and I searched the area for any sign of a sable coat and the white tail with a black tip. We moved slowly, Kit keeping watch on the left and me on the right. I lost count of the number of times we thought we saw something. Twice I jumped out of the car before Kit could even put it in *park*. But the wind and the wet leaves on the ground made mirages out of tree branches that lay across the road.

We drove back through town, and again I checked the store in hopes that Moby had returned. But there was no sign of him. Kit made me stay in the car while he asked the unfriendly new chef and waitress at Cookee's Diner if anyone had reported a stray dog. Even through the rain and the wind, I saw them shake their heads.

When he returned, Kit reached over and covered my hand briefly, before backing out of the parking lot. The heater was on full blast and I was still shivering. The rain fell in a dense sheet and the road turned slick. "It's still early, Trudy. We'll find him."

But it wasn't early. It was late. And I was losing hope. We turned off of M-33 into the parking lot of the Family Fare. Kit's phone cut through the dull thud of the rain. He accepted the call and it came over the speakers of his car.

"Kit, this is J. D. Hardy."

I leaned forward. "J. D., this is Trudy! I'm here! Did you find Moby?"

"Hi Trudy. I got a call from the office in Harrisburg. Someone brought in a dog."

"Harrisburg? How did he get over there?"

"Now, I'm not sure it is Moby. They gave me no other information."

"Is he okay?" I asked before Kit could respond.

"I don't know any of the details."

"Who found him?"

Kit placed a hand on my shoulder. "He doesn't know the details, love. Let him talk."

"You'll have to go to the county offices and ask. They're the only office open right now," J. D. said. His voice crackled. He was probably out on some state highway. "They couldn't tell me much more. It's a busy night. Half the off-duty staff has been called in because of the storm. I'm dealing with several downed wires and fallen limbs."

J. D. gave us the address of the Harrisburg county offices. I couldn't contain the excitement in my voice. "I know where it is. Elizabeth drove me there this morning." Before we signed off, I yelled, "Thank you, J. D. Thank you, thank you!"

Kit made a U-turn in the Family Fare parking lot. As we drove down the two-lane highway toward Harrisburg, I nagged Kit to drive faster. "Kit, hurry; he's got to be so scared."

Kit put a hand on the back of my neck. "Whether it's him or not, we'll find him."

I gripped my hands together and hoped he was right.

We pulled into the dispatch office for Harrison County and I was out of the car before Kit cut the engine. He caught up to me and held the door as we entered.

A man in uniform behind the desk looked up from a phone call. "Do you have an emergency?"

Kit and I spoke at the same time.

"No."

"Yes!"

I started to explain, but Kit put a hand on my arm and pulled me back. "We can wait," he said.

The young man, who looked no more than twenty, studied the screen in front of him. Voices over a speaker interrupted his call. I leaned forward to say something, but Kit squeezed my hand and shook his head. I knew he was right. I clamped my lips shut and bit down to keep from speaking.

We waited, creating a pond on the floor as the man dispatched several officers and made notes in a logbook in front of him. When he was finally finished, he apologized. "Sorry. It's one of those nights . . . What can I do for you?"

"We're looking for a dog that's been brought in. An older collie. Male."

He flipped a page in his logbook and nodded his head.

"Someone did find a dog over on County Road 487."

"Is he all right?"

"This report doesn't say. I can call over to the animal shelter and find out—"

The door to the station burst open and an older man, wearing a floppy red rain hat tied by a string under his chin, tangled with an umbrella and the door.

"What's the deal with 487?" he called out as the umbrella came free. He didn't even notice Kit or me. After he struggled to close the floral umbrella, he shook the slushy rain off a trench coat that opened to reveal a navy sports coat with an emblem on the lapel.

The dispatcher sat up straighter. "The road crew says they'll get to it after they clear the limb that's down over the driveway of the hospital emergency entrance, sir."

"A limb? Surely that can wait. I can't get down 487 and I'm late to a dinner."

"They say they should have it cleared in an hour or so."

"An hour? That's not going to work. I'm missing the roasted pheasant at the leader-appreciation banquet."

"You could take the Huron National Forest roadway, sir."

The man stepped in front of us, his wet shoes squelching on the tile floor. I stared at the back of his head. Thin clumps of hair sprouted from underneath his rain hat. I already hated him.

"Huron would take me a whole forty-five minutes out of my way. Tell them to get on it now, Parker." He reached over the desk for the phone and held it up to the young man, who took it as if it were a hot potato.

"I understand you are in a rush, sir. But county orders are that we clear all access to clinics and hospitals first."

"Oh, for God's sake, it's just a twig. If some kid needs a Band-Aid, they can walk around it up the driveway."

The dispatcher glanced down at the desk and slumped. He started to dial a number.

I poked the rude man in the back and stepped in front of him. "Excuse me. We were about to get some important information."

The man looked at me as if I were an annoying fly.

"Stay out of it, love," Kit said in a low voice.

I was cold and soggy and my dog was waiting. I took a cue on brazenness from the man who was about to eat one of the most beautiful birds in the world. I reached over the desk and pushed the button on the phone, ending the call. "Parker, the dog?"

"*Excuse me?*" The man's voice was so loud he drowned out the rain.

"I will be happy to excuse you, as soon as I find out what is happening with my dog."

"Your—your dog? Are you crazy, lady? There are more important things than worrying about your dog."

Kit tried to pull me off, but I dodged his grasp. I stepped forward until I was nose-to-nose with the pudgy man. "There *are* more important things. Like making sure the driveway of a hospital is accessible. And then my dog!"

"Who do you think you are, young lady?"

The door behind us blew open and several papers flew off the dispatcher's desk. No one was there.

Kit finally managed to wrap an arm around my middle. "If Moby is in a shelter we can wait."

I struggled out of his arms. "I would be happy to wait if there were a real emergency, but not so this carnivorous man can get to his fumb deast."

"My fumb what?" The man turned back to the dispatcher and bellowed, "Pick up the phone again and call, Parker!"

"No Parker, don't do it!" I shouted.

"Trudy, stop," said Kit.

"Trudy?" The man's jowls shook when he spoke.

Kit stepped between us and put his hands up like a preacher trying to calm the masses. "She's upset because her dog has been out in the storm. We understand you have places to be. So—"

The man's lips curled smugly and his chest began to shake as if he thought the situation was funny. "Trudy Brown. I should have known by your red hair. I've heard all about you."

Kit gave up all attempts to reason with the man. He turned to me and placed his hands on my shoulders. "Let's go sit in the corner and wait until they are—"

"Trudy, the dummy who has that bookstore!"

Kit stilled. His face lost all color except for his beautiful blue eyes, which grew very dark behind his rain-splattered glasses. Slowly, he turned around until he faced the man. "What did you say?"

"Now I know why she's so crazy. She's Trudy Brown. The stupid retar—"

Now I was trying to put myself between Kit and this man. "It's not important, Kit. Let's just wait like you said."

But Kit poked the man in the chest with his index finger. "Don't you ever call her that again!"

"He touched me. Did you see that, Parker? He touched me!"

The dispatcher was out of his chair. He inserted himself between both men. "Let's all calm down, everyone."

"Calm down? This man with the funny accent attacked me."

"That was nothing but my finger. I'll be happy to show you what an attack feels like."

"What are you? A drunk Irishman?"

That made Kit madder. He shrugged the deputy's arm off. "I demand you apologize to the lady."

"You're as loony as her. Two retards."

I grabbed the back of Kit's coat and the dispatcher reached for his radio. "Uh, is there a patrol car nearby?" he said into the speaker.

The three men shifted around each other, not exactly touching, but threatening as they slid across the small lake of water in the middle of the floor. That was when I saw the broomstick in the corner of the room.

Chapter 19

"A broom, Trudy? Really?"

"I was trying to keep you apart. It wasn't my fault that man slid and ended up on the floor like a clump of Jell-O."

"His hair came off."

"Only because his stupid-looking rain hat went flying."

"No man likes to see his hair lying in a puddle."

"Then he shouldn't have pushed you."

We sat on a bench in a cell of the Harrison County Jail. It was conveniently located behind the dispatcher's office, so the officer who answered the dispatcher's call didn't have very far to lead us.

I got up and paced back and forth until Kit told me to sit down. "You're making me dizzy!"

I dropped down on the bench with my back to the wall and clutched the bench impatiently. I didn't care if we stayed in the jail all night or all week, for that matter. I just wanted to know if my dog was all right.

Next to me, Kit leaned against the wall, crossing his arms like an unhappy child. "I can take care of myself. I didn't need you to defend me."

"That man was mean and rude."

"He was. But if we had just let him get on with his business, we wouldn't be here."

I lifted my chin and said, "His business of leaving the clinic blocked so he could go eat a dead bird?"

"Get over the dead-bird business. I eat dead birds. And so does Moby, for that matter."

I was silent after that. Ungrateful man.

The jail cell was cold and the concrete walls were pink, of all colors. Like Pepto-Bismol. Some psychologist must have recommended the color. Maybe criminals felt better when they were surrounded by pink. I, for one, only felt a strange chalkiness inside my mouth. It made me thirsty.

Every once in a while I heard voices on the other side of the cell door. The window on the door was made of bars. If they had let me keep my pocketknife I might have been able to use the serrated blade on the metal. Unfortunately, I didn't see a jailbreak in my future.

There was something uniquely uncomfortable about sitting in damp clothing. Bending my knees made me feel like I had been packaged in shrink wrap.

I grew tired of Kit's huffing sighs. "You can play action hero next time. Stop pouting."

"I don't pout."

"Yes, you—"

"Sorry it took me so long to get here." A familiar face appeared on the other side of the door: J. D. Hardy. He unlocked the cell and entered.

"J. D.!" I leaped from the bench.

Kit rose more slowly. "I apologize for bothering you again on such a busy night, J. D.," he said. "Nobody else in town answered their phone."

"I'm not surprised. Instead of canceling the football game in Grayling, the refs kept calling for a delay. Half the town sat in the Grayling High School gymnasium for hours waiting for the weather to clear. It's always been a dead zone, so they probably never got the call."

"Trudy here didn't mean to clobber that man with a broom. It was a bit of a misunderstanding."

J. D. let out a slow breath and grinned at me. "I know all too well how that happens." I had heard rumors about last summer. But I didn't want to ask. J. D. nodded toward the dispatcher's office. "I got the whole story from Parker. I know you aren't entirely to blame. But you chose the wrong man to tangle with."

"Who was he?" I asked.

"John Hamner. He's a judge. Everyone around here calls him 'Judge Jackhammer.' He uses the gavel like he's cutting up concrete on I-75." J. D. kept his voice low.

Kit rubbed the back of his neck and raised an eyebrow at me.

"Well, it looks like the broom got the better end of the jackhammer today."

I curled my hand into a fist and ignored his sarcasm. "Can you tell us anything about Moby?"

J. D. smiled and I warmed under his kind, dark eyes. "He's fine. Elizabeth went straight to the animal shelter after your call. It's definitely Moby. She says to tell you that he wagged his tail when he saw her. And he had a fine dinner of real dog food that he seemed to like. Ate the whole thing."

The relief was so strong and unexpected that I covered my face with my hands to control the explosion. Hot tears mixed with hyperventilating sobs. *Thank you. Thank you. Thank you.* The words repeated themselves over and over in my mind. Never mind that I hadn't prayed in years. All evening my imagination had gone wild with thoughts of what could have happened to Moby. We had been together just a few short weeks, but I couldn't imagine him gone. It wasn't just about the bond we had developed, but it was about the unwavering loyalty and innocent trust he put in me. I would never forgive myself if he had been hurt.

Kit pulled me into the crook of his shoulder. I struggled to get my composure back while he rubbed the back of my neck.

J. D. cleared his throat. "Since neither of you has a prior criminal record, you are being released without bond until your arraignment. Kit, you might want to contact the British consulate to let them know what is going on."

"Bloody hell. Will Judge Jackhammer preside over the arraignment?"

I stepped back from Kit, relieved and ready for a fight. "I'll bring a larger broom if I have to."

J. D. laughed. "I am sure he would love to be the one to decide your future. But that is not legal in this country. Any judge with a connection to the alleged crime must recuse himself. You'll get someone who is impartial."

"So we can go and get Moby now?" I couldn't wait another minute.

"The dispatcher is typing a report. It might take another hour or so. Then you will have to fill out some paperwork and show proof of ownership at the animal shelter. After that you should be fine."

"Proof of what?" I asked.

"Ownership. You know, his license or his last rabies shot from the vet. That kind of thing."

I stared at J. D. and my stomach dropped to my soggy boots.

Kit shook J. D.'s hand. "I can't thank you enough. You've been a real hero, J.D."

"No. Not really . . ."

"Yes, you have. A real hero! Isn't he, Trudy?"

I nodded vaguely. J. D. ran his hand over his mouth to cover a grin at Kit's words. "Don't think twice about it. That is what I'm here for."

J. D. saw my face and paused. "Are you all right, Trudy?"

"Yeah . . ." I said in a weak voice.

When he left, Kit plopped down on the bench and took a deep breath. "It will be a relief to get out of here, get Moby, and spend the rest of the night in a warm bed."

I slunk to the bench and sat down gingerly, afraid to meet his gaze.

"What's wrong?" Kit asked.

"Umm . . . there might be a bit of a problem."

"What kind of problem?" he asked slowly.

"I don't have any paperwork for Moby."

Several seconds passed as he tried to process what I had just said.

"Can you repeat that?" His voice was suddenly sharp.

"I—I don't have anything to show that Moby is mine."

"A license? Registration?"

I shook my head.

"Papers from his previous owner? Dog tags?"

I closed my eyes.

"Did you even take him to a vet to see if he needed shots?"

I dropped my chin to my chest.

Kit took a slow breath. "You didn't even get his vaccinations checked?"

"Nooo . . ." It came out in barely a whisper.

"That was du—" He stopped himself.

But I finished the word for him. "Dumb. I know."

He put his head back and stared at the ceiling. "Damn! What a bloody, bloody mess!"

"Yes." My hair hung limply over my eyes and hot rivers of shame streamed down my face. "I'm a hypo—hippo—you know! With my vegan lifestyle and all my talk of anti-hunting . . . not harming animals. Not even an unfertilized egg. I'm a hippa—what the hell is that word?"

"Hypocrite?"

"A stupid one."

He was up and stomping around the cell. "Stop it. Stop doing that!"

"What?"

He stopped in front of me. "Putting yourself down. You don't even know you're doing it sometimes. You had a tough life, Trudy. Your mother died. Your father dumped you on Aunt Gertrude. She was unsympathetic. Then you ran away. You got the short end of the stick."

"I'm not feeling sorry for myself."

"Shut up and let me talk!"

I leaned back. "Go right ahea—"

"It's time to grow up and stop pretending you're some sort of free spirit who doesn't want to hurt anything. Moby depended on you. And you didn't protect that poor, sweet dog like you should have. All because of some misguided sense of freedom."

"I didn't mean to hurt him. I just didn't think I could take care of him as well as some people."

He stopped in front of me. "Some people? You are missing my point. You know something, Trudy? Even that fat man who was on his way to a pheasant dinner—that man you knocked over the head with a broomstick—even he probably has a pet. If he can do it, why can't you?"

I drew my feet up to the bench and wrapped my hands around my knees. There wasn't a single good excuse I could make for my stupidity.

Kit sat down at the end of the bench, as far from me as he could get. I heard him breathing in large, angry bursts. I buried my head in my knees and we sat like that for a long time.

A half-hour later we emerged from the jail cell to a stack of papers that we were obligated to fill out before we were released. My stack took longer to complete because I couldn't read with everyone looking at me. Kit finally picked up the forms, read them to me, and showed me where to sign. When we were finished, I asked the dispatcher if he knew any way to spring Moby out of the animal shelter without identification.

"You're just lucky that they changed the laws. It used to be up to the county whether they destroyed an unlicensed dog or not."

"*What*?" My heart went cold at the thought that Moby might have been killed in some gas chamber just because of me.

"Yep. It was perfectly legal until the laws were changed."

"Is there any way I can get him back tonight?"

"Nope. You'll have to find someone who can vouch for you and then there will be fines to pay. You'll have to get a license and probably they won't let you have that until you prove he's up on his shots."

"All that?" I asked in a weak voice.

Kit was done with his paperwork. He sent me a withering gaze and said sarcastically, "Funny how most people go through all that rigmarole of licenses and vet visits."

The dispatcher was a little dense. "Well, most people will do anything for their pets. I heard there was a lady in Truhart who left all the money in her bank account to the animal shelter in her pet's name."

"You don't say."

"A lot of people thought she was crazy, but we might have closed the animal shelter if she hadn't done that. Your dog would probably be lost in the system down in Saginaw if it weren't for her."

I shoved my last form toward him and watched his face change. "Brown? Gertrude Brown. Does that ring a bell?"

It took a few seconds, but finally his face changed. "Now that I think of it, that was her name . . ."

"What a coincidence."

His nostrils flared and the corner of his mouth tilted. "Now, that's fate, isn't it? Same name of the lady who left the money. And now your dog is at that same shelter. Kind of ironic."

"Jesus," Kit said under his breath and he walked away.

When we left the office we were met with a blast of cold air and white. I looked up at a gently falling snow. It fell in a muffled hush that would have been soothing after all the pounding rain if my nerves weren't so frayed. We approached the SUV and paused. The windshield was covered in a thin sheet of ice and snow. Kit held up his keys and unlocked the doors of the truck without a word. I wondered if he would ever smile at me again.

"Do you have an ice scraper?" I asked.

"No. I didn't expect I'd have to deal with a snowstorm in the middle of October," he bit back, as if that were my fault.

"It's hardly a snowstorm. Just flurries." I slid into the passenger seat. "Turn on the defrost and the windshield should be clear soon. This isn't uncommon for this time of year."

After several minutes of waiting that seemed like hours with a surly British man sitting next to me, the windshield melted for the wipers to clear the slushy ice. The heat kicked in and I offered Kit his coat. He refused and sat like a block of stone-cold ice.

We backed out of the parking lot and the SUV skidded as we turned onto the two-lane highway.

"Do you want me to drive? I'm used to driving on slippery roads," I offered.

"We have snow in England. I can manage."

"Like once a year. Let me drive, Kit. Really."

"This is a truck. I think it can handle the roads just fine. Better than your little bug."

"But there are things you need to be careful of with a rear-wheel drive."

He ignored me and kept going.

"You are really unpleasant when you're mad." I adjusted the defroster and the speed of the windshield wipers.

We turned down another road that led to Truhart.

"Don't step on the brake when you turn," I said.

Everything would have been fine if Kit hadn't taken his eyes off the road to tell me to mind my own business.

"Watch out!" A large branch lay across the road and he swerved to avoid it.

Several minutes later I stared at a sea of white in front of us and wondered if this night could get any worse.

The world was off-kilter.

And we were in a ditch.

I tried to recover from the shock. Not from the accident, but from the fact that Kit had an unusually broad vocabulary of swearwords. My ears still rang from the string of words he had unleashed when we landed in the ditch.

I shifted uncomfortably. "Do you mind getting off my lap?"

"Are you hurt?"

"I don't think so. But between your driving and your swearing I'll be both paralyzed and deaf before I get out of this truck."

"Shite."

"Are you done cursing?"

"Bugger off, Trudy!"

He braced a hand on the windshield and tried to lift himself from my lap. He winced.

"Are you all right?" I asked.

"Yeah. I just can't move very bloody well." Unfortunately, the way the truck was tilted toward the passenger side, it was impossible for him to take all his weight off me.

I shoved his elbow out of my face. "You shouldn't have removed your seat belt."

"I was trying to open the door so I could get out." Kit fiddled with the door lever.

"Why are you still trying to open the door?" I asked.

"So I can see what can be done about this."

"I'll tell you what can be done about this. We call a tow truck."

He fished his phone out of his coat pocket where he had put it after the dispatcher handed it to him as we were doing paperwork. "It's dead. Yours? Never mind. No cell phone, right?"

"I already heard the speech about being responsible and growing up. Don't start another monologue."

"What a load of rubbish. Who doesn't carry a cell phone these days?"

I kicked him. But as he was squeezed up next to me, the power of my boot was diminished. I shoved him with both hands. "Get off me!"

"I can't. Okay? Your seat belt is in the way. This truck feels like I'm stuck on a waltzer."

"What is a waltzer?"

"You know, that carnival ride with the tilting cars that spin."

"You mean a Tilt-a-Whirl?"

"Are we really having this conversation?"

He was right. My legs were going numb. I might never have the use of them again. "Let me get on the other side of you. I'm lighter."

"Fine."

We struggled to switch positions and my knee landed near his groin as we shifted.

"Ummph! You did that on purpose."

"Ooop—sorry," I said with a satisfied smile. Once we were more comfortable, with me sitting on the high side, I reached over to the dashboard.

"What are you fiddling with now?"

"I'm putting on the hazard lights. And I think this model year comes with an automatic nine-one-one call when there's an accident. Someone will come soon."

"What if they don't?"

He wrote a word that looked like *H-E-L-P* on the foggy window beside him. "Oh, for God's sake, Kit. This is a county road. We aren't going to be stuck in mile-high snowdrifts in the wilderness."

"It happens," he said with a clip to his tone.

"Only in places like Montana or North Dakota. Northern Michigan isn't that kind of place."

"Says a woman who lived here for what? All of one whole year?"

I decided it was best to keep my mouth shut. For the next few minutes we sat, watching our breath cloud up in front of our faces. Kit had cut the engine after the accident. Despite our close proximity, the air felt frigid. I turned on the engine and let the cabin heat for several minutes.

"Don't use up all the gas," he said.

"Ten minutes an hour will be fine. You have half a tank of gas still."

"When did you become such an expert?"

"I know cars. Handling them in emergencies comes with the territory. If the snow were deeper, I'd get out to clear the tailpipe. But it's not." I shut the engine off again. I was feeling downright comfortable for the first time since I had set out in the rain and wind looking for Moby.

"Is that the seat-warmer I feel?" My backside felt quite cozy.

"No. It's me," Kit said. His arm had strayed around my waist because he had nowhere else to put it. I was tired of straining my neck to keep from touching him, so I let it rest on his shoulder. I lost interest in looking for headlights on the road. The cabin had fogged over completely, and I was feeling groggy and comfortable. The anger and bitterness that had saturated the small space just a short time ago was dissolving. Our breathing synced and Kit's hand pulled me closer.

I took the chance that he wasn't mad anymore.

"Kit?" I asked in a small voice.

"Hmmm."

"I'm sorry."

"Hmmm."

I raised my head and looked sideways at him. His eyes were hooded as if he was waiting for something more. "I dragged you into this tonight and it was all my fault you ended up in jail."

He looked away as if he was disappointed by my apology. "Forget about it."

I let my head rest again. "I can't. You were right. I should have taken better care of Moby. He needed more than an occasional meal and a bed. He needed me to do the right thing and give him to someone who could take care of him."

"*You* were taking care of him."

"I don't know how to take care of anyone, Kit."

"That's a piss-poor thing to say."

I sat up and shifted off his lap. "How did a professor get such a colorful vocabulary?"

"Every teenage boy makes it his duty to learn four-letter words. As a student of the English language, I took the job very seriously." He put the arm that had been around me on the back of the seat and lifted his chin. "Don't change the subject."

"I don't remember what we were talking about." I wasn't sure I had the energy to keep any conversation going.

"About you and taking care of things. I am mad because you actually know a lot about nurturing, Trudy. You have a mind like an engineer. You can build stages and create props. Look what you did with the house of horrors."

I pushed myself away from him and felt the warmth leave me.

"And you own a whole wardrobe full of clothes that were made in the last millennium."

"What does that have to do with anything?" I slipped and shifted back to him. It was hard to stay on the high side.

"Clothes don't keep unless you take care of them. You care for your clothes the way a mother cares for her children."

I had never thought about it that way. "I only cared for them because I needed them to last."

"And your car. That crazy old bug that should never in a million years have made it this far across the country . . . you take care of that like it's a baby bird. You practically hand-feed that thing every time you get near it."

He was being overly dramatic.

"You know how to take care of objects, Trudy Brown. Why are you so scared of living things?"

"I don't know," I whispered.

"Come here." Kit pulled me back down into his warm lap and I didn't object. I stared at the white windshield.

"For a guy who spent the first few weeks lying to me, you sure have found your honesty now." My comment was supposed to be sarcastic. But I was very pleased. Kit was honest to a fault now. He didn't know it, but he was just as charming when he dropped the polite act and was himself. More so.

I curled into him and the cab of the SUV felt downright cozy. After several minutes Kit asked, "How did she die?"

I don't know why he asked. Maybe it was always there for him to see. An old wound that I never let heal. I let his question settle in the cold air until I could say the word.

"Cancer."

The white windshield reminded me of her hospital room. White walls. White sheets. Her pale face. "Mom was so busy moving us into our new house in Germany that she put off getting the lump checked out."

"I'm sorry. That must have been really rough." He stroked my hair.

The ticking of the hazard lights blinked off and on. "When she was diagnosed she promised us she would be fine."

"Us?"

"My dad, my brother, and me."

"You don't talk about your brother much."

"Afghanistan. Land mine."

Kit's hand stilled. I didn't want his pity. I didn't want to see the expression on his face. That look that says *You poor, poor thing. They are almost all gone. And now it is just you.*

Then I took a deep breath and relaxed. It wasn't just me. It was hard on everybody.

"My dad lives in New Jersey. He remarried and has two kids. Girls. I have half-sisters." I wasn't completely orphaned.

"Do you see them?"

"I met them once. I was working in a theater in Connecticut and I went down for a weekend. Dad's wife wanted me to come. Get to know my half-sisters. He met her in Korea. She's from there. She's really nice." I kept talking in small sentences. Anything longer made breathing hard.

"You visited just once?"

"Well, they were a new family. I'm not really part of it. I felt . . . weird."

"And the only other relative you had was Aunt Gertrude?"

"Well, now that I think of it, it wasn't so easy on her. She was just really frustrated. I didn't want to learn. And I didn't stick around long enough to let her figure out the problem."

"Ah, yes. The running-away part when you were . . . what?"

"Fifteen. She never actually said I was stupid. She just made me feel that way."

"That's a power you gave her. You didn't have to let her get to you."

"I was fifteen."

"And now you're—what?"

"I get what you're saying." At twenty-seven, maybe it was time to get over my anger. The lightness I felt clutching *Cyrano de Bergerac* yesterday morning wasn't enough. It wasn't just about the books. I had to stop blaming poor brokenhearted Aunt Gertrude for things that were beyond her control. I was tired of being mad at the rest of the world because they could do something I couldn't. No matter how much I would ever work on reading, it would always be a challenge.

I thought about Jenny and her haphazard cheerleading team. The moment they ran out in front of the crowd and began to cheer had terrified me. I didn't want to see them made fun of. But the girls were so brave. What was it Jenny had said? "Don't worry, Miss Trudy. We're used to it."

Maybe I could be that strong. I turned to Kit. "You didn't have to defend me to that jackhammer dude, either. His words didn't hurt me at all."

"He bothered me, though," he said. In the red glow of the blinking hazard lights I could see the tenderness in his expression. He kissed me with a gentleness that made my chest hurt. It was a kiss that held something strong. A gift that I could almost—but not quite—understand.

Kit took off his glasses and studied my face. "Trudy Brown. Do you think you are ready to take responsibility for yourself?"

"Can't I just start with you and Moby?"

"That. Would. Be. Lovely." He kissed me in between each word. His lips moved to my neck. "You take care of me and Moby. We'll help you with the rest."

I understood the feeling that felt like it was ready to burst out of my chest, now. It could be described with a single four-letter word. Not like the ones Kit had used earlier. But one that filled me with such happiness it made me want to scream it to the world. I turned into Kit's lap and wrote the letters with my fingertip on the frosty window behind his head.

Suddenly I was too busy to think. I clung to his jacket and let him trace lines across my shoulder with his lips. Our hands wandered inside each other's clothes, staying warm, and memorizing the feel of each other in the dark.

A light flooded the cab. I shielded my eyes from the brightness and groaned. "We should have turned off the hazard lights."

"I was thinking the same thing," said Kit, giving me a quick kiss.

Doc's voice greeted us from outside. "Hey, you two look like you could use another few minutes."

His flashlight ran along the side window and above Kit's head I could see the outline of the word I wrote under *H-E-L-P*. It was *L-O-V-E*.

Chapter 20

I sat in a chair, watching dawn breaking over Echo Lake. It was a bright morning and the light from the rising sun made the ice and snow-coated trees shimmer. I had never seen anything quite like it.

"You look like Venus with the radiance from the sun in your hair," Kit said from the bed behind me.

I tilted my head back and enjoyed the scenery on the bed as well. He was tousled and sexy, lying in the sheets. "Good morning."

"Up so early?"

"It's such a beautiful morning. I didn't want to miss any of it." I was getting used to early mornings. Last night, I had slept like a baby. The bed had been soft and the pillows felt like—no, they actually *were*—real down. And the warm man beside me felt like he belonged there forever.

Kit rose from the bed and joined me.

"Did last night really happen?" I asked when he lifted me into his lap.

"I think so. I have a piece of paper that says we have an appointment with a judge."

I moaned.

I peeked at the clock on the nightstand. The Furry Friends Rescue Shelter wouldn't open for a couple of hours. It was going to be hard to wait that long.

Last night Doc had pulled the truck out of the ditch for us. He couldn't have been nicer when he found out about Moby and the rest of our horrible evening. "That's about as fine a dog as any I've ever seen, Trudy. Don't worry, no one would let any harm come to him."

I must have looked cold because Doc made me sit in the cab of his tow truck and forced me to eat some of his candy corn while he hooked up Kit's truck and pulled it out of the ditch. I tried not to laugh at Kit as he walked around the truck and attempted to look knowledgeable about ditches and trucks and such. Kit nodded when Doc talked about traction and how to pull the truck out of the ditch. His glasses fogged up in the cold and when he took them off, I knew he couldn't see a thing.

When we finally crashed in his four-poster bed, we were too tired to do anything but fall into an exhausted sleep.

Kit nuzzled my neck and bit my ear. But I was thinking of a dog who was the only thing missing from my perfect morning. "Do you think Moby will be happy to see me?"

"Of course he will," Kit answered, wrapping me in his arms.

"Do you think he'll be mad at me?"

"Why would he be mad?"

"Because I ignored him when he was afraid of the storm. Because I let him down."

He chuckled. "I don't think dogs carry grudges."

"How do you know?"

"I grew up with dogs. They think in very simple ways. Kibble. Petting. Sleeping. Defecating—or pooping, if you prefer. And rabbit."

"Rabbit?"

"Or squirrel, as it is in the States. Whatever happens to be around to chase."

I put my hands on either side of his face and squeezed. "My dog is smarter than that."

"Your dog? I like the way you say that." He pulled my hands away and kissed me.

"Do you think they'll believe he's my dog?"

"I'll vouch for you. And so will Doc. I'm guessing he's already called half the town."

I kicked my feet back and forth impatiently. "I can't wait until ten, Kit."

"Perhaps I can help you pass the time?"

Much later, after we took a shower, I stood in Kit's closet looking for something to wear.

"How can I help you, love?"

I held up a tweed sports coat. "Oh my God! Your clothes even smell wonderful. For once, I don't have a clue where to start."

He helped me with my decision. I borrowed a pair of running leggings, a button-up, and the sports coat with the sleeves rolled up.

When I finished, Kit came out of the bathroom with a towel wrapped around his middle. "You look bloody hot."

Damn. Still not as amazing as him.

When we wandered to the kitchen, he made me coffee and started a pot of oatmeal. A real bed in a real house. Breakfast. I never imagined waking up to such a domestic scene.

The only thing needed to complete the bliss was an old sleeping dog in the corner.

I made my way to the dining room and sat down among all the papers and pictures of Robin Hartchick.

When Kit carried our breakfast in, I was lost in the mystery. "So, other than the Dumpster where the cheerleaders may have tossed it, where do you think the lost manuscript could be?"

He shook his head. "I think she found a way to hide it."

"How?"

"She could have kept it in a secret place. The basement. The rafters. In a floorboard. She might have stored it among all those personal papers that were scattered in the apartment. She might even have typed it up and disguised it to look like something else. Was she tech-savvy? Microfiche and old floppy discs. She could have done a million things with it. But one thing is certain. She did not throw it out."

"How do you know for sure?"

He tensed. "Do you think I'm crazy too?"

I put my hands around his neck and removed his glasses. "Easy, Dr. Darlington. I believe in you. I'm taking care of you, remember?" I used my own version of a cockney accent that made him smile.

His shoulders relaxed. "A woman who turned into a hoarder would not have thrown out a priceless manuscript written by her ex-lover."

Ex-lover. That picture of my aunt as a woman younger than I was now. It made my skin crawl to think of a man like Robin Hartchick using women, riding fame, and of my aunt knowing about his success later on. All his other loves. Never recovering from a pain that happened at such a young age. It was almost haunting.

"Aunt Gertrude could have made millions after Robin Hartchick's death. Your story doesn't explain why she never claimed the lost manuscript."

"It doesn't. But then again, maybe the money didn't motivate her. My guess is that she loved it too much to let it go."

"He sounds like he was a jerk. Does the world really need more Robin Hartchick?"

"He *was* a jerk. But his words were beautiful. They were inspired by your aunt. In some ways I've become more interested in *her* story than Robin's."

"You think his story was about her?"

"It's a real possibility." His shoulders sagged. "But I'm at the end of the search. You have a store to sell." He looked at his watch. "And a dog to claim."

Chapter 21

As soon as I asked about a collie, the young woman behind the counter at the Furry Friends Rescue Shelter smiled. "We've already had five calls this morning. With so many people vouching for you, this shouldn't take too long. But because you never officially registered him, we have to treat this as a new adoption. I hope you understand."

"I do." Heat crept up my neck. She was being very nice, considering my irresponsible behavior. "Can I see him?"

"Sure. There will be paperwork and a fee for last night's boarding. And adoption fees. But I can let you see him now if you want."

She led me down a long corridor. As excited as I was to see Moby, my heart broke for the dogs we passed on the way to Moby's kennel. Some paced and barked repeatedly. Others hung back, too timid and frightened to greet us. Kit followed me and put a hand on my back when I stopped outside Moby's pen. My heart jumped to my throat when I saw him.

He was curled up in the far corner on the hard ground. The woman unlatched the kennel door and I entered. He opened his eyes at the sound of my approaching feet.

I knelt in front of him. "Hi, boy."

He came awake slowly. His tail thumped on the concrete and he struggled to rise on his arthritic hind legs. I reached out to steady him. "I'm here, boy."

He practically fell into my arms. I buried my head in his neck and his body wiggled as he came out of his sleepy haze. I was feeling a million years older than I had just a few months ago, but in my arms Moby transformed into a younger dog, circling around me and barking in rasping, uncontrollable bursts of happiness. He almost knocked me over in his enthusiasm.

From the door, the young woman laughed. "If the phone calls weren't enough, I'd believe your story now. He hasn't acted like this since we brought him in. Even when Miss Lively was here last night."

Moby sniffed and realized that there were others in the kennel. He trotted over to Kit and leaned against his leg for a quick bark before returning to me. I captured him in my arms again, not sure I could let him go.

"Thank you so much for taking care of him." In my mind I also thanked many other people. The ones who called on my behalf. Kit, who stood behind me, grinning at the reunion. My aunt, who wisely left her money to an organization like the Furry Friends Rescue.

Fortunately, the adoption process was quick. Kit stayed with Moby while I took care of the paperwork. Heavyweights like J. D., Sheriff Howe, Marva O'Shea, and even Mayor Bloodworth made the references part easy. I never dreamed I'd have the support of so many Truhart residents. I filled out forms and paid the boarding fee, with Kit's help. I was going to owe him big-time by the end of the day. Moby had been neutered long ago by some responsible owner, so all he needed was a visit to the vet to get rabies shots, a license, and a microchip, which was my decision. I promised to do all that first thing Monday morning.

Moby walked out with a slip lead around his neck provided by the shelter. But we stopped at a pet-supply store in Gaylord on the way home. Moby came in with us and we wandered the aisles looking for the right collar and leash. Everywhere we walked, people commented on our beautiful dog. Kit acknowledged it in his British accent and more than a few comments about Lassie and herding sheep in Scotland followed. Kit took it in with good humor.

We bought a leash, a bone, and a new bowl. I even purchased a collar and had a kind salesgirl make a dog tag for him for free. On it was printed the name *Moby*, my name, and my cell phone number. The one I was going to dig out of my rucksack and charge as soon as I got back to the bookshop.

When the tag was done, I held the collar up and prepared to place it around Moby's neck. "You know what this means, don't you?"

He sat at my feet and raised his chin. Waiting. As if he sensed the gravity of the moment. Warmth spread across my chest. I bent down on one knee and looked him squarely in the eye.

Thinking back at my vow of not owning a living thing, I realized how silly I had been. I had completely missed the point. It wasn't about ownership. It was about belonging together. It came with responsibility, but it was about love.

I slipped the collar around Moby's neck. His tail thumped again and I laughed.

Someone behind me clapped. Another person joined in. Before I knew it, a small crowd stood around us, clapping and laughing at the way Moby was attacking me with his tongue. I was on my backside. Happy to let him run all over me in his excitement. Through a haze of fur, I saw Kit standing over us. His eyes were bright with moisture. There was more that remained to making things better. But I had time.

For now, I had a dog.

It was early afternoon when Kit, Moby, and I made our way back to Truhart. The day was cloudy and brisk. The snow and ice had melted into large puddles that made the truck muddy, but the roads much better.

We drove down the center of Truhart. A new orange street sign read the new temporary name of Main Street: Autumn Lane. Someone had been busy, repairing all the damage done to the Halloween decorations. The scarecrows and the spiderwebs were back in place. And a line of people stretched all the way around the block to get into the house of horrors. When we pulled into the alley I heard a chorus of moans and screams coming from inside the old grocery store. Hopefully, the community center committee was making lots of money for their dream.

Kit stopped the truck in front of the Dumpster. The blue tarp waved in the wind.

"What's that?"

I pushed Moby out of my lap and shrugged.

Kit got out of the truck and I helped Moby down. Kit walked into the delayed headlight beams and inspected the tarp. All that remained from the night before was a fine layer of water in the corners that would come off with a good shake-out. He reached up and yanked on a rope. It was securely tied. All the years of working summer stock had taught me the value of wrapping tarps around props and stage equipment in order to protect them from the elements.

"Wasn't this on Lulu?"

I shrugged. "What's a little snow and ice? She's tougher than she looks."

The smile on Kit's face when he turned toward me was as bright as the sunshine behind his golden head. I grabbed the bag from the pet-supply store and Moby's leash.

I was almost at the back door of the store when Kit grabbed the frame and stopped me. "You did that for me?"

I fumbled with the doorknob and pushed past him into the book-shop. "I was so busy getting that tarp on that I didn't notice how scared Moby was. That's how I lost him."

Kit closed the door. "If you hate books, why did you bother covering the Dumpster?"

"You love books." I released Moby's leash and grabbed his new bowl from the bag. I didn't look at Kit as I poured an extra-large heap of dog food. I added a little warm water to soften it, and placed it in front of Moby. "If some old book is so bleeding important to you, then you should have the chance to find it."

Moby attacked his dog food and I peeked at Kit from the corner of my eye. His head was cocked at an angle and his eyes watched me intently. His earlier smile had been transformed to something else. Something speculative. Something that made me nervous and happy at the same time. For once, I had done something right.

"You decided all that even before last night?"

I grinned and leaned against the stair rail.

"What about the store? You could still sell it to Reeba Sweeney's pawn client and make enough to get a head start on your trip."

I played with the bannister. "She's a bully. She doesn't care what happens to Truhart."

"And you do?"

"She wants to control everything here. I hear she's trying to get the Amble Inn to sell to a casino group."

"But what about Angkor Wat?"

"I'm still going to make that trip. Someday." I could feel his eyes scrutinizing my face. "There's really no rush. I have a dog, you know. And I have you to watch out for. Besides, Angkor Wat is even more run-down than Truhart. Who's to say that one empty ghost town is better than the other?"

Kit walked toward me in a slow stride. Before he could say anything I started up the stairs. "I need to get out of these wet boots. They don't really work with your royal duds I'm wearing."

"You are a bit of a fake, you know that?" Kit said, following me to the bedroom.

"What?"

"You are a fake."

I lifted my chin and crossed my arms. "Says the man who pretended to study birds?"

He leaned against the doorframe and watched me balance on one foot as I changed into a pair of Converse sneakers. "I'm working on that pretending thing. I'm not always good at being honest with myself."

"You're not that bad. I was furious when I called you a liar, Professor. You've actually come a long way since then."

"I'm trying. Your mother talked about walking in other people's shoes? Sometimes I think I spend too much time in other people's shoes."

I stood up from tying my laces. "You?" I wasn't used to seeing him second-guess himself. I crossed the room to stand in front of him.

He started to adjust his glasses, then he thought better and removed them. He looked younger now. "As a professor of literature, I get too caught up in other people's stories. Sometimes I need to remember to live my own story."

"You *are* rather obsessed with other people's words."

"Is it that obvious?" He seemed so vulnerable when he asked me that. I almost loved him more for his insecurity.

"Hmmm. I'm trying to imagine how *your* story would go. The one you make for yourself using your own words, Professor."

He pulled me close. His voice was husky. "It would be about a man and a woman. And it would have a happy ending. Perhaps you would be willing to help me write it?" My knees were suddenly weak and I reached out to him to keep from losing my balance. He grabbed me and held on.

I stared at his strong hand, a lump forming in my throat.

This was a man who never laughed at me when I screwed up my

words. A man who cared about me even when I put hot sauce on his Dinty Moore or wielded a broom that landed us in jail.

"I'm not sure I'm good at writing," I said in a shaky voice.

"You can dictate to me, then." I was terrified of what came next. But I wanted to find out. In the worst way. I lifted my chin and met his blue gaze.

"I love you, Trudy." Four simple words. Hearing them was terrifying. But I was braver than I had been just a few short months ago.

I took a deep breath and let the words come. They turned out to be the easiest words I ever spoke (or wrote).

"I love you too, Kit."

Chapter 22

On the morning of October 31, Kit and I entered the 88th District Courthouse in Alpena. Our lawyer, Flo's brother-in-law, Jacob Tipman, had already recorded our side of the story and presented a document to the judge. He wasn't sure if he could get the case dismissed. But he felt confident that the judge might be amenable to reducing the charges.

Kit looked dashing in his gray wool pants, tweed blazer, and narrow silk tie. I, however, felt dressed for Halloween in a pencil skirt and silk blouse borrowed from Elizabeth Lively. She insisted that nothing in my wardrobe, including my tapestry coat and oversized sweaters, would be appropriate in court.

I wore shiny high-heeled pumps that I found in Aunt Gertrude's closet. They were stylishly retro. Aunt Gertrude would probably laugh to know I was wearing them to my own arraignment. Fate.

In my aunt's shoes and Elizabeth's skirt, my long shanks felt like they went on forever. Judging by the way Kit kept eying my calves, he didn't seem to mind the brevity. The clerk behind the desk must have felt the same. His eyes were glued to my legs as I entered the courtroom. Instead of defending me from the ogling eyes of a stranger, Kit actually winked at me.

We took a seat in the gallery and waited.

Over the past week I had tried my best to block out the upcoming arraignment. Jacob said that we would most likely pay a fine. But he couldn't rule out the possibility of a trial. The worst punishment was Kit's burden. He could lose his visiting-professor status at the University of Michigan in January. Even worse, he could lose his visa. When I asked him if he was worried, he kissed me and told me that he had never felt better. But I caught him on the phone with the university and the consulate twice. I didn't realize I was fidgeting until Kit put a hand on my knee.

The clerk spoke loudly. "All rise for the honorable Judge Alice Sweeney."

My heart sunk like a rock in Echo Lake. So much for my new tactic of impressing the judge with my shapely calves. "He" was a "she."

Even worse, "she" was short, squat, and the spitting image of Reeba Sweeney. I almost fell off my aunt's heels when I saw her walk out the back door and take a seat behind a large desk. Kit stiffened as well. But then I looked closer. There were subtle differences in the shape of her face and nose. The real giveaway was the fact that her eyes showed no recognition when she saw us.

Sisters? Twins? I was going to face a Reeba Sweeney clone. My relief was replaced with nervousness. Was Reeba vindictive enough to complain about me to her sister?

Two defendants were called to the bench first. I was surprised how quickly their cases were heard and subsequent trial dates were set. Jacob had warned us that an arraignment was not a trial. Things moved quickly in the arraignment process.

When it was our turn, Kit and I were asked to stand before Judge Sweeney together. I was surprised to find my knees shaking. Kit took my hand as the judge read the charges.

"Do you understand your rights—"

A commotion broke out from the back of the courtroom. Judge Sweeney's mouth dropped open as she stared at something over my shoulder. She took off her glasses and turned to the clerk. "What . . . is . . . that . . . in the back of my courtroom, Levi?"

I turned around and saw four familiar figures sitting in the back row. They waved when they saw us. Kit's shoulders started shaking as much as my knees had a moment ago. I squeezed his hand and sent him a warning.

The bailiff scanned the group several times, collecting his thoughts. Finally he said, "Your Honor, I see a ghost, a lunatic, a zombie, and a . . . I think it is a clown. But not like any I've ever seen."

"That's what I thought." The judge rubbed her eyes and replaced her glasses.

"Uh, it *is* Halloween, Your Honor."

"So it is." She put a hand over the paperwork in front of her and looked at the ceiling, attempting to guess. "And don't tell me: The defendants are from Truhart."

"Correct. At least temporarily."

She sighed and shook her head. I thought I heard her mumble, "Of course; Truhart," under her breath. Then her lip curled in the corner and she began to laugh. When she recovered, she finished reading the document. Then she looked at me. "I have information from your attorney along with the report from the dispatcher, Bernie Parker. You lost your dog?"

"Yes, I—" I faltered until Kit squeezed my hand. "Uh . . . Yes, Your Honor." Another squeeze. We were doing pretty well with hand-squeeze communication.

"And it says here that Judge Hamner was in a rush to get to his leadership-appreciation banquet. It was the night of the storm. And there was a misunderstanding?"

"Yes, that is correct, Your Honor," said Kit.

Her eyes rose from the report in her hand. She shuffled the papers in front of her, looking for something. When she found it, she said to Kit, "You're British!"

"Yes, Your Honor."

"He's a lord!" Marva called from the back of the room.

Judge Sweeney put a hand to her lip to silence her. Then she smiled at Kit again. "Where are you from in England?"

"My family home is in Knightsbridge. But I recently resided near Cambridge, where I am a professor."

"England." She stapled her fingers together and took a long breath. "I love *Downton Abbey*. I hope to visit the real castle next year. Is that close to Knightsbridge?"

I watched as the judge practically melted in Kit's presence. Who had I been fooling, to think that my considerably nice clothes and long legs might sway a judge, male or female? Kit was the master. I had almost forgotten about his buttery British voice that had ladies swooning across Harrison County.

Judge Sweeney and Kit had a short discussion about *Downton Abbey*. I had no idea what they were talking about. Something about a lord from England marrying an American with money. I was pretty sure Kit's accent grew thicker as he amped up the charm.

From the back of the room, Marva excitedly chimed in, "Ask him if he has met the queen."

That brought the judge back to the present. She put a finger in the air and admonished Marva. "No talking in this courtroom unless I request a response." The clerk, remembering his job, called for silence.

Judge Sweeney pressed her lips together and frowned at her paperwork. After a moment, she asked Kit to approach the stand. They spoke in hushed voices. I held my fist to my mouth and tried not to laugh as she asked him if he actually *had* met the queen. When they finished, he stepped backwards until he was next to me again. Then she was all business again.

"Dr. Darlington, you are aware that if you commit a crime in the United States, you are subject to all the laws and potential punishments that apply in this country?"

Kit ran a hand around his collar. "I understand, Your Honor."

She focused on me next. "Ms. Brown. You were the one holding the broom."

Glad to have the opportunity to talk, I said, "The floor was filthy, Your Honor." Behind me, Corinne snorted.

"Hmm. So you were cleaning when Judge Hamner was . . . ah . . . swept off his feet?"

I stole a glance at Jacob Tipman. He stared straight ahead. I wasn't sure what to say. "Things were . . . messy."

"Your family has donated a considerable sum to the Furry Friends Rescue Shelter."

"That was my great-aunt Gertrude."

"She was a generous woman. That is a very good cause."

She glanced back at her paperwork. I held my breath as Her Honor examined Mr. Tipman's document and the original report. "Did you find your dog?"

"Yes. He's mine now. At first I didn't think I should own any living thing. Until I realized how wrong I was. We should all belong to ea—"

Kit's elbow connected with my ribs. "It was a bit of a personal lesson for Trudy. She's got it all figured out now."

I reached for his hand and nodded. "Especially the part about belonging."

Judge Sweeney removed her glasses and turned to the recorder. "Why don't you strike that last part, Levi."

Then she gazed around the room. "I fail to see any reason why this has to be drawn out in court and waste taxpayers' dollars. Your lawyer has issued an apology on your behalf. Judge Hamner made it to his . . . roast." She said the words with disdain. "I am reducing this to an infraction. You can pay a fee of one hundred dollars to the county clerk. The incident will appear on local police records, but nothing else. No further course of action is needed."

A cheer went up behind us. I threw my arms around Kit and gave him a giant kiss. Then realizing where I was, I pulled away. Judge Sweeney leaned forward with her hands on her desk. "Take that outside, Ms. Brown."

"Sorry, Your Honor. Sorry."

Kit led me away and I wobbled out of the courtroom on Aunt Gertrude's heels.

Later, when we paid the county clerk for the fine, the clerk leaned down and whispered in my ear, "You're lucky you had Judge Sweeney. Sweeney hates that leadership dinner. Refuses to attend every year until they include a vegetarian option on the menu. She's an animal lover and a vegan, don't you know. . . ."

We lingered at the courthouse long enough to thank Jacob Tipman, Flo, Corinne, Elizabeth, and Marva for coming to the arraignment and supporting us. Then we followed the small cavalcade of trucks and SUVs back to Truhart. The house of horrors was due to open its doors for a few short hours before trick-or-treating, and a bonfire was scheduled at the public beach later. Beer, pizza, marshmallows, and vegan chili—in my honor—were being served. It might not be much of a town, but Truhart had a way with celebrations that made a person feel right at home.

We drove Kit's truck down the two-lane county road. "You thought you had Judge Sweeney in the palm of your hand with that cheesy accent," I teased.

He wiggled his eyebrow and said, "Why would a bloke like me do such a cheeky thing?"

"Ha! It turns out the day was saved by the animal lovers of the world. Not the Anglo—anglopeels."

"Anglophiles?"

"That's what I said."

I tickled his neck and kissed him on the cheek, careful not to distract him from his driving. "I love you, Kit. Even when you think you're best friends with the queen."

"I love you too, Trudy. Even when you try to play sexy in heels that you can't walk in."

We took advantage of every stop sign and red light on the way to Truhart to show each other how great our love was.

I had been so sidetracked by giddy relief that I didn't realize we were in front of Books from the Hart until Kit cut the engine. Someone tapped on the windshield and hollered, "Is everyone all right in there?"

I lifted my head from Kit's neck.

"We're here," he said.

"Back where I started." I gazed up at the old building, feeling nothing but pride in the way it had been fixed up. I thought of that first morning in Truhart and my introduction to many of the people I had grown to care about. Life had a funny sense of humor.

That's when I saw Lulu.

She was parked in the no-parking zone, directly across the street from us. "What—"

Kit beamed at me, as if he'd been keeping the secret for too long. "Happy birthday, love—"

I was out of the truck and tripping on my aunt's heels before he could say more.

Lulu looked fabulous. Her chrome was polished, her newly waxed body shone. Even the sidewalls of her tires gleamed in the sunshine. Doc stood on the sidewalk beside her, dangling my Pikachu keychain from his index finger. "Check her out."

I let my hand trail over Lulu, opening the trunk, inspecting everything, and asking Doc all sorts of questions about what he had done to the engine. Finally I stepped away. "How did you do this?"

Doc lifted his chin and nodded to where Kit stood, casually leaning against his truck with his arms crossed. Moby sat next to Kit, now, wagging his tail and happy to be attached by a leash that had an official license on the collar. "Dr. Darlington had me and Vance take care of everything. A new cylinder and valve and a little extra TLC. She drives like a charm, now. Backwards and forwards."

Doc placed the keys in the palm of my hand. "Take her for a ride."

I opened the door. The black cat jumped from underneath the car.

Moby erupted in a series of high-pitched barks and led Kit across the street. The cat disappeared into the brush. "Sorry I scared your cat, Doc."

He scratched his head and looked at me. "My cat's a ginger tom-cat."

That was strange. Maybe Aunt Gertrude's old cat, Piewacket, had a daughter.

I clutched Pikachu and stood with all the loves of my life, wondering if things could ever get better than this.

But they could. Eagerly, I opened the back door.

Together Kit and I lifted Moby into the backseat. Kit walked around to the passenger door and grinned across at me.

He was making all my dreams come true. I wished I could do the same for him. But the bookshop was empty now. We had spent the last week searching the Dumpster and the store. No sign of a lost manuscript. Kit said he didn't mind. But I felt badly.

I threw the pumps in the backseat with Moby. I couldn't stop smiling as I stared at Kit over Lulu's roof. "Thank you."

He lifted his shoulders. "No thanks necessary." He ducked his head and folded his considerable height into the passenger seat.

When I started the engine, she purred like a newborn kitten. Lulu hadn't sounded this good since California. Maybe even since my brother bought her all those years ago.

I rolled down the window and waved. "Thanks, Doc."

He leaned down. "Now be careful, honey. You haven't backed up for a long time. Don't forget to check the rearview mirror. It makes life a lot easier if you can see clearly. Where you're going *and* where you've been."

"I will!"

Looking in the rearview mirror, I could see that Autumn Lane was empty now. Everyone was getting ready for a busy afternoon and evening. I shifted Lulu into reverse and we traveled backwards the full length of Autumn Lane.

"Are we going to travel the whole way in reverse?" Kit looked as comfortable in Lulu as an elephant in a closet. But he was smiling nonetheless.

I shifted into park and revved the smooth engine. "Sorry. It's just so nice to be able to back up."

The sun was moving low in the sky and I flipped down the visor. Something new was there. A postcard of Truhart was paper-clipped next to the brochure of Angkor Wat. A sticky note on the postcard read *Come back and visit us too! Love, Mac.*

I smiled. Mac had been bored serving people he didn't know at the Grande Lucerne. He was back at the diner twice a week. Happy to flip burgers and grill tofu for his friends.

I put a hand on the postcard. "I love this town."

Kit was busy adjusting the seat. "It looks like you might need to have Doc fix the seat adjustment."

I scrunched down to see what was wrong.

"That's not the problem. This is in the way." I pulled out Aunt Gertrude's copy of *Moby-Dick* and handed it to Kit.

He read the spine and sent me a puzzled glance. "What are you doing with a book in your car? I thought you hated reading."

"Don't get all excited. I still do. That was Aunt Gertrude's. She had it when she died and I just couldn't throw it away. She kept it with her wherever she went. Go figure. A book about a whale . . ."

I stopped, unable to finish. My mouth went dry. For a long moment Kit and I stared at each other.

"Do you think . . . ?" How could I have forgotten about the book? All this time it had padded the distance between the seats on the ride from California to Michigan.

Kit turned the book over, examining the worn black cloth binding. He removed his glasses and swallowed several times before he managed to speak. "This . . . this should start with *Call me Ishmael . . .*"

Slowly, he opened the cover and turned the blank pages until he reached the place where the words began. His hands were trembling. His face was pale.

He cleared his throat and tried to speak. His voice was hoarse. "Trudy . . . I can't—"

I grabbed his hand in mine. "It's okay. I'll read it with you."

Together we started:

"The setting sun is like the love of a woman. She'll find her most beautiful light at the end of the day and remind you why you loved her. The memory of that one perfect moment will remain with you throughout your life. And so it was for a man and a woman in a town at the corner of a dark forest on the edge of the world gone slightly mad."

We sat in Lulu's silent interior until Moby's head came between us, taking turns licking our faces.

When Kit lifted his head, the world was in his eyes. I held out the finger I had used to read the page and caught a tear sliding down his cheek. "You seem to have found your lost manuscript, my lord. Are you happy?"

He pulled my finger to his lips. "You read it with me."

I didn't understand why that was important. "It's the lost manuscript."

"It is. But you read it with me, love."

"You read most of it. I don't read so well."

"I know. But I'm honored just the same. You reading it. It was fitting."

I didn't read a lot of things right. Not just books. I didn't always read people and places right either. Not everyone in Truhart thought I was crazy or stupid. Maybe I just let myself think they did because it was easier than trying to understand them. Or to explain myself. And my aunt was just an eccentric, lonely woman. She didn't know how to deal with a rebellious teenage girl like me.

Kit stared down at the book in his lap. "Bloody hell. I can't think of what happens next."

"It appears we have a priceless Robin Hartchick manuscript." I couldn't resist adding something on behalf of Aunt Gertrude. "Cared for by a woman who loved him. A woman he didn't deserve."

He grinned and kissed me. I grabbed the pictures from the visor and stuffed them in the book. "Bookmark that page. We'll read more together later."

Our story was more important to both of us. The one that had a dog. And a handsome man. And a funny little town. And a girl who belonged to all of them.

Our story was just beginning.

I shifted into *drive* and put my foot on the pedal.

The open road was ahead of us.

Author's Note:

Millions of people around the world suffer from some form of dyslexia. While dyslexia is a learning disorder that affects people to varying degrees, it has absolutely no bearing on intelligence. In fact many of the world's greatest minds have suffered from dyslexia. Trudy was diagnosed late in her life, but early intervention is the most successful way parents and teachers can help reduce the long-term impact of dyslexia.

For more information, contact The International Dyslexia Association, (eida.org).

The Bookshop on Autumn Lane is a work of fiction. However, it was inspired by the real life lost manuscripts of Ernest Hemingway. In 1922, while on assignment in Switzerland, Hemingway asked his then wife, Elizabeth Hadley Richardson, to bring his promising, and as yet unpublished, manuscripts to Lausanne so that he could show them to an interested editor. Hadley packed everything—carbons and originals—into a valise and boarded a train for Switzerland. Once settled on the train, she stowed her valise and went to buy water before the train left the station. When she returned, the valise was nowhere to be found. Among the missing manuscripts was an early version of Hemingway's *Nick Adams Stories* that were set in Michigan. He once said the lost manuscripts were some of his best work.

Did you miss Elizabeth and J. D.'s story? Keep reading for a special excerpt of *Skinny Dipping Season,* and a summer that changes everything.

I took another sip. And another.

The last few weeks had been a living hell. But now I was in the middle of nowhere. Not a single soul could bother me. Wiping the wine dribble from my lower lip, I moved into the living room. My insides were warming up and I let my hips sway. I reached for the knob on the radio and turned up the volume. Taking my bottle with me, I went in search of matches.

I lost track of time. A happy glow was spreading upwards through my chest. I caught the beat of the music and twirled around and around, dancing from the kitchen to the living room.

Before I knew it, the bottle was almost empty and the butts of two cigarettes rested in a piece of foil I had turned into an ashtray. Everything was spinning and the room around me was bathed in a fuzzy radiance. A rap song played on the radio, and even though I had absolutely no idea what the words were, I danced to the beat with a passion that Colin, my *ex*, would say I had never been able to exhibit in bed.

I held my cigarette up, ready to attempt my first twerk, when I heard a loud pounding at the window. I froze with my bottom sticking straight out.

A beam of light distorted an image on the other side of the pane, making it look like a monster. Suddenly, the fact that I was alone in the middle of the woods wasn't such a great thing.

I opened my mouth to scream. But it was like a bad horror movie. Nothing came out. A hand pounded on the window again, almost shattering it.

I lowered everything—the bottle, the cigarette, and the ridiculous pose I had been attempting—and finally found my vocal cords. My bloodcurdling scream cut through the bass of the music and gave me the energy to move. I set down the bottle and smashed the butt of the cigarette into the foil wrapper. I tried to remember where my phone was.

Bumping into the ledge of the table, I almost lost my footing. My cell phone was on the counter where I had left it earlier. I grabbed it, praying that there was some sort of cellular service up here.

The pounding increased. Making a split-second decision and hoping I wasn't being rash, I dialed 911, and reached for the volume on the radio. I heard the bored-sounding voice of a woman on the other end. I didn't even let her finish her introductory message. "I think someone is trying to break in!"

There was a pause. "Can you tell me the address?"

What was the address? I didn't even know that. I knew how to get here. Where to turn at the fork in the road where the *Fire Danger* sign stood. But I had little else.

"It's my grandmother's house. Doris Blodget. She used to live here. Crooked Road." From the other room I heard the footsteps on the back porch. No one knew I was here. The house had been empty for years.

"Hurry."

"Ma'am, you need to stay calm."

Were these the fatal last words that every murder victim was forced to hear?

"Easy for you to say." I cradled the phone in my neck and started to open drawers, looking for a weapon.

I could hear a man shouting from outside.

The lady raised her voice. "There is an officer on the way, ma'am."

I grabbed the only weapon I could find, a soup ladle, and peered around the corner of the kitchen.

The pounding had moved to the front door. A deep voice shouted, "Harrison County Sheriff's Department!"

I dropped the phone and tiptoed to the door.

"Lady! Can you hear me? Sheriff's Department," came the muffled voice through the door.

I reached for the doorknob. The sweat on my palms made it difficult to turn the handle. I pulled the door open just enough to be able to see who was on the other side.

The shadows and a red glare behind him obscured his face and all I could see was a vaporized cloud of breath disappearing in the cool night air between us.

"Yes?" I croaked.

"Sheriff's Department."

A badge appeared and there was a moment of silence. "The badge isn't part of a Halloween costume, in case you were wondering . . ."

A strange moment of clarity hit me and my fear turned into something equally painful. I looked over the dark outline at an SUV with blinking red lights.

"Can I come in?" he asked.

Since my arrest in March I had learned a few things about my rights. Things I should have remembered from my high-school civics class. I didn't have to let law enforcement search my vehicle or my house. "Why?" I asked.

"I just want to check—"

"Do you have a warrant?"

I heard him shift restlessly. "Look, lady, you've got—"

"I know my rights and you can't come in without a warrant."

"But—"

"You might look scary and tough, but I won't be bullied." I attempted to close the door, but a hand snaked out and grabbed my own.

"I don't think you understand—"

Something tickled at my nose, but I was too busy trying to smash his hand with the soup ladle to consider it. He was way out of line trying to barge in like this.

Boom! The door burst open, trapping me against the wall in the process. "Hey!"

This was definitely in violation of my rights.

I moved the door out of my way and felt a surge of anger. The man stomped up and down in the middle of the living room. His actions were so strange that I stopped protesting and watched him in confusion. A tiny spark disappeared under his boots and smoke rose from the floor. He put down his flashlight, reached for my bottle of wine, and poured the remaining contents on the carpet. A billowing fog of steam rose up.

"I was drinking that!"

He turned around and our eyes locked. "I'll make sure to mention that in my report," he said.

I looked at a spot in the rug that now sported a nice-sized black hole that was almost the same color as his eyes. It dawned on me that the cigarette must have landed on the rug.

"Well, I didn't realize—" I bit my lip. What an idiot I was. "All you had to do was explain."

"I tried. In between showing you my badge and using your precious bottle as a fire hose. . . ." He brought it to his nose. "What is this stuff? Cough syrup?"

"That is good wine."

He looked at the price sticker and raised his eyebrow. "Obviously."

He set down the bottle. "I've seen too many fires caused by a single spark from a cigarette. That makes the fact that I entered this house to ensure your safety perfectly legal. Look it up."

I struggled for something to say. "You—you could have told me."

"It takes a long time for fire trucks to reach this road and there isn't a lot of time for a—" My cell phone chimed a Disney theme song from the floor where I had dropped it.

His mouth tilted and he must have recognized the song. "Your fairy godmother is calling you," he said in a snarky voice that was completely unnecessary.

I picked up the phone and accepted the call. "Are you all right, ma'am?" As the dispatcher spoke, the officer stepped closer. I was painfully aware of him towering over me. My eyes traveled over him, taking in the hard body underneath the dark jacket, and the badge that he still held.

"I don't suppose you could send someone else?" I asked the dispatcher.

He narrowed his eyes and I added, "Never mind . . . Everything is fine. Thanks."

The dispatcher sounded amused when she hung up. Great . . . I was about to be the newest joke in the county.

I must have looked ready to fall over because Officer Smug took my arm and lowered me to a sitting position on the springless couch. Then he moved about the room, double-checking the house and looking at the boxes against the wall.

"At least my ears have stopped ringing," he said a moment later. "I don't know what was louder, your music or your screaming. What was that thing you were doing?"

I wrapped my hands around my waist and mumbled, "It was a twerk."

"A what?"

"A twerk," I said louder.

He stifled a laugh with a phony cough. "Is that something like an itch?"

I did not appreciate his sense of humor.

He came back to me and leaned down, examining me more closely. The muscles on his square jaw tightened, and then he compressed his lips and did something surprising. He removed his coat and tucked it, still warm from his own body, around my shoulders. I blinked. I must have been shaking. I almost thanked him for his kindness. But I stayed mute as heat burned a path to my face.

For someone who had been so dangerous just minutes ago, this man was now—well, terrifying in a new way.

The lines of his face were chiseled, and his dark, close-cut wavy hair fell across his forehead. He had charcoal eyes and hawklike brows that watched me as if I were a field mouse. A shadow of dark stubble was starting on the lower half of his face. He was probably one of those men who couldn't go a day without shaving, especially if he was supposed to look like one of the good guys. And his broad shoulders were so wide they blocked the light from the ceiling.

Why was I thinking like this? I struggled to find my equilibrium. It had been natural to be scared when I saw him at the window. He could have played a serial killer on TV—the kind who seduced, then killed. Perhaps some women might be attracted to that, but I was more accustomed to clean-cut, preppy men.

He stared as if he was trying to figure out how he was going to deal with a crazy lady like me. The sound of the furnace kicking in again broke the silence.

"Let's start over, shall we? I'm Deputy Sheriff J. D. Hardy. We received a report of a light on here. I don't suppose you want to explain why you're having your own personal party inside a vacant house?"

"Not really." I didn't want to tell him about the events that blew my world apart and the reason I had run away from my former life. Clutching the coat he placed around my shoulders, I tilted my chin down and inhaled, noting the scent of pine and something else I couldn't name.

"Your weapon, although unique, isn't exactly banned," he said, gesturing to the soup ladle I still clutched. "But you are trespassing on private property."

I was only too happy to prove him wrong. "This house belonged to my grandmother—well, my parents now."

"And your name is. . . ."

"Elizabeth Lively. "

"Okay, Beth. You know I am going to need to have that verified."

"Elizabeth. My license is—"

He turned back to the kitchen before I could say a word. Taking in the empty bottle of wine now on the table near my knees and the way he had found me, I realized how this looked.

"I left a message with the real-estate agent to let him know I would be staying here for a while. You can call him to confirm it. The name is on the *For Sale* sign leaning against the side of the house," I explained.

"Yeah. I know him." He held up my purse and seemed to weigh it and shift it, making sure there was nothing dangerous inside. "Can I look for identification or do I need a warrant?" I couldn't figure out if he was trying to be funny or not.

"I'll get it for you."

He watched closely as I put down the soup ladle and sifted through the contents of my large designer purse. Three bottles of hand sanitizer and a package of sanitizing towelettes, sealed facial cleansing wipes, two packs of facial tissues, a clear plastic bag with safety pins, a pack of Band-Aids . . . With every item I shifted around, I felt my face grow hotter. By the time I got to my large wallet, with pockets for change, credit cards, a calendar, a checkbook, and female hygiene products, his mouth was pinching at the corners. It wasn't that strange. Many girls carried this much in their purse. Finally, I removed my driver's license and he picked up his radio from the floor nearby. He made the brief phone call to verify my story.

Taking advantage of the time to pull myself together again, I brought my hands up to my head and tried to smooth my tangled hair. Nobody had been killed, or fired, or ruined. As difficult as this situation was, it was a minor bump in the scheme of things. Especially as it related to the past few months. This could all be fixed. Simple embarrassment was something I was beyond these days. I would explain everything and all would be forgiven.

And then I could be alone again. The thought made me want to cry. My stomach gurgled its agreement.

"It looks like you are who you say you are," Officer Hardy said as he reattached his radio to his belt.

I stared at his chins. Why were there two, suddenly? "It is really just a misunderstanding. I thought you were—"

"Are you planning on staying here very long, Miss Lively? Or is it Mrs.?"

"Miss. I am here for a while." I lifted my shoulders. "I just arrived this afternoon. I don't even drink, really, and I was only doing this ridiculous kind of—well, rebellion, actually . . ."

My voice trailed off. He had slowly lowered himself to one knee. His broad shoulders were at eye level and I resisted the temptation to reach out and touch them so the room would stop spinning.

"This is a nice, quiet kind of town, Miss Lively. We like to keep it that way. If you have a problem with alcohol or any other substance, AA meets every Friday night at a local church."

I swallowed, feeling like a child. "You were banging on the window. It scared me to death. You could have knocked on the front door."

"I did. But you didn't hear me."

I refused to let him see my embarrassment. I had some dignity after all. I pulled his coat from my back, involuntarily inhaling the scent one more time before offering it to him. He took it and dragged it back on and his biceps were momentarily outlined underneath his shirt.

Blinking and looking away, I gestured to the black spot on the floor. "I wouldn't have dropped the cigarette if you hadn't scared me like that."

"All you had to do was answer the door."

I couldn't meet his eyes.

"So while you are looking up the local AA chapter in the directory tomorrow, you might want to check out fire extinguishers too."

A strange feeling overtook me as my stomach rolled over. I wasn't under arrest and with any luck I would never run into this man again. Sure, in the brightness of the light coming from the bare bulb in the ceiling, he managed to look normal and well . . . almost attractive. But earlier it was easy to mistake him for a beast.

Using the last of my draining energy, I stood up and stumbled on my way to the front door. My nerves were frayed and my confidence was deflating by the moment. Not knowing how one was supposed to handle formalities when asking a cop to leave, I reached for the knob. "Thank you for stopping by. I'd like to say it has been a pleasure . . ."

He broke into a caustic smile that was both cruel and strangely appealing. "Have an enjoyable evening doing whatever it was you were doing."

I narrowed my gaze.

Then he leaned in. "Your dancing was fine, but I wouldn't quit your day job."

He said the wrong thing. "M—my dancing may not be any good, but your manners are deplorable."

He was already through the door. He turned on the front step and his face was lost in the shadows.

"I remember Truhart having a nice sheriff," I continued. "I can't imagine what anyone was thinking to put you in charge."

He stepped slowly into the light and a wide smile spread across his face. The hair on the back of my neck stood up and my stomach did somersaults as bile rose in my throat. Why was I having this reaction?

Just then, a breeze blew the stench of the cheap wine and singed carpet my way. I looked at him, wondering if I should warn him.

But it was too late.

The wine and cigarettes were mounting a rebellion all their own. And they were doing it all over Officer Hardy's boots.

CYNTHIA
TENNENT

Skinny Dipping Season

A TRUHART ROMANCE

Keep reading for an excerpt from Cynthia Tennent's first Truhart romance, *A Wedding in Truhart.*

Chapter 1

We were late to the dinner party and I was crushed between my great-aunt and my mother in the backseat of a battered taxi stuck in the slow lane.

"Is my bra twisted, Annie? Something feels like it has a hold on my left bosom and it can't be a man!" The setting sun glared off Aunt Addie's purplish gray hair. I never should have let her dye her own hair last week.

"Let me see what's going on." I shifted my position in the sweltering cab and cringed as I lost a layer of skin on the vinyl seat. Opening the back of my aunt's dress, I took a look at the massive brassiere that was surely more complicated than a seventy-six-year-old woman needed. "You're caught up in the sleeve. Give me a moment to fix this."

"Take your time, my dear. That air is like heaven on my back. Who in their right mind would live in a city that feels like a furnace?"

Our taxi driver convulsively stepped on the brakes and all three of us lurched forward as we crawled through seven lanes of rush-hour traffic on I-75 in Atlanta. I dodged Aunt Addie's head and Mom's shoulder, attempting to fix the bra, and felt a bead of sweat trickle from my armpit to my elbow. The driver leered at me through the rearview mirror.

"Just remember, this weekend is for Charlotte. We can handle a little August heat. Besides, Atlanta will be a lovely place for a wedding next spring," Mom said as I finished with the bra.

"With all your brains and talent I always thought you were going to be the one to live in the big city," said my great-aunt, nudging me with her elbow.

I bit my lip and let Aunt Addie's words roll off me. I'd buried my regrets years ago. The same year we buried Dad.

"I'll remind you about this heat next February when it's ten below and there's three feet of snow on the ground at home," said Mom as she reached behind her back to fasten the top of her own dress. My mother, Virginia Adler, was attractive and calm, even with a layer of perspiration on her face. I had only seen her fall apart once, and a little heat like this wasn't going to rattle her cool composure.

Was it just this morning that we left our inn before dawn and drove three hours to get to the Flint airport? Unfortunately our luckless journey had only begun. Our flight from Flint was behind schedule and the connecting flight in Detroit was delayed too. I guess that's what we should have expected after buying tickets on a website called ElCheapoFare.com. Now, we were getting dressed in the backseat of a steamy cab as we finished the final leg of our journey.

Sometimes I think my family avoids *luck* as if it is a nasty four-letter word. Well, I guess it actually *is* a four-letter word. But so is *love*, and we have plenty of that. I just wished *love* came with air-conditioning and a restroom to change in.

A dinner tonight, wedding-dress shopping tomorrow, and a wedding shower the following night. The long weekend was going to be a whirlwind. I leaned back against the seat and angled my head to catch a breeze coming through the window, marveling at the fact that my baby sister, Charlotte, called this home. It still was hard to imagine anyone from Truhart, population thirteen hundred and dropping, living in a Southern city like Atlanta.

For the past few years, my focus had been on my family and keeping our inn running smoothly. And now I had another goal. I was going to make sure this wedding was everything my little sister dreamed it would be.

At last we pulled up under a large gilded marquee that marked the entrance to the Ambassador Hotel of Atlanta. A man in a dark suit held open the back door of the cab and all three of us awkwardly slid across the sticky seat. By the time my mother disembarked she had to push Aunt Adelaide and me out of the way; we were momentarily frozen in place as we stared through the open glass doors at an opulent room that was nothing like the rustic lobby of our inn back home.

The man cast his eyes over Aunt Addie and her purplish gray hair

piled on top of her head, the way she had worn it since the bicenten-
nial of the nation. Then he cast a glance at the three sorry-looking
carry-on bags the driver had tossed onto the sidewalk.

"May I help you, ladies?"

My mother stood up straighter. "Yes, you can. My daughter and
her fiancé are hosting a special dinner for family and close friends."

"Oh, of course, in the Governor's Room. Will you be staying here
tonight?"

"Actually, no," I said. It had been hard enough to scrape together
money for the airfare; there was no way we could afford this place.

The man nodded and offered to store our luggage, but Aunt Addie
refused to be parted with hers. She insisted that we hold on to them,
and my mother and I knew that arguing with her was futile when she
had that look in her eye. So we followed suit and shouldered the
bags. I cringed to think what Charlotte's guests would think.

Like zombies we shuffled through the main lobby and shivered
when the air-conditioning hit us with a cold blast as we walked up a
long, winding stairway overlooking the lobby. Standing near a curved
bar was a group of elegantly dressed people who stopped talking and
stared as we walked past.

I lifted my chin, trying to look as if we weren't totally out of
place.

Mom wore a pink cotton dress that she'd worn to our church's
fiftieth anniversary last spring. I wore my black go-to skirt with a
wilting gauzy white blouse, a silver chain, and hoop earrings.

And then there was Aunt Addie.

Blue cabbage roses shouted out from her floral polyester dress, in
stark contrast to the chic black elegance of the room around us. Wearing a dress with an elastic waistband that cinched her large girth, and
sensible shoes, she looked like a 1950s throwback. No matter what
Aunt Addie did to herself, she resembled a cross between Minnie Pearl
and Betty White. Out of habit I double-checked my aunt for handwritten price tags from the church thrift store and safety pins that showed
at the hem.

Then I saw Charlotte. She stood in an ornately framed doorway
absently listening to an older man as she chewed on her lip and
looked at her watch. She looked up and our eyes met.

"Annie!" she squealed, rushing our way.

My worries dissolved as I dropped my bag and closed the space between us. I forgot the imposing room and all the curious faces as we crushed each other in an embrace that brought tears to my eyes.

Almost a full year had passed since Charlotte had left Truhart for Atlanta to become the newest sweetheart correspondent on the nationally televised *Morning Show*. Every time I saw her face on TV, I still wanted to reach out and touch the screen to make sure it was real.

"It's so good to see you," we said at the same time.

"Jinx," we said, then laughed.

We pulled apart and Charlotte was immediately captured in a hug from my mother and then Aunt Addie.

"I am so sorry we're late! The plane out of Detroit was delayed and we did the best we could," Mom explained.

"Oh, that's all right, Mom. I'm just glad you're here." The smile Charlotte flashed us assured me she was the same blue-eyed angel who used to pour glitter in the sand traps at our inn's golf course, to make pixie dust. But she had changed as well. Dressed in a black sleeveless dress with a chiffon overlay, her blond hair pulled back in a sophisticated chignon, she appeared every inch the celebrity she was becoming.

"You look wonderful, honey," said Aunt Adelaide, grabbing Charlotte's left hand. "Good Lord, that engagement ring is bigger than a lump of coal in a Christmas stocking. I'll bet that didn't come from the Sears catalogue like mine did."

"And you should see the new car Henry bought me," Charlotte exclaimed.

"Just in time! Annie is really excited to drive that SUV back up to Michigan. A new car for you and our old car back to us," Mom said.

My car had broken down a month ago, and I had been pricing used cars in Gaylord. Now I could reclaim the Ford Escape my dad had bought ten years ago and take it back to Truhart.

"I still can't believe you are getting married," I said.

"Of course I wish you could have told us before you announced it on *The Morning Show*," Mom added.

"That Marva O'Shea still brags about the fact that she knew about it before I did," complained Aunt Addie.

Charlotte frowned. "Oh, Mom, I hope you didn't mind too much!"

We all protested, of course. No point in making Charlotte feel guilty after the fact.

"This must be your family, darling." The three of us stopped to stare as Charlotte's fiancé joined her.

I was prepared to resent this man who was stealing our Charlotte away from Michigan for good. But something in the way he looked at her before he turned to greet us made me love him on sight. Adoration was written all over his face. It was as transparent as the picture window in the lobby of the Amble Inn after spring cleaning week. His blond hair was cropped short to his thinning hair line, and his broad shoulders made up for the fact that he wasn't overly tall. He wore a sharp black suit with a starched white shirt and blue-and-gray striped tie, the perfect complement to Charlotte's sleek style.

"Henry, this is my mother, Virginia, Aunt Adelaide, and, of course, Annie."

I held out my hand politely, but Henry surprised us by swallowing each of us up in a big hug. His Southern drawl came with a whole hunk of charm, and Aunt Addie was already half in love.

"I am so sorry you didn't get a chance to rest before this party," Henry said.

An older woman stepped in front of Henry and held out her hand. I was overwhelmed by a heavy dose of expensive perfume and bling. Her wrists dripped with gold and matched the lamé trim on her form-fitting dress. Her blond hair was pulled back and for a moment I wondered if the tight hairstyle was the reason no wrinkles showed around her eyes. But when she spoke and her generous upper lip barely moved, I had my answer.

"Why, it is so nice that you made the trip to our little part of the world. I am June, Henry's mother." We took turns reaching out for her limp hand and I winced when Aunt Addie shook it too hard and June Lowell flinched. June put her arm around Charlotte's shoulders in a proprietary manner. "We just love Charlotte, our little Northern bride." It sounded so old-fashioned that I resisted the urge to look around for hoopskirts. "Do y'all want to freshen up or change before the party? I know you probably didn't have time."

Something about the way she said the word *party* made my breath catch in my chest. I stole a glance at Charlotte. "This is just close friends and family, right?"

"Well, the Lowells have a lot of friends." I could have sworn that her smile was painted on because it didn't waver. I was conscious of the music and laughter in the room nearby.

Mom placed her hand over her heart. "Would that happen to be the Governor's Room?"

June Lowell's eyes darted to the pin on Aunt Addie's dress, made of lace and shells. She had bought it at last year's church craft show. "Why, yes. Everyone is so excited to meet you. But as I was saying, you are welcome to change in the ladies' lounge."

"No need to change. We're fine," said Mom with that hint of ice in her eyes that I recognized as stalwart Adler pride. "That is, unless you feel we should. We are late enough as it is . . ."

"Oh, you look lovely just as you are, Mrs. Adler. I can see where Charlotte gets her beauty. We wouldn't want to miss your presence for another minute," inserted Henry, giving his mother an annoyed look that lifted him up another notch in my estimation. "Let me get someone to take your bags so you can have a chance to relax."

Henry signaled to one of the waiters, who put down his tray and held out his hand to take Mom's bag. After I handed over my bag, he turned to Aunt Addie. She clutched hers with both hands and narrowed her eyes suspiciously. The young waiter looked startled when he saw her fierce expression, but Mom and I wrestled the bag from her death grip and looped it around his free arm.

A serious-faced young girl appeared at Henry's elbow. "Virginia, Addie, Anne, I would like you to meet my little sister, Jessica," Henry said. The girl was in her early teens and it was obvious that she wished she was anywhere else at the moment.

June pushed Jessica forward and I heard her whisper sharply, "Shoulders!" as the miserable girl readjusted her slouch. She was painfully thin and wore a purple dress dotted with sequins. It looked like something her mother might have picked for her. She held out her hand and greeted each one of us without actually looking us in the eye. Then she reached up to fiddle with her hair.

"Jessica, how nice to meet you," my mother said warmly. "Are you in school in Atlanta?"

"Actually she boards at the Delaworth Academy in Connecticut."

"Boards?" asked Aunt Addie. "Is that some kind of new sport these kids do?"

"No, she lives at a boarding school," corrected June. "We flew her here for the weekend so she could come to the party."

I tried to navigate the conversation away from any comment Aunt Addie might make about boarding school. "It must seem pretty strange to think of your big brother getting married, huh?"

Jessica nodded and looked over at Henry, showing emotion for the first time. Hero worship.

Henry reached over and patted her back. "Actually I keep telling her how great it will be for her to finally have a sister!"

Jessica's glance shifted to Charlotte and I noted how Jessica shut down before Henry led us into the Governor's Room.

As I paused on the threshold of the grand room, some sixth sense made me hesitate and glance to the side. A dark figure caught my eye and the hair on the back of my neck stood up.

I was closer to thirty than twenty, a grown woman who was beyond acting like a star-crossed teenager. But even so, my heart sped up at the knowledge that Nicholas Conrad was coming toward me. Dozens of my diary entries between the ages of eight and fourteen were devoted to him. I knew everything about him: his favorite candy from the vending machine in the golf shack, his batting average on Harrison County High School's baseball team, and the type of car soap he had used on his royal blue 1995 Grand Prix. I knew every girlfriend he took to homecoming and why they weren't good enough for him.

And Nick? He didn't even know my real name.

"Hi, Bump," he said.

CYNTHIA TENNENT

"Charm, humor, loyalty, and love."
— Cindy Myers, author of
The View From Here

A TRUHART ROMANCE

A
Wedding
in
Truhart

Cynthia Tennent was the original book thief, stealing romance novels from underneath her mother's bed when she was just twelve. As an adult, she grew serious and studied international relations, education, and other weighty matters while living all over the world. In search of happy endings, she rediscovered love stories and wrote her own when her daughters were napping. She lives in Michigan with her husband, three daughters, and her collie dog, Jack. You can visit her at www.cynthiatennent.com

CPSIA information can be obtained
at www.ICGtesting.com
Printed in the USA
LVOW10s1533050517
533411LV00001B/132/P